Praise for Sophie Kinsella and the Shopaholic novels

"A hilarious tale . . . hijinks worthy of classic *I Love Lucy* episodes . . . too good to pass up."
—*USA Today*

"Kinsella's Bloomwood is plucky and funny. . . . You won't have to shop around to find a more winning protagonist." —*People*

"[Sophie Kinsella] gives chick-lit lovers a reason to stay home from the mall."
—*Entertainment Weekly*

"Don't wait for a sale to buy this hilarious book." —*Us Weekly*

"Perfect for anyone wishing that bank statements came in more colours than just black and red." —*Daily Mirror* (London)

"If a *crème brûlée* could be transmogrified into a book, it would be *Confessions of a Shopaholic*." —*The Star-Ledger*

Also by Sophie Kinsella

SOPHIE KINSELLA

Mini Shopaholic

a novel

DELL

NEW YORK

Mini Shopaholic is a work of fiction. Names, characters, places, and incidents are the products of the author's imagination or are used fictitiously. Any resemblance to actual events, locales, or persons, living or dead, is entirely coincidental.

2011 Dell Mass Market International edition

Copyright © 2010 by Sophie Kinsella

Published in the United States by Dell, an imprint of The Random House Publishing Group, a division of Random House, Inc., New York.

DELL is a registered trademark of Random House, Inc., and the colophon is a trademark of Random House, Inc.

Originally published in hardcover in the United Kingdom by Bantam Press, an imprint of Transworld Publishers, a division of the Random House Group Limited, London, and in the United States by The Dial Press, an imprint of The Random House Publishing Group, a division of Random House, Inc., New York, in 2010.

ISBN 978-0-440-29653-9

Cover design: Belina Huey
Cover illustration: Anne Keenan Higgins

Printed in the United States of America

www.bantamdell.com

9 8 7 6 5 4 3 2

Mini Shopaholic

Tick Tock Playgroup
The Old Barn | 4 Spence Hill | Oxshott | Surrey

Mrs. Rebecca Brandon
The Pines
43 Elton Road
Oxshott
Surrey

1 September 2005

Dear Mrs. Brandon,

We were delighted to meet you and Minnie yesterday. We are sure she will be very happy at our fun, relaxed playgroup, and we look forward to seeing you next week.

With kind regards,

Teri Ashley
Play Leader

P.S. Please don't worry about the minor paint-squirting incident. We are used to children and we can always repaint that wall.

Tick Tock Playgroup
The Old Barn | 4 Spence Hill | Oxshott | Surrey

Mrs. Rebecca Brandon
The Pines
43 Elton Road
Oxshott
Surrey

4 October 2005

Dear Mrs. Brandon,

Just a few confidential concerns about Minnie. She's a lovely child with real liveliness.

However, she has to learn that she can't wear *all* the dressing-up clothes *every* day, and the "princess" shoes are not suitable for outdoor play. Perhaps we can discuss this at our upcoming parents-and-children activity morning.

With kind regards,

Teri Ashley
Play Leader

P.S. Please don't worry about the minor glue-squirting incident. We are used to children and we can always revarnish that table.

Tick Tock Playgroup

The Old Barn | 4 Spence Hill | Oxshott | Surrey

Mrs. Rebecca Brandon
The Pines
43 Elton Road
Oxshott
Surrey

9 November 2005

Dear Mrs. Brandon,

Thank you for your letter. I'm glad you're looking forward to the parents-and-children activity morning. Unfortunately, there will be no dressing-up clothes for adults, nor will there be any facility for "swapping outfits with other parents," as you suggest.

I'm glad to say that Minnie has broadened her activities in playgroup and is spending a lot of time in our new "Shop" corner.

With kind regards,

Teri Ashley
Play Leader

P.S. Please don't worry about the minor ink-squirting incident. We are used to children and Mrs. Soper can always re-dye her hair.

ONE

OK. DON'T PANIC. I'm in charge. I, Rebecca Brandon (née Bloomwood), am the adult. *Not* my two-year-old daughter.

Only I'm not sure she realizes this.

"Minnie, darling, give me the pony." I try to sound calm and assured, like Nanny Sue off the telly.

"Poneeee." Minnie grips the toy pony more tightly.

"No pony."

"Mine!" she cries hysterically. "*Miiiine* poneee!"

Argh. I'm holding about a million shopping bags, my face is sweating, and I could *really* do without this.

It was all going so well. I'd been round the whole shopping mall and bought all the last little things on my Christmas list. Minnie and I were heading toward Santa's Grotto, and I only stopped for a moment to look at a dollhouse. Whereupon Minnie grabbed a toy pony off the display and refused to put it back. And now I'm in the middle of Ponygate.

A mother in J Brand skinny jeans with an impeccably dressed daughter walks past, giving me the Mummy Once-Over, and I flinch. Since I had Minnie, I've learned that the Mummy Once-Over is even more savage than the Manhattan Once-Over. In the Mummy Once-Over, they don't just assess and price your clothes to the nearest penny in one sweeping glance. Oh no. They also take in your child's clothes, pram brand, nappy bag, snack choice, and whether your child is smiling, snotty, or screaming.

Which I know is a lot to take in, in a one-second glance, but believe me, mothers are multitaskers.

Minnie definitely scores top marks for her outfit. (Dress: one-off Danny Kovitz; coat: Rachel Riley; shoes: Baby Dior.) And I've got her safely strapped into her toddler reins (Bill Amberg leather, really cool; they were in *Vogue*). But instead of smiling angelically like the little girl in the photo shoot, she's straining against them like a bull waiting to dash into the ring. Her eyebrows are knitted with fury, her cheeks are bright pink, and she's drawing breath to shriek again.

"Minnie." I let go of the reins and put my arms round her so that she feels safe and secure, just like it recommends in Nanny Sue's book, *Taming Your Tricky Toddler.* I bought it the other day, to have a flick through. Just out of idle interest. I mean, it's not that I'm having *problems* with Minnie or anything. It's not that she's *difficult.* Or "out of control and willful," like that stupid teacher at the toddler music group said. (What does she know? She can't even play the triangle properly.)

The thing about Minnie is, she's . . . spirited. She has firm opinions about things. Like jeans (she won't wear them) or carrots (she won't eat them). And right now her firm opinion is that she should have a toy pony.

"Minnie, darling, I love you very much," I say in a gentle, crooning voice, "and it would make me very happy if you gave me the pony. That's right, give it to Mummy." I've nearly done it. My fingers are closing around the pony's head . . .

Ha. Skills. I've got it. I can't help looking round to see if anyone's observed my expert parenting.

"Miiiine!" Minnie wrenches the pony out of my hand and makes a run for it across the shop floor. Shit.

"Minnie! *Minnie!*" I yell.

I grab my carrier bags and leg it furiously after Minnie, who has already disappeared into the Action Man section. God, I don't know why we bother training all these athletes for the Olympics. We should just field a team of toddlers.

As I catch up with her, I'm panting. I really have to start my postnatal exercises sometime.

"Give me the pony!" I try to take it, but she's gripping it like a limpet.

"*Mine* poneee!" Her dark eyes flash at me with a resolute glint. Sometimes I look at Minnie and she's so like her father it gives me a jolt.

Speaking of which, where is Luke? We were supposed to be doing Christmas shopping *together.* As a *family.* But he disappeared an hour ago, muttering something about a call he had to make, and I haven't seen him since. He's probably sitting somewhere having a civilized cappuccino over the newspaper. Typical.

"Minnie, we're not buying it," I say in my best firm manner. "You've got lots of toys already and you don't need a pony."

A woman with straggly dark hair, gray eyes, and toddlers in a twin buggy shoots me an approving nod. I can't help giving her the Mummy Once-Over myself, and she's one of those mothers who wears Crocs over nubbly homemade socks. (Why would you do that? Why?)

"It's monstrous, isn't it?" she says. "Those ponies are forty pounds! My kids know better than to even ask," she adds, shooting a glance at her two boys, who are slumped silently, thumbs in mouths. "Once you give in to them, that's the beginning of the end. I've got mine well trained."

Show-off.

"Absolutely," I say in dignified tones. "I couldn't agree more."

"Some parents would just buy their kid that pony for a quiet life. No discipline. It's disgusting."

"Terrible," I agree, and make a surreptitious swipe for the pony, which Minnie adeptly dodges. Damn.

"The biggest mistake is giving in to them." The woman is regarding Minnie with a pebblelike gaze. "That's what starts the rot."

"Well, I never give in to my daughter," I say briskly. "You're not getting the pony, Minnie, and that's final."

"Poneeee!" Minnie's wails turn to heartrending sobs. She is such a drama queen. (She gets it from my mum.)

"Good luck, then." The woman moves off. "Happy Christmas."

"Minnie, stop!" I hiss furiously as soon as she's disappeared. "You're embarrassing both of us! What do you want a stupid pony for, anyway?"

"Poneeee!" She's cuddling the pony to her as though it's her long-lost faithful pet that was sold at market five hundred miles away and has just stumbled back to the farm, footsore and whickering for her.

"It's only a silly toy," I say impatiently. "What's so special about it, anyway?" And for the first time I look properly at the pony.

Wow. Actually . . . it *is* pretty fab. It's made of painted white wood with glittery stars all over and the sweetest hand-painted face. And it has little red trundly wheels.

"You really don't need a pony, Minnie," I say—but with slightly less conviction than before. I've just noticed the saddle. Is that genuine leather? And it has a proper bridle with buckles and the mane is made of real horsehair. *And* it comes with a grooming set!

For forty quid this isn't bad value at all. I push one of the little red wheels, and it spins round perfectly. Now that I think about it, Minnie doesn't have a toy pony. It's quite an obvious gap in her toy cupboard.

I mean, not that I'm going to *give in*.

"It winds up too," comes a voice behind me, and I turn to see an elderly sales assistant approaching us. "There's a key in the base. Look!"

She winds the key, and both Minnie and I watch, mesmerized, as the pony starts rising and falling in a carousel motion while tinkly music plays.

Oh my God, I *love* this pony.

"It's on special Christmas offer at forty pounds," the assistant adds. "Normally this would retail for seventy. They're handmade in Sweden."

Nearly fifty percent off. I *knew* it was good value. Didn't I say it was good value?

"You like it, don't you, dear?" The assistant smiles at Minnie, who beams back, her stroppiness vanished. In fact, I don't want to boast, but she looks pretty adorable with her red coat and dark pigtails and dimpled cheeks. "So, would you like to buy one?"

"I . . . um . . ." I clear my throat.

Come on, Becky. Say no. Be a good parent. Walk away.

My hand steals out and strokes the mane again.

But it's so *gorgeous*. Look at its dear little face. And a pony isn't like some stupid craze, is it? You'd never get tired of a pony. It's a classic. It's, like, the Chanel jacket of toys.

And it's Christmas. And it's on special offer. And, who knows, Minnie might turn out to have a gift for riding, it suddenly occurs to me. A toy pony might be just the spur she needs. I have a sudden vision of her at age twenty, wearing a red jacket, standing by a gorgeous horse at the Olympics, saying to the TV cameras,

"It all began one Christmas, when I received the gift that changed my life. . . ."

My mind is going round and round like a computer processing DNA results, trying to find a match. There has to be a way in which I can simultaneously: 1) Not give in to Minnie's tantrum; 2) be a good parent; and 3) buy the pony. I need some clever blue-sky solution like Luke is always paying business consultants scads of money to come up with . . .

And then the answer comes to me. A totally genius idea which I can't *believe* I've never had before. I haul out my phone and text Luke:

Luke! Have just had a really good thought. I think Minnie should get pocket money.

Immediately a reply pings back:

Wtf? Why?

So she can buy things, of course! I start to type. Then I think again. I delete the text and carefully type instead:

Children need to learn about finance from early age. Read it in article. Empowers them and gives responsibility.

A moment later Luke texts: Can't we just buy her the FT?

Shut up. I type: We'll say two pounds a week shall we?

R u mad? Comes zipping back: 10p a week is plenty.

I stare at the phone indignantly. *10p?* He's such an old skinflint. What's she supposed to buy with that?

And we'll never afford the pony on 10p a week.

`50p a week.` I type firmly. `Is national average.` (He'll never check.) `Where r u anyway? Nearly time for Father Christmas!!`

`OK whatever. I'll be there` comes the reply.

Result! As I put away my phone, I'm doing a quick mental calculation: Fifty pence a week for two years makes £52. Easy enough. God, why on earth have I never thought of pocket money before? It's perfect! It's going to add a whole new dimension to our shopping trips.

I turn to Minnie, feeling rather proud of myself.

"Now, listen, darling," I announce. "I'm not going to buy this pony for you, because I've already said no. But as a special treat, you can buy it for yourself out of your *own pocket money*. Isn't that exciting?"

Minnie eyes me uncertainly. I'll take that as a yes.

"As you've never spent any of your pocket money, you've got two years' worth, which is plenty. You see how great saving is?" I add brightly. "You see how fun it is?"

As we walk to the checkout, I feel totally smug. Talk about responsible parenting. I'm introducing my child to the principles of financial planning at an early age. I could be a guru on TV myself! *Super Becky's Guide to Fiscally Responsible Parenting.* I could wear different boots in each episode—

"Wagon."

I'm jolted out of my daydream to see that Minnie has dropped the pony and is now clutching a pink plastic monstrosity. Where did she get that? It's Winnie's Wagon, from that cartoon show.

"Wagon?" She raises her eyes hopefully.

What?

"We're not getting the wagon, darling," I say patiently. "You wanted the pony. The lovely *pony*, remember?"

Minnie surveys the pony with total indifference. "Wagon."

"Pony!" I grab the pony off the floor.

This is so frustrating. How can she be so fickle? She definitely gets that trait from Mum.

"Wagon!"

"Pony!" I cry, more loudly than I meant to, and brandish the pony at her. "I want the *poneee*—"

Suddenly I get a prickly-neck feeling. I look round to see the woman with the toddler boys, standing a few yards away, staring at me with her pebblelike eyes.

"I mean . . ." I hastily lower the pony, my cheeks burning. "Yes, you *may* buy the pony out of your pocket money. Basic financial planning," I add briskly to the pebble-eyed woman. "What we learned today is that you have to *save up* before you can buy things, didn't we, darling? Minnie's spent all her pocket money on the pony, and it was a very good choice—"

"I've found the other pony!" The assistant suddenly appears again, breathless and carrying a dusty box. "I knew we had one left in the stockroom; they were originally a pair, you see . . ."

There's *another* pony?

I can't help gasping as she draws it out. It's midnight blue with a raven mane, speckled with stars, and with golden wheels. It's absolutely stunning. It complements the other one perfectly. Oh God, we have to have them both. We *have* to.

Rather annoyingly, the pebble-eyed woman is still standing there with her buggy, watching us.

"Shame you've spent all your pocket money, isn't it?" she says to Minnie with one of those tight, unfriendly smiles which proves she never has any fun or sex. You can always tell that about people, I find.

"Yes, isn't it?" I say politely. "That's a problem. So we'll have to think of a solution." I think hard for a moment, then turn to Minnie.

"Darling, here's your second important lesson in financial planning. Sometimes, when we see an amazing one-off bargain, we can make an *exception* to the saving-up rule. It's called seizing the opportunity."

"You're just going to *buy* it?" says the pebble-eyed woman in tones of disbelief.

What business is it of hers? God, I hate other mothers. They always have to butt in. The minute you have a child, it's as if you've turned into a box on an Internet site that says, *Please add all your rude and offensive comments here.*

"Of course I'm not going to *buy* it," I say, a little stonily. "She'll have to get it out of her own pocket money. Darling." I crouch down to get Minnie's attention. "If you pay for the other pony out of your pocket money at fifty pence a week, it'll take about . . . sixty more weeks. You'll have to have an advance. Like an 'overdraft.'" I enunciate clearly. "So you'll basically have spent all your pocket money till you're three. All right?"

Minnie looks a bit bewildered. But then, I expect I looked a bit bewildered when I took out my first overdraft. It goes with the territory.

"All sorted." I beam at the assistant and hand over my Visa card. "We'll take both ponies, thank you. You see, darling?" I add to Minnie. "The lesson we've learned today is: Never give up on something you really want. However impossible things seem, there's always a way."

I can't help feeling proud of myself, imparting this nugget of wisdom. *That's* what parenting's all about. Teaching your child the ways of the world.

"You know, I once found the most amazing opportunity," I add, as I punch in my PIN. "It was a pair of Dolce and Gabbana boots at ninety percent off! Only, my credit card was up to my limit. But did I give up? No! Of course I didn't!"

Minnie is listening as avidly as if I'm recounting *The Three Bears*.

"I went round my flat and searched in all my pockets and bags, and I collected up all my little coins—and guess what?" I pause for effect. "I had enough money! I could get the boots! Hooray!"

Minnie claps her hands, and to my delight, the toddler boys start cheering raucously.

"Do you want to hear another story?" I beam at them. "Do you want to hear about the sample sale in Milan? I was walking along the street one day, when I saw this *mysterious sign*." I open my eyes wide. "And what do you think it said?"

"Ridiculous." The pebble-eyed woman turns her buggy with an abrupt gesture. "Come on, it's time to go home.".

"Story!" wails one of the boys.

"We're not hearing the story," she snaps. "You're insane," she adds over her shoulder as she strides off. "No wonder your child's so spoiled. What are those little shoes of hers, then, Gucci?"

Spoiled?

Blood zings to my face and I stare at her in speechless shock. Where did *that* come from? Minnie is not spoiled!

And Gucci doesn't even make shoes like that.

"She's not spoiled!" I manage at last.

But the woman has already disappeared behind the Postman Pat display. Well, I'm certainly not going to run after her and yell, "At least my child doesn't just loll in the buggy sucking its thumb all day, and by the way have you ever thought about wiping your children's noses?"

Because that wouldn't be a good example to Minnie.

"Come on, Minnie." I try to compose myself. "Let's go and see Father Christmas. Then we'll feel better."

TWO

THERE'S NO WAY on earth Minnie's spoiled. No way.

OK, so she has her little moments. Like we all do. But she's not spoiled. I would *know* if she was spoiled. I'm her *mother.*

Still, all the way to Santa's Grotto I feel ruffled. How can anyone be so mean? And on Christmas Eve too.

"You show everyone how well behaved you are, darling," I murmur determinedly to Minnie as we walk along, hand in hand. "You just be a little angel for Father Christmas, OK?"

"Jingle Bells" is playing over the loudspeakers, and I can't help cheering up as we get near. I used to come to this exact same Santa's Grotto when I was a little girl.

"Look, Minnie!" I point excitedly. "Look at the reindeer! Look at all the presents!"

There's a sleigh and two life-size reindeer and fake snow everywhere and lots of girls dressed as elves in green costumes, which is a new touch. At the entrance I can't help blinking in surprise at the elf who greets us with a tanned cleavage. Is Father Christmas finding his elves at glamour model agencies these days? And should elves have purple acrylic nails?

"Merry Christmas!" she greets us, and stamps my ticket. "Be sure to visit our Christmas Wishing Well and put in your Christmas Wish. Father Christmas will be reading them later on!"

"Did you hear that, Minnie? We can make a wish!" I look down at Minnie, who's gazing up at the elf in silent awe.

You see? She's behaving perfectly.

"Becky! Over here!" I turn my head to see Mum already in the queue, wearing a festive twinkly scarf and holding the handles of Minnie's buggy, which is laden with bags and packages. "Father Christmas just went for his tea break," she adds as we join her. "So I think we'll be another half an hour at least. Dad's gone off to look for camcorder discs, and Janice is buying her Christmas cards."

Janice is Mum's next-door neighbor. She buys all her Christmas cards half price on Christmas Eve, writes them out on January 1, and keeps them in a drawer the rest of the year. She calls it "getting ahead of herself."

"Now, love, will you take a look at my present for Jess?" Mum rootles in a bag and anxiously produces a wooden box. "Is it all right?"

Jess is my sister. My long-lost half sister, I should say. (On Dad's side. It was a bit of a shock at first, but we're all used to it now.) She's coming back from Chile in a few days' time, so we're going to have a second Christmas Day for her and Tom, with turkey and presents and everything! Tom is Jess's boyfriend. He's the only son of Janice and Martin, and I've known him all my life, and he's very . . .

Well. He's really . . .

Anyway. The point is, *they* love each other. And sweaty hands probably don't matter so much in Chile, do they?

It's fantastic that they're coming over, especially as it means we can finally, *finally* have Minnie's christening. (Jess is going to be a godmother.) But I can see why

Mum's stressed out. It's tricky buying presents for Jess. She doesn't like anything that's new or expensive or contains plastic or parabens or comes in a bag that isn't made of hemp.

"I've bought this." Mum opens the lid of the box to reveal an array of posh glass bottles nestling in straw. "It's shower gel," she adds quickly. "Nothing for the bath. We don't want World War Three again!"

There was this slight diplomatic incident last time Jess was over. We were celebrating her birthday and Janice gave her a present of bubble bath, whereupon Jess launched into a ten-minute lecture on how much water a bath uses and how people in the West are obsessed by cleanliness and everyone should just take a five-minute shower once every week, like Jess and Tom did.

Janice and Martin had recently had a Jacuzzi installed, so this didn't go down very well.

"What do you think?" says Mum.

"Dunno." I peer cautiously at the label on the box. "Does it have additives? Does it exploit people?"

"Oh, love, I don't know." Mum looks gingerly at the box as though it's a nuclear armament. "It says 'all-natural,'" she ventures at last. "That's good, isn't it?"

"I think it'll be OK." I nod. "But don't tell her you bought it in a shopping mall. Tell her you bought it from a small independent cooperative."

"Good idea." Mum brightens. "And I'll wrap it in newspaper. What have you got her?"

"I bought her a yoga mat, handmade by peasant women in Guatemala," I can't help saying smugly. "It funds village agricultural projects *and* it uses recycled plastic components from computers."

"Becky!" says Mum admiringly. "How did you find that?"

"Oh . . . research." I shrug airily.

I won't admit I Googled *green worthy present recycle environment lentils gift wrap.*

"Kiss-mas! Kiss-*mas!*" Minnie is dragging at my hand so hard I think she'll pull my arm off.

"Do the Wishing Well with Minnie, love," suggests Mum. "I'll keep your place."

I dump the ponies on the buggy and lead Minnie toward the Wishing Well. It's surrounded by fake silver birch trees with fairies hanging down from the branches, and if it weren't for the screeching kids everywhere, it would be quite magical.

The wishing cards are laid out on a fake tree stump that you can use as a table. I pick up a card, which has *Christmas Wish* printed in swirly green writing at the top, and give one of the felt-tips to Minnie.

God, I remember writing letters to Father Christmas when I was little. They used to get quite long and involved, with illustrations and pictures cut out of catalogs, just in case he got confused.

A pair of pink-faced girls of about ten, all giggly and whispery, are posting their wishes, and just the sight of them gives me a rush of nostalgia. It seems wrong not to join in. I might jinx it or something.

Dear Father Christmas, I find myself writing on a card. *It's Becky here again.* I pause and think for a bit, and then quickly scribble down a few things.

I mean, only about three. I'm not greedy or anything.

Minnie is drawing earnestly all over her card and has got felt-tip on her hands and her nose.

"I'm sure Father Christmas will understand what you mean," I say gently, taking it from her. "Let's post it in the well."

One by one I drop the two cards in. Tiny fake snowflakes are drifting down from above and "Winter Wonderland" is being piped out of a nearby speaker, and I suddenly feel so Christmasy I can't help closing my eyes, clenching Minnie's hand and wishing. You never know . . .

"Becky?" A deep voice penetrates my thoughts and my eyes snap open. Luke is standing in front of me, his dark hair and navy coat dusted with fake snow, a glint of amusement in his eyes. Too late, I realize I've been fervently mouthing, *"Please . . . please,"* with my eyes squeezed shut.

"Oh!" I say, a bit flustered. "Hi. I was just . . ."

"Talking to Father Christmas?"

"Don't be ridiculous." I regain my dignity. "Where've you been, anyway?"

Luke doesn't answer me but starts walking away, beckoning for me to follow.

"Leave Minnie with your mother a moment," he says. "I've got something to show you."

I'VE BEEN MARRIED to Luke for three and a half years now, but I still don't always know the way his mind is working. As we stride along, his mouth is hard, and I almost start to feel nervous. What could it be?

"Here." He comes to a halt in a deserted corner of the shopping mall and gets out his BlackBerry.

On the screen is an email from his lawyer, Tony. It consists of a single word: *Settled.*

"Settled?" For a split second I don't understand—then I have a sudden flash of realization.

"Not . . . *Arcodas*? They've *settled*?"

"Yup." And now I can see a tiny smile glimmering.

"But . . . you never said . . . I had no idea . . ."

"Didn't want to raise your hopes. We've been talking for three weeks. It's not the greatest deal for us, but it's fine. We'll be fine. The point is, it's done."

My legs feel a bit shaky. It's over. Just like that. The

Arcodas case has been hanging over us for so long, it's started to feel part of the family. (Not a good part, obviously. The malevolent old witchy aunt with the warty nose and the nasty cackle.)

It's been two years since Luke went into battle with Arcodas. I say "battle." It wasn't like he firebombed them or anything. He just refused to work for them, as a matter of principle—the principle being that he didn't want to represent a load of bullies who mistreated his staff. He owns a PR company, Brandon Communications, and has had most of his employees for years. When he found out the way Arcodas had been behaving toward them, he was angrier than I've ever seen him.

So he quit, and they took him to court for breach of contract. (Which just proves how awful and overbearing they are.) Whereupon Luke took *them* to court for not paying for the services they'd already received.

You'd have thought the judge would realize instantly who was the good guy and rule in Luke's favor. I mean, hello, don't judges have *eyes*? But instead they had stupid hearings and adjournments, and the whole thing has dragged on and been totally stressy. I have to say, my opinion of lawyers, judges, so-called "mediators," and the whole legal system is a lot lower after all this. Which I would have told them, if they'd only let me speak.

I was *dying* for Luke to call me as a witness. I had my outfit ready and everything (navy pencil skirt, white shirt with ruffle, patent court shoes). And I'd written this brilliant speech, which I still know by heart. It begins: "Ladies and gentlemen of the jury, I ask you to look into your hearts. And then I ask you to look at the two men before you. One honorable, upstanding hero who puts the well-being of his staff before money"— (here I would point at Luke)—"and one odious, sexist man who bullies everyone and has as much integrity as he does dress sense." (Here I would point at Iain Wheeler from Arcodas.) Everyone would be stirred up and would cheer, and the judge would have to bang his gavel and cry, "Order! Order!" And then I was going to cunningly assess the jury, like they do in John Grisham novels, and work out which ones were on our side.

Anyway. All my plans were spoiled when Luke said there wasn't going to be a jury, it wasn't that kind of court. And then he said it was a murky swamp full of dirty tricks and he'd be damned if I got dragged into all this too and I should stay at home with Minnie. So I did, even though the frustration nearly killed me.

Now Luke exhales and pushes his hands through his hair.

"Over," he says, almost to himself. "At last."

"Thank God."

As I reach up to hug him, I can see traces of weariness in his face still. This whole thing has nearly wiped Luke out. He's been trying to run his company, and deal with the case, and keep his staff motivated, *and* win new business.

"So." He puts his hands on my shoulders and surveys me. "We can start to move on. In all sorts of ways."

It takes me a moment to realize what he means.

"We can buy the house!" I catch my breath.

"I put in the offer straightaway." He nods. "They said they'd give an answer by the end of the day."

"Oh my God!" I can't help giving a little jump of excitement. I can't believe this is all happening at last. The case is over! We can finally move out of Mum and Dad's house and have our own family home!

We've tried to move out before. In fact, several times. We've got as far as drawing up contracts for four houses in all, but each one has been doomed. Either the vendor didn't really want to sell (house #3), or they suddenly demanded loads more money (house #1), or the house didn't actually belong to them but to their uncle in Spain and it was all a scam (house #4), or it burned down (house #2). I'd started to think we were jinxed, and then Luke said maybe we should wait till the Arcodas business was over.

"Lucky five?" I raise my eyes hopefully toward Luke, who just crosses his fingers and grins.

This house has got everything going for it. It's in a brilliant road in Maida Vale, and it has a lovely garden with a swing hanging from a tree and is amazingly spacious inside. And it's nearly ours! I feel a sudden burst of exhilaration. I *have* to go and buy *LivingEtc* right now. And *Elle Deco*, and *Wallpaper** . . .

"Shall we get back?" I say casually. "I might pop into Smiths on the way and pick up a few magazines . . ."

And I'd better get *Grand Designs*, and *World of Interiors*, and *25 Beautiful Homes* . . .

"In a minute." Something about Luke's voice alerts me, and I look up to see he's taken a few paces away. His face is averted and his chin is stiff. Something doesn't look right about him.

"Hey, are you OK?" I say cautiously. "There's no bad news, is there?"

"No. But there's something I wanted to . . . run past you." He pauses, his hands cradling the back of his neck, his gaze distant, almost as though he can't bring himself to look at me. "Weird thing happened a few minutes ago. I was in Waterstone's, waiting for the call about Arcodas. Just wandering around . . ." He pauses again, for a long time. "And I found myself buying a book for Annabel. The new Ruth Rendell. She'd have loved it."

There's silence for a moment. I don't know how to respond.

"Luke . . ." I begin tentatively.

"I bought a bloody Christmas present for her." He squeezes his fists into his temples. "Am I going nuts?"

"Of course you're not going nuts! You're just . . ." I break off helplessly, wishing I had something wise and profound to say, trying desperately to remember bits from that book on bereavement I bought.

Because that's the other awful thing that happened this year. Luke's stepmum died in May. She was only ill for a month and then she was gone, and Luke was absolutely devastated.

I know Annabel wasn't his biological mother—but she was his true mum. She brought him up, and she understood him like no one else did, and the worst thing is, he hardly saw her before she died. Even when she was really ill, he couldn't drop everything and rush to Devon, because he had Arcodas hearings in London and they'd been adjourned so many times already it was impossible to delay again.

He shouldn't feel guilty. I've told him so a million times. There was nothing he could do. But even so, I know he does. And now his dad is in Australia with his sister, so Luke can't even make up by spending time with him.

As for his real mother . . . we don't even mention her.

Ever.

Luke's always had a pretty love–hate relationship with Elinor. It makes sense, since she abandoned him and his dad when Luke was tiny. But he was on fairly civil terms with her when she blew it, big-time.

It was around the time of the funeral. He'd gone to see her for some family-business reason. I still don't know exactly what she said to him—something about Annabel. Something insensitive and probably down-right rude, I'm guessing. He's never told me exactly or even referred to the incident again—all I know is, I've never seen him so white, so catatonic with fury. And now we never mention Elinor's name anymore. I don't think he'll ever reconcile with her, his whole life. Which is fine by me.

As I look up at Luke, I feel a little squeeze in my heart. The strain of this year has really hit him hard. He's got two little lines between his eyes which he doesn't lose even when he smiles or laughs. It's like he can't ever look 100 percent happy.

"Come on." I put my arm through his and squeeze it tight. "Let's go and see Father Christmas."

As we're walking along, I casually steer Luke to the other side of the mall. No reason, really. Just because the shops are nicer to look at. Like the bespoke jewelers . . . and that shop with the silk flowers . . . and Enfant Cocotte, which is full of handmade rocking horses and designer wenge cribs.

My pace has slowed right down and I take a step toward the brightly lit window, full of a creeping lust. Look at all these gorgeous things. Look at the tiny rompers, and the little blankets.

If we had another baby, we could get all new lovely blankets. And it would be all snuffly and cute and Minnie could help to wheel it in the pram, and we'd be a real family . . .

I glance up to Luke to see if perhaps he's thinking the same thing as me and will meet my eyes with a soft, loving gaze. Instead, he's frowning at something on his BlackBerry. Honestly. Why isn't he more tuned in to my thoughts? We're supposed to be married, aren't we? He should *understand* me. He should *realize* why I've led him to a baby shop.

"That's sweet, isn't it?" I point at a teddy-bear mobile.

"Mmm-hmm." Luke nods without even looking up.

"Wow, look at that pram!" I point longingly at an amazing-looking high-tech contraption with bouncy wheels that look like they came off a Hummer. "Isn't it great?"

If we had another baby, we could buy another pram. I mean, we'd *have* to. The crappy old pram Minnie had is completely bust. (Not that I want another baby just to get a cool pram, obviously. But it would be an added bonus.)

"Luke." I clear my throat. "I was just thinking. About . . . us. I mean . . . all of us. Our family. Including Minnie. And I was wondering—"

He holds up his hand and lifts his BlackBerry to his ear.

"Yes. Hi."

God, I hate that silent-ring mode. It gives you no warning at all that he's getting a call.

"I'll catch up with you," he mouths to me, then turns back to his BlackBerry. "Yup, Gary, I got your email."

OK, so this isn't a great time to discuss buying a pram for a mythical second baby.

Never mind. I'll wait till later.

As I hurry back to Santa's Grotto, it occurs to me I might be missing Minnie's turn, and I break into a run. But as I skid round the corner, breathless, Father Christmas isn't even on his throne yet.

"Becky!" Mum waves from the front of the queue. "We're next! I've got the camcorder all ready . . . Ooh, look!"

An elf with a bright, vacant smile has taken the stage. She beams around and taps the microphone for attention.

"Hello, boys and girls!" she calls out. "Quiet, now. Before Santa starts seeing all the children again, it's Christmas Wish time! We're going to pull out the wish of one lucky child and grant it! Will it be a teddy? Or a dollhouse? Or a scooter?"

The microphone isn't working properly, and she taps

it in annoyance. Even so, excitement is rippling through the crowd, and there's a surge forward. Camcorders are waving in the air, and small children are swarming through people's legs to see, their faces all lit up.

"Minnie!" Mum is saying excitedly. "What did you wish for, darling? Maybe they'll choose you!"

"And the winner is called . . . Becky! Well done, Becky!" The elf's suddenly amplified voice makes me jump.

No. That can't be . . .

It must be another Becky. There must be loads of little girls here called Becky.

"And little Becky has wished for . . ." She squints at the wishing card. *"A Zac Posen top in aquamarine, the one with the bow, size ten."*

Shit.

"Is Zac Posen a new TV character?" The elf turns to a colleague, looking bemused. "Is that like a spinning top?"

Honestly, how can she work in a department store and not have heard of Zac Posen?

"How old is Becky?" The elf is smiling brightly around. "Becky, sweetheart, are you here? We haven't got any tops, but maybe you'd like to choose a different toy from Santa's sleigh?"

My head is ducked down in embarrassment. I can't bring myself to raise my hand. They didn't say they'd read the bloody Christmas Wishes *out loud*. They should have warned me.

"Is Becky's mummy here?"

"Here I am!" calls Mum, gaily waving her camcorder.

"Shh, Mum!" I hiss. "Sorry," I call out, my face boiling. "It's . . . um, me. I didn't realize you'd be . . . Choose another wish. A child's wish. Please. Throw mine away."

But the elf can't hear me above the hubbub.

"Also those Marni shoes I saw with Suze—not the stack heels, the other ones." She's still reading out loud, her voice booming through the sound system. "Does this make sense to anyone? *And . . ."* She squints more closely at the paper. "Does that say, *A sibling for Minnie?* Is Minnie your dolly, love? Aw, isn't that sweet?"

"Stop it!" I cry out in horror, pushing forward through the crowd of small children. "That's confidential! No one was supposed to see that!"

"And, above all, Father Christmas, I wish that Luke—"

"Shut *up!"* In desperation, I practically dive at the grotto. "That's private! It's between me and Father Christmas!" I reach the elf and wrench the paper out of her hand.

"Ow!" she cries.

"I'm sorry," I say breathlessly. "But I'm Becky."

"You're Becky?" Her mascaraed eyes narrow—then she looks down at the paper again and I see the comprehension dawning. After a few moments her face softens. She folds the paper and hands it back to me.

"I hope you get your Christmas Wish," she says quietly, away from the microphone.

"Thanks." I hesitate, then add, "Same to you, whatever it is. Happy Christmas."

I turn to go back to Mum—and through the thicket of heads I glimpse Luke's dark eyes. He's standing there, near the back.

My stomach flips over. What exactly did he hear?

He's coming toward me now, weaving his way through the families, his expression impenetrable.

"Oh, hi." I try to sound casual. "So . . . they read out my Christmas Wish; isn't that funny?"

"Mmm-hmm." He's giving nothing away.

There's an awkward-ish little silence between us.

He *did* hear his name, I can tell. A wife has an unerring instinct for these things. He heard his name and now he's wondering what I was wishing about him.

Unless maybe he's just thinking about his emails.

"Mummy!" A shrill, unmistakable voice cuts through my head, and I forget all about Luke.

"Minnie!" I turn, and for one frantic moment I can't see her.

"Was that Minnie?" Luke is also alert. "Where is she?"

"She was with Mum . . . *Shit*." I grab Luke's arm and point at the stage in horror.

Minnie's sitting on top of one of Father Christmas's reindeer, holding on to its ears. How the hell did she get up there?

"Excuse me . . ." I barge my way between the parents and kids. "Minnie, get *down*!"

"Horsey!" Minnie kicks the reindeer joyfully, leaving an ugly dent in the papier-mâché.

"Would someone remove this child, please?" an elf is saying into the microphone. "Would the parents of this child please come forward at once?"

"I only let go of her for a minute!" says Mum defensively as Luke and I reach her. "She just ran!"

"OK, Minnie," says Luke firmly, striding up onto the stage. "Party's over."

"Slide!" She's clambered up onto the sleigh. "Mine slide!"

"It's not a slide, and it's time to get down." He takes Minnie round the waist and pulls, but she's hooked her legs through the seat and is gripping on to the sleigh with superhero strength.

"Could you get her off, please?" the elf says, with strained politeness.

I grab Minnie's shoulders.

"OK," I mutter to Luke. "You get the legs. We'll yank her off. After three. One, two, three—"

Oh no. Oh . . . fuck.

I don't know what happened. I don't know *what* we did. But the whole bloody sleigh is collapsing. All the presents are falling off the sleigh onto the fake snow. Before I can blink, a sea of children dashes forward to grab the gifts, while their parents yell at them to "Come back *now,* Daniel, or there won't be any Christmas."

It's mayhem.

"Present!" wails Minnie, stretching her arms out and kicking Luke's chest. "Present!"

"Get that bloody child out of here!" the elf erupts in toxic rage. Her eyes range meanly over me, Mum, and Luke, and even over Janice and Martin, who have appeared out of nowhere, both wearing festive sweaters decorated with reindeer and clutching Christmas Discount Shop bags. "I want your whole family to leave at once."

"But it's our turn next," I point out humbly. "I'm really, really sorry about the reindeer, and we'll pay for any damage—"

"Absolutely," Luke chimes in.

"But my daughter's been longing to see Father Christmas—"

"I'm afraid we have a little rule," the elf says sarcastically. "Any child who wrecks Santa's sleigh forfeits their visit. Your daughter is hereby banned from the grotto."

"Banned?" I stare at her in dismay. "You mean—"

"In fact, *all* of you are banned." With a purple lacquered nail, she points at the exit.

"Well, that's a fine Christmas spirit!" retorts Mum. "We're loyal customers and your sleigh was obviously very poorly made, and I've a good mind to report you to trading standards!"

"Just go." The elf is still standing there, her arm extended rigidly.

In total mortification, I take the handles of the

buggy. We all trudge out in miserable silence, to see Dad rushing up in his waterproof jacket, his graying hair a bit disheveled.

"Did I miss it? Have you seen Father Christmas, Minnie, darling?"

"No." I can hardly bear to admit it. "We were banned from the grotto."

Dad's face falls. "Oh, dear. Oh, love." He sighs heavily. "Not *again*."

"Uh-huh."

"How many is that now?" asks Janice, with a wince.

"Four." I look down at Minnie, who of course is now standing holding Luke's hand demurely, looking like a little angel.

"What happened this time?" asks Dad. "She didn't bite Santa, did she?"

"No!" I say defensively. "Of course not!"

The whole biting-Santa-at-Harrods incident was a complete misunderstanding. And that Santa was a total wimp. He did *not* need to go to the hospital.

"It was Luke and me. We wrecked the sleigh, trying to get her off a reindeer."

"Ah." Dad nods sagely, and we all turn glumly toward the exit.

"Minnie's quite a live wire, isn't she?" ventures Janice timidly after a while.

"Little rascal," says Martin, and tickles Minnie under the chin. "She's a handful!"

Maybe I'm feeling oversensitive. But all this talk of "handfuls" and "rascals" and "live wires" is suddenly pressing on my sore spot.

"You don't think Minnie's *spoiled,* do you?" I say suddenly, and come to an abrupt halt on the marble mall floor. "Be honest."

Janice inhales sharply. "Well," she begins, glancing at

Martin as though for support. "I wasn't going to say anything, but—"

"*Spoiled?*" Mum cuts her off with a laugh. "Nonsense! There's nothing wrong with Minnie, is there, my precious? She just knows her own mind!" She strokes Minnie's hair fondly, then looks up again. "Becky, love, you were exactly the same at her age. *Exactly* the same."

At once I relax. Mum always says the right thing. I glance over at Luke—but to my surprise he doesn't return my relieved smile. He looks as though some new and alarming thought has transfixed him.

"Thanks, Mum." I give her a fond hug. "You always make everything better. Come on, let's get home."

BY THE TIME Minnie's in bed, I've cheered up. In fact, I'm feeling very festive. *This* is what Christmas is all about. Mulled wine and mince pies and *White Christmas* on the telly. We've hung up Minnie's stocking (gorgeous red gingham, from The Conran Shop) and put out a glass of sherry for Father Christmas, and now Luke and I are in our bedroom, wrapping up her presents.

Mum and Dad are really generous. They've given us the whole top floor of the house to live in, so we have quite a lot of privacy. The only slight downside is, our wardrobe isn't *that* big. But it doesn't matter, because I've taken over the guest room wardrobe too—plus I've arranged all my shoes on the bookshelves on the landing. (I put the books in boxes. No one ever read them, anyway.)

I've put up a hanging rail in Dad's study, for coats and party dresses, and stacked some hatboxes in the utility room. And I keep all my makeup on the dining table, which is the ideal size—in fact, it could have been *designed* for makeup. My mascaras fit in the knife drawer, my straightening irons go perfectly on the hostess trolley, and I've put all my magazines in piles on the chairs.

I've also stored just a few teeny things in the garage, like all my old boots, and this amazing set of vintage trunks I bought at an antiques shop, and a Power Plate machine (which I bought off eBay and *must* start using). It's getting a bit crowded in there now, I suppose—but it's not like Dad ever uses the garage for the car, is it?

Luke finishes wrapping a jigsaw puzzle, reaches for a Magic Drawing Easel, then looks around the room and frowns.

"*How* many presents is Minnie getting?"

"Just the usual number," I say defensively.

Although, to be honest, I was a bit taken aback myself. I forgot how many I'd bought from catalogs and crafts fairs and stashed away throughout the year.

"This one's educational." I hastily whip the price tag off the Magic Drawing Easel. "And it was really cheap. Have some more mulled wine!" I pour him another glass, then reach for a hat with two red sparkly pom-poms. It's the cutest thing, and they had them in baby sizes too.

If we had another baby, it could wear a pom-pom hat to match Minnie's. People would call them the Children in the Pom-Pom Hats.

I have a sudden alluring image of myself walking down the street with Minnie. She'd be pushing her toy pram with a dolly in it and I'd be pushing a pram with a real baby in it. She'd have a friend for life. It would all be so perfect . . .

"Becky? Sellotape? *Becky?*"

Suddenly I realize Luke's said my name about four times. "Oh! Sorry! Here you are. Isn't this lovely?" I jiggle the red pom-poms at Luke. "They had them for babies too."

I leave a significant pause, letting the word *babies* hang in the air and using all my powers of marital telepathy.

"This Sellotape is crap. It's all shredded." He discards it impatiently.

Huh. So much for marital telepathy. Maybe I should introduce the subject by stealth. Suze once persuaded her husband, Tarkie, to go on a package holiday to Disneyland so stealthily that he didn't even realize where they were going till they were on the plane. Mind you, Tarkie is Tarkie (sweet, unsuspicious, usually thinking about Wagner or sheep). And Luke is Luke (on the case and always thinking I'm up to something. Which I am *not*).

"So that's fantastic news about Arcodas," I say casually. "And the house."

"Isn't it great?" Luke's face cracks briefly in a smile.

"It's like all the pieces of the jigsaw are falling into place. At least, *nearly* all the pieces." I leave another meaningful pause, but Luke doesn't even notice.

What's the point of peppering your conversation with meaningful pauses if no one notices? I've had enough of being stealthy. It's totally overrated.

"Luke, let's have another baby!" I say in a rush. "Tonight!"

There's silence. For an instant I wonder whether Luke even heard. Then he raises his head, looking astonished.

"Are you *nuts*?"

I stare back at him, affronted.

"Of course I'm not nuts! I think we should have a little brother or sister for Minnie. Don't you?"

"My petal." Luke sits back on his heels. "We can't control one child. How on earth would we control two? You saw the way she behaved today."

Not him too.

"What are you saying?" I can't help sounding hurt. "Do *you* think Minnie's spoiled?"

"I'm not saying that," Luke says carefully. "But you have to admit, she's out of control."

"No, she's not!"

"Look at the facts. She's been banned from four Santa's Grottos." He ticks off on his fingers. "And St. Paul's Cathedral. Not to mention the incident at Harvey Nichols *and* the fiasco at my office."

Is he going to hold that against her forever? They shouldn't have expensive artwork on the walls, is what I say. They're supposed to be working, not walking around looking at art all day.

"She's just spirited," I say defensively. "Maybe a baby would be good for her."

"And drive us insane." Luke shakes his head. "Becky, let's hold our horses on this one, OK?"

I feel crushed. I don't want to hold my horses. I want to have two children in matching pom-pom hats.

"Luke, I've really thought about this carefully. I want Minnie to have a lifelong friend and not grow up an only child. And I want our children to be close in age, not years apart. *And* I've got a hundred quid's worth of vouchers for Baby World which I never spent!" I add, suddenly remembering. "They'll expire soon!"

"Becky." Luke rolls his eyes. "We're not having another baby because we've got some vouchers for Baby World."

"That's not *why* we'd have the baby!" I say indignantly. "That was only an *extra reason.*"

Trust him to pick on that. He's just avoiding the issue.

"So what do you mean? That you *never* want another baby?"

A guarded look flashes over Luke's face. For a moment he doesn't answer but finishes wrapping the pre-

sent, straightening every corner perfectly and smooth-
ing the Sellotape down with his thumbnail. He looks
exactly like someone putting off talking about something which is a sore point.

I watch in growing dismay. Since when was having a
second baby a sore point?

"Maybe I would like to have more than one child,"
he says at last. "In theory. One day."

Well, he couldn't sound less enthusiastic.

"Right," I gulp. "I see."

"Becky, don't get me wrong. Having Minnie has
been . . . amazing. I couldn't possibly love her any
more, you know that."

He meets my eyes directly, and I'm too honest to do
anything except nod silently.

"But we're not ready to have another one. Face it,
Becky, it's been a hell of a year: We don't even have our
own house yet, Minnie's a handful, we've got enough
on our plate as it is . . . Let's just forget about it for now.
Enjoy Christmas, enjoy being the three of us. Talk
about it again in a year's time, maybe."

A year's time?

"But that's ages away." To my horror, my voice shakes
slightly. "I was hoping we might *have* another baby by
next Christmas! I'd even planned perfect names for if
we conceived it tonight. Wenceslas or Snowflake."

"Oh, Becky." Luke takes hold of both my hands and
sighs. "If we could get through one day without a
major incident, maybe I'd feel differently."

"We can easily get through a *day*. She's not that bad!"

"Has there been a single day in which Minnie has not
created havoc of some sort?"

"OK," I say a bit defiantly. "You wait. I'm going to
start a Minnie Incident Book, and I bet we don't have
any entries. I bet Minnie will be an angel tomorrow."

Silently, I resume wrapping presents, breaking off

the Sellotape with extra snap, just to show how hurt I feel. He probably never wanted any children at all. He probably resents me and Minnie. He probably wishes he was still a bachelor, zooming around in his sports car all day long. I knew it.

"So, is that all the presents?" I say eventually, plonking a big spotted bow on the final package.

"Actually . . . I've got one more thing." Luke looks sheepish. "I couldn't resist."

He heads to the wardrobe and rifles at the back, behind his shoes. As he turns, he's holding a scruffy cardboard box. He puts it down on the carpet and gently pulls out an old toy theater. It's made of wood, with faded paint and real little red velvet curtains and even tiny footlights.

"Wow," I breathe. "That's *amazing*. Where did you find that?"

"Tracked it down on eBay. I had one when I was a child, exactly like this. Same sets, characters, everything."

I watch, agog, as he pulls the ropes and the curtains swish creakily back. The stage is dressed with sets for *A Midsummer Night's Dream,* painted in incredible detail. One's an interior scene with pillars, another is a woodland copse with a brook and mossy bank, another is a big forest with distant spires of a castle in the background. There are wooden characters in costumes, and even one with a donkey's head, who must be . . . Puck.

No, not Puck. The other one. Oberon?

OK, I'll quickly Google *A Midsummer Night's Dream* while Luke's downstairs.

"I used to play with this with Annabel." Luke is staring at it as though entranced. "I must have been about . . . six? It was like going into a different world. Look, all the sets are on runners. It's superb craftsmanship."

As I watch him pushing the characters back and

forth, I feel a sudden pang for him. I've never known Luke to display nostalgia for anything, ever.

"Well, don't let Minnie break it," I say gently.

"She'll be fine." He smiles. "We'll put on a father–daughter performance on Christmas Day."

Now I feel a bit guilty. I take it back. Maybe Luke doesn't resent me and Minnie. He's had a hard year, that's all.

What I need to do is have a little Mummy–Minnie chat. Explain the situation to her. And she'll reform her ways and Luke will reconsider, and everything will be perfect.

THREE

OK, CHRISTMAS DOESN'T COUNT. Everyone knows that.

You can't expect a toddler to behave perfectly when it's all so exciting and there are sweets and decorations everywhere. And it's no wonder Minnie woke up at 3:00 a.m. and started yelling for everyone. She just wanted us all to see her stocking. Anyone else would have done the same.

Anyway, I've already torn out the first page of the Incident Book and shredded it. Everyone's allowed to have a false start.

I take a sip of coffee and happily reach for a Quality Street chocolate. God, I love Christmas. The whole house smells of roasting turkey, carols are playing over the sound system, and Dad's cracking nuts by the fire. I can't help feeling a glow as I look round the sitting room: at the tree twinkling with lights and the nativity scene we've had since I was a child (we lost baby Jesus years ago, but we use a clothes-peg instead).

Little Minnie's eyes when she saw her stocking this morning were like saucers. She just couldn't take it in. She kept saying, "Stocking? *Stocking?*" in utter disbelief.

"Becky, love," calls Mum. I head into the hall to see her at the door of the kitchen in her Santa apron.

"Which Christmas crackers shall we have at lunch—novelty games or luxury gifts?"

"What about those ones you got from the German market?" I suggest. "With the little wooden toys inside."

"Good idea!" Mum's face brightens. "I'd forgotten about those."

"Yup, I've got the paperwork here . . ." Luke heads past me toward the stairs, talking on his phone. "If you could run your eyes over the Sanderson agreement . . . Yup. I'll be in the office by three. Just a few things to clear up here first. Cheers, Gary."

"Luke!" I say indignantly as he switches off. "Christmas isn't 'a few things to clear up.'"

"I agree," says Luke, not breaking his stride for a second. "Then again, it's not Christmas."

Honestly. Can't he get into the spirit of it?

"Yes, it *is*."

"In Bloomwood World, maybe. Everywhere else, it's December twenty-eighth and people are getting on with their lives."

He's so *literal*.

"OK, maybe it's not exactly Christmas Day," I say crossly. "But it's our *second* Christmas. It's our special Christmas for Jess and Tom, and it's just as important and you could try to be a bit festive!"

This whole two Christmases thing is fab. In fact, I think we should do it every year. It could be a family tradition.

"My love." Luke pauses, halfway up the stairs, and starts counting off on his fingers. "One, it is not just as important. Two, I need to finalize this agreement today. Three, Tom and Jess aren't even here yet."

A text arrived from Jess and Tom overnight to say that their plane from Chile had been delayed. Since then, Janice has come across to our house approximately every twenty minutes to ask if we've heard anything, and could we possibly look online again, and have there been any reports of accidents or hijacks?

She's even more hyper than usual, and we all know why: She's desperately hoping that Tom and Jess have got engaged. Apparently Tom said in his last email that he had *something to tell her.* I heard her and Mum talking the other day, and Janice is obviously dying to hold another wedding. She's got all sorts of new ideas for floral arrangements and the photos could be taken in front of the magnolia tree and it would "excise the memory of that ungrateful little harlot." (Lucy. Tom's first wife. Total cow, take it from me.)

"On the same subject, why on earth did Minnie get another stocking this morning?" adds Luke, lowering his voice. "Whose idea was that?"

"It was . . . Father Christmas's idea," I say a bit defiantly. "By the way, have you seen how good she's being today?"

Minnie's been helping Mum in the kitchen all morning and she's been absolutely perfect, apart from a tiny moment with the electric mixer, which I won't mention to Luke.

"I'm sure she is—" Luke begins, as the doorbell rings. "That can't be them." He consults his watch, looking puzzled. "They're still in the air."

"Is that Jess?" calls Mum excitedly from the kitchen. "Has anyone texted Janice?"

"It can't be Jess yet!" I call back. "It must be Suze, arrived early." I hurry to the front door and swing it open—and sure enough there's the whole Cleath-Stuart family, looking like a photo spread from the Toast catalog.

Suze is stunning in a black shearling coat, her long blond hair streaming down; Tarquin is the same as ever, in an ancient old Barbour; and the three children are all gangly legs and huge eyes and Fair Isle sweaters.

"Suze!" I fling my arms round her.

"Bex! Happy Christmas!"

"Happy Christmas!" calls out Clemmie, sucking her thumb and holding on to Suze's hand.

"And a happy you near!" chimes in Ernest, who is my godson and already has that bony, upper-class beanpole look going on. ("Happy you near" is an old Cleath-Stuart family saying. Like "Happy bad day" instead of "Happy birthday." There are so many of them, they should issue a crib sheet.) He shoots an uncertain look up at Suze, who nods encouragingly—then he extends a formal hand to me, as though we're meeting for the first time at the ambassador's reception. I solemnly shake it, then scoop him up in a bear hug till he giggles.

"Suzie, dear! Merry Christmas!" Mum hurries into the hall and gives her a warm hug. "And Tark—" She stops in her tracks. "Lord . . ." She glances anxiously at me. "Your lordship . . . ness . . ."

"Ahm . . . please, Mrs. Bloomwood." Tarkie has turned a bit pink. "Tarquin is fine."

Tarkie's grandfather died of pneumonia a couple of months ago. Which was really tragic and everything, but there again, he was ninety-six. Anyway, the point is, Tarkie's dad inherited the title of earl—and Tarkie gets to be a lord! He's Lord Tarquin Cleath-Stuart, which makes Suze "Lady." It's all so grown-up and posh I can hardly get my head round it. Plus, they now have even *more* squillions of money and land and stuff than they had before. Their new house is in Hampshire, only about half an hour away from here. It's called Letherby Hall and it looks just like *Brideshead Revisited*. They don't even live in it full time; they've got a place in Chelsea too.

You'd think Tarkie could stump up for a new scarf. He's unwinding the most threadbare, ratty thing from around his neck—it looks like it was knitted by his old nanny twenty years ago. Well, it probably was.

"Did you get any nice Christmas presents, Tarkie?" I ask.

I've bought him this brillant aromatherapy diffuser thing, which I'm sure he'll love. Well, Suze will love.

"Absolutely." He nods fervently. "Suze bought me a rather wonderful merino tup. Such a surprise."

Tup? Does he mean tux?

"That sounds fab!" I exclaim. "Merino is *so* in right now. You should see the new John Smedley collection; you'd love it."

"John Smedley?" Tarkie seems baffled. "I don't know the name. Is he . . . a breeder?"

"The knitwear designer! You know, you could put a turtleneck under your tux," I say in sudden inspiration. "That's a really cool look. Is it single-breasted?"

Tarkie looks totally at sea, and Suze gives a gurgle of laughter.

"Bex, I didn't give him a tux. I gave him a *tup*. An un-castrated sheep."

An uncastrated sheep? What kind of Christmas present is that?

"Oh, I *see*." I try my hardest to summon some enthu-siasm. "Of course. An uncastrated sheep! Er . . . lovely."

"Don't worry, I gave him a jacket too," adds Suze, grinning at me.

"For when I'm out on my bike," Tarkie chimes in. "It's absolutely super, darling."

I already know better than to say, "Oh, cool, a Bel-staff?" Tarkie doesn't mean "bike" like most people mean "bike." Sure enough, Suze is scrolling through pictures on her phone and turns it to show me a photo of Tarkie in a tweed jacket, perched on a vintage penny-farthing. He's got loads of antique bikes—in fact, sometimes he even lends them to TV companies as props and advises on the way they were ridden in the olden days. (The only thing is, the people don't always listen. And then Tarkie sees the show on TV and they're doing it wrong and he gets all depressed.)

"Why don't all the children come into the kitchen for some squash and biscuits." Mum is rounding up Ernest, Clementine, and Wilfrid like a mother hen. "Where's Minnie? Minnie, darling, come and see your friends!"

Like a fireball, Minnie rockets into the hall from the kitchen, dressed in her scarlet Christmas dress, the sparkly red pom-pom hat, and a pair of pink fairy wings which she's refused to take off since finding them in her stocking.

"Ketchup!" she cries triumphantly, and aims the bottle at Suze's gorgeous coat.

My heart freezes.

Oh no. Oh no, oh no. How did she get hold of that? We always put it on the top shelf now, ever since . . .

"Minnie, no. *No.*" I make a swipe for the ketchup, but she dodges me. "Minnie, give it to me. *Don't you dare*—"

"Ketchup!" The stream of red is streaking through the air before I can even react.

"Nooo!"

"Minnie!"

"Suze!"

It's like *Apocalypse Now;* I see the whole thing as if in slow motion. Suze gasping and shrinking back, and Tarquin diving in front of her, and the ketchup landing in a massive blob on his Barbour.

I don't dare look at Luke.

"Give that to me!" I grab the ketchup out of Minnie's hand. "Naughty girl! Suze, Tarkie, I'm *so* sorry . . ."

"I do apologize for our daughter's terrible behavior," chimes in Luke, a meaningful edge to his voice.

"Oh, no problem," says Suze. "I'm sure she did it by accident, didn't you, darling?" She ruffles Minnie's hair.

"Absolutely," chimes in Tarkie. "No harm done. If I could just . . ." He gestures awkwardly at the tomato ketchup, which is dripping down the front of his Barbour.

"Of course!" I hastily take his Barbour from him. "Well dived, Tarkie," I can't help adding admiringly. "You were really quick."

"Oh, it was nothing." He looks abashed. "Any decent chap would have done it."

It just goes to show how devoted Tarquin is to Suze. He dived in front of her without a moment's hesitation. It's quite romantic, actually.

I wonder if Luke would take a hit of tomato ketchup for me. I might ask him later. Just casually.

"Luke," says Tarquin, a little diffidently, as they shake hands. "Wondered if I could pick your brains about something?"

"No problem." Luke looks surprised. "Shall we go into the sitting room?"

"I'll take the children into the kitchen and sort out this Barbour . . ." Mum takes it from me.

"And, Bex, you can show me all the stuff you got at the sales!" says Suze excitedly. "I mean . . . er . . . talk about the children," she amends hastily as I give her a surreptitious kick.

AS WE SPRAWL on my bed and I start unpacking all the stuff I bought on Boxing Day, it feels like old times, when Suze and I used to share a flat in Fulham.

"*This* is what I'm wearing at the christening." I shake out my brand-new Russian-style dress.

"Fantastic!" says Suze, as she tries on my new leather jacket. "Even better than the picture."

I texted Suze a few photos from the sales, and she gave me her opinions. And in return she sent me some photos of her and Tarkie grouse-beating, or pigeon-shooting, or whatever they were doing. Suze is so sweet and loyal, just like the queen, she never once complains. But, honestly, where would *you* rather be? On some freezing cold moor or in Selfridges with 70 percent off?

"And . . . ta-daah!"

I pull out my prize purchase: my Ally Smith limited-edition cardigan with the famous signature button.

"Oh my God!" squeaks Suze. "Where did you get that? Was it on sale?"

"Sixty percent off! Only a hundred and ten pounds."

"Look at the button." Suze reaches out and strokes it lustfully.

"Isn't it great?" I beam back happily. "I'm going to wear it so much, it'll *easily* pay for itself—"

The door opens and Luke comes in.

"Oh, hi." Instinctively, before I quite realize I'm doing it, I push one of my sale bags under the bed.

It's not that he disapproves, exactly. I mean, it's my money, I earned it, I can do what I like with it. It's just that when Mum and I were up at 7:00 a.m. on Boxing Day, ready to hit the sales, Luke looked at us in bafflement, then looked at all the presents still under the tree, and then said, "Didn't you get enough stuff yesterday?"

Which just shows how little he understands about anything. Christmas presents and the sales are *totally* different. They're like . . . different food groups.

"Bex got the most amazing bargains at the sales,"

says Suze supportively. "Don't you love her new cardigan?"

Luke looks at the cardigan. He turns and studies me for a moment—then the cardigan again. Then he frowns as though something is puzzling him.

"How much was it?"

"A hundred and ten," I say defensively. "Sixty percent off. It's designer, limited edition."

"So . . . you've just spent a hundred and ten pounds on a cardigan which is exactly the same as the one you're wearing."

"What?" I glance down at myself in bemusement. "Of course I haven't. It's nothing like it."

"It's identical!"

"No, it isn't! How can you say that?"

There's a short pause. We're staring at each other as though to say, "Have I married a lunatic?"

"They're both pale cream." Luke ticks off on his fingers. "They both have one large button. They're both cardigans. Identical."

Is he blind?

"But the button's in a different *place,*" I explain. "It changes the whole shape. And this one has flared sleeves. They're nothing like each other, are they, Suze?"

"Completely different." Suze nods fervently.

It's obvious from his expression that Luke doesn't get it. Sometimes I wonder how someone so unobservant can be so successful in life.

"And this button's *red,*" adds Suze helpfully.

"Exactly!" I point to the oversize button with trademark Ally Smith crystals. "That's the whole point of the piece, this amazing button. It's like . . . a signature."

"So you spent a hundred quid on a button."

God, he's annoying sometimes.

"It's an *investment,*" I inform him frostily. "I was just

saying to Suze, I'll wear it so many times, it'll totally pay for itself."

"How many would that be? Twice?"

I stare at him with utter indignation.

"Of course not *twice*. I'll probably wear it . . ." I think a moment, trying to be absolutely realistic. "A hundred times. So each time will cost one pound ten. I think I can afford one pound ten for a designer classic of its time, don't you?"

Luke makes a kind of snorting noise. "Becky, have you ever worn *anything* a hundred times? I'll count it a success if you wear it once."

Oh, ha-di-ha.

"I bet you I'll wear it a hundred times. At least." Determinedly, I shrug off my cardigan and start pulling on the Ally Smith one. "You see? I've already worn it once."

I'll show him. I'll wear it a *thousand* times.

"I must go, Tarquin's waiting for me." Luke shoots Suze a quizzical look. "Quite a business you've inherited."

"Oh, I know," says Suze. "Poor Tarkie was getting in a state about it, so I said, 'Ask Luke, *he'll* know what to do.' "

"Well, I'm glad you did." Luke has been rifling in his cabinet for some papers. He bangs it shut and heads out again. "See you later."

"What was that about?" I say, puzzled. "What business?"

"Oh, it's this Shetland Shortbread thing," says Suze vaguely. "It's quite a big deal, and now it belongs to us . . ."

Hang on a minute. Rewind.

"You own Shetland Shortbread?" I stare at her in amazement. "Those red tins you can buy in Waitrose?"

"Exactly!" says Suze brightly. "It's really scrummy. They make it on one of the farms."

I'm flabbergasted. What else does Suze suddenly now own? Chocolate HobNobs? Kit Kats?

Ooh, that would be cool. I wonder how many free ones she'd get. Maybe . . . a box a year?

No, that's ridiculous. It would be at least ten boxes a year, wouldn't it?

AFTER I'VE SHOWN SUZE all my clothes, I pop downstairs and make some coffee and check that the children are OK. I come back up to find Suze wandering around the cluttered room and picking over my stuff, like she always does. She looks up, holding a pile of old photos which I've been meaning to put in albums. "Bex, I can't believe you're moving out of here at last. It seems like you've been here forever."

"It *has* been forever. Two whole years!"

"What did your mum and dad say?"

"I haven't told them yet." I glance at the door and lower my voice. "I think they'll really miss us when we're gone. In fact . . . I'm a bit worried how they'll take it."

The truth is, Mum and Dad have got used to having us around. Especially Minnie. Every time one of our house purchases fell through, they were secretly glad, Mum once told me.

"God, of course." Suze's face crumples anxiously. "They'll be devastated. Your poor mum will need loads of support. Maybe you can fix up some counseling!" she adds in sudden inspiration. "I bet they have empty-nest workshops or something."

"I do feel guilty." I sigh. "But we can't stay here forever, can we? I mean, we need our own space."

"Of course you do," says Suze supportively. "Don't

worry, your parents will come to terms with it. So come on, show me the house! What's it like? What does it need doing to it?"

"Well, it doesn't really *need* anything done to it," I confess, as I hand her the details. "It's been decorated by a developer."

"Eight bedrooms!" Suze raises her eyebrows. "Wow!"

"I know. It's amazing! It's so much bigger inside than it looks. And it's all been freshly painted and everything. But still, we should put our stamp on it, shouldn't we?"

"Oh, definitely." Suze nods wisely.

Suze is *so* much more with it than Luke, who, by the way, hasn't even been inside the place. I told him we needed to put our stamp on it and he said, "Why can't we be happy with someone else's stamp?"

"I've already made loads of plans," I tell her enthusiastically. "Like, in the hall I thought we could have a really cool hat stand with a single studded Alexander Wang bag hanging from it. It would make such a statement." I scrabble under the bed for the sketch I've done and show it to her.

"Wow," breathes Suze. "That looks amazing. Have you got an Alexander Wang bag?"

"I'd have to buy one," I explain. "And next to it, maybe a console table accessorized with some Lara Bohinc jewelry?"

"I love Lara Bohinc!" says Suze enthusiastically. "Have you got some of her stuff? You never showed me!"

"No, well, I'd have to buy some of that too. But, I mean, it wouldn't be for *me*, would it?" I add hurriedly at her expression. "It would be for the *house*."

For a moment Suze just looks at me. It's the same look she gave me when I wanted us to set ourselves up as telephone fortune-tellers. (Which I *still* think was a good idea.)

"You want to buy a bag and jewelry for your *house*?" she says at last.

"Yes! Why not?"

"Bex, no one buys a bag and jewelry for their house."

"Well, maybe they should! Maybe their houses would look better if they did! And, anyway, don't worry, I'm going to buy a sofa too." I chuck a load of interiors magazines at her. "Go on, find me a nice one."

Half an hour later, the bed is littered with interiors magazines and we're both lying in silence, wallowing in pictures of amazing oversize orange velvet sofas and staircases with built-in lights and kitchens with polished granite mixed with reclaimed wood doors. The trouble is, I want my house to look like *all* of them. All at once.

"You've got a massive basement!" Suze is looking at the house details again. "What's that going to be?"

"Good question!" I look up. "I think it should be a gym. But Luke wants to store his boring old wine there and do wine tastings."

"*Wine tastings?*" Suze pulls a face. "Oh, have a gym. We could do Pilates together!"

"Exactly! It would be so cool! But Luke's got all this valuable old wine in storage, and he's really excited about getting it out again."

That's one thing I'll never understand about Luke: his love of zillion-pound wine, when you could buy a really nice pinot grigio for a tenner and spend the rest on a skirt.

"So, there's one bedroom for you and Luke . . ." Suze is still perusing the details. "One for Minnie . . ."

"One for clothes."

"One for shoes?"

"Definitely. And one for makeup."

"Ooh!" Suze looks up with interest. "A makeup room! Did Luke agree to that?"

"I'm going to call it the library," I explain.

"But that still leaves three bedrooms." Suze lifts her eyebrows significantly at me. "Any plans to . . . fill them up?"

You see? This is why I should have married Suze. *She* understands me.

"I wish." I heave a sigh. "But guess what? Luke doesn't want another baby."

"Really?" Suze looks taken aback. "How come?"

"He says Minnie's too wild and we can't cope with two and we should just enjoy what we've got. He won't budge." I hunch my shoulders gloomily and flick through an article on antique baths.

"Could you just . . . jump him?" Suze says after a while. "And forget to take your pill accidentally-on-purpose and pretend it was a mistake? He'll love the baby when it arrives."

I can't pretend this idea hasn't crossed my mind. Secretly. But I couldn't do it.

"No." I shake my head. "I don't want to trap him. I want him to *want* another baby."

"Maybe he'll change his mind at the christening." Suze's eyes brighten. "You know, it was at Ernie's christening that we decided to have another one. Ernie looked so adorable, and we thought how lovely it would be to give him a brother or sister, so we decided to go for it. Of course, we ended up with *two* more," she adds as an afterthought. "But that won't happen to you."

"Maybe." I'm silent a moment, gearing myself up for the big question. I don't want to ask it. But I have to be brave. "Suze . . . can you be honest with me about something? Really, truly honest?"

"OK," she says a bit apprehensively. "But not if it's about how many times a week we have sex."

What? Where did *that* come from? OK, now I instantly want to know how many times she has sex. It must be never. Or maybe all the time. God, I bet it's all the time. I bet she and Tarkie . . .

Anyway.

"It's not sex." I force myself to return to the topic. "It's . . . do you think Minnie's *spoiled*?"

I can already feel myself wincing with trepidation. What if she says yes? What if my best friend thinks Minnie's a monster? I'll be totally mortified.

"No!" says Suze at once. "Of course Minnie's not spoiled! She's lovely. She's just a bit . . . feisty. But that's good! No children are perfect."

"Yours are," I say morosely. "Nothing ever goes wrong with them."

"Oh my God! Are you kidding?" Suze sits upright and discards the house details altogether. "We're having *such* problems with Ernie. His teacher keeps calling us in. He's hopeless at everything except German, and they don't even *teach* German."

"Oh, Suze," I say sympathetically.

I don't need to ask why Ernie speaks German so well. Tarquin thinks Wagner is the only music worth listening to, and he plays it to all his children, every night. Don't get me wrong, Ernie is my godson and I love him to bits. But last time I visited, he told me the whole story of something called the Something Singers and it went on for hours and I nearly seized up with boredom.

"I've got to go and see the headmistress," Suze continues, looking upset. "What am I going to do if she asks him to leave?"

Forgetting all about my own problems, I put an arm round her shoulders and squeeze, feeling incensed. How dare anyone upset Suze? And who are these morons, anyway? I've seen Ernie's school when I've gone with Suze to pick him up. It's very snooty, with lilac blazers, and costs a million pounds a term or something, and they don't even include lunches. They're probably too busy counting the fees to appreciate real talent.

"I'm sure it'll be fine," I say robustly. "And if they don't want Ernie, then it's obviously a rubbish school."

If I ever see that headmistress, I'll give her my opinion, *very* pointedly. I'm Ernie's godmother, after all. In fact, maybe I should go along to the meeting at the school and express my views. I'm about to suggest this to Suze, when she slaps her hand on the bed.

"I know, Bex! I've got it. You should get a nanny."

"A *nanny*?" I stare at her.

"Who looks after Minnie when you're at work? Still your mum?"

I nod. Since my maternity leave ended, I've worked two and a half days a week at The Look, where I'm a personal shopper. While I'm there, Mum looks after Minnie, which is brilliant because I can just leave her in the kitchen, having her breakfast, and she hardly even notices when I go.

"Does your mum take her to playgroup?"

I make a face. "Not really."

Mum's not into playgroups. She went to Tick Tock once, had a disagreement with a fellow grandmother about who's the best Miss Marple on TV, and never went back.

"So what do they do?"

"Well, it varies," I say vaguely. "They do lots of educational stuff . . ."

This is a slight fib. As far as I can tell, the program never varies. They go shopping and have tea at the Debenhams café, then come home and watch Disney videos.

God, maybe Suze is right. Maybe Minnie needs more routine. Maybe *that's* what's wrong.

"A nanny will knock her into shape," says Suze confidently. "Plus she'll organize her meals and washing and everything, and Luke will see how smooth everything can be. And he'll change his mind instantly. Trust me."

I *knew* Suze would have the answer. This is the solution. A nanny!

I have an image of a cross between Mary Poppins and Mrs. Doubtfire, all cozy with an apron and a spoonful of sugar and lots of wise, homespun words. The whole place will be calm and smell of baking bread. Minnie will become an angel child who wears a pinafore and sits quietly, making constructive Play-Doh, and Luke will instantly drag me off to bed and ravish me.

I mean, it would be worth it just for the ravishing.

"*Everyone's* using Ultimate Nannies at the moment. They're the latest thing." Suze has already opened up my laptop and found the website. "Have a look. I'll pop down and check on the children."

I take the laptop from her and find myself looking at a website called *Ultimate Nannies: raising well-balanced, accomplished children who will be the successes of tomorrow.*

My jaw sags slightly as I scroll down. Bloody hell. These nannies don't look anything like Mrs. Doubtfire. They look like Elle Macpherson. They've all got perfect teeth and perfect abs and intelligent-looking smiles.

Our modern, trained nannies are loving, trustworthy, and educated. They will take full control of your child's routine and cook a balanced menu. They will stimulate your child's development—physically, emotionally, and intellectually. Ultimate Nannies are highly qualified in child nutrition, safety, cultural enrichment, and creative play. Many are fluent in French or Mandarin and/or offer instruction in music, Kumon math, martial arts, or ballet.

I feel totally inadequate as I scroll through pictures of smiley girls with long shiny hair cooking vegetable risottos, bouncing balls in the garden, or dressed up in judo kit. No *wonder* Minnie has tantrums. It's because no one's doing martial arts or making sushi with her. All this time I've totally deprived her. Suddenly, making jam tarts in the kitchen with Mum seems totally lame. We don't even make the pastry ourselves; we get it out of a packet. We *have* to hire an Ultimate Nanny, as soon as possible.

The only thing is—tiny point—do I want some shiny-haired girl dancing around the place in her tight jeans and sushi-making apron? What if she and Luke really hit it off? What if he wants "martial arts" lessons too?

I hesitate for a moment, my hand hovering over the mouse pad. Come on. I have to be mature here. I have to think of the benefits to Minnie. I have to remember that I have a loving, faithful husband and last time I thought he was playing around with a shiny-red-haired girl whose name I won't even deign to remember (you see, Venetia? *That's* how little you mean to me), I'd got it all wrong.

Plus, if the nanny is really sexy and swishy-haired, I can arrange her hours so Luke never sees her. Seized by determination, I fill in the form and press *Send*. This is the answer! Bring in the experts. The only person I'll have to talk round is Mum. She's not keen on nannies. Or day care. Or even babysitters. But that's only because she watches too many real-life dramas about evil nutcase nannies. I mean, not *every* nanny can be a stalker impersonating a dead woman with the FBI on her tail, surely?

And doesn't she want her grandchild to be accomplished and well balanced? Doesn't she want Minnie to be a success of tomorrow?

Exactly.

AS I HEAD DOWNSTAIRS, I find Suze with Luke and Tarquin in the sitting room. There's an empty coffeepot and a massive mound of paperwork on the table, and they've obviously been hard at it.

"You have to think of Shetland Shortbread as a *brand*," Luke is saying. "You're sitting on something that could be a huge global success, but you need to raise its profile. Find a story, a personality, a USP, an *angle*. Establish your brand values." He looks all fired up and enthusiastic, the way he always does when he can see potential in a new project.

Tarquin, on the other hand, looks like a rabbit caught in headlights.

"Absolutely," he says nervously. "Brand values. Ahm . . . Suze, darling, Luke's been terribly helpful. We can't thank you enough."

"Really, it's nothing." Luke claps him on the shoulder. "But you need to sort yourself out, Tarquin. Build an effective business team, strategize, and go from there."

I stifle a giggle. Even *I* know that Tarquin isn't the strategizing sort.

"I'll read those contracts for you and give you my take on them." Luke picks up his BlackBerry. "I know your people have approved them, but as I said, I think you can do better."

"Really, Luke," protests Tarquin feebly. "You've given me far too much time and expertise already—"

"Don't be ridiculous." Luke shoots him a brief smile and switches his BlackBerry on.

Tarquin's bony face is growing flushed. He shoots an

agonized glance at Suze, twists his hands, and clears his throat.

"Luke, I know you have your own company," he suddenly blurts out. "But I'd be delighted to offer you a job. Business manager of the entire estate, all my concerns. Any salary. Any terms."

"A *job*?" Luke looks taken aback.

"Oh yes!" Suze claps her hands with enthusiasm. "Brilliant idea! That would be amazing. We could provide accommodation too, couldn't we?" she adds to Tarkie. "The little castle in Perthshire would be perfect! I mean, not nearly as nice as your house in Maida Vale," she adds loyally. "But as a second home?"

"*Any* terms?" says Luke slowly.

"Yes," replies Tarquin after only a moment's hesitation. "Yes, of course."

"I'll do it for sixty percent of all gross revenues," Luke shoots back.

There's a stunned silence. I can't believe what I'm hearing. Is Luke seriously considering giving up Brandon Communications to run the Cleath-Stuart estate?

Would we live in a *castle*?

Oh my God. We'd be a clan. We could have our own tartan! Hot pink with silver and black. It would be the "McBloomwood of Brandon" tartan, and we'd do Scottish dancing and Luke would wear a sporran . . .

"I . . . ahm . . ." Tarquin glances wildly at Suze. "Ahm. That seems . . . reasonable—"

"Tarquin!" Luke practically explodes. "Of *course* sixty percent is not bloody reasonable! And *that* is why you need a new business adviser you can trust, and *that* is why I'm setting up a meeting for you with some consultants I can highly recommend, and I'm coming along to make sure you understand everything—" He taps at his BlackBerry, then stops as it starts buzzing like an angry bee. "Sorry, a few messages coming in . . ." He peers at the screen, his face jolts in surprise, and he taps something back.

"I knew Luke would never really say yes." Suze makes a rueful face at me. "He'd never abandon his business."

"I know." I nod, although secretly I feel a bit let down. I'd already mentally moved to a Scottish castle and called our second baby Morag.

"Well, you must please let me buy you a titchy," Tarquin is saying to Luke in those posh, stilted tones of his. "Or lunch? Or could I offer you a weekend's shooting? Or . . . or . . . a summer in our house in France? Or—"

"Jesus *Christ*," Luke suddenly says in a low voice. He seems stunned by whatever he's reading on the Black-Berry.

"What?" I say, alert. "What is it?"

Luke looks up and for the first time seems to realize that we're all watching him.

"Nothing." He puts on the smooth smile which means he's not about to discuss it. "Becky, I must go. I'll be late tonight, I'm afraid."

"You can't go!" I say in dismay. "What about our second Christmas? What about Jess and Tom?"

"Give them my love." He's already out of the room.

"What's up?" I call after him. "What's the crisis?" But he doesn't answer, and a moment later I hear the front door bang.

"Who's that at the door?" Mum's voice travels down the corridor. "Is somebody there?"

"It's only Luke," I call back. "He's got to go in to work; there's been an emergency—"

"No, it's not!" I can hear the front door opening and Dad's voice raised. "Jess! Tom! Welcome!"

Jess is here? Oh my God!

I hurry into the hall, followed by Suze, and there she

is. As tall and thin and toned as ever, with a deep tan and cropped hair bleached by the sun, in a gray hoody over faded black jeans.

"Becky." She hugs me, dropping her mammoth rucksack. "Good to see you. We just saw Luke rushing off. Hi, Suze."

"Welcome back! Hi, Tom!"

"Has anyone texted Janice?" Mum hurries out of the kitchen. "Does Janice know?"

"I'll call over the fence," says Dad. "Much quicker than sending a text."

"Quicker than a text?" retorts Mum. "Nonsense! Texts are *instant*, Graham. It's called modern technology."

"You think you could send a text more quickly than I could call over the fence?" scoffs Dad. "I'd like to see you try. By the time you get your phone out—"

"By the time you've walked across, I'll have sent the text!" Mum's already whipped her phone out.

"Janice!" Dad yells as he hurries across the drive. "Janice, Tom is here! You see?" he calls back triumphantly to Mum. "Good old-fashioned instant communication. The human voice."

"I'd forgotten what your parents are like," says Tom in an amused undertone to me, and I grin back. He's looking good. Edgier than before, unshaven and leaner round the cheeks. It's as though he's finally grown into his face. Plus he's chewing gum, so the breath isn't an issue. "Jane," he adds, "I'm heading home anyway, so you really don't need to text my mum—"

Mum ignores him. "*You* think texts are quicker, don't you, Becky, love?" she says firmly as she taps on her phone. "You tell your father to stop living in the dark ages."

But I don't reply. I'm too transfixed by Jess's left hand as she undoes her hoody zip. She's wearing a ring! On her fourth finger! OK, it's not exactly a Cartier solitaire. It's made of bone or wood or something, with what looks like a tiny gray pebble set in it.

Still, it's a ring! On her engagement finger!

I catch Suze's eye, and she's obviously noticed it too. This is so cool. Another family wedding! Minnie can be a bridesmaid!

"What is it?" Mum looks alertly from Suze to me. "What are you—*Oh!*" She suddenly notices the ring too.

Tom has disappeared and Jess is bending over her rucksack, oblivious to us. Mum starts mouthing something long and elaborate above Jess's head. She repeats it several times, looking frustrated that we can't understand. Then she starts gesturing, and I get a fit of the giggles.

"Come into the sitting room!" I manage to say to Jess. "Sit down. You must be exhausted."

Mum nods. "I'll make some tea."

Trust Jess to get engaged all discreetly and not say a word. If it were me I'd have run straight in, saying, "Guess what? Look at my pebble ring!"

"Jess!" Janice's high-pitched voice greets us as she arrives at the front door. Her hair is freshly dyed a virulent auburn, and she's wearing mauve eye shadow, which matches her shoes *and* her bracelet. "Love! Welcome back!"

Her gaze falls instantly on Jess's ring. *Instantly.* Her chin jerks up, and she inhales sharply, then catches Mum's eye.

I'm going to erupt with laughter if I don't get away. I follow Mum into the kitchen, where the children are all sitting in front of *The Little Mermaid.* We make the tea and cut the children some ham sandwiches, all the time whispering about the ring and when Jess and Tom are going to tell everyone.

"We must all act naturally," Mum says, putting two bottles of champagne in the freezer to cool down quickly. "Pretend we haven't noticed. Let them tell us in their own time."

Yeah, right. As we enter the sitting room, Jess is on the sofa, apparently unaware of Janice, Martin, Dad, and Suze sitting in a semicircle opposite, all staring at her left hand as though it's glowing radioactive. As I sit down, I glance out the window and see Tarquin with Ernie in the garden. Tarkie's making weird lunging gestures with his arms, which Ernie is copying beside him. I nudge Suze and say in an undertone, "I didn't know Tarkie did tai chi. He's really good!"

Suze swivels round and peers out the window. "That's not tai chi! They're practicing fly-fishing."

Both Tarkie and Ernie look totally absorbed—in fact, they make a really sweet sight, like a father bear teaching its baby cub to hunt on a TV nature documentary. (Except for the tiny fact that they're trying to catch imaginary fish. With nonexistent rods.)

"You know, Ernie's already caught a trout in our river!" says Suze proudly. "With only a teeny bit of help."

You see. I *knew* he was talented. He's obviously at the wrong school. He should be at fish-catching school.

"So!" says Mum brightly. "Tea, Jess?"

"Yes, thanks." Jess nods.

Mum pours out tea and there's a little pause—a little does-anyone-have-any-announcements-to-make? kind of pause. But Tom and Jess say nothing.

Janice puts her cup to her lips, then puts it down again, then breathes out shakily as though she can't bear the tension. Then her face lights up.

"Your present! Jess, I made you a little something . . ." She practically gallops to the tree, picks up a parcel, and starts ripping off the wrapping paper herself.

"Homemade honey hand cream," she says breathlessly. "I told you I've started making cosmetics, all-natural ingredients . . . Put some on!"

Janice thrusts the hand cream at Jess. We all watch, mesmerized, as Jess takes the ring off, applies hand cream, then puts the ring back on, without saying a word.

Nice try, Janice, I feel like saying. *Good effort.*

"It's great." Jess sniffs her hand. "Thanks, Janice. Good for you, making your own."

"We've all got you eco things, love," says Mum fondly. "We know how you are, with your chlorine dyes and your natural fibers. It's been quite an education for us, hasn't it, Becky?"

"Well, I'm glad." Jess takes a sip of tea. "It's amazing how Western consumers are still so misguided."

"I know." I shake my head pityingly. "They have *no* idea."

"They'll fall for anything with the word *green* in it." Jess shakes her head too. "There's apparently some vile, irresponsible company that sells yoga mats made of toxic computer parts. Trying to peddle them as 'recycled.' Guatemalan kids are getting asthma from making them." She bangs the sofa with her hand. "How can *anyone* be stupid enough to think that's a good idea?"

"God, yes." I swallow hard, my face hot, not daring to look at Mum. "What total utter morons they must be. Actually, I'll just tidy up the presents a bit . . ." Trying to look casual, I head toward the Christmas tree and shove the Guatemalan yoga mat behind the curtains with my foot. That's the last time I believe that so-called bloody "green" catalog. They said they were *helping* people, not giving them asthma! And what am I going to give Jess now?

"My present for you hasn't arrived yet," I say to Jess as I resume my seat. "But it's . . . er . . . potatoes. A great big sack. I know how much you like them. And you can use the sack afterward as organic recycled luggage."

"Oh." Jess looks a bit taken aback. "Thanks, Becky." She takes a sip of tea. "So, how are preparations going for the christening?"

"Brilliantly, thanks." I seize on the change of subject with relief. "The theme is Russian. We're going to have blinis with caviar and vodka shots, and I've got the most gorgeous dress for Minnie to wear—"

"Have you decided about middle names yet?" Mum chimes in. "Because Reverend Parker was on the phone yesterday, asking. You really have to come to a decision, love."

"I will!" I say defensively. "It's just so hard!"

We couldn't quite choose Minnie's middle names when we went to register her birth. (OK, the truth is, we had a slight argument. Luke was totally unreasonable about Dior. And Temperley. And no way was I agreeing to Gertrude, even if it is from Shakespeare.) So we put her down as Minnie Brandon and decided we'd finalize the other names at the christening. The trouble is, the more time goes by, the harder it gets. And Luke just laughs whenever he reads my choices and says, "Why does she need any middle names, anyway?" which is *really* unhelpful.

"So, do you have any news, Tom?" Janice blurts out in sudden desperation. "Has anything happened? Anything to tell? Big, small . . . anything? Anything at all?" She's leaning forward on her chair like a seal ready to catch a fish.

"Well, yes." Tom gives the tiniest of grins. "As it happens, we do." And for the first time, he and Jess exchange one of those shall-we-tell-them? looks.

Oh my God.

They really are! They're engaged!

Mum and Janice have both stiffened on the sofa; in fact, Janice looks like she's about to implode. Suze winks at me and I grin back happily. We'll have such fun! We can start buying *Brides* and I'll help Jess choose her wedding dress, and she's *not* wearing some dreary old recycled hemp thing, even if it is greener—

"Jess and I would like to announce . . ." Tom looks happily around the room. "We're married."

FOUR

EVERYONE'S STILL in a state of shock. I mean, obviously it's great that Tom and Jess are married. It's fab. It's just we all feel like we've missed a step.

Did they *have* to do it in Chile in some teeny register office with only two witnesses and not even let us watch on Skype? We could have had a party. We could have toasted them. Jess says they didn't even have any champagne. They drank some local beer, apparently.

Beer.

There are some things I don't understand about Jess and never will. No wedding dress. No flowers. No photo album. No champagne. The only single thing she got out of her wedding was a husband.

(I mean, obviously the husband is the main point when you get married. Absolutely. That goes without saying. But still, not even a new pair of *shoes*?)

And poor old Janice! As they announced the news, her face rose and fell like a roller coaster. You could tell she was trying desperately to look happy and support-ive, as if a distant wedding in Chile that she wasn't even invited to was exactly what she'd hoped for all along. Except that a tiny tear in the corner of her eye kept giv-ing her away. Especially after Jess said they didn't want a reception at the golf club, or a wedding list at John

Lewis, and point-blank refused to dress up in a hired wedding dress and pose for photos with Janice and Martin in the garden.

Janice looked so miserable, I nearly volunteered to do it instead. It sounded quite fun, actually, and I saw some amazing wedding dresses in the window of Liberty the other day . . .

Anyway. I suppose that wouldn't exactly have been the point.

I finish doing my lip gloss and stand back to survey my reflection. I hope Janice is more cheerful today. It's supposed to be a celebration, after all.

I smooth my outfit down and do a little twirl in front of the mirror. I'm wearing this amazing deep-blue dress with a fake-fur hem, tall button boots, and a fake-fur muff. Plus I've got a long coat edged with braid and a huge fake-fur hat.

Minnie's sitting on my bed, trying on all my hats, which is her favorite occupation. She's in a little fur-trimmed dress too, with white boots that make her look like a skater. I am *so* into this Russian theme—in fact, I'm half toying with getting Reverend Parker to christen her "Minska."

Minska Katinka Karenina Brodsky Brandon.

"Come on, Minska!" I say experimentally. "Time to go and get christened! Take off that hat."

"Mine." She clings on to my red Philip Treacy with the big feather. "*Mine* hat."

She looks so cute, I can't bring myself to drag it off her. Plus I might rip the feather. And does it really matter if she wears a hat?

"OK, darling." I relent. "You can wear the hat. Now, let's go." I hold out my hand.

"Mine." She instantly grabs the Balenciaga bag which was lying on the bed. "Mine. *Miiiine.*"

"Minnie, that's Mummy's bag," I point out reasonably. "You've got your own little bag. Shall we find it?"

"Miiiiiine! Miiiiiiine bag!" she cries furiously, and backs away from me. She's holding on to the Balenciaga bag like it's the last life preserver in the ocean and she's not about to relinquish it to anybody.

"Minnie . . ." I sigh.

To be fair, she does have a point. The Balenciaga bag is way nicer than her own toy bag. Put it this way: If I was being christened, *I'd* want a Balenciaga bag too.

"Well, OK. You have it and I'll take the Miu Miu. But only for today. Now, give me those sunglasses—"

"Miiiiiine! Miiiine!"

She clutches the vintage seventies shades, which she swiped from my dressing table earlier. They're pink hearts and keep slipping down her nose.

"Minnie, you can't go to your christening in sunglasses. Don't be so silly!" I try to sound severe.

Although she *is* rocking quite a good look, what with the hat, the pink shades, and the Balenciaga bag.

"Well . . . fine," I say at last. "Just don't break them."

As we stand in front of the mirror in our Russian dresses, I can't help feeling a swell of pride. Minnie looks so gorgeous. Maybe Suze is right. Maybe today *will* change Luke's mind. He'll see her looking adorable and instantly soften and decide he wants a whole brood of ten.

(Actually, he'd better not. There's no *way* I'm doing the birth thing ten times. Even twice is asking a lot, and the only way I'll get through it another time is by focusing on the matching pom-pom hats.)

Speaking of Luke, where is he? He popped into the office this morning, but he swore he'd be back by eleven. It's quarter to already.

How are u doing? I text him quickly. On way back I hope?

Then I pop my phone into my bag and take Minnie's arm.

"Come on." I beam at her. "Time for your special day."

AS WE HEAD DOWNSTAIRS, I can hear the bustle of the caterers and Dad humming to himself as he does his tie. There are flower arrangements in the hall and glasses being arranged on the hall table.

"I'll call you from the church . . ." Mum is saying to someone as she comes out of the kitchen.

"Oh, hi, Mum." I look at her in surprise. She's wearing the Japanese kimono that Janice brought her back from Tokyo, her hair is scraped back into a bun, and her feet are in little silk slippers. "What are you doing in that outfit? Shouldn't you be changed by now?"

"This is what I'm wearing, love." She pats it self-consciously. "Janice gave it to me, remember? Pure silk. Such good quality."

Have I missed a step here?

"It's lovely. But it's Japanese. The theme's Russian, remember?"

"Oh." Mum looks around vaguely as though distracted by something. "Well, I don't suppose it really matters . . ."

"Yes, it does!"

"Oh, love." Mum makes a face. "You know fur irritates my skin. I've been *longing* to wear this. And Janice has the most exquisite Japanese wedding coat; you'll love it—"

"What, you mean, Janice is coming in a Japanese outfit as well?" I cut her off in indignation.

I should have *known* this would happen. Mum's been pushing a Japanese theme ever since Janice came back from her holiday to Tokyo and started holding sushi-and-bridge evenings. But the point is, I'm in charge, and I said the theme was *Russian*.

"Sorry to interrupt!" A cheerful woman from the caterers comes past with a covered silver tray. "Where shall I put the Asian platters, Jane?"

What?

"Excuse me." I whip round to the caterer. "I ordered Russian food! Caviar, smoked salmon, little Russian cakes, vodka—"

"Plus Asian platters, sushi, and sashimi." The woman looks alarmed. "Isn't that right? And sake."

"Quite right," says Mum hastily. "Take them into the kitchen, thanks, Noreen."

I fold my arms and glare at Mum. "Who ordered sushi?"

"I may have added a few items to the menu," says Mum, looking a bit evasive. "Just for variety."

"But it's a *Russian theme*!"

I feel like stamping my foot. What is the point of having a theme if people ignore it and set up their own, totally different theme, without even telling you?

"We can have two themes, love!" suggests Mum brightly.

"No we can't!"

"It can be Japanese–Russian fusion." She nods triumphantly. "All the celebrities do fusion these days."

"But—" I halt midstream.

Japanese–Russian fusion. Actually . . . that's quite cool. In fact, I wish I'd thought of it.

"You can put some chopsticks in your hair. You'll look lovely!"

"Well, OK," I say at last, a bit grudgingly. "I suppose we could do that." I get out my phone and quickly text

Suze and Danny (who is Minnie's godfather and a total fab fashion designer):

Hey. New theme for today is Russian-Japanese fusion. C u later! xxx

Immediately I get a ping back from Suze.

Japanese?? How do I do that??? Sx

Chopsticks in hair? I reply.

Mum has already produced some black lacquer chopsticks and is trying to stick them into my hair. "We need a hair clip," she says, tutting. "Now, what about Luke?"

"He won't wear chopsticks in his hair." I shake my head. "Whatever the theme is."

"No, silly!" Mum clicks her tongue. "I meant, is he nearly here?"

We both instinctively glance at our watches. Luke has sworn he won't be late for the christening about sixty-five times.

I mean, he won't. He wouldn't be.

God knows what this mammoth, mega work crisis is. He won't say anything about it or even which client it is. But something must have gone fairly pear-shaped, because he's barely even been home in the last couple of days, and when he's called he's only spoken for about three seconds before ringing off. I take out my phone again and text him:

R u nearly back?? Where r u????

A moment later a reply pings back:

Doing best. L

Doing best? What's that supposed to mean? Is he in the car or not? Don't say he hasn't even left the office. I feel a sudden pain under my ribs. He can't be late for his own daughter's christening. He *can't*.

"Where's Luke?" Dad comes past. "Any sign of him yet?"

"Not yet."

"Cutting it a little fine, isn't he?" Dad raises his eyebrows.

"He'll be here!" I muster a confident smile. "There's still plenty of time."

BUT HE DOESN'T ARRIVE and he doesn't arrive. The caterers have finished setting up. Everything's ready. By twenty to twelve I'm standing with Minnie in the hall, staring out at the drive. I was texting him every five minutes, but I've given up now. I feel a bit dreamlike. Where is he? How can he not be here?

"Love, we need to go." Mum has come up softly behind me. "Everyone will be arriving at the church."

"But . . ." I turn to see her face all creased up anxiously. She's right. We can't let everyone down. "OK. Let's go."

As we leave the house, I get out my phone and start to text yet again, my vision a little blurred.

Dear Luke we are going to church. You are missing christening.

I buckle Minnie into her seat in Dad's car and slide in beside her. I can tell that Mum and Dad are almost killing themselves with restraint, not laying into Luke.

"I'm sure he's got a good reason," says Dad at last, as he pulls out of the drive.

There's silence, as obviously none of us can think of what that reason might be.

"What was it again, love?" ventures Mum. "Some crisis?"

"Apparently." I'm staring rigidly out of the window. "Something huge. But it might not happen. That's all I know."

My phone suddenly pings.

Becky so sorry. Can't explain. Still here. Will take helicopter asap. Wait for me. L

I stare at my phone in slight disbelief. Helicopter? He's coming by *helicopter*?

All of a sudden I feel a bit cheered up. In fact, I almost forgive him for disappearing and being so mysterious. I'm about to tell Mum and Dad (very casually) about the helicopter, when the phone bleeps again.

May be a little while yet. Shit about to hit fan.

What shit? I text back, feeling prickles of frustration. What fan?

But there's no reply. Argh, he's so annoying. He always has to be so mysterious. It's probably just some boring old investment fund that made slightly fewer zillions of pounds than it was supposed to. Big deal.

The church is already full of guests as we enter, and I wander around, greeting Mum's bridge friends, half of whom are in Japanese outfits. (I am so having it out with Mum later.) I hear myself saying about fifty times, "Actually, it's a Japanese–Russian fusion theme" and "Luke's just on his way by helicopter," then Mum leads

Minnie off by the hand and I can hear everyone cooing over her.

"Bex!" I turn to see Suze, looking amazing in a purple embroidered coat, fur-trimmed boots, and her hair pinned up with a couple of wooden coffee stirrers from Starbucks.

"This was the best I could do," she says, gesturing at them crossly. "You said Russian! How did Japanese suddenly enter the picture?"

"It was Mum's fault!" I'm about to launch into the whole story when the Reverend Parker approaches, all smart in his swishy white robes.

"Oh, hi there!" I beam. "How are you?"

The Reverend Parker is fab. He isn't one of those super-holy, make-you-feel-bad-about-everything vicars. He's more of a do-have-a-gin-and-tonic-before-lunch vicar. His wife works in the City, and he's always got a tan and drives a Jaguar.

"I'm very well." He shakes my hand warmly. "Lovely to see you, Rebecca. And may I say, it's charming, your Japanese theme. I'm quite a sushi fan myself."

"It's Japanese–Russian fusion, actually," I correct him firmly. "We're having blinis too, and vodka shots."

"Ah, indeed." He beams. "Now, I gather that Luke's been held up?"

"He'll be here very soon." I cross my fingers behind my back. "Any minute now."

"Good. Because I am a *little* pressed for time. And presumably you've decided on your daughter's middle names? Could you possibly write them down for me?"

Oh God.

"Nearly." I pull an agonized face. "I'm so nearly there . . ."

"Rebecca, really," says Reverend Parker a tad impatiently. "I can't baptize your daughter if I don't know her names."

Honestly, talk about pressure. I thought vicars were supposed to be *understanding*.

"I'm planning to finalize them once and for all during the prayers," I explain. "While I'm praying, obviously," I add hastily at his frozen expression. "You know. I might get inspiration from the good book." I pick up a nearby Bible, hoping to get a few brownie points. "Very inspirational. Maybe I'll go for Eve. Or Mary."

The trouble with Reverend Parker is, he's known me for too long. He just raises his eyebrows skeptically and says, "And are the godparents here? Suitable types, I hope?"

"Of course! Here's one." I shove Suze forward, who shakes his hand and immediately starts talking about the church ceiling and whether it's late nineteenth century.

Suze is so great. She always knows what to say to everyone. Now she's talking about the stained glass. Where does she get this stuff? She must have learned it at finishing school, after meringue lessons. I'm not very interested in stained glass, to be honest, so I flick aimlessly through the Bible.

Ooh. Delilah. Now, *that's* a cool name.

"Jesus H. Christ, Becky!" A familiar American accent hits my ears. From behind me I hear a bit of a mild kerfuffle among Mum's friends and someone exclaiming, "Who in God's name is *that*?"

This can mean only one thing.

"Danny!" I whirl round in joy. "You're here!"

It has been *so* long since I've seen Danny. He's looking skinnier than ever and is wearing a Cossack-style swirly coat in leather, with tight black vinyl trousers and army boots. Plus he has a tiny white dog on a lead that I've never seen before. I make to hug him, but he lifts up a hand as though he has some momentous announcement to make.

"This theme?" he says incredulously. "Japanese-slash-Russian-fucking-*fusion*? How much more fucking *inspired* can you get? My new dog is only a fucking *shih tzu*!"

"No way!" Suddenly I remember Reverend Parker, standing a foot away. "Er . . . Reverend Parker . . . this is Danny Kovitz. Another of the godparents."

"Oh jeez." Danny claps a hand over his mouth. "I apologize, Reverend. Loving the church," he adds generously, gesturing around. "Loving your décor. Did someone help you with these colors?"

"You're very kind." Reverend Parker gives him a stiff smile. "But if you could keep down the fruity language during the service?"

"Danny's a famous fashion designer," I throw in hastily.

"Puh-lease." Danny gives a modest laugh. "Not famous. More . . . renowned. *Notorious*. Where's Luke?" he adds to me in a lower voice. "I need him. Jarek's been calling me every day. He's threatening to, like, come *by*." Danny's voice rises in alarm. "You know I don't do confrontation."

Jarek is Danny's former business manager. We met him last year and soon realized he was taking a massive cut of Danny's money for basically doing nothing except wearing Danny's clothes for free and having lots of lunches on expenses. Luke was the one who arranged his termination and lectured Danny about not giving people jobs just because you like their haircuts.

"I thought you changed all your numbers," I say, puzzled. "I thought you weren't going to take any more of Jarek's calls."

"I didn't," he says defensively. "At first. But he had

great tickets for this festival in Bali, so we went to that, and that meant he had my new cell number, so—"

"Danny! You went to a festival with him? After you'd *fired* him?"

Danny looks caught out.

"OK. I fucked up. Where's Luke?" He peers plaintively around the church. "Can Luke talk to him?"

"I don't know where Luke is," I say, more snappily than I mean to. "He's on his way in a helicopter."

"A helicopter." Danny raises his eyebrows. "Quite the action man. Is he going to drop down on a wire like the CIA?"

"No." I roll my eyes. "Don't be silly."

Although, come to think of it, maybe he will. I mean, where else are they going to find a place to land a helicopter?

I get out my phone and text Luke:

R u in helicopter yet? Where r u going to land? On roof?

"Oh my God. Have you seen his *lordship*?" Danny's been distracted by the sight of Tarquin. "Be still my beating crotch."

"Danny!" I hit his arm and glance at Reverend Parker, who thankfully has moved away. "We're in *church,* remember?"

Danny has always had a bit of a thing about Tarquin. And, to be fair, Tarquin looks pretty extraordinary today. He's wearing a white billowy shirt with black breeches and a heavy, military-style coat on top. His dark hair is all ruffled from the wind, which is a great improvement on his normal non-style, and his bony, stoaty face looks almost chiseled in the gloom of the church.

"That's my next collection, right in front of me."

Danny's sketching Tarquin on some old book or other. "English lord meets Russian prince."

"He's Scottish," I point out.

"Even better. I'll throw in a kilt."

"Danny!" I giggle as I catch a glimpse of the sketch. "You can't draw that in church!"

That picture of Tarquin is *not* accurate. In fact, it's obscene. Although I did hear once from Suze's mum that all the Cleath-Stuart men were very well endowed. Maybe it's more accurate than I realize.

"So where's my goddaughter?" Danny rips off the page, folds it up, and begins another drawing.

"She's with Mum somewhere . . ." I look around for Minnie and suddenly spy her about ten yards away, standing with a group of Mum's friends. Oh God, what's she been doing now? She has about five hand-bags looped over her arms and is tugging hard at an elderly lady's shoulder bag, yelling, "Miiine!"

"So sweet!" I hear the lady tinkle with laughter. "Here you are, Minnie, dear." She drapes the shoulder strap around Minnie's neck, and Minnie staggers off, determinedly clutching all the bags.

"Nice Balenciaga," comments Danny. "The perfect accessory when one's being christened."

I nod. "That's why I let her borrow it."

"And you settled for the Miu Miu, which I know for a *fact* you've had for a year, whereas the Balenciaga is new." Danny gives a melodramatic sigh. "I can't think of a more beautiful example of motherly love."

"Shut up!" I give him a push. "Keep drawing."

As I watch him sketching, a sudden thought occurs to me. If Danny really *does* base his next collection on Tarkie, then maybe they could join forces somehow. Maybe they could do a tie-in promotion with Shetland Shortbread! I am such a business brain. Luke will be so impressed. I'm about to tell Suze my great idea, when Reverend Parker's voice booms out.

"Perhaps everyone could take their seats?" He starts ushering us toward the pews. "And then we can start."

Start? Already?

I tug anxiously at his white robe as he swooshes past. "Um, Luke isn't here yet. So if we could just delay a bit longer . . ."

"Dear, we've delayed twenty minutes already." Reverend Parker's smile is a little chilly. "If your husband isn't going to make it—"

"Of course he's going to make it!" I feel stung. "He's on his way. He'll be here—"

"Miiiiiiiine!" A high-pitched, gleeful shriek fills the air, and my whole body stiffens in alarm. My head whips round toward the front of the church, and my stomach seems to drop.

Minnie has climbed over the altar rail and is standing right by the altar, turning each handbag upside down and shaking out the contents. Behind me I can hear the dismayed shrieks of Mum's friends as they see all their things hitting the floor and rolling about.

"Minnie!" I yell, dashing up the aisle. "*Stop that!*"

"Miiiiine!" She's joyfully shaking a Burberry shoulder bag, and coins are cascading out of it. The whole altar is a mess of purses and money and makeup compacts and lipsticks and hairbrushes.

"This is supposed to be your *christening*," I say furiously in Minnie's ear. "You're supposed to be on your *best behavior*. Or you'll *never* get a brother or sister!"

Minnie looks unrepentant, even as all Mum's friends arrive and start exclaiming and tutting and scrabbling for all the bags and money.

On the plus side, at least the kerfuffle delays proceedings. But, even so, Reverend Parker is soon herding everyone into the pews.

"If everyone could please sit down? We really need to get on . . ."

"What about Luke?" whispers Mum anxiously as she takes her seat.

"He'll make it," I say, trying to sound confident.

I'll just have to spin things out till he arrives. There'll be loads of prayers and talking, surely. It'll be fine.

OK. I'M WRITING to the Archbishop of Canterbury. In my opinion, christenings are far, *far* too short.

We're all sitting in the front few rows of the church. We've had about two prayers and a few little bits to say about renouncing evil. We've all sung a hymn, and Minnie has spent the time shredding two hymn books. (It was the only way to keep her quiet. I'll give the church some money.) And now suddenly Reverend Parker has asked us all to gather around the font, and I'm panicking.

We *can't* be up to the splashy water bit yet. I'm not letting Luke miss the big moment.

There's been no sign of him. He isn't replying to any of my texts. I'm hoping against hope that he's switched off his phone because it would interfere with the helicopter controls. My neck is craned, trying to hear for a judder outside.

"Minnie?" Reverend Parker smiles at her. "Are you ready?"

"Wait!" I say desperately, as people start getting to their feet. "Before the actual christening . . . er . . . Minnie's godmother, Susan Cleath-Stuart, wishes to recite a poem for the occasion. Don't you, Suze?"

Suze instantly turns in her seat and whispers, "*What?*"

"*Please,* Suze!" I hiss back. "I need to buy some time, or Luke'll miss it!"

"I don't know any poems!" she mutters as she gets up.

"Just read something out of the hymn book! Something long!"

Rolling her eyes, Suze picks up a hymn book and heads to the front, then smiles around at the audience.

"I would like to recite . . ." She opens the book and riffles through. "'We Three Kings.'" She clears her throat. *"We three kings of Orient are. Bearing gifts we traverse afar . . ."*

Suze is such a star. She reads it at a snail's pace and does all the choruses twice through.

"Very nice." Reverend Parker stifles a yawn. "And now if you could gather round the font—"

"Wait!" I swivel on my seat. "Um, Minnie's godfather, Danny Kovitz, will now . . ." I gaze imploringly at him. "He will also . . . say a poem?" *Please*, I mouth silently, and Danny winks back.

"In honor of my goddaughter's christening, I will perform 'The Real Slim Shady,' by Eminem," he says confidently.

Yikes. I hope Reverend Parker doesn't listen too closely.

Danny isn't the best rapper in the world, but by the time he's finished, everyone's clapping and whooping, even all Mum's bridge friends. So then Danny does an encore, of "Stan" with Suze doing the Dido bits. Then Tom and Jess pitch in with a South American prayer for children, which is actually really moving. And then Dad takes to the floor and sings "Que Sera, Sera" with everyone joining in with the chorus and Martin conducting them with one of Janice's chopsticks.

Reverend Parker is starting to look seriously pissed off.

"Thank you, everyone, for your interesting contributions," he says tightly. "And now if you could gather round the font—"

"Wait!" I interrupt him. "As Minnie's mother, I would just like to make a short speech."

"Rebecca!" snaps Reverend Parker. "We really do have to proceed."

"Just a quick one!"

I hurry to the front of the church, almost tripping in my haste. I'll keep talking till Luke arrives. It's the only way.

"Welcome, friends and family." I gaze around, avoiding Reverend Parker's stony eyes. "What a special day this is. A special, special day. Minnie is being christened."

I pause, as though to let this thought sink in, and quickly check my phone. Nothing.

"But what do we *mean* by that?" I lift a finger, just like Reverend Parker does in his sermons. "Or are we all simply here for the ride?"

There's an interested ripple in the audience, and a couple of people nudge each other and whisper. I'm quite flattered, actually. I hadn't thought my speech would cause such a stir.

"Because it's easy to go through life without ever looking round at the flowers." I give a significant nod, and there are more whispers and nudges.

This reaction I'm getting is amazing! Maybe I could get into preaching! I've obviously got a natural gift for it, and I do have quite a lot of profound ideas.

"It makes you think, doesn't it?" I continue. "But what do we mean by *think*?"

Everyone's whispering now. People are passing BlackBerrys along the pews and pointing at something. What's going on?

"I mean, why are we all here?" My voice is drowned out by the growing hubbub.

"What's happening!" I exclaim. "What are you all

looking at?" Even Mum and Dad are fixated by something on Mum's BlackBerry.

"Becky, you'd better look at this," says Dad in a strange voice. He gets up and passes me the BlackBerry, and I find myself looking at a TV newsreader on the BBC website.

". . . latest on our breaking news that the Bank of London has agreed to emergency funding from the Bank of England. This comes after days of secret talks, in which bosses battled to save the situation . . ."

The newsreader continues talking, but I don't hear what he's saying. I'm gripped by the picture. It's of several men in suits leaving the Bank of England, looking grim. One of them is Luke. Luke was at the Bank of England?

Oh God. Is he at the Bank of England *now*?

The picture on the screen has changed to a group of commentators sitting round a table, looking grave, with that girl TV presenter in the glasses who always interrupts people.

"So, essentially, the Bank of London is *bust*, is that right?" she says in that forceful way she has.

"*Bust* is a very strong word . . ." one of the commentators begins—but I can't hear what else he says, because havoc is breaking out in the church.

"It's bust!"

"The Bank of London's gone bust!"

"But that's where all our money is!" Mum looks a bit hysterical. "Graham, do something! Get it out! Get the money!"

"Our holiday fund!" Janice moans.

"My pension!" An elderly man is struggling to his feet.

"I'm sure we shouldn't overreact," Jess is saying above the hubbub. "I'm sure no one will lose anything; banks are guaranteed . . ." But no one's listening to her.

"My portfolio!" The Reverend Parker rips off his robes and heads for the door of the church.

"You can't just *leave*!" I call after him incredulously. "You haven't christened Minnie yet!" But he totally ignores me—and, to my amazement, Mum is hotfooting it after him.

"Mum! Come back!"

I grab Minnie's hand before she legs it too. Everyone's leaving. Within moments the church is empty, except for me and Minnie, Suze, Tarkie, Jess, Tom, and Danny. We all glance at one another, then, in silent accord, hurry to the exit of the church. We burst out of the big wooden door—and just stand there on the porch, in shock.

"Sweet Jesus," breathes Danny.

The high street is full of people. There must be two hundred, three hundred, maybe. All streaming the same way along the pavement to the tiny branch of Bank of London, outside of which a queue has already formed. I can see Mum anxiously jostling for a place and Reverend Parker blatantly queue-barging in front of an old lady, while a young, panic-stricken guy in a bank teller's uniform tries to keep order.

As I'm gaping at the scene, something attracts my attention. Just down from the Bank of London, directly opposite the church, I glimpse a figure in the throng. Dark helmetlike hair, pale skin, Jackie O–type sunglasses, houndstooth suit . . .

I peer harder in disbelief. Is that . . .

That can't be . . .

Elinor?

But as I'm trying to focus, Elinor—or whoever she was—disappears into the crowd. I rub my eyes and look again, but all I can see now is a policeman who has appeared out of nowhere and is telling people to get off the road.

Weird. I must have imagined it.

"Look at the cop," says Danny in delight. "He's about to lose it. He's going to start Tasering people in a minute."

"Oh my God!" Suze suddenly points upward with a gasp.

This is unreal. Now there are people climbing on the roof of the bank. I exchange flabbergasted looks with Suze. It's like aliens have invaded, or war has broken out, or something. I've never seen anything like it in my whole entire life.

FIVE

WELL, AT LEAST it all makes sense now. At least I can for-give Luke. This is about the first time he's had a so-called "major crisis" at work and it really is a proper, genuine crisis. No one can talk about anything else. Every news channel is covering it.

I've spoken to Luke on the phone and he's going to make it home when he can. But there was no way he could have left any earlier. He was at the Bank of En-gland seeing all sorts of top people. And now he's try-ing to "manage the situation" and "limit the damage." Every single branch of the Bank of London has been besieged. Apparently the prime minister himself is going to make a statement and ask everyone to calm down. (Which, if you ask me, is a big mistake. Mum's already convinced the whole thing is a government conspiracy.)

"Tea?" Dad comes into the snug, where Danny, Suze, Tarquin, Jess, Tom, and I are all sitting, still in a bit of a numb daze. The TV is on Sky News, and they keep playing the same clip, the one with a stern-faced Luke with all his equally stern-faced banker clients.

"So." Dad puts the tray down. "What a to-do. Are you going to rearrange the christening?"

"We'll have to, I suppose." I nod, and look around the room. "When's everyone free?"

"The rest of January's not great." Danny takes out his BlackBerry and squints at it. "Although January *next* year is totally clear," he adds brightly.

"We've got so many shooting parties . . ." Suze fishes for her tiny Smythson diary.

"And remember our trip to the Lake District," Dad chimes in.

God, everyone's so *busy*. In the end, I get everyone to write down when they're available in the next few months. Jess draws a grid and crosses off all the days and works it all out.

"There are three possibles," she says at last. "Eighteenth of February, eleventh of March, or seventh of April, which is a Friday."

"April seventh?" I look up. "That's Luke's birthday."

"I never knew that," says Suze curiously. "I've never even known Luke to *have* a birthday."

"He's not really into birthdays," I explain. "Every time I organize any celebration for him, he cancels it because of some work thing."

It's one of the things about Luke I least understand. He doesn't get overexcited about his presents; he doesn't drop little hints about what kind of treat he'd like; he doesn't do a countdown on the wall calendar. One year he'd actually forgotten it was his birthday when I clattered in with a breakfast tray. How can you *forget* your own birthday?

I glance at the TV screen. There he is, stepping out of the Bank of England again, his forehead furrowed even more deeply than usual. I feel a rush of fondness for him. He's had such a shitty year, he deserves a treat. I should throw him a party. Even if he doesn't want it. Even if he'll try to cancel it.

And all at once the idea hits me.

"Hey! What about if I throw Luke a surprise party?" I look around in excitement. "He'll think we're just having Minnie's christening, reorganized—but it's his birthday party too!"

I have a sudden vision of Luke walking into a darkened room and a whole crowd yelling, "Happy birthday!" And Luke's jaw dropping, and him being absolutely speechless with surprise . . .

Oh God. I have to do this. I *have* to.

"Good one, Bex!" Suze's eyes light up.

"Awesome idea." Danny looks up from his texting. "What theme?"

"I dunno. But something really cool. Something Luke would like."

I've never thrown a surprise party before, but it can't be that hard, can it? I mean, it's just like a normal party except you keep it secret. Easy.

"Becky, are you sure it's a good time to be throwing a party?" says Jess with a frown. "I mean, what if what they say is true?" She gestures at the TV, which is still on the Bank of London story. "What if we're at the beginning of a financial catastrophe?"

Trust Jess. Trust her to bring "financial catastrophe" into a nice talk about a party.

"Well, then everyone will need cheering up, won't they?" I say defiantly. "All the better."

Jess doesn't flicker. "All I'm saying is, you have to be prudent, especially at a time like this. Do you have the money to hold a party?"

Honestly. What is this, *Who Wants to Be a Nosy Elder Sister?*

"Maybe I do." I shrug carelessly. "Maybe I've been saving up a special fund for just such an event."

There's silence in the room, apart from a little snort from Danny. Tom is smirking, and I glower back at him. Have I ever smirked at any of his projects? Did I smirk when he built his ridiculous two-story summer-house in Janice's garden? (Well, actually, maybe I did. But that's not the point. Summerhouses and parties are completely different.)

Worst of all, even Suze is looking a bit pained, as if she doesn't want to laugh but won't be able to help it. She sees me looking at her and flushes guiltily.

"The thing is, it doesn't have to be an expensive party, does it?" she says hurriedly. "You could throw a restrained party, Bex. A thrifty party!"

"That's true." Jess nods. "Tom can make homemade peach wine. It's not bad at all. And I'm happy to cook."

Homemade peach wine?

"And you could have music off an iPod—" suggests Tom.

"*I'm* in charge of the iPod," chips in Danny.

"We could make paper chains . . ."

I'm staring at them all in horror. One tiny bank goes bust and suddenly we're having to act like it's the war and make Spam fritters and stain our legs because we can't afford stockings?

"I don't want to throw Luke some crappy party with homemade peach wine and an iPod!" I exclaim. "I want a *fabulous* party! I want a tent and a band, and caterers, and amazing lights everywhere . . . and entertainment! Jugglers and fire-eaters and stuff."

"But you can throw a nice party without fire-eaters—" begins Suze.

"I don't want something 'nice,' " I say disparagingly. "If I throw Luke a surprise party, I want it to blow him away. I want to knock his socks off. I want him to walk in and be utterly speechless for . . . a whole minute. At least."

All my friends are exchanging looks.

"What?" I'm looking from face to face. "What's wrong?"

"Come on, Becky. It would cost a fortune," says Jess bluntly. "Where would you get the money?"

"I . . . don't know," I say defiantly. "Work extra hard, maybe."

"You'll never keep it secret from Luke," chips in Tom. "Not in a million years."

I feel a surge of indignation at him—in fact, at all of them, even Suze. Why do they have to pour cold water on everything?

"Yes, I will!" I retort furiously. "You watch. I'll organize a fabulous party and I'll totally keep it a secret from Luke—"

"Keep what a secret from Luke?" His deep voice resounds from the hall, and I nearly jump a mile. Bloody hell, how did that happen? I've only been planning this party for two minutes and already I've nearly given it away. I barely have time to shoot an anguished look at Suze before Luke appears through the door. He's holding Minnie and looks surprisingly cheerful.

"How come you're back?" I ask, as he kisses me. "Is it all over?"

"Just grabbing some clean clothes, I'm afraid," he says wryly. "This isn't going to be over anytime soon."

"Um, Luke, that comment you heard me say about 'keeping something secret from Luke'?" I clear my throat. "You're probably wondering what I meant."

"It did cross my mind." Luke raises his eyebrows quizzically.

"Well, it's just that . . . um . . . I didn't want to tell you how crazy it was earlier. At the Bank of London. It was mayhem. I thought it might stress you out. So I was telling everyone to keep quiet about it. *Wasn't* I?"

I glare around the table, and Suze dutifully says, "Absolutely!"

"Don't worry," Luke says wryly. "I've already seen the

worst." He reaches up and ruffles Minnie's hair. "I gather she missed out on her big moment?"

"The vicar ran off to the bank with everyone else! But it's OK," I add carefully, "because we're planning to reschedule the christening. For a future date."

I won't mention the exact date at this point.

"Good." Luke nods without great interest. "Is there any food left?"

I nod. "Loads." I'm about to get up and find him some blinis when Mum comes into the snug, slightly flushed from all the sake she's been drinking.

"Listen, loves," she says to me and Luke. "Reverend Parker's here. He wants to see you. Shall I send him in?"

"Oh, right," I say in surprise. "Of course!"

I've never seen Reverend Parker look sheepish before. His dazzling smile is missing, and he can't quite look either of us in the eyes.

"Rebecca and Luke, I *do* apologize," he says. "Never before have I abandoned a service mid-flow. I can't think what came over me."

"Don't worry," I say magnanimously. "We've got over it."

"I assume you would still like your daughter baptized?"

"Of course we would!" I say eagerly. "In fact, we were just talking about it. We've got it all planned."

"I'm so glad." He looks around the room. "Well, you're all present and correct, so . . ." Before I know what's going on, he produces a little bottle, unscrews it, and sprinkles some kind of water on Minnie's forehead. "Minnie, I baptize you in the name of the Father, and of the Son, and of the Holy Spirit. Amen."

"What?" I say feebly, but he doesn't listen. Now he's making the sign of the cross on her forehead in oil.

"Welcome to the Church, my child. The Lord bless

you and keep you." He feels in his pocket and produces a candle, which he gives to me. "Congratulations, Rebecca." Then he turns to Mum. "Did you say there was sushi?"

I can't speak for shock.

Minnie? Just *Minnie*?

"You mean she's christened now?" I find my voice. "She's *done*?"

"Indeed," Reverend Parker says smugly. "Having started a job, I do like to finish it. Again, I do apologize for the slight hiatus. Good evening, everyone."

He sweeps out before I can even draw breath, and I stare after him, outraged. He didn't even *ask* about middle names. And I'd almost decided!

"Minnie Brandon." Luke hoists her up cheerfully onto his shoulders. "A fine name." I shoot him a baleful look. "I'm going to a grab a bite," he adds. "See you in a sec."

As Luke closes the door behind him, I exhale like a deflating balloon. The others seem a bit shell-shocked too.

"Well, that was a bit sudden," says Tom.

"So we don't need to hold the seventh of April anymore?" says Danny.

"Probably for the best," says Jess. "Becky, I hate to say it . . . but you never would have pulled that party off."

"Yes, I *would*." I glower at her.

"Well, anyway!" says Suze hastily. "It doesn't matter now, because it's not going to happen. It's irrelevant."

I feel a pang of resentment. Everyone's assuming I'll give up on the idea, aren't they? Everyone's assuming I can't do it. These are supposed to be my friends. They're supposed to believe in me.

Well, I'll show them.

"It's not irrelevant. And it *is* going to happen." I look

around the room, feeling my resolve grow. "I'm not going to let that stupid vicar ruin my plans. I'm still going to throw Luke a surprise birthday party. And I'll do it on a budget, and I'll keep it totally secret from Luke, *and* I'll blow his socks off."

I just about manage to stop myself from adding, "So there."

"Bex . . ." Suze glances around at the others. "It's not that we think you *can't* do it—"

"Yes, it is!" I say indignantly. "That's exactly what you said! Well, you'll all be eating your words."

"So, what's going on?" Danny looks up from his BlackBerry, which he's been tapping at yet again. "Is the party on or off?"

"On," I say resolutely. "Definitely on."

People Who Know About Party

Me
Suze
Tarquin
Danny
Jess
Tom

Total = 6

SIX

I'M ALREADY MAKING good progress with this party—in fact, I'm quite proud of myself, bearing in mind I'm not a professional party planner or anything. I've bought a special notebook, which I've disguised by writing *High-heeled boots—possible options* on the front. And I have an extensive to-do list, which goes as follows:

PARTY—TO-DO LIST

Tent—Where get? Where put? How big?
Fire-eaters—Where get??
Jugglers—Where get???
Theme—What?
Food—What? How? (Chocolate fountain?)
Drink—NOT peach wine
Dancing—Need dance floor. Shiny? Black and
   white, lights up like in Saturday Night
   Fever?
Guests—Who? Track down old friends? (NOT
   Venetia Carter or Sacha de Bonneville)
Outfit—Balmain black sequined dress with
   Zanotti crystal sandals and Philippe
   Audibert cuff?

> *Roland Mouret turquoise dress with strappy Prada shoes?*
> *Azzaro red minidress and black Louboutins?*

OK, so a few issues are a bit unresolved as yet. But the *most* urgent thing is to make sure Luke stays free on April 7 and doesn't book a business trip or anything. Which means I'm going to have to rope in an accomplice.

I wait until I have a moment alone in the kitchen, then dial his office number.

"Luke Brandon's office, how may I help?" come the perfectly modulated tones down the phone.

Luke's personal assistant is called Bonnie, and she's been with him for a year. She's in her forties and has mid-blond hair, which she always arranges in the same classic chignon. And she always wears understated tweed dresses and court shoes and speaks in the same soft voice. At Brandon Communications parties, she's the one on the fringes, cradling a glass of water, looking happy just to watch. I've tried to chat to her a couple of times, but she seems quite reserved.

Anyway, apparently she's a total star. Luke had had a couple of disasters before he hired Bonnie, and I've never known anyone to enthuse as much as he did when Bonnie first started. It seems she's incredibly efficient and discreet and almost telepathic at knowing what he's going to need. I might be worried, if it weren't for the fact that I can't actually imagine Bonnie having sex.

"Hi, Bonnie?" I say. "It's Becky here. Luke's wife."

"Becky! How are you?"

That's the other thing: She always sounds pleased to hear from me, even though she must be thinking, *Oh, bloody hell, it's the wife again.*

"I'm good, thanks. And you?"

"I'm very well. Can I put you through to Luke?"

"Actually, Bonnie, it was you I wanted to speak to. I'm throwing Luke a—" I pause and glance around in sudden paranoia, just in case Luke's come back early from work to surprise me and is even now silently creeping up behind me on tiptoes, arms outstretched. But he's not.

Huh. Why doesn't he ever do that?

Just to be doubly sure, I go and shut the kitchen door and pull a chair across it. This is all so cloak-and-dagger. I feel like those French resistance girls in *'Allo 'Allo!*

"Becky, are you still there?" Bonnie's saying. "Becky? Hello?"

"Listen very carefully, I will say this only once." I whisper into the phone in sepulchral tones. "I'm throwing a surprise party for Luke's birthday. It's top secret and you're only the seventh person in the world to know about it."

I almost want to add, "And now I'll have to shoot you."

"I'm sorry, Becky . . ." Bonnie sounds confused. "I can't hear. Could you speak up?"

For God's sake.

"A party!" I say more loudly. "I'm throwing Luke a party on April seventh. And I want it to be a surprise, so could you block off the date in his diary and make something up?"

"April seventh." Bonnie sounds unruffled. "That should be simple enough."

You see? This is why she's a brilliant PA. She behaves as though she's done this kind of thing a million times.

"And I want to invite all his friends from work, so could they all block off their diaries too? But don't make it look suspicious or anything. And don't tell anyone what it's about yet. Maybe you could say it's a big fire drill? And you should have a decoy birthday card going round the office," I add as the thought suddenly crosses my mind. "You know, nearer the time. And if Luke ever mentions his birthday, which he won't, but if he *does,* you should just say—"

"Becky . . ." Bonnie cuts me off kindly. "Should we perhaps meet to discuss all this?"

Result! As I put down the phone, I'm beaming. Everything's falling into place. Bonnie's already offered to put together a guest list and we're having lunch next week. Now I just have to decide on a party venue.

My gaze drifts outside. The garden would be perfect. But we'd never be able to keep it secret from Luke.

"Have you heard the latest?" Mum comes hurrying into the kitchen, followed by Minnie. Her face is pink and she's breathing fast. "It's not just the Bank of London! All the banks are like Swiss cheese! Full of holes! Have you heard, Graham?" she adds agitatedly to Dad, who is just coming in. "The entire banking structure is going to collapse!"

"It's a bad business." Dad nods, flicking on the kettle.

I've stopped watching the news, because it's too depressing, but the Bank of London crisis is still going on like some kind of soap opera. Now they've stopped the Cashpoints working, and a few people have thrown stones at the windows. The prime minister appeared on the TV last night and told everyone to please stop taking their money out. But all that did was make everyone freak out even more. (I knew it would. Didn't I say? They really should make me an adviser at Number 10.)

"Luke says we won't all lose our money," I venture.

"Oh, Luke does, does he?" Mum bristles. "And would Luke like to tell us if any other financial institutions are about to fold? Or would that be too much trouble?"

She's never going to forgive him, is she?

"Mum," I say for the millionth time, "Luke *couldn't* have told us. It was confidential and sensitive. And you would have told the whole of Oxshott!"

"I would *not* have told the whole of Oxshott!" she says sharply. "I would have warned Janice and Martin and a few other dear friends and that is all. And now we'll probably lose everything. Everything." She shoots me a resentful look, as though it's all my fault.

"Mum, I'm sure we won't lose everything." I try to sound confident and reassuring.

"I heard a commentator on the radio this morning predicting anarchy! Civilization will collapse! It's war!"

"Now, now, Jane." Dad pats her on the shoulder. "Let's not overreact. We simply might have to tighten our belts a little. Pull in our horns. *All* of us, Becky." He gives me a significant look.

I can't help feeling a bit offended. What was that look for? Excuse me, I'm an adult. I'm a *mother*. You move back in with your mum and dad and they immediately start treating you like a teenager who's spent her Travelcard money on a pair of leg warmers.

Which I only did *once*.

"Poor Janice has taken to her bed with the strain, you know." Mum lowers her voice discreetly, as though Janice might hear us from inside her house. "It was bad enough for her hearing Jess and Tom's news."

"Poor Janice," Dad and I say, in automatic unison.

"She had her heart set on that wedding. I mean, I know the younger generation likes to do things differently, but, really, is it so hard to walk down an aisle in a veil? Janice had already planned the table decorations *and* the wedding favors. What's she going to do with all that silver fabric?"

Mum keeps on talking, but I've been gripped by a sudden idea.

Janice's garden. Of course! We could put up a tent there and Luke would never suspect a thing! He'd just think Martin and Janice were having their own bash!

". . . and not a single wedding picture for the mantelpiece—" Mum is still in full indignant flow.

"Hey, Mum," I interrupt. "Listen. Don't tell Luke, but I'm going to hold a surprise birthday party for him. And I was thinking—do you reckon Janice would let me do it in her garden?"

There's silence. Both Dad and Mum are eyeing me weirdly.

"A party, love?" Mum sounds tense. "You mean, a few friends over?"

"No! A big party! With a tent and everything."

Now Mum and Dad are exchanging looks.

"What?" I say, rankled.

"It sounds rather . . . big."

"It will be big," I say defiantly. "And brilliant. I'm going to have a dance floor that lights up, and fire-eaters, and Luke will be completely blown away."

I think about this every night; in fact, I always conjure up the same image in my head: Luke staring in shock at the most amazing party in the world and being literally unable to speak. I can't *wait*.

"Fire-eaters?" echoes Mum, looking perturbed. "Becky, love . . ."

"It'll be George Michael all over again," Dad mutters darkly to Mum, and I give a sharp intake of breath. That is *against* our family code. No one was supposed to mention George Michael ever again. We even turn off "Careless Whisper" whenever it comes on.

"I heard that, thank you, Dad." I give him a furious stare. "And it *won't*."

The George Michael incident was so painful, I can

barely bring myself to remember the details. So I won't. Except that I was turning thirteen, and my whole class thought George Michael was entertaining at my birthday party. Because I'd said he was. And they all came with their autograph books and cameras . . .

I feel a bit queasy, just thinking about it.

Thirteen-year-old girls are mean.

And I had *not* made it up, like everyone said. I had *not*. I phoned the fan club, and the man said he was sure George would have loved to be there, and I kind of . . . misunderstood.

"And do you remember the fairies, Graham?" Mum suddenly claps a hand to her head. "All those sobbing, hysterical little girls."

Why do parents have to *remind* you of things all the time? OK, so maybe I shouldn't have told my school friends that I had real fairies in my garden and they were coming to my fifth birthday party and everyone would get a wish. And then I shouldn't have said the fairies had changed their minds because no one had given me a nice enough present.

But I was *five*. You do things when you're five. It doesn't mean you're going to do them when you're twenty-nine.

"Anything else you want to bring up from my past?" I can't help sounding hurt.

"Love." Mum puts a hand on my shoulder. "I'm only saying . . . birthday parties haven't been your strong point. Have they, now?"

"Well, this one will be," I retort, but Mum still looks anxious.

"Just don't make too many *promises*, darling."

"Why don't you take Luke out to dinner instead?" suggests Dad. "The King's Arms does a lovely prix fixe."

OK, I officially give up on all my friends and family. The *King's Arms*?

"I don't want a dreary old prix fixe in a pub! I want to throw Luke a *party*. And I'm going to, even if you think it'll be a disaster—"

"We don't!" says Mum hastily, shooting a glance at Dad. "That's not what we were saying, and I'm sure we can all help—"

"You don't need to," I say haughtily. "I have all the help I need, thank you." And I sweep out of the kitchen before either of them can reply. Which I know is really immature and teenagery of me. But honestly. Parents are so . . . *annoying*.

AND, ANYWAY, they're all wrong, because hosting a surprise party is a doddle. Why don't I do it more often? By that evening, I've got it all sorted. We're having a tent in Janice's garden on April 7. Janice and Martin are totally on board and sworn to utter secrecy. (So is the plumber who was fixing their tap and listening in to the whole conversation. He's absolutely promised not to say a word.)

On the less good side, Mum's even more hysterical than before. She's heard some scare story on the radio about how Britain's national debt is a big black hole and pensions are all going to collapse and basically money won't exist anymore. Or something. So we're having a family conference. Minnie's in bed; a bottle of wine is open, and we're sitting round the table in the kitchen.

"So," Dad begins. "Clearly the world is in something of a . . . state."

"I've just looked in the cellar." Mum sounds a bit tremulous. "We've still got all that bottled water we had for the millennium bug. And eight boxes of canned food, and all the candles. We'd be all right for three months, I think, although what we'd do about little Minnie—"

"Jane, we're not under *siege,*" says Dad testily. "Waitrose is still open, you know."

"You never know! We need to be prepared! It said in the *Daily World*—"

"But there may be financial worries ahead," Dad interrupts, looking grave. "For all of us. So I suggest that we all look at ways that we can C.B."

There's a gloomy silence round the table. None of us is very keen on C.B. It's Dad's shorthand for *Cut Back,* and it's never any fun.

"I know where all the money's going," says Mum adamantly. "It's on those luxury roasted nuts from Marks and Spencer you insist on buying, Graham. Do you know how much they cost? And you sit there in front of the TV, eating handfuls at a time—"

"Nonsense," says Dad heatedly. "You know where our money goes? It's on jam. How many pots of jam do we need? Who needs . . ." He reaches into a cupboard and grabs a pot at random. "Gooseberry and elderflower?"

I bought that, actually, at a crafts fair.

"What do you expect me to do?" exclaims Mum indignantly. "Survive on one miserable jar of cut-price goo made out of food coloring and turnips?"

"Maybe! Maybe we should be shopping at some of those lower-priced stores. We're pensioners, Jane. We can't afford to live the high life anymore."

"It's *coffee,*" says Mum. "Those whatsit capsules of Becky's. Nexpresso."

"Yes!" Dad suddenly wakes up. "I utterly agree. Overpriced waste of money. How much is each one?"

They both turn and stare accusingly at me.

"I need good coffee!" I say in horror. "It's my only luxury!"

I can't live with my parents *and* drink bad coffee. It's not humanly possible.

"If you ask me, it's the TV," I throw back at them. "You have it on too loud. It's wasting energy."

"Don't be ridiculous," retorts Mum tartly.

"Well, it's *not* coffee!"

"I think we could cut out all jam, starting tomorrow," Dad is saying. "All jam, all spreads—"

"Well, if we're going to do that, I'll cut out food, shall I?" Mum's voice is shrill. "I'll just cut out all food, Graham, because that's obviously a waste of money too—"

"Anyway, Nespresso is a million times cheaper than going to a coffee shop," I'm trying to point out. "And you don't even pay for it; I buy it myself on the Internet! So—"

We're all so busy arguing, it's a while before I realize that Luke is in the doorway, watching, his mouth twitching at the edges in amusement.

"Oh, hi!" I leap up, relieved to escape. "How's it going? Are you OK?"

"Fine." He nods. "I just popped up to say good night to Minnie. She was asleep." He smiles ruefully and I feel a twinge of sympathy for him. He hardly ever sees Minnie these days.

"She took all her toys to bed again," I tell him. "Including her dollhouse."

"Again?" He laughs.

Minnie's latest trick is to get out of bed after I've said good night, gather all her toys, and take them back to bed with her, so there's barely any room for her. I went up earlier this evening and found her fast asleep, clasping her wooden pony, with about twenty soft toys and her dollhouse all on top of the duvet, crowding her out of bed.

"Luke!" Mum finally notices him and stops mid-flow through a tirade about how Dad never even has toast for breakfast so what does he know? "We were just discussing the situation."

"Situation?" He raises his eyebrows at me in query.

"We're all trying to think of ways to save money," I explain, hoping Luke might say, "What a ludicrous idea, everything's on the up, let's crack open some champagne." But he just nods thoughtfully.

"That's not a bad idea, the way things are going."

"But how *are* things going?" Mum demands anxiously. "Luke, you know. Is the *Daily World* right or wrong? Because I heard a chap on the radio and he said there would be a domino effect. And we're the dominos!"

"No, we're not." Dad raises his eyes to heaven. "The *banks* are the dominos."

"Well, what are we, then?" Mum glares at him. "The dice?"

"Jane," Luke interrupts tactfully. "You don't want to believe everything you hear in the media. There are some extreme views out there. The truth is, it's still too early to call. What I *can* say is, confidence has plummeted and there's a lot of panic. Not just in banking, in every sector. Whether it's justified . . . that's the question."

I can tell Mum's not satisfied.

"But what do the *experts* say?" she persists.

"Luke is an expert!" I chime in, indignant.

"Economic gurus aren't fortune-tellers, unfortunately." Luke shrugs. "And they don't always agree. What I would say is, it's never a bad idea to be prudent."

"Absolutely." Dad nods approvingly. "That's what I was saying. Our spending has got quite out of hand, Jane, crisis or no crisis. Four pounds, this cost!" He waves the jar of gooseberry jam. "Four *pounds*!"

"Very well." Mum glares at Dad. "From now on, I'll

only shop at the Pound Shop. Will that make you happy, Graham?"

"Me too!" I say supportively.

I've never actually been to a Pound Shop, but they've got to be good. I mean, everything only costs a quid, for a start.

"My darling, we're not quite that penurious." Luke kisses me on the forehead. "The easiest way *we* could save money, if you ask me, would be if you wore some of your clothes more than once."

Not this again.

"I *do* wear them more than once," I say crossly. "You always exaggerate—"

"How often have you worn that cardigan with the red button?" he asks innocently.

"It's—I've—" I stop, a bit stymied.

Damn. Why haven't I worn it? I don't even know where it is. Did I leave it somewhere?

"A hundred times, wasn't it?" Luke looks as though he's enjoying this. "Isn't that what you said?"

"I'm *intending* to wear it a hundred times," I say stonily. "I didn't specify exactly when."

"How many clothes have you got, anyway, stashed away in your cupboards?"

"I . . . er . . ."

"Do you have *any* idea?"

"Too many," snorts Dad. "Are we going to count the boots cluttering up my garage?"

"Any idea at all?" persists Luke.

"I don't . . . It's not . . ." I trail off in confusion.

What kind of question is that, anyway: "How many clothes have you got?" It's totally unreasonable.

"How many clothes have *you* got?" I retort, and Luke thinks for about one microsecond.

"Nine suits, some too old to wear now. Around thirty shirts. Fifty or so ties. I should cull some. Evening wear. I don't need to shop for another year, except for socks." He shrugs. "And I won't. Not in the current climate. I don't think it would send the right signals to turn up to work in a new bespoke suit."

Trust Luke to have an answer.

"Well, you're a *man*. It's different. I work in fashion, remember?"

"I know," he says mildly. "My only point is that if you wore each of your clothes, say, three times, before buying anything new, your clothes bill might go down." He shrugs. "You said you wanted ideas to save money."

I didn't want *those* kinds of ideas. I wanted ideas involving things I'm not interested in, like petrol or insurance. But now I'm a bit stuffed.

"Fine!" I fold my arms. "I'll wear every single item in my wardrobe three times before I even think of going shopping again. Satisfied?"

"Yes." He flashes me a smile. "And I'm giving up my car plans. Just for now."

"*Really?*"

"Like I say." He shrugs. "It's not the moment."

I feel humbled. Luke was planning to get a new car as a celebration as soon as the Arcodas case was over. It was, like, the prize. We'd gone for a test drive in one and everything.

Well, I suppose if he can do that, I can wear my clothes three times before I go shopping again. It's not such a hardship.

Anyway, I probably haven't got *that* many. I try to visualize my wardrobe. I mean, it's just a few tops and jeans and dresses, isn't it? And a few things crammed in at the back. I'll get through them all in a couple of weeks.

"We'll still be able to buy clothes for Minnie, won't we?" I look up in sudden alarm. "And she can still have her pocket money?"

I've got quite used to Minnie having pocket money when we're out and about. She spent another six months' advance in the Bambino sale and got the most *gorgeous* half-price sparkly Wellingtons. Plus, it's teaching her financial planning, because I've got it all written down in a book.

"Of course Minnie can have her pocket money!" Luke laughs. "And if she needs new clothes, she needs them. She's a growing girl."

"Fine," I say, trying not to feel envious.

It's all right for children. I wish *I* grew out of all my stuff every three months and had to replace it all.

"Anyway, Becky, I thought the Bloomwood style was Make More Money." Luke breaks in to my thoughts. He pulls out a chair and pours himself a glass of wine. "Maybe you could go back to work full-time now that we're getting a nanny."

Argh! No! It's as though he's fired a shot into the air with no warning; in fact, I feel myself physically recoil. Why did he have to mention the word *nanny* like that, with no preamble? I was going to soften Mum up first, maybe via general chitchat about au pairs.

"Nanny?" Mum's voice is instantly sharp. "What nanny? What are you talking about?"

She manages to make *nanny* sound like *serial killer*.

I hardly dare look at her.

"We just thought . . . it might be a good idea to try to get some expert help . . ." I cough. "I mean . . ."

"Minnie's spoiled," puts in Luke flatly. "She needs some structure and regulations."

Mum looks mortally offended.

"She's not spoiled by *you*, Mum, obviously," I add hurriedly. "It's just . . . they have these amazing people called Ultimate Nannies who help to raise a well-balanced, accomplished child. They're qualified in martial arts and everything."

"Martial *arts*?" echoes Mum incredulously. "What does she need martial arts for, poor little love?"

"And they're trained in routines and child development . . ." I glance desperately at Luke for support.

"We think it's what Minnie needs," says Luke firmly. "We're going to interview some candidates next week, and I'm sure we'll all get along marvelously."

"Well." Mum seems at a loss for words. "Well." She takes a swig of wine. "I see. Everything's changing."

"Of course, arrangements would have had to change substantially anyway," begins Luke, "bearing in mind that we'll be—oof!" He breaks off as I kick him hard on the ankle and glare at him.

Does he have *no* tact? Is he just going to blurt out everything, right here, right now?

We *can't* tell Mum we're moving out. Not on top of everything else. It'll be the final straw. It'll destroy her. She'll sink into depression and probably spiral into some kind of breakdown.

"What?" Mum looks beadily from face to face. "Bearing in mind you'll be what?"

"Nothing!" I say quickly. "Um, shall we go and watch telly?"

"Becky?" I can see Mum's face working with alarm. "What is it? What aren't you telling me?"

Oh God, now I'm torn. If we don't tell her the truth, she'll think something really awful's happened. And, after all, it is a family conference. Maybe this *is* the right time to break the news.

"OK." I take a deep slurp of wine for courage. "Here's the thing, Mum. Luke and I have found a lovely family house in Maida Vale. And we've had an offer accepted. And this one looks like it's really going ahead. Which means we'll be . . ." I take a deep breath, hardly able to say it. "Mum, we're moving out."

There's a stunned, disbelieving silence in the room. No one seems able to speak.

I shoot an agonized look at Luke. This is awful. I knew it would be bad, but I never thought it would be this bad.

"You're . . . going?" Mum says at last, her voice cracking slightly. "You're actually leaving us?"

She's devastated. It's obvious. I can already feel the tears rising inside.

"Yes, we're going. In about four weeks' time, probably." I swallow, my throat tight. "We have to have our own space. You must understand that, Mum. But we'll come and visit loads, and you'll still see Minnie, I promise, and—"

Mum doesn't seem to be listening.

"They're going! They're *going*." She grabs Dad's arm. "Did you hear that, Graham?"

Hang on. She doesn't sound *that* devastated. In fact, she sounds . . . delighted.

"Is this true?" Dad narrows his eyes.

"Looks like it." Luke nods.

"We can start having dinner parties again," says Mum breathlessly. "We can use the table! We can have guests to stay!"

"I can use my workshop," Dad chimes in faintly. "At last."

"I'll get my wardrobe back! And the utility room!" Mum seems almost giddy with excitement. "Oh, Graham!" To my astonishment, she plants a kiss on Dad's cheek. "I have to call Janice and tell her the good news!"

Good news? What about the empty-nest syndrome? What about spiraling into depression?

"But you said you didn't want us to go!" I say indignantly. "You said you were relieved those other houses fell through, because you would have missed us so much!"

"We were *lying*, love!" says Mum merrily. "We didn't want to hurt your feelings. Hello, it's me, Janice!" She turns to her mobile. "They're going! Yes! Four weeks! Tell the others!"

OK. Now I really am offended. Has the whole *neighborhood* been waiting for us to go?

JEANS (cont'd)

J Brand—cropped
J Brand—boot leg
Goldsign—skinny dark
7 For All Mankind—
   distressed (two sizes too
   small)
Balmain—black distressed
Notify—black
Notify—black (still in bag,
   never worn)
Theory—skinny stretch
7 For All Mankind—studded
7 For All Mankind—cutoffs
Acne—frayed at knee
Acne—ripped (tags still on)
Cavalli—frayed and se-
   quinned (still in bag)
Paige Premium Denim—
   boyfriend
True Religion—gray wide leg

EXERCISE WEAR

Stella McCartney yoga pants
Stella McCartney sleeveless
   top
Black ballet leotard
   (unworn)
Pink point ballet shoes
   (unworn)
Black leggings—Sweaty
   Betty
Gray leggings—Nike
   (still in bag with receipt)
Black leggings "Anti-
   cellulite" (never worn)
Gray leggings—American
   Apparel
Hip Hop graffiti dance pants
   (unworn)
Sequined ice dance
   costume
American football outfit
   (for Halloween party)
Fred Perry tennis dress
   (white)
Fred Perry tennis dress
   (pale blue)
Professional drag-racing
   suit (still in box)

continued on next
page . . .

Ms. Rebecca Brandon
The Pines
43 Elton Road
Oxshott
Surrey

18 January 2006

Dear Rebecca,

Thank you for your letter to the Chancellor of the
Exchequer, which was passed to me.

On his behalf, may I thank you for the sentiment that you
"know how he feels" and your thoughts on how to "get
out of this mess." Your father's principles of "C.B." and
"M.M.M." seem sound, as does the advice to "look
around and sell some things you don't need."

Thank you also for the kind gift of *Controlling Your Cash*
by David E. Barton—a book I was unfamiliar with. I am
unaware of whether the Chancellor owns a copy but will
certainly pass it on to the Treasury, along with the advice
to "write down everything that he spends."

With thanks again for your interest.

Yours sincerely,

Edwin Tredwell
Director of Policy Research

SEVEN

WHY HAVE I GOT so many clothes? Why? *Why?*

I've finally collected them from around the house and counted them all. And it's a total disaster. There's no way I'm going to get through them all in two weeks. Two years, more like.

How can I have so many pairs of jeans? And T-shirts? And old cardigans that I'd forgotten about?

On the plus side, I found a Whistles coat that will look fab with a belt. And some True Religion skinny jeans which were still in their plastic bag, stuffed under a pile of Lancôme gift sets.

But, on the downside, there are about eighteen gray T-shirts, all scraggy and shapeless. I don't remember buying *any* of them. And some really mortifying sales buys. And the worst thing is, Luke told Jess I was doing an audit of my clothes and she decided to come over and help me. So I couldn't do what I was planning, which was to hide all the clothes I hate in a plastic bag and smuggle them out of the house.

Jess was relentless. She made me write down a list of every item and wouldn't let me discount anything. Not the disastrous hot pants, not the revolting maroon leather waistcoat (what was I *thinking?*), not even all those old promotional T-shirts and shoes I've got free off magazines. And that's before we get to the weird Indian clothes I bought on our honeymoon.

If I have to wear that maroon leather waistcoat in public three times, I'll *die*.

Morosely, I look down at myself. I'm in one of my zillion unworn white shirts, with a pair of black trousers and a waistcoat layered over a long cardigan. This is the only way I'm going to survive—by layering as many pieces as possible every day and getting through them that way. Even so, according to Jess's calculations, I won't need to go shopping until October 23. And it's still only January. I want to *cry*. Stupid, stupid banks.

I was secretly hoping this whole financial-crisis thing would be one of those very quick affairs that come and go and everyone says, "Ha-ha, silly us, what a fuss we made about nothing!" Like that time when there was a report of an escaped tiger on the loose in Oxshott and everyone got hysterical, and then it turned out to be someone's cat.

But no one's saying, "Ha-ha, silly us." It's all still in the papers and everyone's still looking worried. This morning Mum very ostentatiously ate her toast without jam, shooting little resentful looks at Dad the whole time. I was sunk in gloom, trying not to look at the Christian Dior ad on the back of Dad's newspaper, and even Minnie was subdued.

And when I get to work, things are even more depressing. I run the personal-shopping department at The Look, which is a department store on Oxford Street. It didn't start off too well, but recently it's been on a roll. We've had loads of events, and great coverage in the media, and profits have been up—in fact, we all got bonuses!

But today the place is desolate. The women's fashion floor is silent, and nearly all our appointments in the personal-shopping department have been called off. It's a pretty depressing sight, a whole row of bookings with *Canceled* written beside them.

"Everyone said they'd got a cold," reports Jasmine, my colleague, as I'm leafing through the appointment book in dismay. "You'd think they could make up something more original."

"Like what?"

Jasmine taps her pale-green nails, which totally clash with her violet leopard-print eyes. (Colored lenses are her new fashion habit. Her own eyes are one blue, one green, so she says she's already used to people staring at them and wondering if they're real.)

"Like they have to go to rehab," she says at last. "Or their coke-addict husband beat them up and they've had to go to a secret women's refuge. That's what I'd say."

God,'Jasmine is warped. We couldn't be more different, the two of us. Jasmine behaves as though she doesn't care about anything, including her own clients. She tells people they look shit, they've got no style, their clothes should go in the bin . . . then she'll toss some garment to them with a shrug and they'll put it on and look so spectacular, they *can't* not buy it. Sometimes they'll get all gushy or try to give her a hug, and she'll just roll her eyes and say, "Jeez."

"Or they could be honest." Jasmine throws back her long, bleached-blond hair. "They could say, 'I haven't got any money, the bastard bank lost it all.' You do realize this place'll close down?" she adds almost cheerily, gesturing around. "In fact, this whole country's over. It's a fucking mess. I'll probably move to Morocco." She eyes my shirt suspiciously. "Isn't that Chloé, two seasons ago?"

Trust Jasmine to notice. I'm debating whether to say, "No, it's a tiny label you don't know about," or, "Yes, it's vintage," when a voice says timidly, "Becky?" As I hear my name, I turn round and peer in surprise. It's Davina, one of my regular clients, hovering at the entrance. I barely recognize her, what with her mac, head scarf, and sunglasses.

"Davina! You came! Great to see you!"

Davina is in her thirties and a doctor at Guy's Hospital. She's a world expert on eye disease and pretty much a world expert on Prada shoes too—she's been collecting them since she was eighteen. Today she had an appointment to find a new evening dress, but, according to the appointment book, she'd called it off.

"I shouldn't be here." She looks around warily. "I told my husband I'd canceled. He's . . . worried about things."

"Everyone is," I say understandingly. "Do you want to take your coat off?"

Davina doesn't move.

"I don't know," she says at last, sounding tortured. "I shouldn't be here. We had a row about it. He said, what did I need a new dress for? And that it wasn't the time to be splashing the cash. But I've won a Taylor Research Fellowship. My department's throwing me a reception to celebrate." Her voice suddenly throbs with emotion. "This is huge, this fellowship. It's an incredible honor. I worked for it, and I'll never get one again, and I've *got* the money for a dress. I've saved it up and it's all secure. We don't even bank with Bank of London!"

She sounds so upset, I feel like giving her a hug. The thing about Davina is, she doesn't do things lightly. She thinks about every piece she buys and goes for really classic well-made things. She's probably been looking forward to getting this dress for ages and ages.

What a meanie her husband is. He should be *proud* of his wife, getting a prize.

"Do you want to come in?" I try again. "Have a cup of coffee?"

"I don't know," she says again, her voice tiny. "It's so difficult. I shouldn't be here."

"But you are here," I point out gently. "When's the reception?"

"Friday night." She takes off her sunglasses to massage her brow and suddenly focuses past me, on the rail in my fitting room. It's holding all the dresses I pulled out for her last week. I told Jasmine to have them ready this morning.

There are some gorgeous pieces on that rail. Davina would look amazing in any one of them. I can see the lust growing in her eyes.

"Are those—"

"Just a few options."

"I can't." She shakes her head desperately. "I *can't* turn up in something new."

"But would your husband *know* it was new?" I can't resist saying. I see this thought register in her head.

"Maybe not," she says at last. Her brow is clearing a little . . . then it wrinkles anxiously again. "But I can't possibly come back home with any shopping bags. Or have anything delivered. *Or* have anything delivered to work. All the junior staff will chatter and want to see, and it'll get back to my husband. That's the downside of both working in the same hospital."

"So how can you buy a dress?" says Jasmine bluntly. "If you can't take anything home or have it delivered?"

"I don't know." Davina looks a bit crestfallen. "Oh, this is hopeless. I shouldn't have come."

"Of course you should!" I say firmly. "We're not in the business of giving up. Come in and have a cup of coffee and look at the dresses. And I'll think of something."

• • •

THE MINUTE Davina puts on the Philosophy by Alberta Ferretti, we both know. She *has* to have it. It's a black and bitter-chocolate sheath with a trailing wisp of chiffon, and it's five hundred pounds and worth every single penny.

So now it's up to me to work out how we do it. And by the time she's dressed again and eaten the sandwiches I ordered for her, I have the answer. We are hereby introducing a new, specialist personal-shopping service at The Look called SIP (Shop In Private). I've made all the arrangements for Davina, plus I've come up with several extra innovations. I've even typed up a quick email about it, which begins: *Do you feel guilty about shopping in these troubled days? Do you need a new level of discretion?*

I don't want to boast, but I'm quite proud of all my ideas. Customers can come to the personal-shopping department, select their new clothes, and then, in order to remain discreet, choose from a number of delivery options:

1. Have clothes on standby, ready to be biked over to client's house at a suitable specified time (i.e., when no one else is in).

2. Have clothes delivered in a cardboard box labeled *Computer Paper* or *Sanitary Products*.

3. Have a member of staff (i.e., Jasmine or me) pose as a friend, visit home, and offer clothes as "unwanted cast-offs."

4. Have a member of staff (i.e., Jasmine or me) pose as a cleaning lady, visit home, and secrete clothes in hiding place to be previously arranged.

5. For a more substantial fee, members of staff from The Look (Jasmine and me) will set up a "charity stall" at a location to be arranged,* where the client may "purchase" clothes for a nominal price in front of spouse or partner.

*This option may work better for groups of shoppers.

Davina's going for the *Computer Paper* option. By the time she left, her eyes were sparkling with excitement and she gave me a massive hug, saying she'd send me pictures of the reception and I'd absolutely made her day. Well, she deserves it. She looks amazing in that dress and she'll remember the occasion all her life. As I set off for my lunch with Bonnie, I feel pretty chuffed with myself.

The only teeny doubt which occasionally shoots through my head is that I haven't run the Shop In Private scheme past any of my bosses. Like the CEO or head of marketing or director of operations. Strictly speaking, I should have got a new initiative like this approved before I launched it to the public. But the thing is, they're *men*. They'd never understand. They'd probably just make lots of stupid objections and time would tick away and we'd lose all our customers.

So I'm doing the right thing. Yes. I'm sure I am.

I'm meeting Bonnie at a restaurant near the Brandon Communications offices. As I arrive, she's sitting at a table, looking as understated as ever in a beige tweed dress and flat patent pumps.

Every time I've met Bonnie, she's always seemed remote and spotless, almost not human. But I *know* there's a hidden side to her—because I've seen it. At the last Brandon C Christmas party, I happened to notice her when the rest of us were on the dance floor singing madly to "Dancing Queen." Bonnie was sitting alone at a table, and as I watched, she surreptitiously helped herself to one of the hazelnut chocolates left on the plates. Then another one. She went around the whole table, discreetly Hoovering the hazelnut chocolates, and even folded the wrappers neatly and put them in her evening bag. I never told anyone about it, not even Luke—because something told me she would have been mortified to have been seen. Let alone teased about it.

"Becky," she greets me, in her low, well-modulated voice. "How lovely to see you. I've ordered some sparkling water."

"Fab!" I beam at her. "And thanks so much for helping out."

"Oh, it's no trouble. Now, let me show you what I've done so far."

She pulls out a plastic folder and starts fanning printed papers across the table.

"Guests . . . contacts . . . dietary requirements . . ."

I goggle at the pages in amazement. Luke's right: Bonnie's awesome. She's compiled a full list of guests from Luke's business and personal address books, complete with addresses, phone numbers, and a short paragraph on who each person is.

"Everyone in the company has blocked off the evening of April seventh," she continues. "I've taken Gary into my confidence, and we've invented a full company training session. Here you are . . ."

Speechlessly, I look at the sheet of paper she proffers. It's a schedule for a *Brandon Communications Training Session,* beginning at 5:00 p.m. and lasting into the evening, with *drinks* and *group activities* and *discussion circles.* It looks so genuine! There's even the name of some *facilitating company* printed at the bottom.

"This is brilliant," I say at last. "Absolutely fantastic. Bonnie, thank you so, *so* much—"

"Well, it means you don't have to tell anyone at the company the truth just yet." She gives a little smile. "These things are better kept under wraps for as long as possible."

"Absolutely," I agree fervently. "The fewer people who are in on the secret, the better. I've got a list of exactly who knows, and it's tightly controlled."

"You seem to have things very well in hand." She smiles encouragingly. "And how are the party arrangements themselves going?"

"Really well," I say at once. "I mean . . . I haven't *quite* finalized everything . . ."

"Have you thought about employing a party planner?" inquires Bonnie mildly. "Or one of the concierge services? There's one in particular that several of my employers have used, called The Service. Very efficient; I can recommend them."

She takes out a notepad and scribbles down a number. "I'm sure they'd help with organizing, sourcing, providing staff, whatever you need. But it's only a suggestion."

"Thanks!" I take the paper and put it in my purse. That might not be a bad idea, actually. I mean, not that I need any *help.* But just to tie up any loose ends.

The waiter arrives; we both order salads, and he refreshes our water. As Bonnie sips meticulously, I can't help eyeing her with curiosity. If you think about it, this is the Other Woman in Luke's life. (Not in a Camilla Parker-Bowles kind of way. Definitely not. I'm not falling into that trap again of thinking Luke's having an affair and hiring private detectives and getting myself all stressed out over nothing.)

"Did you want some wine, Becky?" says Bonnie suddenly. "I have to remain professional, I'm afraid . . ." She gives a regretful smile.

"Me too." I nod, still fixated by Bonnie.

She spends more time with Luke than I do. She knows all about huge areas of his life that he never bothers telling me about. She probably has all sorts of interesting insights on him.

"So . . . what's Luke like as a boss?" I can't resist asking.

"He's admirable." She smiles and takes a piece of bread from the basket.

Admirable. That's so typical. Discreet, bland, tells me nothing.

"How is he admirable, exactly?"

Bonnie gives me a strange look, and I suddenly realize I sound as if I'm fishing for compliments.

"Anyway, he can't be Mr. Perfect," I add hurriedly. "There must be things he does that annoy you."

"I wouldn't say that." She gives another closed smile and sips her water.

Is she going to bat away every question like that? I suddenly feel an urge to get underneath her professional veneer. Maybe I could bribe her with a hazelnut chocolate.

"Come on, Bonnie!" I persist. "There must be *something* that annoys you about Luke. Like, I get annoyed when he answers the BlackBerry all the time in the middle of conversations."

"Really." Bonnie gives a guarded laugh. "I couldn't say."

"Yes, you could!" I lean across the table. "Bonnie, I know you're a professional, and I respect that. And so am I. But this is off the record. We can be honest with each other. I'm not leaving this restaurant till you tell me something that annoys you about him."

Bonnie has turned pink and keeps glancing toward the door as though for escape.

"Look," I say, trying to get her attention. "Here we are together, the two women who spend the most time with Luke. We know him better than anyone else. Shouldn't we be able to share our experiences and learn from each other? I won't *tell* him or anything!" I add, realizing I might not have made this clear enough. "This is strictly between you and me. I swear."

There's a long pause. I think I might be getting through to her.

"Just one thing," I cajole. "One teeny, tiny little thing . . ."

Bonnie takes a gulp of water, as though stiffening her nerves.

"Well," she says at last. "I suppose the birthday card situation is a *little* frustrating."

"Birthday card situation?"

"The staff birthday cards, you know." She blinks at me. "I have a stack of them for him to sign for the whole year, but he won't get round to it. Which is understandable, he's very busy—"

"I'll get him to do them," I say firmly. "Leave it to me."

"Becky." Bonnie blanches. "Please don't, that's not what I meant—"

"Don't worry," I say reassuringly. "I'll be really subtle."

Bonnie still looks troubled. "I don't like you to be involved—"

"But I am involved! I'm his wife! And I think it's monstrous that he can't be bothered to sign his own staff's birthday cards. You know why it is?" I add knowledgeably. "It's because he doesn't care about his own birthday, so he thinks no one else does either. It wouldn't even *occur* to him that anyone cared."

"Ah." Bonnie nods slowly. "Yes. That makes sense."

"So, when's the next company birthday? Who's next on the list?"

"Well, actually . . ." Bonnie turns a little pinker. "It's my own birthday, in two weeks' time."

"Perfect! Well, I'll make sure he's signed the cards by then—" A new thought strikes me. "And what's he going to get you as a present? What did he get you for Christmas? Something really nice, I hope."

"Of course! He got me a lovely gift!" Bonnie's bright voice is a bit forced. "This beautiful bracelet."

She shakes her arm and a gold link bracelet falls down from under her sleeve. I stare at it, speechless. Luke bought her this?

I mean, it's not a bad bracelet. But it's *so* not Bonnie's coloring or style or anything. No wonder she's hidden it up her sleeve. And she probably feels she has to wear it to work every day, poor thing.

Where did he get it, anyway, totallyblandpresentsforyoursecretary.com? Why didn't he ask *me*?

Things are becoming clearer to me. We need to coordinate, Bonnie and me. We need to work as a team.

"Bonnie," I say thoughtfully. "Would you like to have a *proper* drink?"

"Oh no—" she begins.

"Come on," I say coaxingly. "Just one tiny glass of wine at lunchtime doesn't make anyone unprofessional. And I promise I won't mention it."

"Well." Bonnie relents. "Perhaps I will have a small vermouth on the rocks."

Yay! Go, Bonnie!

BY THE TIME we've finished our salads and are sipping coffees, we're both a million times more relaxed. I've made Bonnie laugh with stories of Luke doing yoga on our honeymoon, and she's told me about some previous boss trying the lotus position and having to go to the hospital. (She was too discreet to mention who it was. I'll have to Google.) And, most important, I've hatched my plan.

"Bonnie," I begin as the waiter presents us with the bill and I swipe it before she can protest. "I just want to say again, I'm *so* grateful to you for helping me with the party."

"Really, it's no trouble at all—"

"And it's made me realize something. We can help each other!" My voice rises in enthusiasm. "We can pool our resources. Think what we can achieve if we work in partnership! Luke doesn't need to know. It can be our own private arrangement."

As soon as I say "private arrangement," Bonnie looks uncomfortable.

"Becky, it's been very pleasant spending time with you," she begins. "And I do appreciate your wishing to help; however—"

"So let's keep in touch, OK?" I interrupt. "Keep my number on speed dial. And anything you want me to nudge Luke about, let me know. Big or small. I'll do whatever I can."

She's opening her mouth to protest. She *can't* backtrack now.

"Bonnie, please. I really care about Brandon Communications," I say with sudden warmth. "And it might just be that I can make a difference to things. But I'll only know that if you keep me in the loop! Otherwise I'm powerless! Luke tries to protect me, but he doesn't realize he's shutting me out. Please let me help."

Bonnie looks taken aback by my little speech, but it's kind of true—I have felt shut out by Luke, ever since he wouldn't let me go to the trial. (OK, *not* trial. Hearing. Whatever it was called.)

"Well," she says eventually, "I didn't see it quite like that. Of course, I'd be glad to let you know if I ever think there's anything you could . . . contribute."

"Fab!" I beam. "And, in return, maybe you could do the odd favor for me?"

"Of course." Bonnie looks as though she can't quite keep up. "I'd be glad to. Did you have anything specific in mind?"

"Well, yes, actually, I *did* have one small request." I take a sip of cappuccino. "It would really, really help me out if you could do it."

"To do with the party?" Bonnie is already getting out her notebook.

"No, this isn't to do with the party. It's more general." I lean across the table. "Could you tell Luke that a gym is better than a wine cellar?"

Bonnie stares back at me, flummoxed. "I'm sorry?" she says at last.

"We're buying this house," I explain, "and Luke wants a wine cellar in the basement, but I want a gym. So could you persuade him a gym is a better choice?"

"Becky." Bonnie looks perturbed. "I *really* don't think this is appropriate—"

"Please!" I wheedle. "Bonnie, do you realize how much Luke respects your opinion? He listens to you all the time. You can influence him!"

Bonnie seems almost at a loss for words. "But . . . but how on earth would I even bring up the subject?"

"Easy!" I say confidently. "You could pretend to be reading an article about it and you could casually say how you'd *never* buy a house that converted the whole basement into a wine cellar and you'd much prefer a gym. And you could say you think wine tastings are really overrated and boring," I add.

"But, Becky—"

"And then we'd really be helping each other out. Girlpower." I smile at her as winningly as I can. "The sisterhood."

"Well . . . I'll do my best to bring it up in conversation," says Bonnie finally. "I can't promise anything, but—"

"You're a star! And anything else you want me to do or say to Luke, just text. Anything at all." I offer her the plate of chocolate mints. "Here's to us! The Becky and Bonnie team!"

EIGHT

AS I WALK DOWN the street after lunch, I feel exhilarated. Bonnie's amazing. She's the best assistant Luke's ever had, by a million miles, and we're going to make a fabulous duo. Plus, I've already phoned that concierge company she recommended and been put through to their party division. Everything's going so easily!

Why on earth have I never used a concierge service before? They all seem really pleasant and it's as though nothing's too much trouble. We *have* to become members. According to the disembodied voice that talks while you're waiting, they can do anything, from getting sold-out theater tickets, to chartering a plane, to getting someone to bring you a cup of tea in the middle of the Najavo Desert.

You know. If you wanted one.

"Hi!" A cheery-sounding guy comes onto the line. "My name's Rupert. Harry explained the brief: You're looking for the ultimate surprise party for your husband."

"Yes! With fire-eaters and jugglers and a tent and a disco."

"OK, let's see." He pauses and I can hear the flipping of pages. "We recently organized a birthday party for three hundred in a series of bedouin tents. We had jugglers, fire-eaters, three international buffets, dancing on a starlit floor, award-winning cameramen to capture the event, and the birthday girl arrived on an elephant . . ."

I'm breathless, just listening to the list.

"I want that one," I say. "That exact one. It sounds fab."

"Great." He laughs. "Well, maybe we could meet up, finesse the details, and you could look at the rest of our event portfolio."

"I'd love to!" I say joyfully. "My name is Becky, I'll give you my number . . ."

"Just one small detail," adds Rupert pleasantly after I've dictated my mobile phone number. "You'll have to join The Service. I mean, obviously we can fast-track your membership—"

"I'd love to," I say firmly. "I was thinking of doing it anyway."

This is so cool. We're going to have a private concierge service! We'll be able to get in to concerts and all the best hotels and secret clubs. I should have done this *years* ago—

"So, I'll email those forms to you this afternoon," Rupert's saying.

"Fab! How much does it cost?" I add as an afterthought.

"The annual fee is all inclusive," replies Rupert smoothly. "We don't sting you for any extra charges, unlike some of our competitors! And for you and your husband, it would come in at six."

"Oh, right," I say uncertainly. "Six . . . hundred pounds, you mean?"

"Thousand." He gives a relaxed laugh. "I'm afraid."

Six thousand pounds? Just for the annual fee? Yikes. I mean, I'm sure it's worth it, but . . .

"And . . ." I swallow, hardly daring to ask. "That

party we were talking about. With the tents and the jugglers and everything. About how much would that cost?"

"That came in *under* budget, you'll be pleased to hear"—Rupert gives a little laugh—"and the total was two hundred and thirty."

I feel wobbly. Two hundred and thirty thousand pounds?

"Becky? Are you still there? Obviously we can work with budgets a lot smaller than that!" He sounds cheery and lighthearted. "A hundred grand would normally be our starting point—"

"Right!" My voice is a bit shrill. "Great! Well . . . you know what, actually . . . thinking about it . . . I'm still at a very early planning stage. So maybe I'll call you back and we can have a meeting at a . . . later date. Thanks so much. Bye."

I switch off my phone before my cheeks can turn any redder. Two hundred and thirty thousand pounds? For a party? I mean, I really love Luke and everything, but two hundred and thirty thousand—

"Becky?"

I look up and jump a mile. It's Luke. What's Luke doing here? He's standing about three yards away, staring at me in astonishment. To my sudden horror I realize I'm holding the transparent folder full of guest lists, conference details, and everything else. I'm about to give the whole bloody thing away.

"What a surprise!" He comes forward to kiss me, and I feel a spurt of panic. I hastily try to stuff the folder away but in my confusion drop it on the pavement.

"Let me." He bends down.

"No!" I yelp. "It's private! I mean, it's confidential. Personal shopping details of a member of the Saudi royal family. Highly sensitive." I hastily scrabble for it, folding it up as best I can and shoving the whole lot in my bag. "There!" I bob up again and smile fixedly. "So . . . how are you?"

Luke doesn't answer. He's giving me one of those looks. One of those something's-going-on looks.

"Becky, what's up? Were you coming to see me?"

"No!" I retort sharply. "Of course not!"

"So what are you doing in this area?"

Immediately I realize my crucial mistake. I should have said I *was* coming to see him.

"I . . . um . . ." I try to think quickly of a good reason for being in EC2 at lunchtime. "I'm trying to get to know the city better. I'm doing it post code by post code. You should see SE24—it's fab!"

There's silence.

"Becky." Luke runs both hands through his thick dark hair. "Be honest with me. Are you in some kind of . . . financial trouble? Have you been seeing someone?"

What?

"No!" I exclaim, offended. "Of course not! At least . . . no more than normal," I add, feeling the need to be honest. "That is *so* typical of you, Luke. You bump into me on the street and immediately assume I'm in debt!"

I mean, I am in debt. But that's hardly the point.

"Well, what am I *supposed* to think?" he replies heatedly. "You act shifty, you're hiding paperwork from me; obviously something's going on."

Oh God, oh God, I have to deflect him . . .

"OK!" I say. "You got me. I was . . . I was . . ." My mind gropes frantically. "Having Botox."

Luke's face drops, and I take the opportunity to zip my bag shut.

"Botox?" he says in disbelieving tones.

"Yes," I say defiantly. "Botox. I wasn't going to tell you. And that's why I was acting weird."

There. Perfect.

"Botox," he says again. "You had *Botox*."

"Yes!"

I suddenly realize I'm speaking with too much animation. I try to make my face all rigid and stary, like middle-aged celebrities. But too late: Luke's peering closely at my face.

"Where did you have it?"

"Er . . . here." I point gingerly to my temple. "And . . . there. And here."

"But . . ." Luke looks puzzled. "Aren't the lines supposed to disappear?"

What? He's got a nerve. I don't have any lines! Like maybe the *teeniest* odd little line, which you can hardly see.

"It's very subtle," I say pointedly. "It's the new technique. Less is more."

Luke sighs. "Becky, how much did you pay for this? Where did you have it done? Because there are girls at work who've had Botox, and I have to say—"

Oh God. I'd better get him off the subject of Botox quickly, or he'll be saying, "Let's go to the clinic right now and get our money back."

"I only had a tiny bit of Botox," I say hurriedly. "I was really there about . . . another procedure."

"Something *else*?" Luke stares at me. "What, for God's sake?"

My mind is utterly blank. Procedure. Procedure. What do people have done?

"Boobs," I hear myself saying. "A boob job."

From his aghast expression, perhaps that wasn't the right way to go.

"A *boob* job?" he manages at last. "You had a—"

"No! I was just . . . *thinking* about having one."

"Jesus Christ." Luke rubs his brow. "Becky, we need to talk about this. Let's get off the street." He takes my arm and leads me toward a nearby bar. As soon as we're inside the door, he turns and takes me by the shoulders so hard, I gasp in surprise.

"Becky, I love you. However you look. *Whatever* shape you are. And the thought that you felt you had to go off secretly . . . it kills me. Please, please, please, don't ever do that again."

I never expected him to react like that. In fact, he looks so upset, I feel terrible. Why did I have to make up something so stupid? Why couldn't I have said I was meeting a client at her office? A million good excuses are coming to mind now, none of which involve clinics or boob jobs.

"Luke, I'm sorry," I falter. "I never should have thought about it. I didn't mean to worry you—"

"You're perfect," he says almost fiercely. "You don't need to change one hair. One freckle. One little toe. And if it's me that's made you feel you should do this . . . then there's something wrong with *me*."

I think this is the most romantic thing Luke has ever said to me, ever. I can feel tears rising.

"It was nothing to do with you," I gulp. "It was . . . you know. The pressures of society and everything."

"Do you even know this place is *safe*?" He reaches for the bag. "Let me have a look. A lot of these so-called surgeons are irresponsible cowboys. I'm going to get our company doctor—"

"No!" I instinctively pull my bag close to my chest. "It's OK, Luke. I know it's safe—"

"No, you don't!" he almost shouts in frustration. "It's major fucking surgery, Becky! Do you realize that? And the idea that you would go off like this in secret, risking your life, without even *thinking* of me or Minnie—"

"I wouldn't risk my life!" I say desperately. "I'd never have surgery without telling you! It's one of those lunchtime keyhole ones, where they just give you an injection."

"You think that makes it OK?" He doesn't let up an iota. "That sounds even more dodgy to me. What exactly does it involve?"

I'm sure I've read something about lunchtime boob jobs in *Marie Claire*, only I can't quite remember the details now.

"It's very minimal. Very safe." I rub my nose, playing for time. "They mark the area and inject a kind of special foam into the . . . um, capillaries. And it . . . er . . . expands."

"You mean they *inflate*?" He stares at me.

"Kind of." I try to sound confident. "Just a bit. You know. A size or two." I make what I hope is a realistic gesture at my chest.

"Over what sort of time period?"

I scrabble around for something convincing.

"About . . . a week."

"Your breasts inflate over the course of a *week*?" He seems staggered at this idea. Shit. I should have said an hour.

"It depends on your body type," I add hastily, "and your . . . personal breast metabolism. Sometimes it only takes five minutes. Everyone's different. Anyway, I won't be doing it. You're right, I should never have gone off in secret." I gaze up at him with my most heartfelt expression. "I'm sorry, Luke. I owe it to you and Minnie not to put myself at risk and I've learned my lesson now."

I was hoping Luke might give me a kiss and tell me how perfect I am again. But his face has kind of changed. He doesn't seem *quite* so upset and tortured as he did before. In fact, he's eyeing me with a familiar kind of expression.

Something near suspicion.

"What's the name of the clinic?" he says lightly.

"I can't remember now." I cough. "Anyway, let's not talk about it anymore. I feel so bad, Luke—"

"You could look at the paperwork." He gestures at my bag.

"I'll look later," I nod. "Later. When I'm less upset at the worry I caused you."

Luke's still just giving me that look of his.

Oh God. He's twigged, hasn't he? At least, he's twigged I wasn't at a boob-job clinic.

"Do you want a drink?" he says abruptly.

"Er . . . OK," I say, my heart pounding. "Do you have time?"

"I can sneak fifteen minutes." He glances at his watch. "Don't tell my assistant."

"Of course not." I give a slightly unnatural laugh. "Not that I even know her!"

"You do know her." Luke gives me a puzzled look as he heads to the bar. "Bonnie. You've met."

"Oh, right. Of course."

I subside into a chair and unfurl my clenched fingers from my bag. This whole secret-party lark is totally stressy, and I've only just started.

"Cheers." Luke has returned to the table with two glasses of wine, and we clink glasses.

For a while there's a silence as we sip. Luke keeps eyeing me over the top of his glass. Then, as though coming to a decision, he puts it down.

"So, some good news. We've got a couple of new clients. *Not* financial."

"Ooh!" I look up with interest. "Who?"

Let it be Gucci, let it be Gucci . . .

"The first is a climate technology company. They're lobbying for investment in a new carbon-absorption project and want us to come on board. Could be interesting."

Carbon absorption. Hmph.

"Great!" I say warmly. "Well done! What about the other one?"

"The other one is quite a coup . . ." he begins, his eyes sparkling. Then he hesitates, glances at me, and sips his wine. "Actually, that's not quite firmed up yet. I'll let you know when it is. Don't want to jinx it."

"Well, congratulations anyway." I lift my glass. "I guess you need a bit of good news at the moment."

"It's not great out there." He raises his eyebrows wryly. "How about your shopping department? I can't imagine that's done great the last few days either."

"Well, actually—" I'm about to tell him about my fab new system where people can hide their shopping from their husbands.

Then I stop. On second thought, maybe I won't.

"We're holding up," I say instead. "You know."

Luke nods and takes another sip of wine, leaning back in his chair. "It's nice to have a few moments, just the two of us. You should come this way more often. Although maybe not to the plastic-surgery clinic." Again he shoots me that skeptical look.

Is he going to push it? Or not? I can't tell.

"So, did you see the email about the nannies?" I change the subject quickly. "Aren't they fab?"

"Yes!" He nods. "I was impressed."

We've already had a load of CVs sent through from Ultimate Nannies, and each one looks better than the last! One speaks five languages, one has sailed across the Atlantic, and one has two degrees in history of art. If one of them can't make Minnie well balanced and accomplished, I don't know who can.

"I'd better go." Luke gets to his feet and I grab my bag. We head to the street, and Luke pauses to kiss me. "See you later, Becky."

"See you." I nod.

I'm off the hook. He's just going to leave it. Even

though there's no way in a million years he believes the boob-job story.

Thanks for trusting me, I want to message silently back into his head. *I wasn't doing anything bad, promise.*

I hold my breath and watch him walk away till he's rounded the corner. Then I collapse on a nearby bench, pull out a compact mirror, and start studying my face in detail.

OK, Luke knows nothing about anything. I could *easily* have had Botox. Look at that totally smooth bit, right by my hair. He must be blind.

I GET BACK to The Look to find Jasmine on the phone.

"Yeah, two o'clock, no problem," she's saying. "See you then." She puts the receiver down and gives me a look of triumphant joy. (That's to say, one corner of her mouth raises reluctantly in a smile. I've learned to read Jasmine pretty well.) "Well, your plan's working. Three clients have uncanceled their appointments."

"Fantastic!"

"And there's a customer waiting right now," Jasmine adds. "No appointment. Says she want to see you, no one else. She's lurking around the floor till you get back."

"OK," I say in surprise. "Well, just give me a minute."

I hurry to my dressing room, put my bag away, and freshen up my lip gloss, wondering who it might be. People do quite often drop in without an appointment, so it could be anybody. God, I hope it's not that girl who wants to look like Jennifer Aniston, because the truth is, she's never going to in a million years, however many halter tops she buys—

"Rebecca."

A familiar, haughty voice interrupts my thoughts.

For an instant I can't react. I think I might be dreaming. The back of my neck is prickling as I finally turn round—and there she is. Immaculate as ever in a pistachio-colored suit, rigid hair, equally immobile face, and her crocodile Birkin dangling from one skinny arm.

It was her, shoots through my mind. *It was her outside the church.*

"Elinor!" I manage. "What a . . . surprise."

This would be the understatement of the year.

"Hello, Rebecca." She looks around the dressing room disdainfully, as though to say, "I expected no better," which is a nerve, as it's just been redecorated.

"Er . . . what can I do for you?" I say at last.

"I wish to—" She stops, and there's a long, frozen silence. I feel as though we're in a play and we've both forgotten our lines. "What the hell are you doing here?" is what I really want to say. Or, frankly, just "Hhhnnnnhh?"

This silence is getting ridiculous. We can't stand here forever like two mannequins. Elinor told Jasmine she was a customer. Well, fine. I'll treat her like a customer.

"So, are you after anything in particular?" I take out my notepad, as if she was any other client. "Day wear, perhaps? We have some new Chanel pieces in, which I believe might be your style."

"Very well," says Elinor after a lengthy pause.

What?

She's going to try on clothes? Here? Seriously?

"OK," I say, feeling a bit surreal. "Fine. I'll select some pieces that I think would . . . er . . . suit you."

I go to collect the clothes myself, return to the dressing room, and hand them to Elinor.

"Feel free to try on as many or as few as you like," I say politely. "I'll be right outside if you need any advice or help."

I close the door quietly and give a silent scream. Elinor. Here. What the fuck is going *on*? Am I going to tell Luke about this? The whole thing is too freaky. I suddenly wish I'd pressed Luke more on what exactly happened between them and what heinous thing she said. Should I be telling Elinor dramatically to get out now and never darken the door of The Look again?

But if I did that, I'd probably get fired.

After about a minute, the door opens again and Elinor appears, holding the whole armful of clothes. She can't have tried them on; she hasn't had nearly enough time.

"Shall I take those for you?" I force myself to stay polite.

"Yes. They were satisfactory." She nods.

For a moment I think I can't have understood.

"You mean . . . you want to take them?" I say disbelievingly. "You're going to *buy* them?"

"Very well. Yes." She frowns impatiently, as though this conversation is already irritating her.

Eight grand's worth of clothes? Just like that? My bonus is going to be *fantastic*.

"OK! Well, that's great!" I'm trying to suppress my glee. "Any alterations needed or anything?"

Elinor shakes her head with the barest of movements. This is officially the most bizarre appointment I've ever known. Most people, if they were going to spend eight grand on clothes, would at least come out and do a twirl and say, "What do you think?"

Jasmine passes by with a rack of clothes, and I see her eyeing Elinor incredulously. She is quite a sight, Elinor, with her pale, tight, over-made-up face, veiny hands laden with rocks, and her steely, imperious gaze. She's looking older too, I abruptly realize. Her skin is looking thin and papery, and I can see a couple of gray wisps at her temple, which the hairdresser obviously missed. (I expect he'll be shot at dawn.)

"So, is there anything else I can help you with? Evening wear? Accessories?"

Elinor opens her mouth. Then she closes it, then opens it again. She looks as though she's really struggling to utter something, and I watch in apprehension. Is she going to mention Luke? Does she have some piece of bad news? There *has* to be a reason she's come here.

"Evening wear," she murmurs at last.

Yeah, right. That's really what you were about to say.

I fetch her six evening dresses and she chooses three. And then two bags. And a stole. The whole thing is becoming farcical. She's spent about twenty grand and she still won't look me in the eye and she *still* won't say whatever she's come here to say.

"Would you like any . . . refreshments?" I say at last, trying to sound normal and pleasant. "Can I get you a cappuccino? A cup of tea? A glass of champagne?"

We've run out of categories of clothes. She can't buy anything else. She can't stave it off any longer. Whatever *it* is.

Elinor's just standing there, her head bowed slightly, her hands clutched around the handle of her bag. I've never known her to be this subdued. It's almost scary. And she hasn't insulted me once, I realize in sudden astonishment. She hasn't said my shoes are shoddy or my nail polish is vulgar. What's up with her? Is she *ill*?

At last, as though with a huge effort, she raises her head.

"Rebecca."

"Yes?" I say nervously. "What is it?"

When she speaks again, it's so quietly I can barely hear her.

"I wish to see my grandchild."

• • •

OH GOD, oh God, oh God. What do I do?

All the way home, my head is spinning. Never in a million years did I think this would happen. I didn't think Elinor was even *interested* in Minnie.

When Minnie was born, Elinor didn't bother visiting us for about three months. Then she just pitched up one day with her driver waiting outside, glanced into the crib, said, "Is she normal?" and, when we'd said yes, left. And whereas most people give you gorgeous things like teddies or cute booties, Elinor sent the most hideous antique doll, with ringlets and scary eyes, like in a horror film. It was so creepy, Mum wouldn't have it in the house, and in the end I sold it on eBay. (So Elinor had better not ask to see it or anything.)

And all this was before the big row between her and Luke, since when we've barely mentioned her name. About two months before Christmas, I tried to ask if we'd be giving her a present, and Luke nearly bit my head off. I haven't dared mention her since.

Of course, there's one easy option ahead of me. I could throw her card in the bin and pretend I never saw her. Blank the whole thing from my mind. I mean, what could she do about it?

But somehow . . . I can't bring myself to. I've never seen Elinor look vulnerable before; not like she did today. During those tense moments when she was waiting for me to answer, I couldn't see Elinor the ice queen; I only saw Elinor the lonely old woman with papery hands.

Then, as soon as I said, "OK, I'll ask Luke," she immediately reverted to her normal subzero manner and started telling me how inferior The Look was to shops in Manhattan and how the English don't understand service culture and how there were specks on the carpet in the dressing room.

But somehow she's got under my skin. I can't ignore her. I can't throw her card away. She may be a total bitch ice queen, but she *is* Minnie's grandmother. They are flesh and blood. (You know. If Elinor had any of either.)

After all, it's possible Luke might have mellowed. What I need to do is raise the subject very carefully. Very, very gently, like waving an olive branch in the air. And I'll see what happens.

So that night, I wait up till Luke gets back, has kissed Minnie good night, has had a whiskey, and is getting undressed, before I broach anything.

"Luke . . . about your mother," I begin tentatively.

"I was thinking about Annabel today too." Luke turns, his face softened. "Dad emailed me some old pictures of her today. I'll show you."

Oh, great start, Becky. I should have been clear *which* mother. Now that he thinks I've brought up the subject of Annabel, it's impossible to segue neatly into Elinor.

"I was just thinking about . . . um . . . family ties." I change tack. "And family traits," I add in sudden inspiration. "Who do you think Minnie takes after most? She totally gets being a drama queen from Mum, and she has your eyes—in fact, she probably takes after everyone in the family a little bit, even . . ." I hesitate, my heart thumping. "Even your biological mother. Elinor."

"I sincerely hope not," says Luke curtly, and bangs a drawer shut.

OK. So he doesn't sound mellow.

"But Elinor is her grandmother, after all," I persist. "Minnie's bound to take after her in some way or other—"

"I don't see that." He cuts me off. "Nurture's what counts. I was always Annabel's son, never that woman's."

Yikes. *That woman.* Things are even worse than I thought.

"Right," I say feebly.

I can't pipe up with, "How about we take Minnie visiting with Elinor?" Not now. I'll have to leave it for the moment.

"So, did you have a good rest of the day?" I change topic.

"Not bad." He nods. "And you? Get back all right?"

"Yes, fine," I say innocently. "I got a cab. Thanks for asking."

"Strange area to have a cosmetic-surgery clinic, I was thinking," he adds casually. "Not what you would expect in the financial district."

I make the mistake of meeting his eye—and there's a telltale glint in it. I *knew* he was on to me.

The only way forward is to brazen it out.

"Are you crazy?" I retort. "It makes total sense. Look at all those haggard City workers walking around. You know, a recent magazine survey showed that City workers are more prematurely aged than any other sector, by twenty percent."

I've made this up, but Luke doesn't know that, does he? And I bet it's true.

"You know what?" I add, having a sudden bright thought. "The same survey said that if people feel cherished by their bosses, they age less quickly. *And* they work better."

"I'm sure." Luke is checking his BlackBerry.

"And it said that one way to accomplish this is for bosses to give their employees personalized, signed birthday cards," I persist. "Isn't that interesting? Do you give people personalized cards at Brandon Communications?"

"Uh-huh." Luke barely nods.

What a nerve. I feel like saying, "No, you don't! They're all in a pile in your office, unsigned!"

"Oh, good." I force myself to sound casual. "Because apparently people feel really happy to know their boss has signed the card themselves and it hasn't just been done by an assistant or anything. It raises their endorphins by fifteen percent."

Luke pauses in his tapping. Yes! I've got through to him.

"Becky, you do read a lot of crap."

Crap?

"It's called *research,* actually," I say with dignity. "I thought you might be interested in how a tiny little thing like a signed birthday card could make all the difference. Because a lot of bosses would forget. But obviously not you."

Ha. Take that, Mr. Too-Busy-to-Sign.

For a moment Luke is silenced.

"Fascinating," he says at last. But then he reaches for a pencil and makes a note on the to-do list he carries around in his pocket. I pretend not to notice, but inside I smile a satisfied little smile.

OK, now I feel we're done with this conversation. And I really don't want to reprise the one about Botox. So, with an elaborate yawn, I lie down on the pillows to go to sleep.

But as I close my eyes, a vision of Elinor is still lingering in my head. I actually feel *guilty* about her, which is very weird and a brand-new experience for me. But I can't work out what to do about it now.

Oh well. I'll think about it tomorrow.

From: Bonnie Seabright
Subject: Cards
Date: 23 January 2006
To: Becky Brandon

Luke has signed all the birthday cards! Many thanks! Bonnie!

From: Becky Brandon
Subject: Re: Cards
Date: 24 January 2006
To: Bonnie Seabright

No problem! Let me know if anything else is bugging you.

Becky xxx

PS—Have you managed to mention the gym yet?

Ms. Rebecca Brandon
The Pines
43 Elton Road
Oxshott
Surrey

6 February 2006

Dear Rebecca,

Thank you for your letter of 1 February.

The Chancellor has indeed made a recent speech in which he highlighted the importance of retail to the British economy.

Unfortunately, at this time there are no specific OBEs or Damehoods "for shopping," as you suggest. Should such an honor be introduced, I will be sure to put your name forward.

I therefore return with thanks your package of receipts and store tags, which I looked at with interest and agree shows "real commitment to sustaining the economy."

Yours sincerely,

Edwin Tredwell
Director of Policy Research

NINE

A WEEK LATER, I still haven't decided what to do about Elinor. The truth is, I've barely given her a thought, I've been so busy. We've been deluged by customers wanting to use our secret shopping service! It's amazing! The TV news headlines might be all dismal about how the high street is dead and no one's shopping—but they should come to our department; it's buzzing!

And I'm even more preoccupied than usual today, because our Ultimate Nanny is starting.

She's called Kyla, and she's fab. She has a degree from Harvard and a master's in child care, and she's a qualified teacher in Mandarin and tennis and the flute and the guitar and singing and . . . something else, which I've forgotten. The harp, maybe. She originally came over to Britain with an American family, but they relocated back to Boston. She decided to stay because she's doing a part-time dissertation at Goldsmiths and has family over here. So she only wants to work three days a week, which is perfect for us.

And she's got these real buck teeth.

I mean, *huge*. Like a moose.

Not that her looks are relevant, either way. Obviously. I'm not some sort of prejudiced, lookist person.

I would have hired her even if she'd had a million-dollar supermodel's smile.

But still. Her teeth warmed me to her for some reason. Plus, her hair isn't remotely swishy.

Which, by the way, was *not* on my interview-points list. When I wrote *No swishy hair,* I was referring to something else completely, and Luke did *not* have to start teasing me. I just happened to notice Kyla's hair— out of interest—and it's a very dull bob with a few grays.

So basically she's perfect!

"Julie Andrews is going to be here soon, is she?" Mum comes into the kitchen, where Minnie is doing Play-Doh and I'm idly browsing eBay. She catches sight of the page and draws breath sharply. "Are you shopping, Becky?"

"No!" I say defensively.

Just because I'm on eBay, it doesn't mean I'm going to *buy* anything, does it? Obviously I don't need a pair of turquoise patent Chloé shoes, worn once, PayPal only. I'm keeping up to date with what's out there, that's all. Like you keep up with current events.

"I hope you've got Minnie's lederhosen ready," Mum adds. "And your whistle."

"Ha-ha," I say politely.

Mum's still really prickly about us hiring a nanny. She got even more offended when Luke and I wouldn't let her do the interviews with us. She hovered outside the door, tutting and clicking her tongue and looking each candidate up and down disparagingly. Then, when she read Kyla's CV, with all the stuff about the guitar and singing, well, that was it. She instantly christened Kyla "Julie Andrews" and has been making little oh-so-funny jokes ever since. Even Janice is in on it and has started calling Luke "Captain von Trapp," which is *really* annoying, because that makes me either the dead wife or the baroness.

"If she wants to make clothes out of the curtains, can you tell her to use the ones in the blue room?" Mum adds.

I'll pretend I didn't hear that. And, anyway, my phone is ringing. It's Luke's ID on the screen—he must want to know how it's going.

"Hi!" I say as I answer. "She's not here yet."

"Good." He sounds crackly, as though he's in a car. "I just wanted to say something to you before she arrives. Becky, you must be *honest* with her."

What's that supposed to mean?

"I'm always honest!" I say, a tad indignantly.

"This nanny needs to know the extent of the problem," he continues, as though I haven't even spoken. "We've hired her for a reason. There's no point pretending Minnie's a saint. We need to give her the history, explain the trouble we've had—"

"OK, Luke!" I say, a bit crossly. "I don't need the lecture. I'll tell her everything."

Just because I wasn't *totally* forthcoming about Minnie at the interview—I mean, what am I supposed to do, slag off my own daughter? So I slightly fibbed and said Minnie had won best-behavior prize at toddler group for six weeks running. And Luke said that was defeating the entire object of the exercise, and we had a . . . heated discussion.

"Anyway, she's here," I say as the doorbell goes. "I'd better run. See you later."

As I open the door, Kyla's standing there, holding a guitar, and I have to stifle a giggle. She *does* look just like Julie Andrews, except in jeans. I wonder if she danced up the road, singing "I have confidence in me."

"Hi, Mrs. Brandon." Her buck teeth are already exposed in a friendly grin.

"Please call me Becky!" I usher her in. "Minnie can't wait to see you! She's doing Play-Doh," I add a little smugly as I lead her to the kitchen. "I like to start her off with something constructive in the morning."

"Wonderful." Kyla nods vigorously. "I did a lot of Play-Doh work with Eloise, my former charge, when she was a toddler. She was so talented at it. In fact, she won a prize in a local art competition for one of her creations." She smiles reminiscently. "We were all so proud."

"Great!" I smile back. "So here we are . . ." I open the door with a flourish.

Shit. Minnie isn't doing Play-Doh anymore. She's abandoned all the pots and is banging merrily at my laptop.

"Minnie! What are you doing?" I give a shrill laugh. "That's Mummy's!"

I hurry over—and as my eyes focus on the screen, my blood runs cold. She's about to bid £2,673,333,333 for the Chloé shoes.

"Minnie!" I grab the laptop away from her.

"Miiiine!" yells Minnie furiously. "Mine shoooooes!"

"Is Minnie doing some computer art?" Kyla heads toward me with a pleasant smile, and I hastily whip the laptop away.

"She was just working with . . . numbers," I say a bit shrilly. "Would you like some coffee? Minnie, do you remember Kyla?"

Minnie gives Kyla a snooty look and starts banging the Play-Doh pots together.

"I'll be making my own Play-Doh from now on if that's OK, Mrs. Brandon," Kyla says. "I prefer to use organic flour."

Wow. Organic homemade Play-Doh. You see, *this* is why you have an Ultimate Nanny. I can't wait to boast about her at work.

"And when do you think you'll start teaching her Mandarin?" I ask, because I know Luke will ask.

Luke is really into Minnie learning Mandarin. He keeps telling me how useful it will be for her in later life. And I think it'll be cool too—except I'm also a bit apprehensive. What if Minnie gets fluent in Mandarin and I don't understand her? Do I need to learn it too? I keep picturing a teenage Minnie cursing me in Mandarin, while I stand there frantically flicking through a phrase book.

"It depends on her aptitude," replies Kyla. "I started Eloise at eighteen months, but she was an exceptional child. Very bright and receptive. And so willing to please."

"She sounds great," I say politely.

"Oh, Eloise is a wonderful child." Kyla nods fervently. "She still Skypes me every day from Boston for calculus and Mandarin practice. Before her athletic training, of course. She's a gymnast now too."

OK, I'm already a bit sick of this Eloise. Calculus, Mandarin, *and* gymnastics? That's just showing off.

"Well, Minnie's very bright and receptive too. In fact . . . she wrote her first poem the other day," I can't resist adding.

"She *wrote* a poem?" For the first time, Kyla sounds impressed. Ha. Suck on that, Eloise. "She's writing already?"

"She said it to me and I wrote it down for her," I explain after a slight pause. "It was a poem in the oral tradition."

"Tell me your poem, Minnie!" Kyla exclaims brightly to Minnie. "How did it go?"

Minnie glowers at her and stuffs Play-Doh up her nose.

"She probably doesn't remember anymore," I say quickly. "But it was very simple and lovely. It went . . ."

I clear my throat for effect. " 'Why do the raindrops have to fall?' "

"Wow." Kyla seems bowled over. "That's beautiful. So many *levels* in there."

"I know." I nod earnestly. "We're going to put it on our Christmas cards."

"Good idea!" enthuses Kyla. "You know, Eloise produced so many wonderful handcrafted Christmas cards, she sold them for charity. She won the philanthropy prize at her school. You know St. Cuthbert's, Chelsea?"

St. Cuthbert's, Chelsea, is the school where Ernie goes. God, no wonder he's miserable there if it's full of Eloises.

"Fantastic! Is there anything Eloise *can't* do?" There's the tiniest edge to my voice, but I'm not sure Kyla notices.

"So I guess today Minnie and I will just hang out together, get to know each other . . ." Kyla chucks Minnie under the chin. "She's obviously super-intelligent, but is there anything else I should know about her? Any foibles? Little problems?"

I smile fixedly back for a few moments. I know what Luke said. But there's no way on *earth* I'm saying, "Yes, actually, she was banned from four Santa's Grottos and everyone thinks she's wild and my husband won't have another child as a result." Not after hearing all about Saint Eloise.

And, anyway, why should I prejudice Minnie's case? If this nanny is any good, she'll work Minnie's little quirks out and solve them herself. I mean, that's her job, isn't it?

"No," I say at last. "No problems. Minnie's a lovely, caring child, and we're very proud to be her parents."

"Great!" Kyla exposes her buck teeth in a wide smile. "And does she eat everything? Vegetables? Peas, carrots, broccoli? Eloise used to love to help me make risotto with vegetables from the garden."

Of course she did. I expect she's got a bloody Michelin star too.

"Absolutely," I reply without a flicker. "Minnie *adores* vegetables. Don't you, darling?"

Minnie has never eaten a carrot in her life. When I once tried to hide them in a shepherd's pie, she sucked off all the shepherd's pie and spat the carrots one by one across the room.

But I'm not admitting that to Miss Perfect Pants. If she's such a hotshot nanny, then she'll be able to make Minnie eat carrots, won't she?

"So maybe you'd like to pop out for a while, while Minnie and I get to know each other!" Kyla addresses Minnie brightly. "Want to show me your Play-Doh, Minnie?"

"OK!" I say. "See you later."

I back out of the kitchen with my cup of coffee, almost straight into Mum, who's skulking in the corridor.

"Mum!" I exclaim. "Were you *spying* on us?"

"Does she know 'Edelweiss' yet?" she says with a sniff. "Or are we still on 'Do, a Deer'?"

Poor old Mum. I really should try to cheer her up.

"Look, why don't we go out shopping or something?" I suggest on impulse. "Kyla wants to get to know Minnie, and Dad'll be here in the house in case she has any problems."

"I can't go shopping!" retorts Mum touchily. "We're impoverished, remember? I've already had to cancel all our Ocado orders, you know. Your father was adamant. No more luxury quiches, no more smoked salmon . . . We're on strict rations." Mum's voice trembles slightly. "If I go anywhere, it'll have to be the Pound Shop!"

I feel a sudden pang of sympathy for her. I'm not surprised Mum's so miserable these days.

"Well, then, let's go to the Pound Shop!" I try to jolly her along. "Come on, it'll be fun!"

BY THE TIME I've put my coat on, Mum has phoned Janice and she's decided to come along to the Pound Shop too. And when we get outside, I find Jess waiting with her, dressed in an ancient ski jacket and jeans.

"Hi, Jess!" I exclaim as we start walking along. "How are you?"

I haven't seen Jess for ages. She and Tom went to spend some time in Cumbria last week, and I didn't even know she was back.

"I'm going nuts," she says in a savage undertone. "I can't stand it. Have you ever tried living with Janice and Martin?"

"Er . . . no." I can't imagine Janice and Jess would get on too well. "What's up?"

"First she wouldn't stop trying to make us have another wedding. Now she's given up on that; she wants us to have a baby."

"Already?" I want to giggle. "But you've only been married five minutes!"

"Exactly! But Janice won't stop dropping hints. She sits there every evening, knitting something yellow and fluffy, but she won't say what it is." Jess lowers her voice darkly. "It's a baby blanket, I know it is."

"Well. Here we are." Mum breaks in to our conversation as we arrive at the corner of the high street.

There's a Pound Shop to our right and a 99p Shop opposite. For a moment we survey both in doubtful silence.

"Which one shall we go to?" ventures Janice at last. "The 99p Shop is *slightly* cheaper, obviously . . ." She peters out.

Mum's eyes keep being drawn across the road to

Emma Jane Gifts, a gorgeous boutique full of cashmere knitwear and handmade ceramics, which we both love pottering around. I can even see a couple of Mum's friends from bridge in there, giving us little waves. But then Mum pulls herself up firmly as though going into battle and swivels toward the Pound Shop.

"I have certain standards, Janice," she says with quiet dignity, like a general saying he'll dress for dinner even though bombs are dropping all around him. "I don't think we need to sink to the 99p Shop quite yet."

"OK," whispers Janice nervously.

"I'm not ashamed to be seen here," adds Mum. "Why should I be ashamed? This is our new way of life, and we're all just going to have to get used to it. If your father says we have to exist on turnip jam, then so be it."

"Mum, he didn't say we had to have turnip jam—" I begin, but Mum is already sweeping in, her head held proudly high. I exchange glances with Jess and follow.

Wow. This place is bigger than I thought. And there's such a lot of stuff! Mum has already taken a basket and is putting tins of some dodgy-looking meat into it with jerky, resentful movements.

"Your father will just have to adjust his taste buds to suit his wallet!" she says, clattering another one in. "Maybe nutrition is something we can't afford anymore! Maybe vitamins are only for the super-rich!"

"Ooh, chocolate bourbons!" I say, spotting some. "Get some of those, Mum. And Toblerones!"

Hey. There's a rack of cotton wool balls over there. It would be crazy not to stock up on them. I mean, it wouldn't make economic sense. And there are makeup applicators and even eyelash curlers! For a pound! I grab a basket and start filling it.

"Jane!" A breathless voice greets us and I see Janice clutching a load of packets labeled *solar garden lights*. "Have you seen these? They *can't* cost a pound, surely."

"I think everything's a pound—" I begin, but she's already tapping the shoulder of a salesgirl.

"Excuse me," she says politely. "How much is this item?"

The salesgirl shoots her a look of ineffable contempt. "Pahnd."

"And this?" She gestures at a garden hose.

"Pahnd. Everyfink's a pahnd. *Pahnd* Shop, innit?"

"But . . . but . . ." Janice seems about to expire with excitement. "This is incredible! Do you realize how much these would cost in John Lewis?"

There's a gasp from the next aisle along, and I look up to see Mum brandishing a load of plastic storage boxes. Her martyred air has vanished and her eyes are bright. "Janice! Tupperware!"

I'm about to follow them when I notice a rack of glittery snakeskin belts. This is unbelievable. I mean, a belt for a pound! It would be criminal not to. And there's a whole load of hair extensions and wigs . . . God this place is *brilliant*. Why have I never come here before?

I put five belts and a selection of wigs into my basket and throw in a few bits of "famous brands" makeup (even though I haven't heard of any of the brands), then wander down to find myself in front of a rack labeled *Secondhand Supplies—Catering Returns, Sold as Seen.*

Wow. Look at this. There are loads of place cards and table confetti and stuff. Perfect for a party.

I stare at them silently for a few moments, my mind circling round and round. Obviously I can't buy the stuff for Luke's party at the Pound Shop. It would be really cheapskate and stingy.

But they only cost a pound. And they're proper catering supplies. And would he mind?

Put it this way: The less I spend on place cards and

party poppers . . . the more I can spend on champagne. And everything's a pound. A *pound*!

Oh God, I can't pass this up. It's too good an opportunity. Hastily, I start shoving packets of place cards, party poppers, table confetti, and napkin holders into my basket. I won't tell anyone I got them at the Pound Shop. I'll say I got them from a specialist entertainment company.

"Do you need another basket?" Jess appears by my side.

"Oh, thanks." I take it and add some pop-up candelabra decorations, which I've just noticed. They look a bit manky, but no one'll notice if the lights are dim enough.

"Is this for Luke's party?" She nods at my basket with interest. "How are the preparations going?"

Oh, bloody hell. I can't have Jess telling everyone the decorations came from the Pound Shop.

"No!" I say quickly. "Of course this isn't for Luke! I'm just . . . getting inspiration. Aren't you buying anything?" I add, noticing she doesn't have a basket. "Aren't you going to stock up on Jiffy bags or something?"

I would have thought this place would be right up Jess's street. She's the one always giving me lectures about spending too much and why don't I buy in bulk and live off potato peelings?

"No, I don't buy things anymore," says Jess matter-of-factly.

Did I mishear that?

"What do you mean, you 'don't buy things'?" I say, still loading up my basket. "You must buy things. Everyone buys things."

"Not me." She shakes her head. "Since living in Chile, Tom and I have taken the decision to be zero consumers, or as near as possible. We barter instead."

"You *barter*?" I turn and stare at her. "What, with beads and stuff?"

Jess gives a snort of laughter. "No, Becky. Everything. Food, clothing, heating. If I can't barter for it, I don't do it."

"But . . . who with?" I say incredulously. "No one barters anymore. That's, like, the Middle Ages."

"You'd be surprised. There are a lot of like-minded people out there. There are networks, websites . . ." She shrugs. "Last week I bartered six hours of gardening for a British Rail voucher. That got me up to Scully. It cost me nothing."

I stare at her, gobsmacked. In fact, to be honest I feel a teeny bit affronted. Here we all are, feeling really virtuous because we're shopping in the Pound Shop. And Jess has to trump everyone by not shopping at all, ever. That's *so* typical of her. Next she'll probably invent some form of anti-shopping. Like antimatter, or antigravity.

"So . . . could *I* barter?" I say, as a thought hits me.

"Of course you could," says Jess. "In fact, you *should.* You can get anything and everything. Clothes, food, toys . . . I'll send you links to the websites I use most."

"Thanks!"

Yes! I resume filling my basket, full of exhilaration. This is the answer. I'll *barter* for everything I need for Luke's party. It'll be easy. And those posh, zillion-pound party organizers can sod off. Who needs them when you have a Pound Shop and a bartering website?

Ooh. *Star Wars* fairy lights, two strings for a pound! And some Yoda shot glasses.

I pause thoughtfully. Maybe the party could have a *Star Wars* theme. I mean, I'm not sure Luke's *exactly* into *Star Wars* . . . but I could get him into it, couldn't I? I could rent the DVDs and suggest we join the fan club, and I expect he'd be a total enthusiast by April 7.

Except there are also some really fab disco ball garlands. And some jeweled pewter-effect platters reading *King Arthur's Court,* with matching goblets. Oh God, now I'm torn.

Maybe it could be a seventies disco–*Star Wars*–King Arthur fusion themed party?

"You could barter for those too," Jess says, watching me disapprovingly as I pick up a disco ball garland. "Or, even better, make decorations with recycled materials. It's far more environmentally friendly."

"I know," I say patiently. "I should have dreary old paper chains made of newspaper."

"I'm not talking about paper chains made out of newspaper!" She looks offended. "There are lots of creative decorating ideas on the Web. You can reuse silver foil, decorate plastic bottles . . ."

Silver foil? Plastic bottles? What am I, six years old?

"Look, Jess!" Janice's bright voice interrupts us and I look up to see her rounding the corner, clutching a small packet. "I've found some vitamins! Folic acid! That's supposed to be good for you young girls, isn't it?"

I exchange looks with Jess.

"Only if they're planning to become pregnant," says Jess icily.

"Well, I'll just pop it in my basket, anyway." Janice's casual air is fooling no one. "And look at this! It's a baby-name book! A thousand names for only a pound! Girls *and* boys."

"I don't *believe* this," mutters Jess, hunching her arms around herself defensively.

"What do you need a baby-name book for, Janice?" I ask.

"Well!" Janice's cheeks grow pink, and she looks from me to Jess. "You never know . . ."

"I *do* know!" Jess suddenly erupts. "Listen, Janice.

I'm not pregnant. And I'm not *going* to be pregnant. Tom and I have decided that when we have a family, we'll be adopting a disadvantaged child from South America. And it won't be a baby, and it'll have a South American name. So you can keep your bloody folic acid and your baby-names book!"

She stalks off, out of the shop, leaving me and Janice both absolutely gobsmacked.

A South American child! That is so *cool*.

"Did she just say . . . they're *adopting*?" says Janice at last, her voice quivering.

"I think it's a fab idea!" I say firmly. "Hey, Mum!" I call over to Mum, who's filling a basket full of dried flowers. "Jess is going to adopt a South American child!"

"Ooh!" Mum's eyes light up. "How lovely!"

"But what about all my knitting?" Janice looks ready to burst into tears. "I've made a whole newborn layette! Yellow and white, in case of either sex, and little Christmas outfits up to age six!"

OK, Janice is officially insane.

"Well, no one asked you to, did they?" I point out. "Maybe you could give them all to charity."

I think I'm turning into Jess. I've even got her hardness in my voice. But honestly! Why on earth was Janice knitting baby clothes before Jess and Tom were even *engaged*?

"I'll talk to Tom." Janice seems to come to a decision. "He's only going along with this silly plan to please Jess. He'll want a child of his own, I know he will. He'll want to carry on our gene pool. Martin's family dates back to Cromwell, you know. He's had a family tree done."

"Janice," I begin, "I *really* wouldn't get involved—"

"Look!" Her gaze suddenly focuses on the shelf in front of her. "A pair of gardening gloves! Padded! For a *pound*!"

• • •

AS WE HEAD BACK from our outing, everyone's in an up-beat mood. We had to splash out on a taxi home be-cause we had too many shopping bags to carry—but we've saved so much money, what's a taxi fare?

Janice hasn't mentioned babies or gene pools again but keeps pulling items out of her bags and showing them to us.

"A full dental kit with mirror! For a pound!" She looks around the taxi to make sure everyone is as in-credulous as she is. "A miniature tabletop snooker set! For a *pound*!"

Mum seems to have bought the entire stock of Tup-perware, loads of kitchen utensils and big casseroles, several bottles of L'Oréal shampoo with Polish writing, some artificial flowers, a big box of birthday cards, and a really cool mop with a pink stripy handle, which Minnie will love.

And, right at the end, I found a whole load of posh wooden hangers. Three for a pound, which is a *total* bargain. They'd cost at least two quid each anywhere else. So I bought a hundred.

With the help of the taxi driver, we stagger into the house and drop our bags in the hall.

"Well!" Mum says. "I'm exhausted after all that hard work! Do you want a cup of tea, love? And one of those bourbon biscuits . . ." She starts rooting around in one of the Pound Shop bags, just as Dad comes out of his study. For a moment he stares at us, his jaw slack.

I suppose seventeen carrier bags does look like quite a lot. You know, if you weren't expecting them.

"What's this?" he says at last. "What's all this?"

"We've been to the Pound Shop," I say brightly. "We did really well!"

"Jane . . ." Dad is looking incredulously from bag to

bag. "We're supposed to be *saving* money, if you re-member."

Mum raises her head from the bag full of food, her cheeks red. "I *have* been saving money. Didn't you hear? I've been shopping at the Pound Shop!"

"Did you buy the whole bloody *place*?" Dad's looking at the sea of plastic bags. "Is there anything left?"

Uh-oh. Mum's inhaling, with one of her I've-never-been-so-insulted-in-all-my-life breaths.

"If you want to know, Graham, I've been buying us tinned shepherd's pie and bargain biscuits, since we can't afford Ocado anymore!" She brandishes the bour-bons at him. "Do you know how much these cost? Five packets for a pound! Is that wasting money?"

"Jane, I never said we couldn't afford Ocado," begins Dad testily. "I merely said—"

"But next time I'll go to the 99p Shop, shall I?" Her voice rises shrilly. "Or the Ten Pence Shop! Will that satisfy you, Graham? Or maybe *you'd* like to do the household shopping. Maybe you'd like to struggle on a budget to keep this family fed and clothed."

"Fed and clothed?" retorts Dad scoffingly. "And how is this keeping them fed and clothed?" He reaches for the pink stripy mop.

"So now we can't afford basic hygiene, is that it?" Mum is pink with outrage. "Now we can't afford to mop our floors?"

"We can mop them with the cupboardful of mops we've *already got*!" Dad erupts. "If I see one more use-less cleaning gadget in this house . . ."

Oookay. I think I might just quietly edge away be-fore I get drawn into this and they each start saying, "Becky agrees with me, don't you, Becky?"

Anyway, I'm *dying* to see how Kyla and Minnie are get-ting on.

They've been together for two solid hours. Kyla's

bound to have had a positive effect on Minnie already. Maybe she's started Minnie on Mandarin or French. Or embroidery!

I tiptoe up to the kitchen door, hoping to hear the sound of Minnie singing a madrigal or saying, *"Un, deux, trois,"* in a perfect accent, or maybe doing a bit of quick Pythagoras. But, instead, all I can hear is Kyla saying, "Minnie, come on. Come *on*, now!"

She sounds a bit weary, which is weird. I had her down as one of those endless-energy, broccoli-juice-type people.

"Hi!" I call out, and push the door open. "I'm back!"

Blimey. What's up? Kyla's completely lost her sparkle. Her hair is disheveled, her cheeks are flushed and there's a smear of mashed potato on her shirt.

Minnie, on the other hand, is sitting in her high chair with a plate of food in front of her, looking like she's having a whale of a time.

"So!" I say brightly. "Did you have a good morning?"

"Great!" Kyla smiles—but it's one of those automatic smiles that doesn't reach her eyes. In fact, if truth be told, her eyes are saying, "Get me out of here now."

I think I'll just ignore them. I'll pretend I don't understand Eye. Or Clenched Hands Round the Chair Back.

"Have you started on any languages yet?" I say encouragingly.

"Not yet." Kyla flashes her teeth again. "In fact, I'd like to have a chat, if that's OK?"

I'm tempted to say, "No, get going on the Mandarin," close the door, and run. But that wouldn't be the act of a responsible mother, would it?

"Of course!" I turn with a winning smile. "What's up?"

"Mrs. Brandon." Kyla lowers her voice as she comes

toward me. "Minnie's a sweet, charming, intelligent child. But we had a few . . . issues today."

"Issues?" I repeat innocently, after only the tiniest of pauses. "What kind of issues?"

"There were moments today when Minnie was a little stubborn. Is that normal for her?"

I rub my nose, playing for time. If I admit that Minnie's the stubbornest person I've ever come across, then that just lets Kyla off the hook. She's supposed to *cure* Minnie's stubbornness. In fact, why hasn't she done it already?

And, anyway, everyone knows you shouldn't label children; it gives them complexes.

"Stubborn?" I wrinkle my brow as though baffled. "No, that doesn't sound like Minnie to me. She's never stubborn with me," I add for good measure. "She's always a little angel, aren't you, darling?" I beam at Minnie.

"I see." Kyla's cheeks are flushed and she looks a bit beleaguered. "Well, I guess it's early days for us, isn't it, Minnie? The other thing . . ." She lowers her voice. "She won't eat any carrots for me. I'm sure she's just playing up. You said she eats carrots, right?"

"Absolutely," I say emphatically. "Always. Come on, Minnie, eat your carrots!"

I head over to the high chair and look at Minnie's food. Most of the chicken and potatoes have gone, but there's a stack of beautifully cooked carrots, which Minnie's eyeing as though they're the Black Death.

"I don't understand where I'm going wrong." Kyla sounds quite hassled. "I never had this kind of problem with Eloise . . ."

"Could you possibly get down a mug for me, Kyla?" I say casually. As Kyla reaches up to the cupboard, I whip a carrot off the plate, stuff it in my mouth, and swallow it in one gulp.

"She just ate one," I say to Kyla, trying not to sound too smug.

"She *ate* one?" Kyla whips round. "But . . . but I've been trying for fifteen minutes!"

"You'll get the knack," I say kindly. "Um, could you possibly get a jug down as well?" As she turns away, I stuff another carrot in my mouth. To give credit to Kyla, they *are* pretty yummy.

"Did she just eat another one?" I can see Kyla avidly counting the carrots on the plate. It's a good thing I'm a fast chewer.

"Yes!" I clear my throat. "Good girl, Minnie! Now eat the rest for Kyla . . ."

I hastily head across the kitchen and start making some coffee. Behind me I can hear Kyla, determinedly upbeat.

"C'mon, Minnie! Lovely carrots. You ate two already, so let's see how fast you can eat the rest of them!"

"Noooooo!" Minnie yells at her, and I turn to see her batting the fork away. "Nooooo ca-rrot!"

Oh God. She's going to start hurling all the carrots across the room in a minute.

"Actually, Kyla," I say quickly, "could you be a real star and take some shopping upstairs for me? All the bags in the hall. And I'll supervise Minnie."

"Sure." Kyla wipes her brow. "No problem."

The minute she's gone, I hurry to Minnie's high chair and start cramming all the carrots into my mouth. For God's sake, why did she have to cook so *many* of the bloody things? I can barely get my mouth closed around them, let alone chew them—

"Becky?" I freeze in dismay as I hear Kyla's voice behind me. "Your mom said to bring these bags into the kitchen, is that OK?"

I don't know what to do. My cheeks are bulging with carrots.

OK, it's fine. I'm facing away. She can't see my mouth.

"Mmm-hmm," I manage.

"Oh my gosh! Did she eat all the carrots?" Kyla drops the shopping bags. "But that's so quick! What happened, did she just start wolfing them down?"

"Mmm-hmm." Keeping my head averted, I give what I hope is an expressive shrug.

Now Kyla's coming over to the high chair. Hastily, I back away till I'm at the window, facing out. God, this is hideous. My jaw is starting to ache from holding in all the carrots, and my face is growing hot with the effort. I risk a quick chew, then another—

"No *way*." Kyla's voice comes out of nowhere. Shit! She's about two feet away, staring at my face. How did she creep round there without me noticing? I sneak a quick glance at my reflection in the stainless-steel fridge.

Oh God. The end of a carrot is poking out of my mouth.

For a moment Kyla and I stare at each other. I don't quite dare push it back into my mouth.

"Minnie didn't eat any carrots, did she?" says Kyla, politely but with an edge.

I stare back desperately. If I speak, will carrots fall on the floor?

"I may have helped her out," I say indistinctly at last. "A little."

I can see Kyla looking from me to Minnie and back again with increasing incredulity.

"I'm getting the feeling she didn't write a poem either, did she?" she says, and now there's a definite sarcasm to her voice. "Mrs. Brandon, if I'm going to work effectively with a family, I need full and candid lines of communication. I need honesty. And there's obviously not much chance of that here. Sorry, Minnie. I hope you find a carer who works out for you."

"You can't just *leave*—" I begin in dismayed, muffled tones, and three carrots fall out of my mouth onto the floor.

Damn.

From: cathy@ultimatenanniesuk.com
Subject: Re: Tiny favor
Date: 8 February 2006
To: Becky Brandon

Dear Mrs. Brandon,

Thank you for your phone message. We're sorry that things did not work out for you with Kyla.

Unfortunately, we are not able to issue Post-its to all our staff, as you suggest, so that if your husband rings up, "The story is that Kyla broke her leg." Regarding an instant replacement who looks like Kyla, I'm afraid this will not be possible either.

Perhaps you could telephone me if you wish to discuss this matter further.

With kind wishes,

Cathy Ferris
Director, Ultimate Nannies

OXSHOTT MARKETPLACE.COM

**The official website for people in the Oxshott area
who want to barter.**

"It's fun, it's free, it's for everybody!!!"

GENERAL ITEMS

Ref10057
Wanted: Big tent for two hundred people (one night's hire)

Offered: Two Marc Jacobs handbags, really cool, v.g. condition

Barterer: BeckyB
Click for more details, including photos

Ref10058
Wanted: Dance floor which lights up (one night's hire)

Offered: 20 assorted gift sets, never used: Clarins, Lancôme, Estée Lauder, etc.

Barterer: BeckyB
Click for more details, including photos

Ref10059
Wanted: Organic hemp sleeping bag and tent

Offered: 16 bottles homemade peach wine

Barterer: JessWebster
Click for more details. No photos

Ref10060
Wanted: 100 bottles of champagne

Offered: Power Plate machine, unused, never tested, plus plastic abdomenizer, Supermodel Stepper, and *Get Fit in Three Days!* DVD with skipping rope and book

Barterer: BeckyB
Click for more details, including photos

Ref10061
Wanted: Fireworks display (spelling out *Happy Birthday, Luke* at the end)

Offered: Original art deco cocktail cabinet from Manhattan antiques shop, cocktail shakers included

Barterer: BeckyB
Click for more details, including photos

Ms. Rebecca Brandon
The Pines
43 Elton Road
Oxshott
Surrey

10 February 2006

Dear Rebecca,

Thank you for your letter of 8 February and for all your
suggestions.

Bartering is certainly one idea to aid the economy.
However, I am not sure how practical it would be for the
Chancellor to barter "some old stuff in museums that we
don't need" for "loads of French cheeses that we could all
share out." I also fear it would be unfeasible to barter "a
minor member of the Royal Family" with the USA, in
return for "enough J. Crew clothes for everyone."

Nevertheless, I thank you for your continuing interest in
our economy.

Yours sincerely,

Edwin Tredwell
Director of Policy Research

TEN

HUH. SOME NANNY AGENCY that is. I'm thinking of complaining to the Nanny Ombudsman. Nanny agencies should be *confidential*. They should be *discreet*. Evidently the story of the mother and the carrots has been forwarded to every single nanny agency in town. Suze rang up apologetically and said everyone at St. Cuthbert's was talking about it and it's the new urban legend, except the way the story goes now, it ends up with Kyla and me throwing carrots at each other.

Luke wasn't impressed, no matter how many times I explained that Kyla was totally unsuitable for us, anyway. And apparently the agency might find it "difficult" to find a replacement Ultimate Nanny. So I've had to ask Mum to step in, and she got all huffy and said, "Oh, I'm good enough for you now, am I?"

And to make things worse, last night I finally looked properly at my bargain party supplies from the Pound Shop. I opened the place cards first of all—and they were personalized with *Happy Birthday, Mike*. Two hundred of them.

For a while I considered introducing "Mike" as a nickname for Luke. I mean, why shouldn't he have a nickname? And why shouldn't it be Mike? I reckoned if I started sending him little emails calling him "Mikey," and got Mum and Dad to call him "Mike," and maybe even gasped, "Oh, Mike, Mike!" a couple of times during sex, I could probably get him used to it before the party.

But then the napkin holders had *Congratulations, Lorraine* all over them, so I gave up on that plan.

At least there are *some* positives at the moment. My bartering venture is already a triumph—in fact, Jess is right, it's amazing! Why on earth do people ever buy things when they can barter? I've had loads of responses to my ads, and I've got several appointments this evening. At this rate I'll have the whole party sorted out in no time, for no money!

Jess sent me links to some eco-decorating websites as well, and although most of the ideas are rubbish, I did find one that was quite cool. You cut old plastic bags into strips and make pom-poms—and they look really good. And they're free! So I've started making those, whenever Luke isn't around. Luckily, I have a large supply of plastic bags already. The Selfridges pom-poms look amazing, all bright and yellow, and the green Harrods ones are really smart too. Now I just need a few white ones. (I might have to go and stock up at Harvey Nichols Food Hall. I mean, it's quite expensive there, but then, that's the price of being green.)

And the other big plus is our new house, which is all still going forward. I've come here in my lunch hour to show it to Suze—and it looks even better than it did before.

"Bex, I love it!" Suze comes clattering down the stairs, her face bright. "It's so *light*! And the upstairs is massive! All those bedrooms! They seem to come out of nowhere!"

"It's incredible, isn't it?" I beam proudly.

"It just shows what architects can do." She shakes

her head wonderingly. "And no glitches? No problems?"

Poor Suze has heard the saga of every other house we've tried to buy.

"Nothing! We're exchanging next week and completing two weeks after that. We've booked the van and everything." I beam at Suze. "This one is meant to be."

"You must be so *relieved*." Suze gives me a hug. "I can't believe you've finally got a house!"

"I know." I tug at her arm. "Come and see the garden!"

We head outside and across the lawn to the back, where there's a huge spreading oak tree and a swing and a load of climbing equipment on bark chippings.

"All your kids will be able to come and play here," I say proudly.

"They'll love it!" Suze gets on the swing and starts pushing herself back and forth.

"How's Ernie?" I suddenly remember. "How was the meeting at school?"

"We haven't had it yet." Suze's face falls. "I'm dreading it. I've got to go to school for an event next week, and I know the headmistress will collar me—" She breaks off. "Hey, Bex, will you come too? You could be my buffer. She can't be mean to me if you're standing there, can she?"

"Of course I'll come!" I can't wait to have a go at this headmistress, to be honest.

"It's an art exhibition. All the kids have done paintings and we go and have a cup of coffee and look at them," says Suze. "And then we have to make a donation to the school."

"I thought you paid fees," I say, puzzled. "Why do you need to make a donation?"

"The fees are only the *beginning*," says Suze, as though I understand nothing. "Then there's the fund-raising and the school charity and the collections for the teachers. I spend my whole life writing out checks."

"And then, on top of that, they're mean to you?"

"Yes." Suze looks a bit miserable. "But it is a very good school."

God, this whole school malarkey sounds a nightmare. Maybe I'll find an alternative. Maybe I'll educate Minnie at home. Or not at *home*. That would be boring. We could do our lessons in . . . Harvey Nicks! God, yes. Perfect. I can just see myself now, sitting at a little table, sipping a latte, and reading Minnie interesting bits of culture from the paper. We could do sums with the sugar cubes and geography in the International Designer Room. People would call me the Girl Who Teaches Her Child in Harvey Nicks, and I could start a whole international trend of in-shop schooling—

"Hey, Bex." Suze has stopped swinging and is squinting suspiciously at my velvet top. "Is that my top? Is that the one I lent you when we first moved in together?" She's getting off the swing. "And I asked you for it back and you said it got burned accidentally in a bonfire?"

"Er . . ." I automatically take a step backward.

That story's ringing a bell. Why did I say I burned it? I can't remember now, it's so long ago.

"It is!" She's examining it closely. "It's that Monsoon top! Fenny lent it to me and I lent it to you and you said you couldn't find it and then you said it had got burned! Do you know what a hard time Fenny gave me about that?"

"You can have it back," I say hastily. "Sorry."

"I don't want it back *now*." She peers at me incredulously. "Why are you wearing it, anyway?"

"Because it was in my wardrobe," I say morosely. "And I've agreed to wear everything in my wardrobe three times before I go shopping for clothes again."

"*What?*" Suze sounds staggered. "But . . . why?"

"It was after the bank went bust. We made a deal. Luke's not buying a car and I'm not buying any new clothes. Not till October."

"But, Bex." Suze looks concerned. "Isn't that bad for your health? I mean, isn't it *dangerous* to go cold turkey? I saw this TV show once. People go shaky and have blackouts. Have you felt shaky at all?"

"Yes!" I stare at her, riveted. "I felt really shaky when I walked past the Fenwick sale the other day!"

Oh my God. It never occurred to me that by giving up shopping I could be jeopardizing my *health*. Should I see a doctor?

"And what about Luke's party?"

"Shhh!" I say fiercely, looking around the empty gardens in paranoia. "Don't *tell* everyone! What about it?"

"Aren't you going to get a new dress?" mouths Suze silently.

"Of course I am—" I stop dead.

That hadn't even occurred to me. I can't get a new dress for Luke's party, can I? Not while our deal is still on.

"No," I say at last. "I can't. I'll have to wear something out of my wardrobe. I promised him."

Suddenly I feel a bit flat. I mean, not that I was holding the party just so I could have a new dress. But still.

"So . . . how *is* the party going?" asks Suze after a pause.

"Really great!" I say at once, in a brushing-off way. "All fine. I'll send you an invitation when they're ready."

"Good! And . . . you don't need any help or anything?"

"Help?" I say a bit sharply. "Why would I need help? It's all totally under control."

I'll show her. Wait till she sees my shopping-bag pom-poms.

"Excellent! Well, I look forward to it. I'm sure it'll be brilliant." She starts swinging again, not meeting my eye.

She doesn't believe me, does she? I *know* she doesn't. I'm about to challenge her when a shout draws my attention.

"There they are! There are the devils!" A middle-aged man with a red face is coming out of the house next door to this one, gesticulating at me.

"Who's that?" murmurs Suze.

"Dunno," I say in an undertone. "We've never met the neighbors. The estate agents said an old man lived there. They said he was ill and never left the house . . . Can I help you?" I raise my voice.

"Help me?" He glares at me. "You could help by explaining what you've done to my house! I'm calling the police!"

Suze and I exchange wary glances. Am I moving in next to a nutter?

"I haven't done anything to your house!" I call back.

"Well, who's stolen my bedrooms, then?"

What?

Before I can answer, our estate agent bustles out to the garden. He's called Magnus and wears chalk-striped suits and has a very low, discreet voice.

"Mrs. Brandon, I'll deal with this. Is there a problem?" he says, "Mr. . . . ."

"Evans." The man approaches Magnus and they have a conversation over the garden fence, which I can hear only tiny snippets of. But since those snippets include the words *sue, outrageous,* and *daylight robbery,* I'm agog.

"You don't think anything's *wrong,* do you?" I say anxiously to Suze.

"Of course not!" she says at once in reassuring tones.

"It's probably just some little neighborly misunderstanding. One of those things you can clear up over a cup of tea. Maybe it's about . . . the hedge!" she adds hurriedly, as Mr. Evans starts shaking his fist at Magnus.

"Do you get that upset about a hedge?" I say uncertainly.

The conversation is getting louder and the snippets are bigger.

". . . *take a sledgehammer myself . . . evil devils need punishing . . .*"

"Very well." Magnus looks deathly as he comes hurrying over the grass to us. "Mrs. Brandon. There has arisen a small matter involving the bedrooms of your property. According to this neighbor, several of them have been . . . appropriated from his property."

"What?" I stare at him blankly.

"He believes that someone has knocked through the adjoining wall and . . . stolen his bedrooms. Three of them, to be precise."

Suze gasps. "I *thought* it looked too big!"

"But you told us it had eight bedrooms! It was on the house details!"

"Indeed." Magnus is looking more and more uncomfortable. "We were informed by the developer that this was an eight-bedroom house, and we had no reason to dispute this—"

"So he just bulldozed into next door's upstairs and stole all the rooms and no one even *checked*?" I stare at him incredulously.

Magnus looks even more worried.

"I believe the developer obtained the proper permissions from the council—"

"How?" Mr. Evans looms up, clearly bored of waiting. "By forging documents and greasing palms, that's how! I come back from the States and go upstairs for a nap and what do I find? Half my top floor missing! Blocked up! Someone's come in and stolen my property!"

"Why didn't someone notice?" says Suze robustly. "Wasn't it a bit careless of you to let them do that?"

"My father's deaf and nearly blind!" Mr. Evans looks even more incensed. "His carers pop in and out, but what do they know? Preying on the vulnerable, that's what it is." His face is almost purple, and his yellowing eyes are so menacing I quail.

"It's not my fault! I didn't do anything! I didn't even know! And you can have your bedrooms back," I add rashly. "Or . . . we could buy them off you, maybe? It's just, we're pretty desperate. We're living with my parents and we've got a two-year-old . . ."

I'm gazing desperately at Mr. Evans, willing him to soften, but he looks even more ax-murdery than before.

"I'm phoning my lawyer." He wheels around and stalks back to the house.

"What does this mean?" I demand. "What happens next?"

Magnus can't look me in the eye.

"I'm afraid this will be complicated. We'll have to consult the deeds, take legal advice, the house may have to be put back the way it was, or perhaps Mr. Evans will come to an arrangement . . . I think you will be able to sue the vendor successfully, and indeed there may be a fraud prosecution . . ."

I'm staring at him in growing dismay. I don't care about a fraud prosecution. I want a house.

"So we won't be able to exchange next week?"

"The whole deal is off for now, I'm afraid."

"But we need a house!" I wail. "This is our fifth house!"

"I'm sorry." Magnus takes out his phone. "Please excuse me, I need to alert our legal team."

As he walks away, I look at Suze. For a moment, neither of us speaks.

"I don't believe it," I say at last. "Are we *jinxed*?"

"It'll all work out," says Suze hopefully. "Everyone will just sue each other and you'll get the house in the end. And, on the plus side, if you *do* have to stay with your mum a bit longer, think how thrilled she'll be."

"She won't!" I say in desperation. "She'll be livid! Suze, she doesn't have empty-nest syndrome after all. We got it all wrong."

"What?" Suze looks shocked. "But I thought she was going to really miss you and get suicidal."

"It was all an act! She can't wait for us to go! The whole *neighborhood*'s waiting." I clutch my head in despair. "What am I going to do?"

There's silence as we both look round the wintry garden.

Maybe we could be squatters, I find myself thinking. Or set up a big tent in the garden and hope no one notices us. We could be alternative-lifestyle people living in our yurt. I could call myself Rainbow, and Luke could be Wolf, and Minnie could be Runs on Grass in Mary Janes.

"So what are you going to do?" Suze breaks me out of a fantasy where we're sitting by a campfire and Luke is chopping wood in old leather trousers, with *Wolf* tattooed on his knuckles.

"Dunno," I say despairingly. "I'll just have to think of something."

AS I GET BACK HOME that day, I find Mum and Minnie in the kitchen, both in aprons, icing cupcakes. (Mum got the icing set at the Pound Shop. And the cakes.) For a moment they're so engrossed and happy that they don't see me—and with no warning, I have the weirdest flashback to Elinor standing in that dressing room, looking old and sad and lonely and asking if she could see her grandchild.

She hasn't even seen Minnie since she was in her cradle. She's missed *so* much of Minnie's life already. Which I know is her own fault, and I know she's a bitch. But even so . . .

Oh God. I feel so torn. Should I let Minnie get to know her? Not that I could see Elinor icing cupcakes exactly. But they could do something together. Look through the Chanel catalog, maybe.

Minnie's concentrating so hard on putting multicolored sprinkles onto her cakes, I don't want to disturb her. Her face is pink with effort, and her little nose is screwed up and there are sprinkles stuck to her cheek with butter icing. As I watch her, my heart feels all crunchy. I could stand here watching her forever, carefully shaking her small pot. Then suddenly she sees me and her face lights up.

"Mummy! Spinkles!" She holds out the pot of sprinkles proudly.

"Well done, Minnie! *Look* at all your lovely cupcakes!" I swoop down and give her a kiss. Her face is dusted in icing sugar—in fact, there seems to be a thin layer of icing sugar over pretty much everything in the kitchen.

"Eat." Now Minnie is hopefully offering me a cupcake. "Eat spinkles." She starts cramming it into my mouth.

"Yum!" I can't help laughing as crumbs fall down my chin. "Mmm."

"So, Becky!" Mum looks up from her piping bag. "How was the house?"

"Oh!" I come to. "Great."

Which is kind of true. It *was* great, apart from the fact that some of it is stolen.

"And you're still all set to move in?"

"Well." I rub my nose, and sprinkles fall on the floor. "There might be a *tiny* delay . . ."

"Delay?" Mum sounds immediately tense. "What kind of delay?"

"I'm not sure yet," I backtrack hastily. "It may be nothing."

I watch Mum warily. Her shoulders have stiffened. That's not a good sign.

"Well, of course, if there *was* a delay," she says at last, "you'd stay on here. We wouldn't dream of anything else."

Oh God. She sounds so noble and self-sacrificing. I can't bear it.

"I'm sure it won't come to that!" I say quickly. "Although if it did . . . we could always . . . rent?" I hardly dare say the word—and sure enough, she snaps on it like a shark scenting blood.

"*Rent?* You're not *renting,* Becky. It's just throwing money away!"

Mum's pathologically opposed to renting. Every time I've tried to suggest that Luke and I rent, she's behaved as though we're deliberately paying money to a landlord to spite her. And when I say, "Loads of people in Europe rent," she just sniffs and says, "Europe!"

"Becky, *is* there a problem?" Mum stops icing and looks at me properly. "Are you moving out or not?"

I can't tell her the truth. We're going to have to move out. Somehow.

"Of course we're moving out!" I say brightly. "Of course we are! I only said there *might* be a delay. But there probably won't. We'll be gone in three weeks." And I hurry out of the kitchen before she can ask anything else.

OK. So I have three weeks to sort out the house situation. Or find another solution. Or buy a yurt.

GOD, YURTS ARE EXPENSIVE. I've just looked them up on-line. Thousands of pounds, for a bit of tarpaulin. So I'm not sure we'll be doing that. I'm not sure *what* we'll be doing.

But I won't think about it right now, because I'm about to do my first bit of bartering. Mum and Dad are out, Luke's got a business dinner, and Minnie's in bed, so the way is clear. I'm quite excited! Here begins a whole new way of life. Zero consumption, green, ethical bartering in the local community. The way life *should* be. I'll probably never go shopping again. People will call me the Girl Who Never Goes Shopping.

My first barterer, called Nicole Taylor, is coming round at seven o'clock with a tent, and I'm giving her two Marc Jacobs bags in return, which I think is a fair swap, especially as I never use them anymore. I've wrapped them up in tissue paper and put them in the original packaging, and even thrown in a Marc Jacobs key ring to be generous. The only hitch I can foresee is that it might be hard getting the tent into the garage if it's really massive. But I'm sure I'll manage somehow.

Then I've got a fire-eater called Daryl, who's swapping his services for a Luella clutch (which seems a bit weird, but maybe he wants it for his girlfriend or something). And a juggler who's getting a pair of Gina sandals. And some woman who cooks canapés, who's going to swap them for a Missoni coat. (I'll be quite sorry to see that go, but the original Banana Republic one I put up didn't get a single offer.)

The one I'm most excited about is the fire-eater. He said he'd do a demonstration and everything. I wonder if he's going to come along in a spangly costume! The doorbell rings, and I feel a flurry of excitement as I hurry to the front door. This must be the tent!

"Hello!" I fling the door open, half-expecting to see a great big wedding-style tent, fully erected on the front lawn and all lit up.

"Hiya." A thin girl looks at me sidelong from the front step. She's only about sixteen, with lank hair hanging on either side of a pale face, and she doesn't seem to have a tent with her, unless it's folded up very small.

"Are you Nicole?" I say uncertainly.

"Yeah." She nods and I get a waft of spearmint gum.

"Have you come to barter a tent for two Marc Jacobs bags?"

There's a long pause, as though she's mulling this over.

"Can I see the bags?" she says.

This isn't going quite as I expected.

"Well, can I see the tent?" I counter. "How big is it? Could I get two hundred people in it? Is it stripey?"

There's another long pause.

"My dad owns a tent company," she says at last. "I can get you one, I swear."

She can *get me one*? What kind of rubbishy bartering is this?

"You were supposed to be bringing it with you!" I say indignantly.

"Yeah, well, I couldn't, could I?" she says sulkily. "But I'll get you one. When d'you need it? Are those the bags?" Her eyes have fallen greedily on the Marc Jacobs carriers by my feet.

"Yes," I say reluctantly.

"Can I have a look?"

"I suppose so."

She unwraps the first—a gray tote—and gasps, her

whole face lighting up. I can't help feeling a pang of empathy. I can tell she's a fellow handbag lover.

"God, I love this. I *have* to have it." She's already got it on her shoulder and is twisting it this way and that. "Where's the other one?"

"Look, you can only have them if you get me a tent—"

"Hey, Daryl." Nicole lifts a hand at another lank teenager, who's coming into the drive. This one's a boy in skinny jeans with dyed black hair and a rucksack on his back.

Is *this* the fire-eater?

"Do you know him?" I say a bit disbelievingly.

"We're at sixth-form college together, doing fashion studies." Nicole chews her gum. " 'S where we saw your ads, online."

"Hi." Daryl shuffles up and raises a limp hand in a kind of greeting. "I'm Daryl."

"You're really a fire-eater?" I look at him dubiously. I was picturing someone more macho, with a permatan and gleaming teeth and a sequined jockstrap. But then, I shouldn't judge. Maybe this Daryl grew up in the circus or something.

"Yeah." He nods several times, his eyes twitching.

"And you want my Luella clutch in exchange?"

"I collect Luella pieces." He nods fervently. "Love Luella."

"Daryl designs bags," puts in Nicole. "He's, like, *really* talented. Where did you buy this?" She's still entranced by the Marc Jacobs bag.

"Barneys in New York."

"Barneys?" she gasps. "Have you been there? What's it like?"

"Actually, I used to work there."

"No *way*." Now Daryl is goggling at me in awe. "I'm saving up to go to New York."

"We both are." Nicole nods vigorously. "I got up to a hundred and sixty pounds before Christmas. Only then it was the sales. And I went into Vivienne Westwood." She winces.

"I went into Paul Smith." Daryl sighs. "Now I'm down to thirty quid."

"I'm down to minus eighty," says Nicole gloomily. "I owe my dad. He was like, 'What do you need another jacket for?' and I was like, 'Dad! It's Vivienne *Westwood*.' And he looked at me, like 'Huh?'"

"I know exactly how you feel," I can't help chiming in sympathetically. "They just don't understand. Which jacket was it? *Not* that fabulous red one with the lining?"

"Yeah!" Her face lights up. "It was! And these amazing shoes. I've got a photo somewhere . . ." She starts scrolling through her phone.

She's just like me! I have photos of all my favorite clothes.

"Can I hold the Luella?" ventures Daryl as I admire Nicole's Westwood shoes.

"Of course! Here it is." I hand him the Luella clutch, and Daryl gazes at it reverently for a moment. "So . . . maybe we should get down to business. Could you demonstrate your fire-eating? It's for a party. I want a really cool display."

There's a tiny pause, then Daryl says, "Yeah. Sure. I'll show you."

He puts his rucksack on the ground, rifles in it for a moment, then produces a long wooden stick, which he sets alight with a Zippo.

That doesn't look anything like a normal fire-eater's stick. It looks like a bamboo cane out of the garden.

"Come on, Daryl." Nicole is watching him with concentration. "You can do it."

Daryl throws back his head, exposing a skinny neck,

and lifts up the stick. With a trembling hand, he brings the flame within a few inches of his mouth, then flinches and jerks it away.

"Sorry," he mumbles. "Bit hot."

"You can do it!" encourages Nicole again. "Come on. Just think *Luella*."

"OK." His eyes are closed and he seems to be psyching himself up. "I'm doing it. I'm doing it."

The stick is half on fire by now. OK, there's no *way* this guy is a proper fire-eater.

"Wait!" I exclaim as he lifts the flaming stick up again. "Have you ever done this before?"

"Learned it off YouTube," says Daryl, his face sweating. "I'll do it."

YouTube?

"Exhale, Daryl," chimes in Nicole, looking anxious. "Remember, *exhale*."

He lifts the stick up again, his hand shaking. Orange flames are billowing up like an inferno. In a minute he's going to set us all alight.

"C'mon," he's muttering to himself. "*C'mon*, Daryl."

"Stop it!" I shout in horror. "You'll hurt yourself! Look, you can have the Luella clutch, OK? You can *have* it! Just don't burn your face!"

"Really?" Daryl lowers the stick, looking a bit white and trembly, then suddenly jumps as the flame licks his hand. "Ow! Fuck!" He drops it to the ground, shaking his hand, and we watch it slowly burn itself out.

"You're not a fire-eater at all, are you?" I say at last.

"Nah." He scuffs his foot. "Just wanted the clutch. Can I really still have it?"

I can't blame him. To be honest, if I saw an ad offering a designer bag in return for fire-eating skills, I'd probably pretend I could fire-eat too. But, still, I can't help feeling deflated. What am I going to do about Luke's party now?

"OK." I sigh. "You can have it."

I look at Nicole, her face all hopeful, her arm still wrapped round the gray Marc Jacobs bag. The truth is, I never use either of those bags anymore. And something tells me I'm never going to get a tent for them.

"And, Nicole, you can keep the Marc Jacobs bags if you like."

"Legend!" She nearly explodes with joy. "For real? Do you want me to . . . wash your car or anything?"

"No, thanks!" I can't help laughing.

Nicole's face is glowing. "This is *awesome*. Oh, look, there's Julie."

"Don't tell me," I say. "Another friend of yours."

A blond teenage girl is coming up the drive, holding three colored balls.

"Hi!" She smiles hesitantly. "I'm the juggler? For the Gina sandals?"

"Can you juggle?" I say bluntly.

"Well . . ." She looks anxiously at Nicole, who grimaces back and shakes her head. "Um . . . I'm a quick learner?"

AS DARYL, Nicole, and Julie head back down the drive, I sink down on the front step and stare out, hugging my knees. I can't help feeling gloomy. Some bartering that was. I mean, it's not that I *begrudge* giving away stuff—in fact, it was a pleasure to see my things going to good homes. And all three of them were really grateful.

But, still, it wasn't exactly a successful transaction, was it? If you ask me, bartering's crap, and I don't know why I ever believed Jess. I'm down three designer bags and a pair of sandals, and I haven't got anything to show for it. The party isn't any further forward . . . and we haven't got a house . . . and we've got to move out . . . My head is sinking farther and farther forward, and it's a few moments before I hear a gentle voice saying, "Rebecca?"

I look up to see a woman in a neat jacket and skirt holding out a tray of food.

"It's Erica," she says. "From Oxshottmarket place.com? With the canapés for the Missoni coat? I thought I'd bring a selection and you could make your choice."

I struggle to my feet and stare at her suspiciously for a moment. "Can you actually cook?"

Erica laughs. "Take a bite"—she gestures at the tray—"and you tell me."

Silently, I reach forward, take a canapé, and bite into it. It's prawn and chili on shortcrust pastry, and it's delicious. And so is the avocado and mozzarella roll.

By the time I've finished them all, I feel a million times better. It turns out Erica's a proper caterer! She's going to do a whole selection and serve them herself. *And* the Missoni coat looks fabulous on her, especially when I throw in a patent belt and some knee-high shiny Prada boots (which always cut into my shins and I never wear anyway) and redo her hair.

And she said if I want to expand to catering the whole party, she's willing to barter some more!

I'm glowing all over with pride. It worked! Here I am, bartering in my local community, being totally green and worthy, using the world's resources the way we were *meant* to. Without money, without credit cards, without waste. Wait till I tell Jess!

Happily, I drift inside and check on Minnie. Then I turn on my laptop and, just out of interest, summon up Erica's catering website. Wow. It's really impressive. There she is, looking all smart and professional in her apron. And there's a page of testimonials . . . and here's a list of party menus . . . and . . .

What?

I stare at the Web page in shock. I don't believe this.

The Missoni coat, Prada boots, and belt that I bartered were worth a total of sixteen hundred quid *at least*—and it says here I could get exactly the same lot of canapés for twelve hundred in her *Special Nibbles Deal*.

I've spent four hundred quid too much. No *wonder* she was so keen.

As I close down the computer, I'm absolutely seething. I was right the first time. Bartering's a stupid, rubbish system, and there was a *reason* it went out of fashion, and I'm never doing it again, ever. What's wrong with *money*?

DR. JAMES LINFOOT

36 HARLEY STREET   LONDON WI

Rebecca Brandon
The Pines
43 Elton Street
Oxshott
Surrey

17 February 2006

Dear Rebecca,

Thank you for your letter of 15 February.

I am indeed a specialist in the heart and lungs and was sorry to hear of your symptoms. However, I think it unlikely they have been brought about by "shopping cold turkey."

I do not agree that it is imperative that you "buy a few little things for the sake of your health." Nor can I issue you a "prescription to go shopping."

I suggest you visit your local GP if symptoms persist.

Kind regards,

James Linfoot

Ms. Rebecca Brandon
The Pines
43 Elton Road
Oxshott
Surrey

20 February 2006

Dear Rebecca,

Thank you for your letter of 16 February.

I can understand your unhappiness at your unfortunate recent bartering experience. I will indeed, if I get the chance, warn the Chancellor that "bartering is not the way to go after all." Please do not worry: He has not already embarked on "swapping all our stuff with France's."

If it is any consolation, the inefficiencies of illiquid financial instruments have always been a source of frustration to investors. Coincidentally, I am currently writing a paper entitled "A History of the Valuation and Pricing of Illiquid Investments since 1600" for *The British Journal of Monetary Economics*. With your permission, I would like to use your example of bartering disappointment as anecdotal "flavor." I will, of course, credit you in a footnote if you so wish.

Yours sincerely,

Edwin Tredwell
Director of Policy Research

Alaris Publications LTD

P.O. Box 45   London E16 4JK

Ms. Rebecca Brandon
The Pines
43 Elton Road
Oxshott
Surrey

27 February 2006

Dear Rebecca,

Thank you for your demo CD: "Becky's Inspirational
Speeches," which we have listened to. They were certainly
very lively and some of the anecdotes most amusing.

You assert that your "profound and spiritual message
comes across loud and clear." Unfortunately, after several
careful listens, we were unable to detect exactly what that
message was. Indeed, there seemed to be several messages
in your text—some contradicting the others.

We will not therefore be releasing a 12-part set and
advertising it on the TV, as you suggest.

Yours truly,

Celia Hereford
Director (Mind-Body-Spirit)

ELEVEN

IT'S HAPPENING. It's actually, definitely happening. The party invitations have gone out! No turning back now.

Bonnie emailed the final guest list over yesterday, to my secret party email account. As I ran my eye down it, I suddenly felt a bit nervous. I'd forgotten how well connected Luke is. Some really important, grown-up people have been invited, like the chairman of Foreland Investments and the whole board of Bank of London. There's even someone called the Right Reverend St. John Gardner-Stone, who sounds petrifying and I can't believe he was ever a friend of Luke's. (I quickly Googled him—and when I saw his massive bushy beard, I believed it even less.)

Two hundred important people coming for a party. And I don't have a tent yet. No one else responded to my barter ad, and there's no *way* I can afford one from a posh hire company. My stomach clenches with anxiety every time I think about it. But I have to stay positive. I'll get one somehow. I just have to. And I've got the canapés and the Pound Shop table confetti, and I've made forty pom-poms already—

Could I *make* a tent? Out of shopping bags?

I have a sudden vision of a perfect patchwork

canopy, with hundreds of designer names shining all over it . . .

No. Let's be realistic. Pom-poms are my limit.

On the plus side, my latest fab plan is to get the party sponsored. I've written loads of letters to the marketing directors of companies like Dom Perignon and Bacardi, telling them what a great opportunity it will be for them to become involved with such a glitzy, high-profile event. If just a few of them send us some free stuff, we'll be set. (And obviously I've sworn them to secrecy. If any of them blab, they're *dead*.)

I glance nervously down at myself and brush a speck off Minnie's little pink tweed coat. We're walking along Piccadilly, and I've never felt so apprehensive in all my life. Two hundred yards away is the Ritz, and in the Ritz is Elinor, waiting in a suite, and that's where we're headed.

I still can't quite believe I've done this. I've set up a secret meeting. I've said absolutely nothing to Luke. It feels like the most massive betrayal. But at the same time . . . it feels like something I've got to do. I've got to give Elinor a chance to know her grandchild. Just one.

And if it's a disaster or if Elinor says anything appalling, I'll whisk Minnie away and pretend it never happened.

The Ritz is as grand and beautiful as ever, and I have a sudden flashback to coming here with Luke for a date, before we were even going out together. Imagine if I'd known then that we'd end up getting married and having a daughter. Imagine if I'd known I'd end up betraying him with a secret meeting with his mother—

No. Stop it. Don't think about it.

As we walk into the Ritz, a dark-haired bride is standing a few feet away, wearing the most amazing sheath dress with a long sparkly veil and tiara, and I feel a pang of lust. God, I'd love to get married again.

I mean, to Luke, obviously.

"Pin-cess." Minnie is pointing at the bride with her chubby finger, her eyes like saucers. "Pin-cess!"

The bride turns and smiles charmingly down at Minnie. She takes a little pink rosebud out of her bouquet, rustles over to us, and hands it to Minnie, who beams back, then reaches for the biggest, most succulent rose.

"No, Minnie!" I grab her hand just in time. "Thanks so much!" I add to the bride. "You look lovely. My daughter thinks you're a princess."

"Pince?" Minnie is looking all around. "Pince?" The bride meets my eye and laughs.

"There's my prince, sweetheart." She points to a man in morning dress who's approaching over the patterned carpet.

Yikes. He's short, squat, balding, and in his fifties. He looks more like a frog. I can tell from Minnie's puzzled frown that she's not convinced.

"Pince?" she says again to the bride. "Where pince?"

"Congratulations and have a lovely day!" I say hastily. "We'd better go . . ." And I hurriedly lead Minnie away, her little voice still piping up, "Where pince?"

I'm half-hoping the man at the reception desk will say, "Sorry, Elinor Sherman's gone out for the afternoon," and we can forget all about it and go to Hamleys instead. But Elinor has clearly primed the staff, because the man immediately leaps to attention, says, "Ah yes, Mrs. Sherman's visitors," and escorts me up in the lift himself. And so, before I know it, I'm standing in an elegant carpeted corridor, knocking on the door, my hand trembling.

Maybe this was a terrible idea. Oh God. It was, wasn't it? It was a terrible, terrible, *bad* idea—

"Rebecca." She opens the door so suddenly, I squeak in fright.

"Hi." I clutch Minnie's hand tighter, and for a moment we all just stare at one another. Elinor's dressed in white bouclé, with giant pearls round her neck. She seems to have got even thinner, and her eyes are weirdly wide as she looks from me to Minnie.

She's *scared*, I realize.

Everything's turned on its head. I used to be petrified of *her*.

"Come in." She stands aside and I gently lead Minnie in. The room's beautiful, with grand furniture and a view over Green Park, and there's a table laid with a teapot and a posh tiered cake stand full of little éclairs and things. I guide Minnie to a stiff sofa and lift her onto it. Elinor sits down too, and there's a silent moment so twitchy and uncomfortable I almost feel like screaming. At last Elinor draws breath.

"Would you like a cup of tea?" she says to Minnie.

Minnie just gazes back with huge eyes. She seems a bit cowed by Elinor.

"It's Earl Grey," Elinor adds to Minnie. "I will order a different variety if you would prefer."

She's asking a *two-year-old* what kind of tea she likes? Has she ever had any dealings with a two-year-old before?

Well. Actually, probably not.

"Elinor . . ." I put in gently. "She doesn't drink tea. She doesn't really know what tea is. Hot!" I add sharply as Minnie makes a lunge for the teapot. "*No*, Minnie."

"Oh." Elinor seems put out.

"She can have a biscuit, though," I add quickly.

I quite like the look of those biscuits myself. And the cakes.

With the very tips of her fingers, Elinor places a biscuit on a gold-embossed plate and hands it to Minnie. Is she crazy? A priceless porcelain plate from the Ritz—and a toddler? I almost want to cover my eyes as I imagine Minnie dropping the plate, hurling the plate, crushing the biscuit to crumbs, basically causing chaos . . .

But, to my amazement, Minnie's sitting bolt upright, her plate on her lap, the biscuit untouched, her gaze still fixed on Elinor. She seems mesmerized by her. And Elinor seems a bit mesmerized by Minnie too.

"I am your grandmother, Minnie," she says rigidly. "You may call me . . . Grandmother."

"Gran-muff," says Minnie hesitantly.

I feel a bolt of panic in my heart. I can't have Minnie going around saying "Gran-muff." Luke will want to know what or who "Gran-muff" is.

I can't even pretend she's talking about Mum, because Minnie calls her "Grana," which is totally different.

"No," I say hurriedly. "She can't call you Grandmother or Gran-muff or anything like that. She'll only say it at home and Luke will find out. He doesn't know I'm here." I feel the tension creep into my voice. "And he *can't* know. OK?"

Elinor is silent. She's waiting for me to continue, I realize. I really am calling all the shots here.

"She can call you . . ." I search my mind for something innocuous and impersonal. "Lady. Minnie, this is Lady. Can you say *Lady*?"

"Lady." Minnie gazes at Elinor uncertainly.

"I'm Lady," says Elinor after a pause, and I feel a sudden twinge of pity for her, which is ridiculous, because this is all her own fault for being such an ice-queen bitch. Still, it's a bit tragic to be sitting in a hotel suite, being introduced to your own grandchild as "Lady."

"I bought an amusement." Elinor gets up abruptly and heads into the bedroom. I take the opportunity to brush down Minnie's skirt and cram an éclair into my mouth. *God,* that's delicious. "Here you are." Elinor stiffly proffers a box.

It's a jigsaw of an Impressionist painting. Two hundred pieces.

For God's sake. There is no way on earth Minnie can make a puzzle like this. She's more likely to eat it.

"Lovely!" I say. "Maybe we could do it together!"

"I'm fond of jigsaws," says Elinor, and my jaw nearly drops open. This is a first. I've never heard Elinor say she's fond of *anything* before.

"Well . . . er . . . let me open it . . ."

I open the box and shake the pieces onto the table, fully expecting Minnie to snatch them and post them into the teapot or something.

"The only way to do a jigsaw is to be methodical," says Elinor to Minnie. "First we turn the pieces over."

As she begins doing so, Minnie grabs for a handful.

"No," says Elinor, and shoots Minnie one of those chilly glances which used to make me want to shrivel. "Not like that."

For a moment, Minnie is motionless, the pieces still clutched in her tiny hand, as though working out just how serious Elinor is. Their eyes are fixed on each other, and they both look deadly determined; in fact—

Oh my God, they look like each other.

I think I'm going to hyperventilate or pass out or something. I've never seen it before—but Minnie has the same eyes and the tilt of her chin and the same imperious stare.

My worst fear has come true. I've given birth to a mini-Elinor. I grab a tiny meringue and munch it. I need the sugar, for the shock.

"Give the pieces to me," says Elinor to Minnie—and, after a pause, Minnie hands them over.

How come Minnie's behaving so well? What is *up?*

Elinor has already begun arranging the pieces on the

table, her gaze focused. Blimey. She's serious about liking jigsaw puzzles, isn't she?

"How is Luke?" she says without looking up, and I stiffen.

"He's . . . he's . . . fine." I take a sip of tea, suddenly wishing it was laced with brandy. Just the mention of Luke has made me jumpy. I shouldn't be here; Minnie shouldn't be here; if Luke ever found out . . . "We'll have to go soon," I say abruptly. "Minnie, five more minutes."

I can't believe I'm acting with such confidence. In the past it was always Elinor sweeping in and out on her own terms and the rest of us dancing attendance around her.

"Luke and I had a . . . disagreement." Elinor's head is bowed resolutely over the pieces.

I'm a bit thrown. Elinor doesn't usually bring up tricky family subjects.

"I know," I say shortly.

"There are elements of Luke's character I find"—she pauses again—"hard to comprehend."

"Elinor, I really can't get into this," I say uncomfortably. "I can't talk about it. It was between you and Luke. I don't even know what happened, except that you said something about Annabel—"

Is it my imagination or does Elinor twitch slightly? Her hands are still shuffling jigsaw pieces, but her eyes are distant. "Luke was devoted to . . . that woman," she says.

That woman again. "Yes, and that's exactly what he calls you," I feel like saying.

But of course I don't. I just sip my tea, watching her with more and more curiosity. Who knows what's going on underneath that lacquered hair? Has she been thinking about her row with Luke all this time? Has she finally realized how she's wrong-footed herself? Has she *finally* realized what she's been missing out on?

I've never known such a mystery as Elinor. I'd so love to climb inside her head, just once, and see what makes her tick.

"I met her only once." Elinor raises her head with a questioning expression. "She did not seem particularly refined. Or elegant."

"Is that what you said to Luke?" I can't help exclaiming furiously. "That Annabel wasn't refined or elegant? No wonder he walked out on you. She *died,* Elinor! He's *devastated.*"

"No," says Elinor, and now there's a definite little spasm under her eye. It must be the only square millimeter which isn't Botoxed. "That is not what I said. I am merely trying to understand his overreaction."

"Luke never overreacts!" I retort angrily.

OK, this isn't quite true. I have to admit Luke has been known to overreact to things on occasion. But, *honestly,* I feel like hitting Elinor over the head with her silver teapot.

"He loved her," she says now—and I can't tell if it's a statement or a question.

"Yes! He loved her!" I glare at Elinor. "Of course he did!"

"Why?"

I stare at her suspiciously, wondering if she's trying to score some kind of point—but then I realize she's serious. She's actually asking me why.

"What do you mean, *why*?" I snap in frustration. "How can you ask *why*? She was his *mother!*"

There's a sharp silence. My words seem to be sitting in the still air. A prickly, awkward feeling creeps over me.

Because, of course, Annabel wasn't Luke's mother.

Strictly speaking, Elinor's his mother. The difference is, Annabel knew how to *be* a mother.

Elinor has no idea what being a mother is about. If she did, she wouldn't have abandoned Luke and his father in the first place, when Luke was still tiny. If she did, she wouldn't have turned away that day he came to New York at age fourteen. I'll never forget him telling me about the way he waited outside her apartment building, desperate to meet the mythical, glamorous mother he never saw. The way she came out at last, immaculate and beautiful like a queen. He told me that she saw him across the street, that she *must* have known exactly who he was . . . but pretended she didn't. She just got in a taxi and disappeared. And they never saw each other again till he was an adult.

So of course he got a bit obsessed with Elinor. And of course she let him down, again and again. Annabel totally understood it and was endlessly patient and supportive—even when Luke grew up and became in thrall to Elinor. She knew he was dazzled by his natural mother; she knew he'd get hurt by her. All she wanted to do was protect him as much as she could, just like any mother would.

Whereas Elinor . . . Elinor has no idea about anything.

Half of me wants to say, "You know what, Elinor? Forget it. You'll never understand." But the other half wants to rise to the challenge. I want to try to *make* her understand, even if it turns out to be impossible. I take a deep breath, trying to organize my thoughts. I feel like I'm explaining a foreign language to her.

"Annabel loved Luke," I say at last, folding my napkin into pleats. "Unconditionally. She loved him for all his good points and all his flaws. And she didn't want anything in return."

In all the time I've known Luke, Elinor has only been

interested in him when he could do something for her or raise money for her stupid charity or cast her some reflected glory. Even the wedding she put on for us in the Plaza was all about her and *her* position in society.

"Annabel would have done anything for Luke." I'm staring determinedly down at my napkin. "And she would never have expected any reward or result. She was proud of his success, of course she was, but she would have loved him whatever he'd done. *Whatever* he'd achieved. He was just her boy and she loved him. And she never switched that love off. I don't think she could."

I'm feeling a bit tight around the throat. Even though we hardly ever saw her, Annabel's death hit me too. Sometimes I can't quite believe she isn't here anymore.

"And, by the way, just so you know, she *was* elegant and refined," I can't help adding, a little savagely. "Because when Luke starting spending more time in New York and getting to know you, she never said anything except positive things about you. She loved Luke so much, she'd rather do that and have him happy than ever let him know she was hurt. That's a pretty elegant and refined way to behave, if you ask *me*."

To my horror, my eyes are damp. I shouldn't have got into this. I wipe at them furiously and take Minnie's hand.

"We've got to go, Min. Thanks for the tea, Elinor."

I'm scrabbling for my bag. I have to get out of here. I don't bother putting Minnie's coat on but just grab it, and we're nearly at the door when Elinor's voice hits the back of my head.

"I would like to see Minnie again."

In spite of myself, I turn to look at her. She's sitting bolt upright in the chair, her face as pale and expressionless as ever. I can't tell if she even heard anything I said, let alone whether it went in.

"I would . . ." She seems to be speaking with a struggle. "I would appreciate your kindness if you were to arrange another meeting between myself and Minnie."

She would "appreciate my kindness." God, how the tables have turned.

"I don't know," I say after a pause. "Maybe."

Thoughts are jumbling round my head. This wasn't supposed to be the beginning of some regular arrangement. It was supposed to be a one-off. I already feel like I've betrayed Luke. And Annabel. And everyone. What am I even *doing* here?

But at the same time I can't rid myself of that image: Minnie and Elinor staring silently at each other with the same mesmerized gaze.

If I don't let them ever see each other, am I simply repeating what happened with Luke? Will Minnie get a complex and blame me for not letting her see her grandmother?

Oh God, it's all too complicated. I can't cope. I want a normal, straightforward family, where grannies are kindly creatures who sit by the fire and do knitting.

"I just don't know," I say again. "We have to go."

"Good-bye, Minnie." Elinor stiffly lifts a hand, like the queen.

"Bye bye, Lady," says Minnie brightly.

The little pocket of Minnie's dress is stuffed with jigsaw pieces, I suddenly notice. I should take them out and give them back to Elinor. Because otherwise she might spend ages trying to do a jigsaw that's incomplete. And that would be really annoying and frustrating for her, wouldn't it?

So as a mature, adult person, I should give them back.

"Bye, then," I say, head out of the door, and pull it shut.

• • •

ALL THE WAY HOME I'm swamped with guilt and paranoia. I cannot tell a *soul* where I was today. No one would understand and Luke would be devastated. Or furious. Or both.

As I head into the kitchen, I'm braced for an instant quiz on where Minnie and I have been all afternoon, but Mum just looks up from her seat at the table and says, "Hello, love." There's something about her high-pitched, edgy tone which makes me give her a second glance. Her cheeks are a suspect pink color too.

"Hi, Mum. Everything OK?" My eyes drop to the navy-blue sock in her hand. "What are you doing?"

"Well!" Clearly she's been waiting for me to ask. "I would have thought it was obvious! I'm darning your father's socks, since we're too *impecunious* to afford any new clothes—"

"I didn't say that!" Dad strides into the kitchen behind me.

"—but now he says they're 'unwearable'!" Mum finishes. "Does that look 'unwearable' to you, Becky?"

"Er . . ."

I examine the sock she thrusts at me. Not to be rude about Mum's darning—but it does look a bit lumpy, with great big stitches in bright blue wool. *I* wouldn't fancy putting it on.

"Couldn't you get some new socks at the Pound Shop?" I suggest.

"New socks? And who's supposed to pay for those, may I ask?" demands Mum shrilly, as though I've suggested Dad gets the finest bespoke monogrammed socks from Jermyn Street.

"Well . . . er . . . they only cost a pound . . ."

"I've ordered some from John Lewis," says Dad with an air of finality.

"John Lewis!" Mum's voice shrills even higher. "We can afford John Lewis now, can we? I see: It's one rule for you, Graham, and another for me. Well, as long as I know where I stand . . ."

"Jane, don't be *ridiculous*. You know as well as I do that a pair of socks isn't going to ruin us . . ."

Surreptitiously, I take Minnie by the hand and lead her out of the kitchen.

Mum and Dad are so scratchy at the moment, Mum in particular. Luckily, I gave Minnie an early supper at Pizza Express on the way home, so she just needs to have her bath and some milk. Then, when she's in bed, I can log on to my secret email account and see if there are any replies yet—

"Becky." Luke's voice makes me jump like a scalded cat. There he is, coming down the stairs. What's he doing home this early? Does he know about Elinor? What does he suspect?

Stop it. Stay calm, Becky. He doesn't suspect anything. He had a meeting with a client in Brighton, that's all.

"Oh, hi there!" I say brightly. "Minnie and I were just . . . out."

"That would make sense." Luke gives me a quizzical glance. "How's my girl?" He reaches the bottom of the stairs and swings Minnie up into his arms.

"Lady," says Minnie seriously.

"Lady?" Luke tickles her chin. "Which Lady, poppet?"

"Lady." Her eyes are huge and reverent. "Puzz-le."

Argh! Since when did Minnie know how to say *puzzle*? Why does she have to expand her vocabulary *now*? What other words will she suddenly come out with? *Elinor? Ritz Hotel? Guess what, Daddy, I went to see my other grandmother today?*

"Puzz-le." She plucks the puzzle pieces out of her pocket and presents them to Luke. "Lady."

"How funny!" I laugh quickly. "We were looking at puzzles in a toy shop and there was one of the Mona Lisa. *That* must be why she's saying *puzzle* and *lady*."

"Tea," adds Minnie.

"And we had tea," I chime in desperately. "Just us. Just the two of us."

Don't say "Grand-muff," for God's sake don't say "Grand-muff" . . .

"Sounds good." Luke drops Minnie to the floor. "By the way, I had a phone message from Michael's assistant."

"Michael!" I say absently. "That's great. How's he?"

Michael is one of our oldest friends and lives in the States. He was Luke's business partner for ages, but now he's more or less retired.

"I don't know. It was a bit strange." Luke takes out a Post-it and gives it a puzzled glance. "It was a bad line, but I *think* the assistant said something about April seventh? About not being able to make a party?"

Party?

Party?

The world seems to freeze. I'm pinioned, staring at Luke in horror. My heart seems to be thumping loudly inside my head.

What was Michael's assistant doing *phoning*? She was supposed to *email*. It's supposed to be a *secret*. Did I not write that big enough? Did I not make it clear?

"Has he invited us to something?" Luke looks perplexed. "I don't remember getting an invitation."

"Me neither," I manage, after what seems like six hours. "Sounds like the message got garbled."

"We couldn't make it out to the States anyway." Luke is frowning at the message. "It's just not feasible. And I think I've got something on that day. A training conference or something."

"Right." I'm nodding frantically. "Right. Well, why

don't *I* get back to Michael about it?" I take the Post-it from Luke, trying very hard not to snatch it. "Leave it to me. I want to ask after his daughter, anyway. She sometimes comes to The Look when she's in town."

"Of course she does. Where else would she go?" Luke gives me a disarming smile, but I can't return it.

"So . . . would you mind giving Minnie her bath?" I try to speak calmly. "I've got a quick call I need to make."

"Sure." Luke heads for the stairs. "C'mon, Min, bath time."

I wait until they've reached the landing, then leg it outside to the drive, speed-dialing Bonnie's number.

"Disaster! Catastrophe!" I barely even wait for her to say hello. "The assistant of one of the guests rang up about the party! She left a message with Luke! I mean, I managed to save the situation . . . but what if I hadn't?"

"Oh goodness." Bonnie sounds shocked. "How unfortunate."

"I wrote on the invitation, *Don't call!*" I'm gabbling almost hysterically. "How much clearer could I have been? What if other people start calling? What do I do?"

"Becky, don't panic," says Bonnie. "I'll have a think about this. How about we have breakfast tomorrow to formulate a plan? I'll tell Luke I'm coming in late."

"OK. Thanks so much, Bonnie. See you tomorrow."

Slowly, my pulse rate starts to subside. Honestly, organizing a surprise party is like doing hundred-yard sprints with no warning the whole time. They should offer it instead of personal training.

Ooh, maybe I'll end up super-fit with no effort. *That* would be cool.

I put my phone away and am heading back into the house when I become aware of the grinding sound of an engine. A big white van is pulling in to the drive, which is weird.

"Hi." I approach hesitantly. "Can I help you?"

A guy in a T-shirt leans out of the cab of the van. He's in his late forties, with dark stubble and a massive tattooed forearm.

"You the bartering girl? Becky?"

"What?" I peer at him in surprise. What's going on? I haven't even put any ads in recently. Unless he's got those latest Prada shades and wants to swap them for a blue Missoni scarf.

Which somehow I doubt.

"My daughter promised you a tent? Nicole Taylor? Sixteen-year-old?"

This is Nicole's *dad*? I suddenly notice a nasty frown between his eyes. Shit. He looks quite scary. Is he going to tell me off for bartering with someone underage?

"Well yes, but—"

"Whole story came out last night. My wife wanted to know where she got them bags you gave her. Nicole should never have done it."

"I didn't realize she was so young," I say hastily. "I'm sorry—"

"You think a tent costs the same as a couple of handbags?" he says menacingly.

Oh God. Does he think I was trying to pull some kind of scam?

"No! I mean . . . I don't know!" My voice jumps with nerves. "I was just hoping someone might have a spare tent they didn't want, you know, lying around the place—"

I break off as I realize my voice might be carrying up to the bathroom window. Shit.

"Can we whisper, please?" I edge nearer the cab. "It's all supposed to be a secret. And if my husband comes out . . . I'm buying fruit off you, OK?"

Nicole's dad shoots me an incredulous look, then says, "How much are them bags worth, anyway?"

"They cost about a thousand pounds new. I mean, it depends how much you like Marc Jacobs, I suppose . . ."

"Thousand quid." He shakes his head in disbelief. "She's a bloody little *lunatic*."

I don't dare chime in, either to agree or disagree. In fact, now I think about it, he might be talking about me.

Abruptly, Nicole's dad focuses on me again. "All right," he says heavily. "If my daughter promised you a tent, I'll supply a tent. I can't lay on the full monty, you'll have to put it up yourself. But we're quiet at the moment. I'll sort you something."

For an instant I can't believe what I've heard.

"You'll get me a *tent*?" I clap a hand over my mouth. "Oh my God. Do you know how you have just saved my life?"

Nicole's dad gives a short laugh and hands me a card. "One of the lads'll be in touch. Tell him the date, say Cliff knows about it, we'll sort you out." He grinds the van into gear and starts reversing out of the drive.

"Thanks, Cliff!" I call after him. "Tell Nicole I hope she's enjoying the bags!"

I want to dance around. I want to whoop. I've got a tent! And it didn't cost thousands, and it's all sorted. I *knew* I could do it.

CENTRAL DEPARTMENTAL UNIT
FOR MONETARY POLICY

5th Floor • 180 Whitehall Place • London SW1

Ms. Rebecca Brandon
The Pines
43 Elton Road
Oxshott
Surrey

28 February 2006

Dear Rebecca,

Thank you for your prompt reply. It is most kind of you to issue permission so readily.

Unfortunately, *The British Journal of Monetary Economics* is not an illustrated periodical and does not have a "photo editor" or "stylist," as you suggest. I will therefore be unable to use the photographs of the Missoni coat, belt, and boots that you so kindly enclosed and return them with thanks.

Yours sincerely,

Edwin Tredwell
Director of Policy Research

TWELVE

THIS TIME WE'VE GONE for a central London restaurant, well away from Luke's office. As I arrive I can see Bonnie, already at a corner table, looking immaculate in a coral-colored suit and the seed-pearl earrings which I made Luke buy her as a birthday present. She looks perfectly comfortable sitting there on her own, her head erect, calmly sipping a cup of tea. Like she's sat on her own in restaurants a million times before.

"The earrings look great!" I say, sliding in to the seat opposite.

"They're exquisite!" says Bonnie, touching one. "I do hope you got my thank-you message, Becky. How on earth did you do it?"

"I was really subtle," I say proudly. "I found them online and told Luke I wanted them for myself. Then I said, 'Actually, no! They'd suit someone with different coloring. Someone like your assistant, Bonnie, maybe!'"

I won't mention that I had to say it about five times, louder and louder, before Luke even looked up from his laptop.

"You're very adept." Bonnie sighs. "I haven't had quite so much luck with your basement gym, I'm afraid. I have *tried* to mention it—"

"Oh, don't worry about that anymore. The house is

off for the moment, anyway." I pick up the menu, then put it down distractedly. "I'm more bothered about the party. Can you *believe* what happened last night?"

"People are so lax when it comes to invitations." Bonnie tuts with disapproval. "They never read instructions properly."

"So what am I going to do?" I'm hoping Bonnie will have thought of some clever solution already—and, sure enough, she nods calmly.

"I have a suggestion. We contact each invitee personally, reiterate the top-secret nature of the party, and head off any further mishaps."

"Yes," I say slowly. "Yes, that's a good idea. I'll take the list to work tomorrow."

"May I suggest, Becky, that I do the telephoning?" says Bonnie gently. "If you do, you will give the impression that you are the point of contact. But you should *not* be the point of contact. We need to separate you from the guests as much as possible, to prevent any further slipups."

"But that would be too much work! You can't do that!"

"I don't mind at all. Really, I'd be glad to." She hesitates. "It's rather fun!"

"Well . . . thanks!"

A waiter is hovering and I order a double cappuccino. I need the caffeine. This party is harder work than I thought. My hand muscles are aching from cutting out plastic bags for pom-poms (I'm up to seventy-two) and I'm constantly paranoid Luke's going to stumble across my folder of notes. Last night I dreamed that he came back home just as I was making his birthday cake in a giant mixing bowl, and I had to pretend it was breakfast and he kept saying, "But I don't want cake for breakfast."

Which is a stupid dream, because there's no *way* I'm making a birthday cake for two hundred people.

Oh God. I need to add that to the list. *Order birthday cake*.

"Becky, dear, relax," says Bonnie, as though reading my mind. "Minor scares will always happen. But it seems to me you have this party remarkably well contained. You know, Luke has a very loyal staff," she adds quietly. "They'll be delighted to have this chance to show their appreciation of him."

"Oh!" I feel a tiny glow. "Well . . . that's good, anyway."

"I've never had a boss who stuck up for his staff with such *resolve*. If ever there's a difficult client or a complaint, Luke insists on taking the meeting himself. He says it's his name above the door and he should take the flak. Of course, this can also be a weakness," she adds thoughtfully, sipping her tea. "I think he should probably delegate more."

I can't help looking at Bonnie anew. How much does she observe, sitting quietly in the corner, watching everyone?

"This new carbon-thingy client sounds cool," I say, hoping to prod her into saying more.

"Oh yes. Luke was thrilled with the result. Of course, he tried to downplay his hopes—but I always know if a meeting is important to him," Bonnie suddenly gives a little smile, "because he reties his tie."

"*Yes!*" I exclaim in delighted recognition. "He does that at home too!"

We smile at each other, and I take a sip of my cappuccino. In some ways it feels weird, talking about Luke behind his back. But in other ways it's quite nice, having someone to share with. No one else knows Luke's everyday quirks.

"Have you always made friends with the wives of your bosses?" I can't help asking. "Or husbands?"

"Not really." She looks almost amused. "They wouldn't have seen me as . . . friend material, I don't think."

I've seen pictures of Lady Zara Forrest, the wife of Bonnie's previous employer. She runs a spa in Notting Hill and is always doing interviews. I can't see her hanging out and chatting with Bonnie.

"Well, I suppose it's more natural for you to be friends with other people in the company," I say quickly. "It seems to have a really good atmosphere . . ."

"Yes," says Bonnie. "Although, of course, as Luke's personal assistant, I'm in a tricky position. I have to be guarded on some matters. So it's natural that there's a little distance between me and the others." She smiles. "It's always been that way."

She's lonely.

It hits me with a thud. Of course, she might have a massive social life outside work—but somehow I don't think so. Luke once told me how available she is over the weekend, how she always replies to emails within the hour, and how helpful it is to him. Maybe it is great for him. But what about her?

"Well, I'm so glad *we've* got to know each other better," I say warmly. "I told you we'd be a good team. I'm working on the air-conditioning situation, by the way."

Luke keeps his office *far* too cold. I'm not surprised Bonnie's shivering.

"Thank you!" She dimples. "And is there anything else I can do for you?"

"There must be something . . ." I take a few sips of cappuccino, mulling it over. "Oh yes! You know that new shower gel Luke's using? Doesn't it smell awful?"

"Shower gel?" Bonnie seems thrown. "Well, I couldn't comment . . ."

"You *must* have smelled it. The rosemary and gin-seng one? I hate it, but he says it wakes him up. Well, if you said you hated it too, he might stop using it."

"Becky, dear." Bonnie peers at me. "I couldn't possibly mention something as personal as *shower gel.*"

"Yes, you could! Of course you could! Believe me, Luke respects your views on everything. He wouldn't get offended. And that blue tie of his with the cars on it—can you tell him that's hideous too?"

"Becky, really—"

"Come on." I smile winsomely at her, wife-to-PA. "You *must* hate that tie too."

"Well . . ." Bonnie looks uncomfortable. Of course she does. I unwrap my little biscuit and crunch it, pondering.

A new, radical thought has come to me. There's another major way I could get her to influence Luke for me. Possibly.

"Bonnie . . . are you an only child?" I say at last.

"No, I have a brother."

Perfect!

"Well, if you get the chance . . . could you mention your brother to Luke and say how having a sibling has been really important to you? And maybe ask him if he wants any more children after Minnie and say how lovely it would be if he did? And how he should get a move on?"

Bonnie looks thunderstruck.

"Becky! This *really* isn't my business—I *really* couldn't—"

"Yes, you could!" I say encouragingly. "I so want another baby, and I know he does too, deep down, and he'd totally listen to you."

"But—"

"Just if you get the chance," I say reassuringly. "If it comes up in conversation. Shall we get the bill?"

As we leave the restaurant, I give Bonnie an impulsive hug.

"Thanks so much for everything, Bon. You're the best!"

I should have hooked up with Bonnie *ages* ago. Next I'll get her to tell Luke we need to go to Mauritius.

"Not at all." She still looks a bit flustered but smiles at me. "And please don't worry about the party. I'm sure Luke doesn't suspect anything."

"I'm not so sure." I glance up and down the street in sudden paranoia. "Did I tell you he bumped into me after our lunch? I told him I'd gone for Botox, but he didn't believe me, and now he keeps giving me these little looks, as though he knows I'm up to something—" I stop at Bonnie's expression. "What?"

"*Now* it makes sense!" she exclaims. She draws me aside, out of the flow of people on the pavement. "Becky, that day we met, Luke came back to the office and asked me if any designer clothes shops had opened in the area. I assumed it was some kind of retail research. But now I wonder if he thought you were secretly . . ." Bonnie trails off tactfully.

"Shopping?" I say incredulously. "He thought I was *shopping*?"

"It's possible, don't you think?" She twinkles. "It could be rather a good cover."

"But . . . but you don't understand! I've promised not to shop! We've had this agreement ever since that bank went bust! And I'm totally keeping to it!"

My mind is whirling with indignation. Did Luke think I was breaking my promise and covering up with a story about Botox? Is *that* why he kept looking so suspiciously at my bag?

I feel like marching into his office, throwing down my purse like a gauntlet, and declaring, "Rebecca

Brandon née Bloomwood keeps her word, sir!" And
challenging him to a duel, maybe.

"Oh, dear." Bonnie looks troubled. "Becky, this is
only surmise—"

"No, I'm sure you're right. He thinks I was shopping
Well, *fine*. Let him." I lift my chin firmly. "I'll use it as a
decoy."

After all, the more Luke suspects I'm secretly shopping, the less he'll suspect I'm secretly organizing a
party. As I head off down the street, I'm full of resolve
If "shopping" is what Luke thinks I'm up to . . . then
"shopping" is what he'll get. Big-time.

AS I HEAR Luke's key in the lock that evening, I'm ready
for him. I'm wearing a vivid lime-green sweater that
I've never worn (total mistake, what was I *thinking?*)
and still has the shop tag hanging from the label. On
top of that, I've got the leather jacket that I bought in
the sales, with its Whistles label carefully reattached
and poking out, plus a scarf, a necklace, and a bright
orange belt, none of which I've ever worn.

I mean, I *was* planning to wear them. You know.
When the right moment came.

I've dragged down some posh carrier bags from the
top of the wardrobe and put them under the kitchen
table, just peeking out. I've stuffed some Prada-logoed
tissue paper into the kitchen bin and half hidden some
old receipts behind the microwave. Minnie is following
me around in her pajamas and dressing gown, eating a
honey sandwich and watching in wonderment. As I
hear Luke heading toward the kitchen, I say, "Shhh!" to
her, just in case.

"Shhh!" she instantly replies, putting her finger to
her lips. "Shhh, Mummy!" She looks so serious, I can't
help laughing. Then I set up position in the kitchen,

checking out my reflection in the stainless-steel fridge
with my best fashionista pose. When Luke comes in, I
give quite a convincing jump.

"You startled me, Luke!" I say, and hastily rip off my
jacket, making sure the pink Whistles tag bobs into
view. "I was just . . . um . . . This is nothing. Nothing at
all!" I squash the jacket into a ball and whip it behind
my back, as Luke gives me a puzzled look. He heads to
the fridge and gets out a beer.

Ooh. Maybe I should have put the receipts in the
fridge.

No. Too obvious.

"Shhh, Daddy!" says Minnie importantly to Luke,
her finger still on her lips. "Hide-seek."

That's what she thinks I was doing. (Hide-and-seek
is Minnie's favorite game. Except it isn't like normal
hide-and-seek. You only count to three and you have to
tell her where you're going to hide. And when it's her
turn she always hides in the same place, which is the
middle of the room.)

"I'll play in a minute, poppet. Interesting sweater,"
he says to me, raising his eyebrows. As well he might,
since I look like a lime-green jelly bean.

"It's ancient!" I say at once. "I bought it ages ago. You
can ask Suze. Ring her up now if you don't believe me!
Go on!"

"Becky . . ." Luke gives a little laugh. "I never said I
don't believe you. Why are you so paranoid?"

"Because . . . no reason!" I edge over to the table and
kick the carrier bags underneath in a surreptitious yet
obvious manner. I can see Luke's eyes zip down and
register them.

Ha! Result!

"So, what were you up to today?" he says easily,
reaching for the bottle opener.

"Nothing! I didn't go anywhere! God, you're always

quizzing me, Luke." I stuff the necklace inside my jumper as though to hide it.

Luke opens his mouth to speak—then seems to decide against it and instead uncaps his beer.

Take the cap to the bin, I silently will him. *Go on, take it to the bin* . . .

Yes!

I really should be a choreographer. Just as Luke's about to pull out the bin, I leap across the kitchen with spot-on timing and plant a hand on the handle to stop him.

"I'll do that," I say super-casually. "Don't worry. I'll take care of it."

"I'm just putting it in the recycling." Luke seems puzzled. He makes to open the bin and I let just a bit of Prada tissue paper become visible before I grab the handle again.

"I said I'll do it!" I say feverishly.

"Becky, it's fine." He wrenches the whole bin drawer open, and the Prada tissue paper gusts up with the draft as though to say, "Here I am! Look at me! Prada!"

For a moment neither of us speaks.

"Gosh, what's that doing there?" I say in a high-pitched, unnatural voice, and start stuffing it down again. "That's old. Really, really old. I mean, I can't even remember the last time I went into a Prada. Or bought anything Prada. Or anything!"

I'm stumbling over my words and I've never sounded so guilty in my life.

In fact, I'm beginning to *feel* guilty. I feel like I've just been shopping and maxed out my credit card and all the stuff is hidden under the bed.

"Becky." Luke passes a hand over his brow. "What the hell is going on?"

"Nothing!"

"Nothing." He gives me a skeptical look.

"Nothing at all." I try to sound firm and confident. Although I'm now wondering if I've overdone it.

Maybe he's not fooled by my act for a moment. Maybe he's thinking, *Well, she obviously hasn't been shopping, so what else could she be trying to hide, aha, I know—a party!*

For a few moments we just look at each other. I'm breathing hard, and my hand is still clenched round the handle of the bin drawer.

"Found?" Minnie's voice breaks the spell. She's standing in the middle of the room with her hands over her eyes, which is how she hides.

"Becky!" Dad appears at the door. "Darling, you'd better come. You've got a delivery."

"Oh, right," I say, taken aback. I wasn't expecting a delivery. What can this be?

"Found?" Minnie's voice rises to a wail. "*Found?*"

"*Found* you!" Luke and I hastily say in unison. "Well done, Minnie!" I add, as she opens her eyes and beams proudly at us. "Very good hiding! Who's this delivery from?" I turn to Dad again.

"It's a van from fashionpack.co.uk," says Dad, as we follow him out to the hall. "Quite a lot of stuff, apparently."

"Really?" I wrinkle my brow. "That can't be right. I haven't been shopping on fashionpack.co.uk. I mean, not recently."

I can see Luke eyeing me quizzically, and I flush. "I *haven't*, OK? It must be a mistake."

"Delivery for Rebecca Brandon," the delivery guy says as I reach the front door. "If you could sign here . . ." He holds out an electronic device and a stylus.

"Wait a minute!" I hold up my hands. "I'm not signing anything. I didn't order anything from you! I mean, I don't *remember* ordering anything—"

"Yeah, you did." He sounds bored, as though he's heard this before. "Sixteen items."

"Sixteen?" My jaw drops.

"I'll show you the receipt if you like." He rolls his eyes and heads back to the van.

Sixteen items?

OK, this makes no sense. How can I have ordered sixteen items from fashionpack.co.uk and not even remember? Am I getting Alzheimer's?

A minute ago I was pretending to be guilty about shopping, and now it's all coming true, like some kind of bad dream. How can this be happening? Did I somehow *make* it happen?

I notice Luke and Dad exchanging looks above my head.

"I didn't do it!" I say, rattled. "I didn't order anything! It must have been some kind of weird computer glitch."

"Becky, not the computer-glitch excuse again," says Luke wearily.

"It's not an excuse, it's true! I didn't order this stuff."

"Well, *someone* clearly did."

"Maybe my identity's been stolen. Or maybe I was sleep-shopping!" I say in sudden inspiration.

Oh my God. Now, that makes *total* sense. It explains everything. I'm a secret sleep-shopper. I can see myself rising silently from my bed, coming downstairs with a glassy stare, logging on to the computer, tapping in my credit-card details . . .

But then, why didn't I buy that fab bag from Net-a-Porter that I've been lusting after? Does my sleep-shopping self have no taste?

Could I write a note to my sleep-shopping self?

"Sleep-shopping?" Luke raises an eyebrow. "That's a new one."

"No it's not," I retort. "Sleepwalking's a very common

ailment, I think you'll find, Luke. And I expect sleep-shopping is too."

The more I think about this theory, the more sure I feel that it's true. It would explain so much about my life. In fact, I'm starting to feel a bit resentful toward all those people who've given me a hard time over the years. I bet they'd change their tune if they knew I suffered from a highly specialized medical condition.

"It's very dangerous for you to wake the person when they're in a trance," I inform Luke. "It can give them a heart attack. You just have to let them carry on."

"I see." Luke's mouth starts to twitch. "So if I see you buying up the whole of Jimmy Choo online in your PJs, I have to stand back and let you do it, otherwise you'll die of a coronary?"

"Only if it's in the middle of the night and I've got a glassy stare," I explain.

"My darling." Luke gives a short laugh. "It's *always* in the middle of the night and you *always* have a glassy stare."

He has such a nerve.

"I do *not* have a glassy stare!" I begin furiously, as the guy returns from the van.

"Here you are." He shoves a piece of paper at me. "Sixteen Miu Miu coats in green."

"Sixteen coats?" I stare at the page disbelievingly. "Why on earth would I order sixteen coats, all the same color and size?"

To be honest, I have *looked* at this coat online, and I even put it in my basket, but I never actually—

My thoughts stop mid-flow. A terrible picture is coming to me. My laptop, left open in the kitchen. The page open. Minnie, clambering onto a chair . . .

Oh my God, she *can't* have done it.

"Minnie, did you press the buttons on Mummy's computer?" I turn to Minnie in horror.

"You're kidding." Luke looks staggered. "She couldn't do that!"

"She could! She can use a mouse easily. And that website has got a one-click button. If she just bashed at the keyboard enough times and clicked enough times . . ."

"You mean to say, Minnie ordered these?" Dad looks equally flabbergasted.

"Well, if I didn't, and Luke didn't—"

"Where shall I put them?" the delivery guy interrupts us. "Inside the front door?"

"No! I don't want them! You'll have to take them back."

"Can't do that." He shakes his head. "If you want to return 'em, you'll have to take delivery, use the return form, and send 'em back."

"But what's the point of taking delivery?" I say in frustration. "I don't want them."

"Well, next time you don't want something, can I suggest you don't order it?" says the delivery guy, and gives a hoarse chuckle at his own wit. Next thing I know, he's lifting a big box down from the back of the van. It's about the size of Dad.

"Is that all of them? Actually, it's not as bad as I thought—"

"That's one." The guy corrects me. "Come individually packaged on a hanging rail, they do." Already he's hefting down another one. I stare in horror. What are we going to do with sixteen great big boxes of coats?

"You are a naughty, naughty girl, Minnie." I can't help taking it out on her. "You do not order Miu Miu coats off the Internet. And I am going to . . . to . . . cut your pocket money this week!"

"Miiine box!" Minnie reaches longingly toward the boxes, her honey sandwich back in her hand.

"What's all this?" Mum appears out of the front door.

"What are these?" She gestures at the massive boxes. They look like upturned coffins, standing there in a row.

"There's been a mix-up," I say hurriedly. "They're not staying. I'm going to return them as soon as I can."

"That's eight . . ." The guy hefts another one down. He's enjoying this, I can tell.

"There are sixteen in all," says Dad. "Maybe we can fit some in the garage."

·"But the garage is full!" says Mum.

"Or the dining room . . ."

"No." Mum starts shaking her head wildly. "No. No. Becky, this really is enough. Do you hear me? It's enough! We can't deal with any more of your stuff!"

"It's only for a day or two—"

"That's what you always say! That's what you said when you moved in here! We can't do it anymore! *We can't deal with your stuff anymore!*" She sounds hysterical.

"It's only another two weeks, Jane." Dad takes hold of her shoulders. "Come on now. Another two weeks. We can do it. We're going to count it down, day by day, remember? One day at a time. Yes?"

It's like he's coaching her through labor or a prisoner-of-war camp. Having us to stay is the equivalent of a *prisoner-of-war camp*?

And all of a sudden I'm stricken with mortification. I can't put Mum through this anymore. We have to go. We have to move out right now, before she loses it completely.

"It's not two weeks!" I say hurriedly. "It's . . . two days! That's what I was about to tell you. We're moving out in two days!"

"Two *days*?" echoes Luke incredulously.

·"Yes! Two days!" I avoid his gaze.

Two days should give us enough time to pack. And find somewhere to rent.

"What?" Mum lifts her head from Dad's chest. "Two days?"

"Yes! The house suddenly all came together, so we're moving out. I meant to tell you."

"You're really going in two days?" falters Mum, as if she can't let herself believe it.

"Promise." I nod.

"Hallelujah," says the delivery guy. "If you could sign, madam?" His eyes swivel to his lorry. "Oy! Young lady!"

I follow his gaze and gasp. Shit. Minnie's climbed up into the cab of his lorry.

"Drive!" she yells joyously, her hands on the wheel. "Miiiine drive!"

"Sorry!" I hurry to get her down. "Minnie, what on *earth* are you—" I clap a hand to my mouth.

There's honey smeared all over the steering wheel. Honey and crumbs are decorating the seat and the window and the gear stick.

"Minnie!" I say furiously, under my breath. "You naughty girl! What have you *done*?" A horrible thought strikes me. "Where's your sandwich? What have you done with it? Where did you—"

My gaze falls on the built-in tape player.

Oh . . . bloody hell.

THE LORRY DRIVER was amazingly nice, bearing in mind he'd just delivered sixteen coats to someone who didn't want them and then her daughter shoved a honey sandwich inside his tape machine. It only took about half an hour to clean everything up, and we've promised him a state-of-the-art replacement.

As the lorry disappears out of the drive, Mum and

Dad head into the kitchen to make a cup of tea and Luke practically hauls me upstairs.

"Two days?" he demands in a whisper. "We're moving out in two *days*?"

"We have to, Luke! Look, I've got it all planned. We'll find a rental place and we'll tell Mum we're moving in to the house and everyone will be happy."

Luke is regarding me as though I have a screw loose.

"But she'll want to visit, Becky. Hadn't you thought of that?"

"We won't let her! We'll put her off until the house has been sorted out. We'll say we want everything to be perfect first. Luke, we don't have any choice," I add defensively. "If we stay here any longer, we'll give her a nervous breakdown!"

Luke mutters something under his breath. It sounds a bit like, "You're going to give *me* a bloody nervous breakdown."

"Well, have you got a better idea?" I retort, and Luke is silent.

"And what about Minnie?" he says at length.

"What do you mean, what about Minnie? She'll come with us, of course!"

"I didn't mean that." He clicks his tongue. "I meant, what are we going to do about her? I take it you're as concerned by what just happened as I am?"

"By the honey sandwich?" I say in astonishment. "Come on, Luke, relax. It was one of those things, all children do it—"

"You're in denial! Becky, she's getting wilder every day. I think we need to take extreme action. Don't you agree?"

Extreme action? What's *that* supposed to mean?

"No, I don't." I feel a little chilly around my spine. "I don't think she needs 'extreme action,' whatever that is."

"Well, I do." He's looking grave and not quite meeting my eye. "I'm going to make some calls."

What calls?

"Luke, Minnie isn't some kind of *problem*," I say, my voice suddenly shaky. "And who are you calling, anyway? You shouldn't call anyone without telling me first!"

"You'd tell me not to!" He sounds exasperated. "Becky, one of us has to do *something*. I'm going to sound out a couple of child experts." He pulls out his BlackBerry and checks it, and something inside me flips.

"What experts? What do you mean?" I grab his BlackBerry. "Tell me!"

"Give that back!" His voice rises harshly, and he pulls the BlackBerry out of my grasp.

I stare at him in shock, blood pulsing through my cheeks. He meant that. He really didn't want me to see. Is this about Minnie? Or . . . something else?

"What's the secret?" I say at last. "Luke, what are you hiding?"

"Nothing," he says defensively. "There's work in progress on there. Rough stuff. Sensitive stuff. I don't like anyone seeing it."

Yeah, right. His eyes keep flicking to his BlackBerry. He's lying. I know it.

"Luke, you're keeping something from me." I swallow hard. "I know you are. We're a couple! We shouldn't have secrets from each other!"

"You can talk!" He throws back his head and laughs. "My darling, I don't know whether it's shopping, or some massive debt, or you really *are* having Botox— but there's *something* going on that you don't want me to know about. Isn't there?"

Shit.

"No, there is not!" I say hotly. "Absolutely not!"

Please let him think it's shopping, please let him think it's shopping . . .

There's an odd, tingly pause, then Luke shrugs.

"Fine. Well, then—neither of us is hiding anything."

"Fine." I lift my chin. "Agreed."

THIRTEEN

AS SOON AS I get up the next morning, I call Bonnie's line and leave an urgent message for her to call back. *She'll* tell me what's going on. Downstairs at breakfast there's a prickly atmosphere, and Luke keeps glancing warily at me as though he's not sure how to proceed.

"So!" he suddenly says in fake cheerful tones. "Big day today. I'm trying to arrange a meeting with Sir Bernard Cross's right-hand man, Christian Scott-Hughes. We feel Sir Bernard might be sympathetic to the climate-technology cause."

God, he's transparent. He's not going to tell me about whatever-it-is on the BlackBerry, so instead he's offering me some boring old piece of information about climate technology and he thinks that'll fool me.

"Fab," I say politely.

Actually, I *am* quite impressed. Sir Bernard Cross is massive. (In both senses: He's always in the news because of being a billionaire philanthropist with lots of extreme views, and he weighs about 350 pounds.)

"Christian Scott-Hughes is Sir Bernard's executive director and hugely influential," Luke is saying. "If we can win him round, then we're a long way down the road."

"Why don't you go and meet Bernard Cross himself?" I say, and Luke gives a little laugh.

"My darling, Sir Bernard doesn't just 'meet people,'" he says. "That's like saying, 'Why don't we meet the queen herself?' You don't do that. You go through layers. You work the system."

I don't get that at all. If I wanted to see the queen, I'd aim to see the queen. But there's no point saying that to Luke, because he'll give me some lecture about how I don't understand the complexities of his business, like that time when I suggested matchmaking all his single clients.

And, anyway, I don't really care one way or the other about Sir Bernard Big-Belly.

"How about you?" He drains his coffee. "Work OK?"

"Booming, *actually*," I say smugly. "Our appointment book is fuller than it's ever been, and the managing director just sent me an email telling me how brilliant I am."

Luke gives an incredulous laugh. "I don't know how you do it. Every other sector is dead, but you're still managing to sell expensive designer clothes . . ." His face suddenly blanches. "Becky, please tell me you're not selling them all to yourself."

I gasp with affront. Number one, I made a promise, which I am *keeping*. Number two, if I was doing that, then why would I be standing here in a skirt which I bought five years ago from Barneys?

"If you *really* want to know," I say haughtily, "we at The Look have a unique approach to fashion selling, which is seeing us through the difficult times."

I won't explain that "unique" means "we hide the clothes in computer-paper boxes." Luke doesn't need to hear every tedious little detail of my job, does he?

"Well, all power to you, then." Luke gives me a disarming smile. "I have to go. Give my love to Suze."

I'm meeting Suze before work to see Ernie's art exhibition at his school and—hopefully—bump into his headmistress. (I've prepared all sorts of cutting remarks. She'll be quaking in her boots by the time I've finished with her.) And then we're both going on to The Look for the big promotional tie-in meeting.

This is the other reason my star is so high at work at the moment: My idea about linking Danny's new collection with Shetland Shortbread totally worked! The whole collection is centered around tartan, so it's perfect. They're doing a special offer and joint publicity, and it's all in association with the British Wool Marketing Board. The promotional shoot took place on Tarkie's farm, with super-thin models standing amid herds of Tarkie's sheep. And the best bit is, it was all my idea, and now everyone's really impressed.

Jasmine said the other day that maybe they'd even make me a board director! Of course, I instantly gave a modest little laugh and said, "Oh, rubbish." But I've already worked out what I could wear for my first board meeting—this amazing pale-yellow jacket from the new Burberry Prorsum collection, over dark pinstriped trousers. (I mean, you're allowed to buy new clothes if you get on the *board* of something. Even Luke must know that.)

ON MY WAY to St. Cuthbert's, two emails that make me want to whoop arrive on my BlackBerry. The first is from Bonnie, which she obviously sent last night. It says we've had forty-three acceptances already. Forty-three! I can't *believe* Luke is so popular!

No. That came out wrong. Obviously I *can*.

But, still, forty-three in two days! And that's not even counting all the Brandon Communications staff, who still don't know there's a party but think they're going to a conference.

And the other is from Kentish English Sparkling Wine. They want to provide drinks for the party! They're sending me fifty bottles! All they ask is that they can issue a press release and publish photos of Luke and his guests enjoying their high-quality product. I mean, I've never tasted Kentish English Sparkling Wine, but I'm sure it's delicious.

I can't help feeling proud as I stride along. I am doing *so* well. I've got the tent, the drinks, the canapés, the pom-poms, *and* I've booked a professional fire-eater called Alonzo, who doubles as a country-and-western singer, if we want it. (He doesn't sing country-and-western songs *while* he's fire-eating. He gets changed and calls himself Alvin.)

St. Cuthbert's is in one of those posh white squares with lots of railings and stucco, and I'm nearly at the school gate when my mobile rings with Suze's ID.

"Suze!" I greet her. "I'm just outside. Where shall I meet you?"

"I'm not there! I'm at the doctor's." Suze sounds despairing. "Ernie has a terrible earache. We've been up all night. I won't be able to come to The Look either."

"Oh, poor you! Well . . . should I leave?"

"No, don't be silly! Go to the exhibition and grab yourself a cake. They'll be delicious. Half the mothers have done a Cordon Bleu course. And you could always look at Ernie's painting," she adds, as though it's an afterthought.

"Of *course* I'll look at Ernie's painting!" I say firmly. "And we must meet up as soon as Ernie's better."

"Definitely." Suze pauses. "So . . . how are you?" she adds. "How are the party preparations going?"

"Great, thanks," I say ebulliently. "All under control."

"Because Tarkie and I had this great idea, if you're serving coffee . . ."

I feel a flash of annoyance. No one will believe I can do this, will they? Everyone assumes I'm totally incompetent and can't even serve coffee properly.

"Suze, for the last time, I don't need your help!" The words shoot out before I can stop them. "I can do it on my own! So leave me alone!"

Instantly I regret sounding so harsh. There's silence at the other end, and I can feel my cheeks turning pink.

"Suze . . ." I swallow. "I didn't mean—"

"You know, Bex, sometimes people *want* to help." Suze cuts me off, her voice suddenly trembling. "And it's not always about *you*, OK? It's not because we think you can't do it. It's because Luke isn't only your husband, he's our friend too, and we wanted to do something nice for him. Tarkie suggested getting the Shetland Shortbread guys to come up with a special shortbread recipe just for Luke. And we thought we could serve it at the party with the coffee. But, fine, if you're that prickly we won't. Forget it. I have to go."

"Suze—"

It's too late. She's gone. I try redialing but get the busy signal.

Oh God. She sounded really hurt. Maybe I was a bit defensive. But how was I supposed to know she had special shortbread?

For a few moments I stand there, wincing. Should I text her?

No. She's too angry with me. I'll wait till she's cooled down a bit. And maybe had a night's sleep.

There's nothing I can do now. I might as well go in and have a cake.

I head through the school gates, past all the babbling mothers, and follow signs to the exhibition. It's being held in an airy hall with a parquet floor, and I can already see what Suze means about the cakes. There's a whole trestle table of candy-colored macaroons and mini chocolate brownies, and lots of very toned mummies in low-slung jeans, holding cups of coffee and eyeing up the goodies with hostile eyes. Not a single one is eating a cake—so why do they bother to have them?

"Hi!" I approach the trestle table, where a well-groomed blond woman is serving. "I'd like a chocolate brownie, please."

"Of course!" She hands me a tiny sliver of brownie in a napkin. "Five pounds please."

Five quid? For two bites?

"All for the school!" She trills with laughter that sounds like icicles and puts my fiver into a felt-covered cash box trimmed with gingham. "Now, are you a new reception mummy? Because we *are* expecting the decorated gingerbread houses by Tuesday, and response *has* been a bit disappointing—"

"I'm not a mummy," I hastily correct her. "At least, not here. I'm just a visitor. My daughter isn't at school yet."

"Ah. I see." The interest in her eyes dies a little. "So where will your daughter be going?"

"I don't know." My voice is muffled by the brownie, which is absolutely scrumptious. "She's only two."

"Two months." The woman nods knowingly. "Well, you'll have to get your skates on—"

"No, two." I swallow the brownie. "Two years old."

"Two years old?" The woman seems riveted. "And you haven't started?"

"Er . . . no."

"You haven't got her down anywhere?" She stares at me with wide, twitchy eyes. *"Nowhere?"*

OK, this woman is freaking me out, with her super-white teeth and stressy manner. I mean, I know schools get full up and everything. But, come on, even the waiting list for that new Prada bag was only a year. No school can be more exclusive than a limited-edition Prada bag, surely?

"Thanks so much for the brownie!" I quickly walk away. Now I feel all anxious, like I've missed the boat and I didn't even know there *was* a boat. They should have *Vogue* for schools. They should have this month's Must-Have and Latest Trends and timings for all the waiting lists. Then you'd *know*.

Anyway, I'm not going to get obsessive about this. We'll get Minnie into a lovely school, I know we will.

I wonder where Madonna sends her kids to school. I mean, not that I'd send Minnie to a school because of the celebrities. Obviously not.

But still. Maybe I'll look it up online. Just out of interest.

I buy myself a coffee and then head toward the art. Most of the paintings are of flowers, and when I get to Ernie's picture, right in the corner, I'm a bit startled. It's . . . different. It's very dark and splodgy and shows a sheep on a dark background that might be a moor . . .

Ah. Looking more closely, I think the sheep is dead.

Well. There's nothing *wrong* with painting a picture of a dead sheep, is there? And the blood trickling from its mouth is quite realistic. I'll say that to Suze, when we've made up. Yes. I'll say "I loved the blood! It had such . . . movement!"

". . . absolutely revolting!"

"Gross!"

I become aware of a cluster of little girls also looking at the painting. One of them has perfect blond French plaits and a hand clamped over her mouth.

"I feel sick," she declares. "You know who painted this? *Ernest*."

"He's *always* drawing sheep," says another one derisively. "It's all he can do."

The others break into bitchy giggles, and I stare at them, livid. They all look like junior versions of Alicia Bitch Long-Legs. A bell rings and they hurry off, which is a good thing; otherwise, I probably would have said something undignified and immature involving the word *cows*.

Suddenly I notice a woman with dark hair in a bun and a queenly air. She sweeps the room, smiling graciously at people and making short conversations. I watch on tenterhooks as she nears me.

Yes! I thought so. On the lapel of her cardigan is a badge saying *Harriet Grayson, MA, Headmistress*. This is the one who's been giving Ernie a hard time.

Well, I'll give *her* a hard time. Especially as I still feel guilty about snapping at Suze.

"Hello." She smiles at me and extends her hand. "I'm afraid you'll have to remind me—are you in reception?"

"Oh, I'm not a parent at the school," I begin. "I'm . . ."

I was going to launch into, "I'm Ernest Cleath-Stuart's godmother, and I've got a few things to say to you." But now I have an even better idea. No one knows me here, do they?

"Actually . . . I'm a professional art scout," I say coolly.

"An *art* scout?" She looks taken aback.

"Yes, Professor Rebecca Bloomwood from the Guggenheim junior department. I'm sorry, I don't have my card." I shake her hand in a brisk, professional way. "I'm over here on business. We scouts like to visit school art events incognito, assess the new talent coming through. And I've found some, right here."

I point at Ernie's dark, splodgy painting, and the headmistress follows my gaze uncertainly.

"That's by Ernest Cleath-Stuart," she says at last. "An interesting child, Ernest—"

"*Incredibly* gifted, as I'm sure I don't need to explain to you." I nod gravely. "Look at the subtle way he plants his message in the . . . the texture." I gesture at the sheep. "Look at the form. So easy to underestimate. But as a professional, I saw it at once."

The headmistress's brow is wrinkled as she peers at the painting.

"Quite," she says at last.

"I'm sure an excellent school such as yours is drawing out this unique child and nurturing him." I smile at her with gimlet eyes. "Because, believe me, you have something very special there. Does he have a scholarship for art?"

"Ernest? A *scholarship*?" The headmistress seems poleaxed at the very idea. "Well, no . . ."

"I foresee other schools wishing to poach this extraordinary talent." I give her another gimlet smile and glance at my watch. "Unfortunately I must go now, but thank you for your time—"

"Let me show you some work by our other pupils!" says the headmistress, hurrying along beside me as I head toward the door. "This is by a very talented little girl called Eloise Gibbons, who's now left us." She gestures at a painting of a field full of poppies, which looks just like a van Gogh.

"Derivative," I say dismissively, barely shooting it a glance. "Thank you so much. Good-bye."

I stride swiftly out of the school gates and head down the pavement, clamping my lips together so I don't laugh. Ha. Maybe they'll start to appreciate Ernie now. And I meant it! OK, it was a bit weird—but I still thought Ernie's dead sheep was the best thing in the whole place.

• • •

AS SOON AS I arrive at The Look, I can tell Danny's already here, from the limo parked outside and the cluster of girls on the ground floor, comparing autographs on their T-shirts.

I head up to the conference room on the top floor—and as I walk in, the big meeting is already in progress. There are plates of Shetland Shortbread everywhere and images of the new collection up on the walls, and the table is full of business people. Danny is in the middle of it, looking like a peacock in a bright blue and green coat over jeans. As he sees me, he waves and pats the chair next to him.

All the top executives from The Look are here, plus some people I don't recognize, who must be from Shetland Shortbread. Luke's friend Damian, who has become a consultant to Tarkie, is here as well. Brenda from our marketing department is doing a PowerPoint presentation, and she's on some kind of graph comparing preorders of the new Danny Kovitz collection to last year's.

"Absolutely thrilling," she's saying. "We've never had a reaction like it. So, thank you, Danny Kovitz, for a wonderful partnership; thank you, Shetland Shortbread, for coming on board—and here's to us all working together!"

"Awesome job you guys have done," says Danny. "Hey, Becky, you should have come to Scotland for the shoot! We had a blast! Did my bagpipes arrive yet, Zane?" He turns to a boy with dyed red hair, who is hovering behind his chair. He must be one of Danny's five zillion assistants.

"Um . . ." Zane is already whipping out his phone, looking anxious. "I can check . . ."

"You bought some bagpipes?" I can't help giggling. "Can you play the bagpipes?"

"As an *accessory*. Believe me, they're gonna be the new It bag. Hey, you should have bagpipes in the store display." Danny turns to Kathy, the head of merchandising, who instantly grabs her notepad, writes down *Bagpipes,* and underlines it three times.

"We're also tremendously excited by the prelaunch publicity we're getting," Brenda continues. "We've already had mentions in *Vogue* and the *Telegraph,* and I understand Lord Cleath-Stuart has recently done an interview with *Style Central* magazine."

"Tarkie's in *Style Central*?" I stare at her, wanting to giggle. *Style Central* is the most cutting-edge bible for avant-garde designers and fashion editors who live in places like Hoxton. And Tarkie is . . . well . . . Tarkie. I mean, he still wears the cricket sweater he had at Eton.

"He did it with me," chips in Danny reassuringly. "Don't worry, I did most of the talking. *Great* pictures," he adds. "He wasn't afraid to push the boundaries. There's, like, a real experimental edge to Tarquin, you know?"

"Really?" I say dubiously. Is this the same Tarquin we're talking about? Tarquin who still washes his face with carbolic soap, no matter how many bottles of designer face wash Suze buys him?

"Well, now." Trevor, our managing director, speaks for the first time, and everyone turns to listen. "While we're all gathered here, I would like to single out another person at this table. Becky was the inspired member of our staff who came up with this collaboration— introducing Danny Kovitz to the store in the first place, and now forging a relationship with Shetland Shortbread. Well done, Becky!"

There's a smattering of applause and I start to beam

modestly around, but Trevor holds up his hand to stop it.

"Not just that. As we're all aware, times are hard for the high street at the moment. However, Becky's department has demonstrated a *rise* in sales over the last month of seventeen percent!"

He pauses for effect, and everyone else shoots me looks of either awe or hatred. Gavin, our menswear director, has gone all red around the neck and has a sulky frown.

"And Becky's customer testimonials are incredible," Trevor adds. "Jamie, would you like to read some out?"

"Absolutely!" Jamie from customer services nods enthusiastically. "Here's one from Davina Rogers, a doctor. *Dear Sir, I would like to commend you on your personal-shopping department and, in particular, Rebecca Brandon. Her farsighted and discreet approach to shopping in these times has made all the difference to me. I will be returning many times.*"

I can't help glowing with pleasure. I had no idea Davina would write a letter! She emailed me a picture of herself at her reception—and she did look spectacular in that Alberta Ferretti dress.

"Here's another one," Jamie reaches for another printout. "*Finally someone understands what women need and want when they shop! Thank you so much, Chloe Hill.*"

I remember Chloe Hill. She bought up about ten pieces from the new Marc Jacobs collection and left them in the store. We arranged that the next evening Jasmine would go round to her house with the clothes in a bin bag and pretend to be a neighbor returning to New Zealand, off-loading unwanted clothes. Apparently Chloe's husband was there and was totally fooled. (The only hitch came when he suggested Chloe might give some of the clothes to their housekeeper and accused her of being small-minded when she said, "Not in a million years.")

"In honor of this achievement," Trevor is saying now, "we would like to present Becky with this small token and ask her: How on earth did you do it?"

To my astonishment, he produces a bouquet of flowers from under the table, passes it across to me, and leads a round of applause.

"There's no doubt who we'll be announcing as Employee of the Year next month," Trevor adds with a twinkle. "Congratulations, Becky."

"Wow." I can't help blushing with pleasure. "Thanks very much."

Employee of the Year! That's so cool! You get five grand!

"And now, seriously." Trevor barely waits a beat. "How *did* you do it, Becky? Can you explain the secret of your success?"

The applause dies away. Everyone around the table is waiting alertly for me to answer. I bury my face in the flowers and smell them, playing for time.

Thing is . . . I'm not sure I *want* to explain the secret of my success. Something tells me no one here would understand about delivering clothes to customers in bin bags. And even if they did, they'd all start asking tricky questions, like when did we start this initiative and who approved it and how does it accord with company policy?

"Who knows?" I look up at last with a smile. "Maybe all my customers are just trying to support the economy."

"But why only in your department?" Trevor looks frustrated. "Becky, we want to harness your methods and apply them to *all* departments, whether it's because of a particular product . . . a technique of selling . . ."

"Maybe it's the department layout," suggests a young guy in glasses.

"Yes, good idea!" I say quickly.

But Brenda is shaking her head. She's quite bright, Brenda; that's the trouble.

"Customer service is the key, in my opinion," she says. "You're obviously pressing the right buttons somewhere. Could I come and observe you for a few days?"

Oh my God. No *way* do we want Brenda skulking around. She'd instantly realize what we were doing and blab to Trevor.

"I don't think so," I say hastily. "Jasmine and I work very well as a team, with no one else. My worry is that if we start messing with the formula, we might jeopardize the success we've got."

I can see the word *jeopardize* lodge in Trevor's brain.

"Well, let's leave it for now," he says heavily. "Just keep doing what you're doing. Good work, everyone." He pushes his chair back and looks at me. "Danny and Becky, would you like a spot of lunch? We've booked a table at Gordon Ramsay, if that suits?"

"Yes please!" I say joyfully.

Lunch at Gordon Ramsay with the managing director! Employee of the Year! I am *so* heading toward the board of directors. As Trevor takes a call on his mobile, Danny pushes his chair over to mine.

"So, how's the party going?"

"Shhh!" I glare at him. "Not so loud!"

"I was at this fashion bash in Shoreditch last week and I thought of you." He offers me some gum. "I don't know what security firm you're using, but Fifteen Star Security is in *really* terrible form. The bouncers were, like, totally aggressive, and the valet parking was a shambles. So if you've booked them, you might want to think again."

For a moment I can't quite find an answer.

Bouncers? Valet parking? I haven't even *thought* about bouncers and valet parking.

"Well, I certainly won't use *that* company, then," I say, as convincingly as I can.

"Cool." Danny swings his feet up onto a chair. "Who are you using?"

"I'm just . . . er . . . firming up on security arrangements."

It's fine. Don't panic. I'll simply add it to the list: *Book bouncers and valet parking.*

"The guest bathrooms were *great,* though," he adds enthusiastically. "They were in a separate tent, and everyone got a foot massage. Are you hiring foot masseurs?"

I can't reply. I'm too gripped by horror.

Restrooms. *Shit.* How could I have forgotten restrooms? Was I expecting two hundred people to use Janice's en suite?

Surreptitiously, I write *Book loos* on my hand with a Biro.

"Of course I'm having foot masseurs." I try to sound nonchalant. "*And* hand masseurs. And . . . Reiki people."

I'm not letting some stupid fashion bash in Shoreditch beat *my* party.

"Excellent." His eyes gleam. "And Luke has no idea?"

"None. And keep your voice down!"

"Well, that won't last. No one ever threw a surprise party that was a genuine surprise."

"Yes, they did!" I retort crossly, but Danny is shaking his head.

"Take it from me, Becky. Some moron'll blab. Hey, look what I made for my goddaughter." He pulls out a little tartan T-shirt with MINNIE ROCKS in hot-pink letters.

It's always the same with Danny. Just as you're about to clonk him over the head for being so annoying, he does something really sweet and you fall in love with him all over again. I can't help throwing an arm around him and giving him a hug.

But, oh God. What if he's right?

AS I'M ARRIVING HOME, my mobile rings, and it's *finally* Bonnie calling me back.

"Bonnie!" I retreat into the bushes. "How are you?"

"I'm well, thank you." Bonnie sounds strained, and not like her usual self. "All's well."

I peer at the phone dubiously. "Bonnie, what's wrong? You sound really hassled."

"Well, the truth is . . ." Bonnie sighs. "Luke didn't react well when I tried to mention his shower gel just now. In fact, he became quite irritable with me."

"Oh, sorry," I say, guiltily. "Well, don't worry about that anymore. It was worth a try. How's the party going on your end?"

"We've had lots more acceptances today! I've made a file of all the details and special requests."

"Special requests?" I echo uncertainly.

"We've had requests for vegetarian food, kosher food, wheat-free food . . . I assume your caterers can take care of that? In addition, one guest needs a waiting area for his driver, another needs a baby-feeding area, one government minister would like to send in his security people first to sweep the area . . ."

"Right! No problem!"

I'm trying to sound confident and can-do, but inside I feel a bit daunted. Since when did birthday parties get so *complicated*?

"Becky?"

"Sorry." I wrench my mind back. "Bonnie, there's

something else. I need to ask you something." I take a deep breath. "Is Luke hiding something from me?"

There's silence and my heart plunges. I *knew* it.

"Is it about Minnie? Be honest."

"No, dear!" She sounds taken aback. "I haven't heard Luke talking about Minnie at all!"

"Oh." I rub my nose. "Well, something to do with work, then?"

There's another silence. The answer is obviously "yes." Suddenly I have an ominous feeling about this.

"Bonnie, I thought you were my friend," I say at last. "Why can't you tell me what's going on? Is it bad? Is it another court case?" My mind is racing with awful possibilities. "Is Luke in trouble? Is he *bankrupt*?"

"No!" Bonnie cuts in hastily. "Please, Becky, don't think anything like that!"

"Well, what am I supposed to think?" My voice rises in agitation. "I know Luke wants to shield me from all the bad things, but how can I help him if I don't know what's going on?"

"Becky, please don't get upset! It's not bad! It's simply . . . a new client."

"Oh."

The wind is slightly taken out of my sails. That's not what I was expecting. Although, now I remember it, Luke did mention another new client, didn't he? But why is it a huge secret?

"Who is it?"

"I can't tell you," Bonnie says reluctantly. "Luke specifically asked me not to mention it. He thought you might get . . . overexcited. He wanted to be sure it would work out first."

"Overexcited?" I stare indignantly at the phone. "Bonnie, you *have* to tell me."

"I can't."

"Yes, you can! We're a team, remember?"

"I can't." Bonnie sounds pained. "Becky, you must realize that Luke is my boss—"

"And I'm your *friend*. Friends are more important than bosses! Everyone knows that."

There's silence, then Bonnie whispers, "Becky, I should go. I'll talk to you tomorrow."

She rings off and I watch the light in my phone die away. I walk over to the willow tree in the middle of the front lawn and sit on the old wooden bench. To be honest, I feel unsettled. What's going on with Luke? And how am I going to manage this party? I thought I was doing so well; I was so pleased with myself. But now I'm feeling panicky.

Security guards. Valet parking. Kosher food. Restrooms. Foot masseurs. Oh God, oh God. How am I going to afford all this? Why have I spent so long making stupid pom-poms? What *else* do I need to think about?

Suze would know. Suze goes to posh parties all the time. But I can't ask her. Not now.

On impulse, I open my BlackBerry and scroll down the acceptance list. The more names I read, the worse I feel. Why can't Luke have *normal* friends? Why do they all have to be so posh and important? These people will be used to grand receptions in smart venues. They're used to marble pillars and string quartets and waiters in white coats . . .

"Becky?" Mum is standing at the front door, with a concerned look. "Are you OK, love?"

"I'm fine," I say brightly. "Just . . . thinking."

There's no way in a million years I'm admitting I'm worried about the party.

Mum disappears again and I nibble my thumbnail. Well, I don't have any choice, do I? I'll have to book the bouncers and the restrooms and the masseurs and everything else. And just pay for it . . . somehow.

I wince as I think over my finances. I can't take the money out of the joint account, because Luke will see. And I can't take it out of my own account, because there's nothing to take out. There's no way the bank will extend my overdraft. Not at the moment. And I've already maxed out half my cards. All the credit companies are so *stingy* these days.

Could I contact my old bank manager, Derek Smeath, and plead for a special emergency party overdraft? He'd understand, surely. And he always liked Luke, and I could invite him to the party—

I sit bolt upright. No. I've got it. I'll ask Trevor for my Employee of the Year money in advance. He can't refuse me, can he? Not after all those nice things he said about me.

In fact, while I'm at it . . . why don't I ask him for a raise?

I'm so relieved, I almost laugh out loud. Why didn't I think of that before? He's just presented me with flowers, for God's sake. My department is the best by miles. It's bucking all the trends. It's *obvious* I should get a raise. I'll ask for a confidential meeting and I'll calmly ask for a small yet significant raise, and together with the Employee of the Year money, that will pay for everything.

Maybe a medium-size yet significant raise. Even better.

And meanwhile I'll Google *expensive luxury party-planning details*, just to see what else I've forgotten.

Feeling a million times better, I get up from the bench and am heading inside as a text bleeps on my phone. I pull it out, to see it's from Bonnie.

Becky dear. I have been torn by guilt. I feel you are right. Your friendship has come to mean a great deal to me and the major part of any friendship has to be trust. I will there-

fore trust you and send by separate text the
name of the new client which Luke is keeping
from you (for all the best reasons I must assure you).

   Please delete these texts straightaway
after reading. I hope and believe that you
will respect the fact that I am risking a
certain amount by divulging this information.
Please try not to give away to Luke the fact
that you know it. Some self-restraint may be
required on your part.
   Your affectionate friend
   Bonnie

I feel so touched as I read the words. Bonnie is my
friend. And I'm her friend. And that's what's important.
I hardly even care about the name of the client anymore. I mean, it'll only be some boring big-shot finance
type I've never heard of, probably.

As for saying I'll need self-restraint . . . for God's
sake. I think sometimes people who work in PR start to
believe their own hype. I press *Reply* and start texting
back:

Dear Bonnie Thank you so much. You are a
great friend to me. Don't worry I will not
give away to Luke by a smidgen that I know
the name of this client and I really don't
think self-restraint will be a problem—

A bleep interrupts me. Ooh, that might be Bonnie's
second text. I might as well go and have a look before I
continue. I click on it and wait for the message to ap-
pear on the screen.

It consists of two words only. For a moment I stand

stock still, blinking, not quite able to process what I'm seeing.

Sage Seymour.

Sage Seymour the movie star? *She's* the new client? But . . . but . . . how on earth . . .

No. It can't be true. It's ridiculous. Luke doesn't represent movie stars.

But then, Bonnie wouldn't say it, unless—

Sage Seymour?

How did this happen? How did he go from representing boring old banks to actresses? And why has he kept so quiet about it?

I'm almost hyperventilating. I keep looking up and then looking down at the screen again, just to check it still says the same thing.

Sage Seymour's the coolest movie star *ever.* She was in that one about the Nazis. She wore that amazing nude beaded dress to the Oscars. I've always, always, always wanted to meet her.

And Luke's *met* her? He's *working* with her?

Why didn't he TELL ME?

Sage Seymour—Google Search

Suggestions:

Google Earth

Google Maps

Google.com

Google Wave

Google Translate

Google Chrome

Google Voice

Recent Searches:

sage seymour luke brandon

sage seymour luke brandon new publicist

sage seymour becky brandon

sage seymour fashion

jimmy choo 50 percent off

madonna children school

claudia schiffer children school

expensive luxury party planning details

budget luxury party planning details

valet parking oxshott

alexander wang handbag

alexander wang handbag sale

venetia carter discredited and ruined

sage seymour pink swimming pool

sage seymour new best friend

FOURTEEN

I CANNOT BELIEVE Luke hasn't told me about Sage Seymour.

I would never, ever, *ever* keep such a big secret from him. In fact, I'm quite shocked. Is this how he thinks a marriage works? With one person knowing a movie star and not telling the other one?

Obviously I can't let him know that I know, because that would be betraying Bonnie's confidence. But I *can* give him cutting little glances now and then, as though to say, "Yes, well, someone's got a great big secret, haven't they?"

"Becky, is something wrong?" Luke looks at me, puzzled, as he passes by, hefting two massive carrier bags to the removal lorry. The guys have been here for an hour and we're nearly all packed up.

"No!" I say tartly. "What could possibly be wrong?" Luke scans my face for a minute, then sighs.

"Oh God. I get it." He dumps the bags down and puts his arms around me. "I know it's a difficult day for you. Of course, it'll be great to have our own space—but we've been happy living here. It's the end of an era."

"It's not about the 'end of an era'!" I want to yell at

him. Why would I care about that? It's "Why didn't you let me meet the famous movie star?"

I can't believe I've missed such an amazing opportunity. We could all have had dinner together by now. We probably would have really hit it off. Sage and I would have exchanged phone numbers and become best friends and she would have invited me out to her home in Malibu, where she's got that shell-pink-mosaic swimming pool. It looks *amazing*.

I can just see us, floating on lilos, drinking smoothies, chatting about life. She could have told me how she gets her hair that amazing treacly color, and I could have told her exactly where she went wrong with that last boyfriend of hers. (Because I totally disagree with that columnist in *Heat* magazine—the split was *not* inevitable.) And then we could have gone shopping and been snapped by paparazzi and started a whole new trend with scarves or something.

But Luke's keeping me out of it. On purpose. He doesn't *deserve* a surprise party. I'm so grouchy, I almost feel like telling him.

"Becky?" I look up to see Jess coming into the drive. "Good luck with your new house," she says matter-of-factly. "Here's a housewarming present."

She hands me a massive bulky bag made of strong brown paper, and I peep inside. Bloody hell. What on earth is that?

"Wow, thanks! Is it . . . candy floss?" I say uncertainly.

"Insulation lagging," says Jess. "Houses in this country are shockingly poor on insulation. Put it in your loft. Save some energy."

"Lovely!" I pat it gingerly. "So, how are you? I've hardly seen you."

"I've been visiting friends. I try not to stay here for

more than a night at a time." Jess lowers her voice darkly. "She's doing my head in. Tom's too."

"Janice?" I whisper back sympathetically. "Is she still going on about you having a baby?"

"Worse! She knows she can't talk about it, because Tom'll shout her down. So she's resorted to other measures."

"What measures?" I say, intrigued.

"She gave me this herbal drink the other day. She said I seemed 'run-down.' But I didn't trust her, so I looked it up online. It's only a natural fertility drug and libido enhancer." She looks outraged. "Tom had already drunk three cups!"

"No way!" I feel like giggling, except Jess is so fierce, I don't dare.

"I wish this was us, moving out to our own place." She looks wistfully at the van.

"Well, why don't you?"

"We'll be going back to South America in a few weeks." Jess shrugs. "There's no point, and we don't have any spare cash. But, I'm telling you, if she does one more thing—"

"Come and stay with us!" Impulsively, I squeeze her arm. "We'll have a fab time, and I promise not to feed you any fertility drugs."

"Really?" Jess looks surprised. "But your mum and dad said you didn't want anyone visiting your house till it was ready."

"Er . . . kind of." I clear my throat.

I haven't had a chance to explain the situation to Jess. I'll call her later, when we're at the rented place.

"Ready to go?" Luke is calling. He dropped our car off at the house yesterday, so we're going in the removal truck. It's the coolest thing *ever*. It's got a row of seats at the front so there's room for all of us, even Minnie. She's already strapped in to her booster with her snack box and is passing raisins one by one to the removal driver. (He's called Alf and luckily seems a very patient guy.)

We should *so* buy a great big truck, I think idly. I mean, it's the perfect family car. You'd never have to worry about having too much shopping again. We could all sit in the front and people would call us the Family in the Cool Truck, and—

"*Becky?*"

Oh. Oops. Everyone's waiting.

I head over to Mum and give her a hug. "Bye, Mum. And thanks so much for putting up with us."

"Oh, love." Mum waves it off. "Don't be silly." She glances at Dad. "Shall we . . ."

Dad nods and clears his throat self-consciously. "Before you go, darling, I'd just like to say a few words," he begins. Luke descends from the cab of the lorry with a questioning look and I shrug back. I had no idea Dad was planning to make a speech.

"I thought this day would never happen." Dad's voice rings round the tarmac drive. "Our daughter has bought a house!" He pauses momentously. "We're very, very proud, aren't we, Jane?"

"We used to say, 'Who on earth would ever give our little Becky a mortgage?'" Mum chimes in. "We were quite worried, love! But now you've got a beautiful house in Maida Vale!"

I can't look at Luke. I'm standing there in silence, chewing my lip, feeling more and more uncomfortable. I mean, I know we will have a house soon. So I haven't *exactly* lied. But still.

"And so, in honor of the occasion . . ." Dad clears his throat again, suddenly sounding choked up. "Becky, we'd like you to have this." He hands me a present, wrapped up in tissue paper.

"Oh my God! You shouldn't have!" I pull the tissue off—and it's the picture of the lady with the flowers.

The painting that's been hanging on the upstairs landing for as long as I can remember.

"Wh-*what*?" I look up in shock. "I can't take this! This belongs here!"

"Oh, sweetheart." Mum suddenly looks misty-eyed. "When you were a little girl, you always said you wanted that picture in your room. And I used to say, 'You can have it when you're a grown-up lady with your very own house.'" She dabs at her eyes. "And now here you are, darling. A grown-up lady with your very own house."

I've never felt more guilty in my life.

"Well . . . thanks, Mum," I stutter. "I'm really honored. It'll have pride of place in our home."

"Maybe in that lovely hallway!" suggests Mum. "It would look beautiful with that fireplace." Mum's looked at the house's details online so many times, she probably knows it better than me.

"Yes, maybe." My face is boiling by now.

Oh God. This is unbearable. We must get on to the lawyer and speed everything up. And as *soon* as we're in the proper house, we'll have them over, and we'll put the picture up and everything will be OK.

"You will tell us when we can visit," says Mum longingly.

"Well . . . we'll come and see *you* very soon," I say, avoiding a direct answer. "I'll call you later, Mum."

Luke and I clamber up into the cab of the lorry and Alf looks over. He's so wizened he looks about a hundred and three, although apparently he's only seventy-one. He's already told us he's got a bad hip and a dodgy shoulder and a dicky chest, so the other lads are meeting him at the site to help move the boxes. "Ready?" he rasps, his gold tooth glinting.

"Yes, let's go."

"Young lady want her raisins back?" He's got a whole

fistful of them, I suddenly notice. Some of them chewed.

"Minnie!" I scold. "I'm *so* sorry, let me take those from you . . ." I hastily cram the raisins back into Minnie's snack box, then breathe out as the lorry rumbles out of the drive.

"So, Mrs. Homeowner," says Luke sardonically. "You must be feeling very proud."

"Shut up!" I clasp my head in my hands. "Look . . . it'll be OK. I'll give it a couple of days and then I'll phone home and make something up about the house needing renovation and say we're renting somewhere. They'll be fine. And then as soon as we *do* get the house we'll have a big dinner for everyone."

"Christmas dinner, maybe." Luke nods. "Next year."

"What?" I stare at him in horror. "Don't be silly! It's not going to take *that* long to get the house. The lawyer said it would all be sorted out quickly!"

"Which in lawyer-speak means Christmas next year."

"No, it *doesn't*—"

"Is that your mum?" interrupts Alf conversationally.

"What?"

"Blue Volvo? They're following us." He nods at the wing mirror and I stare into it in disbelief. There they are. Driving along, right behind us. What's Mum doing, following us?

I whip out my phone and speed-dial her number.

"Mum, what are you *doing*?" I say with no preamble.

"Oh, Becky!" Her voice rings out. "You've ruined the surprise! Graham, I *told* you to stay farther back! They've seen us!"

"Mum, listen to me." I know I sound jumpy, but I can't help it. "You're not supposed to be coming with us. We said we'd *tell* you when we were ready for you to come and visit."

"Becky, love!" Mum laughs. "This is your first house! The first property you've ever owned! We don't mind what state it's in!"

"But—"

"Darling, I know what you said. And, to be honest, we were planning to let you have your privacy. But then we couldn't resist it! We couldn't let you just slip off without helping you. I've brought some tea cakes, and Dad's got his tools. We'll help you get shipshape in no time . . ."

My heart is thudding. There's no way I can let them turn up to some crummy rented townhouse. Not after Dad's speech.

"We could even pop round and meet your new neighbors!" Mum's still talking cheerily. "They might turn out to be good friends to you, Becky. I mean, look at Janice and me, friends after thirty years. I can remember the day we moved in, and Janice came round with a bottle of sherry . . . Ooh, Dad says, can you remind him of the address in case we get separated?"

My mind works like a spring trap.

"Mum, I can't hear you . . . I'm losing you . . ." I rub the phone against my bag to make a kerfuffly noise, then switch it off and look at Luke. "It's OK. They don't know the address." I turn urgently to Alf. "We need to lose them."

"*Lose* them?"

"Yes! Like in cop films. Duck down a side alley or whatever."

"A side alley?" He sounds startled. "What side alley, dear?"

"I don't know! Find one. You know, like in car chases!" Doesn't he *watch* movies?

"I think my wife wants you to drive very fast down a narrow one-way street the wrong way, knock over a barrow of fruit, send crowds of people screaming, roll the van 360 degrees, and manage to elude my parents-in-law *that* way," says Luke in a deadpan voice. "I'm assuming you are a stunt removal driver?"

"Shut up." I hit him on the chest. "Do you realize the situation we're in?"

"If it were up to me, we wouldn't be in this situation," he says calmly. "Because we would have told your parents the truth in the first place."

We pull up at a set of traffic lights. Mum and Dad pull up alongside and wave merrily, and I wave back with a sick grin.

"OK," I instruct Alf. "When the lights change, you go!"

"Love. This is a lorry, not a Ferrari."

The lights change, and I start gesturing *Go, go!* with my hands. Alf shoots me a baleful look and puts the truck into gear unhurriedly.

Honestly. I feel like offering to drive myself.

"Sorry, folks. Fuel stop." Alf pulls in to a service station and, sure enough, Mum and Dad's Volvo follows us. A few moments later, Mum has got out of the car, bustled over, and is knocking on the door of the cab.

"Everything all right?" she calls up.

"Of course!" I wind down the window and smile brightly. "Just getting some petrol."

"I've got Janice on the line. You wouldn't mind if she came along too, would you, love?"

What?

Before I can answer, Mum's turned back to the phone. "Yes, we're at the BP with the café. . . . See you in a tick!" She turns to me. "Janice and Martin were in the car already, coming back from Yogacise. There they are!" She waves frantically as a black Audi turns in at the service-station entrance. "Yoo-hoo!"

"Becky!" Janice leans out of the window as the Audi

approaches. "You don't mind, do you, dear? Your mum's told us *all* about the house. So exciting!"

"You follow us," Mum is telling Martin. "And we'll follow the truck."

I don't believe this. We've got a convoy.

"Put *Maida Vale* in your sat nav, Martin," Mum's saying bossily. "That way, even if we *do* get separated— Becky, what's the exact address?" she calls over to me.

"I . . . er . . . I'll text you . . ."

I've got to tell her the truth. I've got to. Right now.

"The thing is, Mum . . ." I swallow and look over at Luke for support, but he's got out of the truck and is taking a call on the forecourt.

"No, it's *not* fucking OK," I can hear him saying.

Oh God. He looks really angry. What's going on?

"Becky." I jump as Janice appears out of nowhere, blinking at me through the cab window. She's wearing a bright-pink yoga outfit, which hurts my eyes, together with knee-highs and clogs. It's a look which some edgy nineteen-year-old model could just about carry off. "I wanted a little discreet word, while Luke is out of the way." She lowers her voice almost to a whisper. "It's about the p-a-r-t-y. I was reading *Hello!* the other day. That 'Royal Fashion' party. Did you see it?"

I nod absently, watching Luke. He's moved away from the cab, but I'm pretty sure he's yelling at somebody. And I'm pretty sure I wouldn't like Minnie to hear his language.

Is he having a row with Sage Seymour? Is he breaking things off with her before I've even had a chance to meet her and become her best friend? If so, I will *kill* him.

". . . and they had a touch-up area for all the celebrities!" Janice finishes with a flourish. "You see?"

I must have missed a beat somewhere.

"Sorry, Janice." I smile apologetically. "I wasn't quite following you."

"I'm a *makeup artist,* love," she says, as though it's obvious. "And I'd like to volunteer to host a little touch-up area myself. I'll make up all the guests! It will be my gift to Luke."

I'm speechless. Janice is *not* a makeup artist. She did one course at the adult-learning institute and learned how to apply peach blusher and highlighter in badger stripes to a plastic dummy's cheeks. And now she wants to make up people at my party?

"Janice . . . that's so sweet," I say as convincingly as I can. "But you mustn't miss the fun."

"We'd have shifts!" she says triumphantly. "I've got a team of chums, you know! We were all in the course together, so we all use the same techniques."

The idea of a team of Janices, all clutching palettes of frosted eyeshadow, makes me feel a bit faint.

"Right," I manage. "Well, that would be really . . . something."

OK. I need to put this on my to-do list, right at the top. *Do not let Janice do any makeup on the guests.*

"Better go," she breathes dramatically. "Luke approaching at one o'clock."

Before I can say anything else, she's slipped away to her car, just as Luke gets back into the driver's cab.

"Unbelievable." He's breathing fast and his jaw is rock-hard. "Unbe*liev*able."

"What is it?" I say nervously. "And don't swear in front of Minnie."

"Becky, I've got bad news." Luke looks directly at me. "The townhouse has fallen through. We can't have it."

For a nanosecond I think he must be joking. But his face doesn't flicker.

"But . . ."

"Some fucking moron at the office rented it to another tenant. They've already taken possession and our agent has only just realized."

"But it's *ours!*" My voice is rising in panic. "We *need* that house!"

"I know. Believe me, they know it too. They're finding us an alternative within the hour or we're checking in to a hotel at their expense." He exhales. "What a total fuckup."

I feel a bit light-headed. This can't be happening.

"I'd better tell your parents—" Luke makes to get out.

"No!" I almost squeal. "We can't!"

"Well, what do *you* suggest doing?"

I can see Mum waving at me from the Volvo, and a moment later a text comes through on my phone.

Ready to go love?

"Let's just drive to Maida Vale." I lick my dry lips. "We might as well. And hopefully the agents will call on the way. We can busk it somehow."

Alf has hoisted himself back into the cab. "Ready, folks?"

"Yes," I say, before Luke can speak. "Drive. Go."

It'll take us an hour to get to Maida Vale, I'm thinking. At least. And in the meantime, they'll sort us out with another house and we'll go there and it'll all be fine. It has to be.

EXCEPT IT ONLY TAKES forty minutes to reach Maida Vale. I can't believe it. Where's all the traffic gone? Is there a conspiracy against us?

We're driving up the main shopping road and we still don't have a house. My exterior is strangely calm, even though my heart is galloping with panic. As long as we keep driving, we're OK.

"Go more slowly," I tell Alf yet again. "Go some winding back route. Go down there!" I point at a narrow little street.

"No left turn," says Alf, shaking his head.

We've told Alf the whole story. Or, at least, he worked it out for himself, after Luke had a shouting match with the agent. (Luckily, Minnie's fallen asleep. Two-year-olds can sleep through *anything*.) Luke's started calling other rental agencies as well—but so far no one's got a house available that can be moved into within the next twenty minutes. I feel like screaming with frustration. Where are all the houses? And where's all the *traffic*?

I glance into the wing mirror, in case by any chance Mum and Dad have peeled off or got lost—but there they still are, sticking to us like glue. Luke's listening to a message on his phone and I gaze hopefully at him, but he shakes his head.

"So where d'you want me to go now?" Alf pauses at a junction, rests his arms on the throbbing steering wheel, and looks at me.

"I don't know," I say desperately. "Could you . . . circle?"

"*Circle?*" He gives me a sardonic look. "Do I look like an airplane?"

"Please. Just for a bit."

Shaking his head, Alf signals left and turns down a residential street. We go along the canal, then up another residential street, and are almost immediately back where we started.

"That was too quick!" I say in dismay.

Sure enough, a moment later a text comes through from Mum:

Darling is your driver lost? We've been down this
road before. Dad says what's the address he'll use
his sat nav.

"Becky." Luke has come off the phone. "We can't just
drive round Maida Vale until we have a house."

"Any luck, squire?" says Alf. He seems to have a new
respect for Luke, ever since he heard him swearing at
the agent. In fact, despite all his sardonic little looks, I
think he's enjoying the drama.

"None," replies Luke. "Becky, we're going to have to
come clean."

"No. Not yet. Let's . . . let's stop for lunch!" I say in
sudden inspiration. "We'll find a coffee shop or something. Luke, here's the plan. I'll keep Mum and Dad en-
tertained, and you go and see the agent and *force* him
to give us a house."

Alf rolls his eyes with forbearance and is soon trying
to maneuver the lorry into a space opposite a *Café
Rouge*. I watch the others pulling over too and see Janice getting out to guide Martin, with lots of beckoning
and pointing and "Careful, Martin!"

I unbuckle Minnie and we all get out, stretching our
legs. I feel like we've been on some massive road trip,
not just driven up from Oxshott.

"Hi!" I wave at the others, trying to look relaxed and
cheery, like this was always the plan.

"What's going on, love?" Mum is first to reach us. "Is
this it?" She's peering at all the flats above the shops, as
though one might suddenly turn out to be a family
house with a basement and a garden and two parking
spaces.

"Trust Becky to live among the shops." Martin gives
a chortle at his own wit.

"No, this isn't where we're going to live!" I laugh as
naturally as I can manage. "We're stopping for lunch."

There's a baffled silence.

"*Lunch*, love?" says Janice at last. "But it's only ten-twenty."

"Yes, well. The . . . um . . . the lorry driver has to have lunch. It's union regulations," I improvise, and shoot a meaningful look at Alf. "Isn't it, Alf?"

"But we must be only a few minutes away from the house," says Mum. "This is ridiculous!"

"I know," I say hurriedly. "But the union's really strict. We don't have a choice."

"Don't blame me," says Alf, playing along. "I don't make the rules."

"For goodness sake," says Dad impatiently. "I've never heard such nonsense." He turns to Alf. "Now, look here. Couldn't you drop Becky at the house and *then* have lunch?"

"Rules is rules," says Alf, shaking his head implacably. "I break 'em, I'm up before a disciplinary tribunal, and that's my job on the line, that is. I'll go and have my well-earned break and you let me know when you're ready to go, all right, my love?" He gives me a wink and heads into Café Rouge.

God, he's fantastic. I feel like giving him a hug.

"Well!" Mum seems outraged. "*Now* we know what's wrong with this country! Who wrote these rules, anyway? I'm writing to the *Daily World*, and to the prime minister . . ." As we troop into Café Rouge, she casts Alf a baleful look, and he waves cheerfully back.

"Everyone should order lots," I say as we find a table. "I mean, we'll be here awhile, waiting for Alf. Have a sandwich, a croissant, a steak—it's all on me . . . Minnie, *no*." I hastily remove the sugar lumps before she can grab them all.

"Where's Luke?" says Mum suddenly.

"He's at the estate agent's," I say truthfully.

"Getting the keys, I expect," says Dad, nodding cheerfully. "I think I'll have a panini."

I TRY TO spin out lunch for as long as I can. But no one wants steak at ten-twenty in the morning, and there are only so many croissants you can eat. We've each had two cappuccinos, and Luke still hasn't texted any good news, and Minnie's already bored with all the toys in the play box. And now, to my alarm, Mum and Dad are getting fidgety.

"This is ridiculous!" Mum says, as she watches Alf order yet another hot chocolate. "I'm not waiting round here for some jobsworth driver to finish his lunch! Graham, you wait here, and Becky and I will walk to the house. We can walk from here, can't we, love?"

I feel a stab of alarm.

"I don't think that's a good idea, Mum," I say hurriedly. "I think we should wait for Luke and all go in the van."

"Don't be silly! We'll call Luke and tell him we're going straight there. We can pick the keys up on the way. What's the address? Is it near?"

Mum's already gathering her things together and picking up Minnie's mittens. This isn't good. I need to keep everyone contained in Café Rouge.

"I'm not sure exactly where it is," I say hastily. "Really, it would be much better to wait. Let's have another coffee—"

"No problem!" Janice has produced a little A–Z, bound in red leather. "I never travel anywhere without it," she explains brightly. "Now, what's the name of your new road, Becky? I'll be able to locate it in a trice!"

Shit.

Everyone's looking at me expectantly. The minute I

say the name of the road, they'll walk there and find out the truth.

"I . . . um . . ." I rub my nose, playing for time. "I . . . can't remember."

"You can't *remember*?" says Janice uncertainly. "Your own address?"

"Love," says Mum with barely concealed impatience. "You must know where you live!"

"I just don't remember the exact name of the street! I think it begins with . . . *B*," I add randomly.

"Well, ring Luke!"

"He's not answering," I say hastily. "He must be busy."

Mum and Dad are exchanging looks, as though they never realized they had such a half-wit for a daughter.

"I'm not sitting here any longer!" Mum clicks her tongue. "Becky, you said it was only a few streets away from the shops. We'll just walk around, and you're bound to recognize it when we come to it. Graham, you wait here for Luke."

She's standing up. There's nothing I can do. I shoot an agonized glance at Alf and call, "Just going for a walk!"

"Now, *think*, Becky," says Mum, as we all pile out to the street except Dad. "Which direction is it?"

"Er . . . that way, I think." I immediately point in the opposite direction of the house, and we all start trooping along.

"Is it Barnsdale Road?" Janice is running a finger down the A–Z index. "Barnwood Close?"

"I don't *think* so—"

"Becky, love!" Mum erupts. "How can you not remember the name of your own street? You're a *homeowner*. You have to take *responsibility*! You have to—"

"Daddy!" says Minnie in sudden joyful tones. "Daddeee!"

She's pointing inside the nearby glass frontage of the estate agent's office. There's Luke, right in the window, laying into Magnus, who looks absolutely terrified.

Shit. Why did I come this way?

"Is that your estate agent?" Mum glances up at the RIPLEY AND CO. sign. "Well, that's all right! We can go in, find out the address, and get the keys from them! Well done, Minnie, darling!"

"Luke seems rather cross about something," Janice observes, as Luke starts making savage gestures at Magnus. "Is it the fixtures and fittings, love? Because my advice is, it's not worth it. Let them *take* the shower curtain. Don't end up in court, like my brother did—"

"Come on, Becky!" Mum is halfway toward the door. "What's wrong?"

I'm rooted to the spot.

"Mum . . ." My voice is a bit strangled. "There's . . . something I need to tell you. About the house. The truth is . . . I haven't been totally honest."

Mum stops dead. As she turns, there are little spots of pink on her cheeks.

"I knew it. I *knew* there was something. You've been hiding something from us, Becky! What is it?" Her face drops as though with a sudden horrific thought. "Is there no off-street parking?"

I hear sharp inhalations from both Janice and Martin. In Surrey, parking is practically a religion.

"It's not that. It's . . ." My breath is coming so quickly I can barely talk. "It's . . ."

"Mrs. Brandon." A man in a suit whom I don't recognize is hurrying out of the estate agent's, onto the pavement. "David Ripley, managing partner." He holds out a hand. "Please don't stand out here in the cold. Let me offer you a cup of coffee at least. I'm well aware of your unfortunate situation, and believe me, we are doing *everything* in our power to find you a home, as *soon* as possible."

I can't look at Mum. I can't look at anyone. The only thing that can save me now is a freak tornado.

"Find Becky a home?" Mum echoes uncertainly.

"We're devastated about the rental property mix-up," David Ripley continues. "Your deposit will be re-funded immediately—"

"*Rental* property?"

The sharpness in Mum's voice gets through even to David Ripley, who turns at once.

"I'm so sorry, is this your mother?" He extends a hand. "How do you do. Let me assure you, we're doing everything we can to house your daughter—"

"But she's *got* a house!" says Mum shrilly. "She's *bought* a house! We're here to pick up the keys! Why else do you think we're all here in Maida Vale?"

David Ripley looks from Mum to me in confusion.

"I'm so sorry—is there something I haven't been told?"

"No," I say, hot with mortification. "My mother hasn't quite got . . . the whole picture. I need to talk to her."

"Ah." David Ripley lifts his hands with a delicate ges-ture and backs off toward the office. "Well, I'll be inside if you need me."

"Mum . . ." I swallow hard. "I know I should have told you . . ."

"Martin," murmurs Janice, and they discreetly move away to look at a travel agent's window. Mum is just standing there, her brow contorted with incomprehen-sion and disappointment.

Suddenly I feel like crying. My parents were so proud of me, buying my first-ever house. They told all their friends. And here I am, screwing everything up, as usual.

"There was a delay with the house," I mumble, staring at the pavement. "And we couldn't bear to tell you, because you were so hassled with us cluttering up the place at home. So we rented somewhere—except then that house fell through too. So . . . we're homeless." I force myself to raise my head. "I'm sorry."

"We've driven all this way . . . and you haven't got a house?"

"Yes. I mean, we will get one, but—"

"You mean . . . you deliberately misled us? You let Dad make his little speech? You let us give you the painting? And it was all *lies*?"

"It wasn't *lies*, exactly—"

"Well, what else was it?" Mum explodes, and I flinch. "Here we all are, traipsing around Maida Vale; Janice and Martin have made all this effort; we've all brought housewarming presents—"

"I told you not to come!" I say defensively, but Mum doesn't seem to hear.

"Everything you do, Becky, is a fiasco! Everything is a fantasy! What's your father going to say? Do you know how disappointed he'll be?"

"We will get a house!" I say desperately. "We will, I promise! And you can have the painting back until then."

"This is *just* like George Michael—"

"It is *not*!" I cut her off, stung. "It is *not* George Michael all over again." I furiously brush away a tear. "It's only . . . a little hitch."

"It's always a little hitch, love! Always!" Mum sounds beside herself. "The party will be just the same—"

"No, it *won't*!" I almost roar. "And I never *asked* you to drive all this way, did I? Or buy me presents. And if you don't want to come to Luke's party, Mum, then you needn't! In fact, please don't!"

Tears are streaming down my face by now, and I can

see Janice and Martin studiously staring at the special offers to Morocco as though they're gripped by them.

"No!" Minnie's gazing up at me in distress. "No cry!"

"OK." Luke's voice suddenly rings out, and I look up to see him striding toward us. "I've sorted it. They're putting us up—" He breaks off and looks from face to face. "What's up? What's happened?"

Mum says nothing, but her mouth tightens.

"Nothing," I mutter miserably. "We were just . . . talking."

"Right," says Luke, clearly flummoxed. "Well, I've negotiated a two-bedroom serviced apartment at The West Place until they find us alternative accommodation."

"The West Place!" Janice turns round from the travel agent's window. "We saw that on TV! Remember, Martin, that lovely new hotel with the rooftop spa? With all the mosaics?"

"Yes, well, I wasn't taking any shit." Luke flashes her a brief smile. "We can move in today; the stuff will go into storage . . ." He trails off, clearly aware of the tension in the air. "So . . . is that OK by you? Becky?"

"Mum should take it." The words come out of my mouth even before I've properly thought them through. "Mum and Dad should have it."

"O-kaay," says Luke hesitantly. "Well, that's certainly one way to do it . . ."

"We've put Mum and Dad out for all this time, and now we've let them down. We should let them enjoy the luxury apartment. And then . . . regroup."

I'm staring into the middle distance; I can't bring myself to look at Mum. Luke's head is swiveling between us as though for clues; I can see Janice mouthing something urgently at him.

"Jane?" Luke says finally. "Would that suit you? To stay in The West Place for a little while?"

"It would suit very well," says Mum in clipped, un-natural tones. "Thank you, Luke. I'll just call Graham and tell him."

Mum obviously can't look at me either. Well, good thing we won't be living together anymore.

"I'll take Minnie to look at the shops," I say, taking Minnie's hand. "Let me know when it's time to go home."

WE EVENTUALLY make it home by four o'clock. Mum and Dad went back first and packed some things, and Luke settled them into the serviced apartment, which apparently is amazingly swanky. Not that I want to hear about it.

I've made Minnie her supper and put on Peppa Pig and am sitting by the fire, staring morosely into the flames, when Luke arrives back. He heads into the room and watches me for a moment.

"Becky, come on. What's up between you and your mum?"

"Shhh!" says Minnie crossly, and points at the TV. "Peppa!"

"Nothing." I turn away.

"Something's going on," Luke persists, crouching down beside my chair. "I've never known you and your mum like this before."

I look at him silently as answers crowd into my mind.

She thinks I can't throw you a party. She thinks it'll all be a failure.

And, deep down, I'm petrified she might be right.

"Just mother–daughter stuff," I say eventually.

"Huh." He raises a skeptical eyebrow. "Well, I'm glad we've got some time alone. There's something I want to talk to you about."

He draws up a chair and I watch, a little apprehensively.

"You were right, Becky," he says frankly. "I was keeping something from you. And I'm sorry. But I wanted to be sure before I said anything."

Instantly, my mood lifts. He's going to tell me about Sage Seymour! Yes! Maybe we're all going to meet up tonight! Maybe he wants to take us out for dinner at The Ivy or somewhere! I know she's filming at Pinewood Studios at the moment, because I Googled her (simply because I take an interest in my husband's career, like any supportive wife would do).

Oh, this will *totally* make up for a shitty day. And I can wear that Nanette Lepore dress I've never worn, with my pink Vivienne Westwood shoes.

"Don't worry, Luke." I beam at him. "I know you have to be discreet."

Maybe she'll ask me to be her personal shopper! Maybe Luke has recommended me! I could dress her for the Golden Globes. I could *go* to the Golden Globes. I mean, she'll need someone to make sure her hem's straight—

"I've recently been in touch with a contact I have. A guy who represents . . . celebrities," Luke says slowly.

"Really?" I try to sound offhand. "What sort of celebrities?"

"Have you by any chance heard of someone called . . ."

Have I *heard* of her? Is he nuts? She's got an Oscar, for God's sake! She's one of the most famous women in the world!

"Of course I have!" I blurt out excitedly, just as he says:

". . . a woman called Nanny Sue?"

For an instant we stare at each other in confusion.

"Nanny *Sue*?" I echo at last.

"She's a child-care expert, apparently." Luke shrugs. "Has a show on TV? I hadn't heard of her myself."

I'm so frustrated, I feel like slapping him. Number one, *obviously* I've heard of Nanny Sue, and he hasn't only because he doesn't watch enough TV. Number two, why are we talking about her and not Sage Seymour?

"Yes, I have," I say grudgingly. "I've got her book. What about her?"

"It seems she's planning to start a new private enterprise. A kind of . . ." He hesitates, not meeting my eye. "A children's behavior-management camp."

He can't be serious.

"You want to send Minnie to a *boot camp*?" The words almost stick in my throat. "But . . . but . . . that's ridiculous! She's only two! They wouldn't even take her!"

"Apparently in exceptional cases they will accept children as young as that."

My mind is swirling in shock. There I was, sitting happily, thinking he was about to tell me we're having cocktails with a movie star tonight. And instead he's saying he wants to send our daughter away?

"Is it"—I swallow hard—"*residential*?"

I feel hollow at the thought. He wants to send her to boarding school for naughty children. I have a sudden image of Minnie in a braided blazer, her head cowed, sitting in the corner and holding a sign saying, *I must not order sixteen coats off the Internet.*

"Of course not!" Luke seems shocked. "It'll simply be a program for children with particular behavioral issues. And it's only an idea." He rubs the back of his neck, still not looking at me. "I've already spoken to this Nanny Sue. I explained the situation and she seemed very understanding. She'll come and assess

Minnie for us if we like and make a recommendation. So I made an appointment."

"You *what*?" I can't believe this. "You've already *spoken* to her?"

"I was just finding out what the options were." At last Luke meets my gaze. "Becky, I don't like the idea any more than you do. But we have to do *something*."

"No, we don't!" I want to yell. "And we especially don't have to invite strangers into our home to tell us what to do!"

But I can tell: He's set on this. It's just like that time on our honeymoon when he decided we should take the train to Lahore, not fly. He's not going to budge.

Well, fine. He can hire all the child-care gurus he likes. No one's taking Minnie away from me. Let Nanny Sue come and do her worst. I'll see her off. Just watch me.

DR. JAMES LINFOOT

36 HARLEY STREET   LONDON W1

Rebecca Brandon
The Pines
43 Elton Street
Oxshott
Surrey

3 March 2006

Dear Rebecca,

Thank you for your letter of 1 March.

I have never heard of "sleep-shopping." I therefore cannot
give you the Latin name for it, nor write to your husband
and tell him he must "respect your medical condition."

I suggest you visit your local GP if symptoms persist.

Kind regards,

James Linfoot

FIFTEEN

SO NOW I'M NOT talking to Mum and I'm barely talking to Luke either.

It's more than a week later. Nanny Sue's coming today, and I'm totally prepared. I feel like a gladiator, ready to go into the arena with all my swingy metal spikes and bludgeons. But I'm still livid with Luke. In fact, the more time goes on, the angrier I feel. How could he have arranged all this without consulting me? We're at breakfast and we've hardly spoken two words to each other. Certainly neither of us has mentioned Nanny Sue.

"Do you want some more milk, Minnie?" I say in chilly tones, and reach past Luke for the jug. Luke sighs.

"Becky, we can't go on like this. We have to talk."

"Fine. Let's talk." I shrug. "What about? The weather?"

"Well . . . how's your work?"

"It's OK." I stir my coffee noisily.

"Excellent!" Luke sounds so hearty I want to cringe. "Things are good for us too. Looks like we'll be finalizing a meeting with Christian Scott-Hughes any day now. The client's been wanting to line something up with him for more than a year, so they're thrilled."

Whoopee-doo. Like I'm interested in some boring old meeting with Christian Scott-Hughes.

"Great," I say politely.

"Unfortunately, I'm going to have to bollock my personal assistant today. Not so good." He sighs. "Didn't see that one coming."

What? He's doing *what*?

I raise my head, unable to keep up my distant demeanor anymore. He's going to bollock *Bonnie*? How can he bollock Bonnie? She's perfect! She's lovely!

"But . . . I thought you loved her," I say, trying to sound only mildly interested. "I thought she was the best assistant you've ever had."

"I thought so too. But recently she's become . . ." Luke hesitates. "I can only describe it as inappropriate."

I can't imagine Bonnie being inappropriate for one moment.

"What do you mean? What's she done?"

"It's odd." Luke passes a hand over his brow, looking perplexed. "Most of the time she behaves with impeccable discretion and tact. And then all of a sudden she'll lurch into territory that, frankly, is none of her business. Like commenting on my *shower gel,* of all things." Luke frowns. "I really think that's unprofessional behavior, don't you?"

I feel the color creep into my cheeks. "Er . . . I suppose . . ."

"There have been other comments too, even more intrusive and personal. To be honest, I haven't hired her to give me opinions about my family or house. Or choice of ties."

Shit. *Shit.* This is all my fault. Except I can't exactly say that, can I?

"Well, I think you should give her another chance," I say hastily. "You don't want to upset her, do you? She was probably just making conversation. I'm sure she'll never be intrusive again. In fact, I'm positive."

Because I'll instantly ring her up and tell her to lay off the suggestions.

Luke gives me a strange look. "Why does it matter to you? You hardly know her."

"I just feel very strongly that people should be given a chance! And I think you should give this assistant another chance. What's her name again, Bobbie?" I add innocently.

"Bonnie," Luke corrects me.

"*Bonnie.*" I nod. "Of course. I've really met her only once, at the Christmas party," I add for good measure.

I shoot a surreptitious glance at Luke, but he doesn't seem suspicious. Thank God.

"I must go." He gets up, wiping his mouth. "So . . . I hope it goes well today." He kisses Minnie. "Good luck, poppet."

"She's not running the Olympics," I retort curtly. "She doesn't need luck."

"Well, anyway, let me know how it goes." He hesitates awkwardly. "Becky, I know how you feel about . . . today. But I really think this could be the breakthrough we need."

I don't even bother answering him. There's no way some child-catching, boot-camp expert is having any "breakthrough" in my family.

BY TEN O'CLOCK I'm ready for her. The house is prepared, and I'm prepared, and even Minnie is all dressed up in her most innocent-looking Marie Chantal pinafore.

I've done my research. First of all, I looked up Nanny Sue's website and read every page. (Unfortunately, there's nothing about the boot camp on there yet, just a message saying: *My new series of behavior-management programs for children and adults will be launched soon—check for details.* Huh. I'm not surprised she's being cagey.)

Then I bought all her DVDs and watched them back-to-back. And it's always the same pattern. What happens is, there's a family with kids haring about and parents arguing and usually an old abandoned fridge in the garden or dangerous electrical sockets or something. Then Nanny Sue comes in and watches carefully on the side and says, "I want to see who the Ellises really *are*," which means, "You're doing loads of stuff wrong, but I'm not going to tell you what yet."

The parents always end up having a screaming match and then sobbing on Nanny Sue's shoulder and telling her their life history. And every week she gets out her little box of tissues and says gravely, "I think there's more to this than child behavior, isn't there?" and they nod and spill all about their sex life or job troubles or family tragedy and they play sad music and you end up crying too.

I mean, it's a total formula, and only complete suckers would end up falling for her tricks.

And now, presumably, she's going to crank up the drama and take all the children away to boot camp, somewhere really tough like Utah or Arizona, and it'll make even better telly when they're reunited.

Well, not here. No way.

I look around the kitchen, checking that everything is in place. I've put up a massive gold star chart on the fridge, and I've labeled the bottom step of the stairs the *Naughty Step,* and there's a stack of educational toys on the table. But with any luck my first salvo will work and she won't even get this far.

What you *can't* do with Nanny Sue is say, "My child doesn't have any problems," because then she catches

you out and finds some. So I'm going to be even clev-
erer than that.

The doorbell rings and I stiffen.

"Come on, Min," I murmur. "Let's go and get rid of
the nasty child expert."

I open the door—and there she is. Nanny Sue herself, with her trademark blond bob and neat little features and pink lipstick. She looks smaller in real life
and is wearing jeans, a striped shirt, and a padded
jacket like horse riders wear. I thought she'd be in her
blue uniform and hat, like she is on the telly. In fact,
I'm half-expecting the theme music to begin and a
voice-over to say: "Today, Nanny Sue has been called to
the house of the Brandons . . ."

"Rebecca? I'm Nanny Sue," she says in her familiar
West Country burr.

"Nanny Sue! Thank God! I'm so glad to see you!" I
say dramatically. "We're at our wits' end! You have to
help us, right here, right now!"

"Really?" Nanny Sue looks taken aback.

"Yes! Didn't my husband explain how desperate we
are? This is our two-year-old, Minnie."

"Hello, Minnie. How are you?" Nanny Sue crouches
down to chat to Minnie and I wait impatiently till she
rises again.

"You won't believe the problems we've had with her.
It's shameful. It's mortifying. I can hardly admit it." I let
my voice wobble slightly. "She refuses to learn how
to tie up her shoelaces. I've tried . . . my husband's
tried . . . everyone's tried. But she won't!"

There's a pause, during which I keep my anxious-
mother look perfectly intact. Nanny Sue looks a little
perplexed. Ha.

"Rebecca," she says. "Minnie's still very young. I
wouldn't expect any child of two to be able to tie her
own laces."

"Oh!" I instantly brighten. "Oh, I *see*. Well, that's all right, then! We don't have any other problems with her. Thank you so much, Nanny Sue, please do invoice my husband. I mustn't keep you any longer— good-bye."

And I slam the front door before she can reply.

Result! I high-five Minnie and am about to head to the kitchen for a celebratory Kit Kat when the doorbell rings again.

Hasn't she gone?

I peep through the spy hole and there she is, waiting patiently on the doorstep.

What does she want? She's solved our problems. She can go.

"Rebecca?" Her voice comes through the door. "Are you there?"

"Hello!" calls Minnie.

"Shhh!" I hiss. "Be quiet!"

"Rebecca, your husband asked if I could assess your daughter and report my findings to both of you. I can hardly do that on a one-minute acquaintance."

"She doesn't need assessing!" I call back through the door.

Nanny Sue doesn't react, just waits with the same patient smile. Doesn't she *want* a day off?

I'm feeling a bit thrown, to be honest. I thought she'd hoof off. What if she tells Luke I wouldn't let her in? What if we end up having another big row?

Oh God. Maybe it'll be simpler if I just let her in, let her do her so-called "assessing," and get rid of her.

"Fine." I throw open the door. "Come in. But my daughter *doesn't* have any problems. And I know exactly what you're going to do and what you're going to say. And we already have a Naughty Step."

"Goodness." Nanny Sue's eyes spark a little. "Well, you're ahead of the game, aren't you?" She steps in and beams at Minnie, then at me. "Please don't be apprehensive or worried. All I'd really like to observe is a normal day for both of you. Act naturally and do what you would usually do. I want to see who the Brandons really *are*."

I knew it! She's set us our first trap. On telly, either the family hasn't got a plan for the day or their child refuses to turn off the TV, and they all start fighting. But I am *so* ahead of her. I prepared for this moment, just in case—in fact, I've even rehearsed it with Minnie.

"Gosh, I don't know," I say in musing tones. "What do you think, Minnie? Some home-baking?" I click my tongue. "But I've just remembered, we're out of organic stone-ground flour. Maybe we could make houses out of cardboard boxes, and you could paint them with nonleaded paint."

I look meaningfully at Minnie. This is her cue. She's supposed to say, "Walk! Nature!" I coached her and everything. But, instead, she's gazing longingly at the TV in the sitting room.

"Peppa Pig," she begins. "*Mine* Peppa Pig—"

"We can't see a real pig, darling!" I interrupt hastily. "But let's go on a nature walk and discuss the environment!"

I'm quite proud of the nature-walk idea. It counts as good parenting *and* it's really easy. You only have to walk along and say, "There's an acorn! There's a squirrel!" every so often. And Nanny Sue will have to admit defeat. She'll have to give us ten out of ten and say she can't improve on a perfect family, and Luke will be totally sussed.

When Minnie's dressed in her coat and boots (tiny pink Uggs—*so* sweet), I reach in my bag and produce four dark-gray velvet ribbons, sewn in a bow and backed with Velcro. I did them last night, and they look really good.

"We'd better take the Naughty Ribbons," I say ostentatiously.

"Naughty Ribbons?" inquires Nanny Sue politely.

"Yes, I noticed from your TV show that you don't use the Naughty Step while you're out and about. So I've created a 'Naughty Ribbon.' They're very simple but effective. You just Velcro them on to the child's coat when they're naughty."

"I see." Nanny Sue doesn't venture an opinion, but that's obviously because she's seething with jealousy and wishes she'd thought of it first.

Honestly, I think I might become a child expert. I have far more ideas than Nanny Sue does, *and* I could give fashion advice too.

I usher her out of the house and we start heading down the drive. "Look, Minnie, a bird!" I point at some creature flapping out of a tree. "Maybe it's endangered," I add solemnly. "We have to *protect* our wildlife."

"A pigeon?" says Nanny Sue mildly. "Is that likely to be endangered?"

"I'm being *green*." I give her a reproving look. Doesn't she know anything about the environment?

We walk along for a while and I point out a few squirrels. Now we're approaching the parade of shops at the end of Mum's road, and I can't help glancing right, just to see what they have in the antiques shop.

"Shop!" says Minnie, tugging on my hand.

"No, we're not going shopping, Minnie." I give her an indulgent smile. "We're going on a nature walk, remember? Looking at *nature*."

"Shop! Taxi!" She sticks her hand confidently out into the road and yells even louder, *"Taxi! Taxeeee!"* After a moment, the taxi at the head of the rank rumbles toward us.

"Minnie! We're *not* getting a taxi! I don't know why

she's done that," I add quickly to Nanny Sue. "It's not like we take taxis all the time—"

"*Tax-eee!*" Minnie is getting that red-cheeked, angry bull look. Oh God. I can't risk a tantrum in front of Nanny Sue. Maybe we *could* take a taxi somewhere.

"Minnie!" comes a cheerful, booming voice. "How's my best little customer?"

Damn. It's Pete, who usually drives us to Kingston when we go shopping.

I mean, not that we go *that* often.

"Pete sometimes drives us to the . . . the . . . educational soft-play center," I say to Nanny Sue.

"So." Pete leans out of his window. "Where is it today, my beauties?"

"Star-bucks," enunciates Minnie carefully before I can speak. "Starbucks—shops."

"Your usual, then?" Pete says cheerfully. "Hop in!"

I feel my face flood with color.

"We're not going to Starbucks, Minnie!" I say shrilly. "What a . . . a crazy idea! Could you take us to the educational soft-play center, please, Pete? That one in Leatherhead that we go to all the time?"

My eyes are fixed desperately on his, willing him not to say, "What are you talking about?"

"Muffin?" Minnie turns hopeful eyes on me. "Muffin Starbucks?"

"No, Minnie!" I snap. "Now, you be a good girl or you'll get a Naughty Ribbon." I take the Naughty Ribbon out of my bag and brandish it ominously at her. Instantly Minnie holds her hands out.

"Mine! Miiiine!"

She wasn't supposed to *want* the Naughty Ribbon.

"Maybe later," I say, flustered, and shove it back in my bag. This is all Nanny Sue's fault. She's putting me off.

We get in and I buckle Minnie up, and Pete pulls away from the curb.

"Rebecca," says Nanny Sue pleasantly, "if you *do* have errands to do, please don't feel constrained by me. I'm very happy to go to the shops or do whatever you would normally do."

"This is it!" I try to sound natural. "This is our normal routine! Educational play! Have a snack, darling," I add to Minnie, and produce a spelt biscuit which I got from the health-food shop. She looks at it dubiously, licks it, then chucks it on the floor and yells, "Muffin! Muffin *Starbucks*!"

My face flames red.

"Starbucks is . . . the name of our friend's cat," I improvise desperately. "And Muffin is the other cat. Minnie's such an animal lover, aren't you, darling?"

"Have you seen the great white elephant?" Pete's voice comes cheerily from the front. "They've opened it at last!"

We've arrived at the junction where the road joins the dual carriageway and are sitting in a line of traffic. Suddenly I see what Pete's pointing at. It's a massive black-and-white billboard, reading:

HEATHFIELD VILLAGE!
NEW LUXURY OUTLET MALL OPENS TODAY!

Wow. They've been talking about opening that place for ages. My eyes slide farther down the billboard.

SPECIAL INTRODUCTORY OFFERS TODAY!
FREE GIFT FOR EACH CUSTOMER!
NEXT EXIT!

Free gift for each customer?

I mean, it's probably nothing to get excited about.

It'll be a tiny scented candle or one single chocolate or something. And the place is probably nothing much either. Anyway, I'm not even *interested* in some new shopping mall, because we haven't come out to go shopping, have we? We've come out to do educational, bonding things.

"Look at the clouds," I say to Minnie, and point out the opposite window self-consciously. "Do you know how clouds are made, darling? It's with . . . er . . . water."

Do I mean water vapor? Or steam?

"Burberry," says Pete with interest. "Now, that's good quality stuff. My son-in-law, he gets all the fakes from Hong Kong, and he says—"

Burberry? My head jerks round and I see another massive billboard—this time listing all the designers in the outlet.

Burberry. Matthew Williamson. Dolce & Gabbana. Oh my God.

Anya Hindmarch. Temperley. *Vivienne Westwood?* All at discount prices? *Yards* away?

The taxi edges forward again, and I feel a pull of alarm. We'll be past the exit in a minute. It'll be too late.

OK, let's think this through properly. Let's be rational. I know we're supposed to be going to Leatherhead and bouncing around a ball pit. But the thing is . . . Nanny Sue said she didn't mind if we went shopping. She actually *said* it.

Not that I'd buy anything for myself. Obviously. I'm keeping my promise. But this is a brand-new, state-of-the-art discount shopping center with free gifts. We can't just *drive past.* It's . . . it's . . . wrong. It's ungrateful. It's against the laws of nature. And I'm allowed to buy things for Minnie, aren't I? It's part of the duties of a mother to keep her child clothed.

I glance at the list again. Petit Bateau. Ralph Lauren Girls and Boys. Funky Kid. Baby in Urbe. I feel a bit breathless. This is a no-brainer.

"You know, I do need to get Minnie some new socks." I try to sound offhand. "So we could pop into this new mall instead of the soft-play. Just an idea. What do you think?"

"It's up to you." Nanny Sue lifts her hands. "Entirely."

"So, um, Pete, could you take us to the outlet mall instead?" I raise my voice. "Thanks so much!"

"Better clear my boot, then, hadn't I?" He turns and flashes a grin at me. "Ready for all the bags."

I smile weakly back. I'll tell Nanny Sue later that he has a really quirky sense of humor.

"Are you fond of shopping, then, Rebecca?" says Nanny Sue pleasantly.

I pause as though trying to think this over.

"Not *fond*," I say eventually. "I wouldn't say *fond*. I mean, it's got to be done, hasn't it? Keeping the store cupboard full." I shrug ruefully. "It's a necessary chore for any responsible mother."

We pull up at the main entrance, which has massive glass doors leading into a huge airy atrium. There are palm trees and a water feature crashing down a steel wall, and as we enter I can already see *Valentino* and *Jimmy Choo* glinting at me in the distance. The air is filled with the smell of cinnamon pastries and cappuccino machines firing up, mingled with expensive leather and designer scents and . . . *newness*.

"So where do you need to go?" says Nanny Sue, looking around. "It was socks, wasn't it?"

"I . . . um . . ."

I can't quite think straight. Mulberry is straight ahead and I've just seen the most amazing bag in the window. "Um . . ." I force myself to focus. "Yes. Socks."

Children's socks. *Not* Valentino. *Not* Jimmy Choo.

Not Mulberry. Oh God, I wonder how much that bag is . . .

Stop it. Don't look. I'm not buying anything for myself. I'm not even thinking about it.

"Mine! Miiiiiine dolly!" Minnie's voice jerks me back to the present. She's standing outside Gucci, pointing to a mannequin.

"It's not a dolly, darling, it's a mannequin! Come on." Firmly, I take her hand and lead her toward the mall guide. "We're going to get you some socks."

We head toward the Kids' Zone, which is where all the children's stores are clustered. There's a clown greeting customers, and stalls laden with toys, and the whole area feels like a fairground.

"Book!" Minnie has immediately made a beeline for one of the stalls and grabbed a big pink book with fairies on the front. "Mine book."

Ha! I glance smugly at Nanny Sue. My daughter went for the educational book, not the trashy plastic!

"Of course you can buy a book, Minnie," I say loudly. "We'll take it out of your pocket money. I'm teaching Minnie financial planning," I add to Nanny Sue. "I write down all her pocket-money expenditures."

I take out my little pink Smythson notebook with *Minnie's Pocket Money* on the front. (I had it printed specially. It was quite expensive, but then, it's an investment in my daughter's financial responsibility.)

"Man!" Minnie has grabbed a puppet in addition to the book. "Mine man! Miiiine!"

"Er . . ." I look doubtfully at the puppet. It is quite sweet, and we don't have any puppets. "Well, OK. As long as you get it out of your pocket money. Do you understand, darling?" I speak super-clearly. "It has to come out of your *pocket money.*"

"Goodness!" says Nanny Sue as we head to the till. "How much pocket money does Minnie get?"

"Fifty pence a week," I reply, reaching for my purse. "But we have a system where she can have an advance and pay it back. It teaches her budgeting."

"I don't understand," persists Nanny Sue. "In what sense is she budgeting?"

Honestly. She's quite slow, for a so-called expert.

"Because it all goes in the *book*." I scribble down the cost of the book and the puppet, slap the notebook shut, and beam at Minnie. "Let's find you some socks, darling."

God, I love Funky Kid. They change their décor each season, and today the whole place is done up like a barn, with wooden beams and bales of fake straw. It has fantastic clothes for kids, like quirky knitted cardigans with hoods and padded coats with appliqué patches. I find some adorable socks with cherries and bananas round the hems, half price at £4.99, and put two pairs of each into my basket.

"There," says Nanny Sue briskly. "Well done. Shall we go to the checkout?"

I don't reply. I've been distracted by a rail of little pinafores. I remember these from the catalog. They're mint-green needlecord, with a white cross-stitch border. They're absolutely gorgeous, and they're 70 percent off! I quickly look through the rails—but there aren't any in size 2–3. Of course there aren't. They've been snapped up. Damn.

"Excuse me?" I ask a passing sales assistant. "Do you have any of these in size two–three?"

At once she makes a face. "Sorry. I don't think we got any in that size. It's so popular."

"Does Minnie need a pinafore?" inquires Nanny Sue, coming up behind me.

I'm getting a bit sick of Nanny Sue and her pointless questions.

"They're tremendously good value," I say smoothly. "I always think that, as a responsible parent, you should look for bargains, don't you agree, Nanny Sue? In fact"—a sudden inspiration has come to me—"I think I'll stock up for next year."

I grab a pinafore in size 3–4. Perfect! Why didn't I think of that before? I take a red pinafore too and head toward a rack of pale-pink raincoats with flower hoods. They don't have any small sizes at all—but I find a size 7–8. I mean, Minnie will need a coat when she's seven, won't she?

And there's a really lovely velvet jacket, size 12, for only £20, down from £120! It would be a *total* mistake not to get it.

I can't believe how farsighted I'm being as I fill my basket with more and more clothes. I've practically bought all Minnie's key pieces for the next ten years, at rock-bottom prices! I won't need to buy her anything else!

As I pay for the lot, I feel a glow of self-satisfaction. I must have saved *hundreds*.

"Well!" Nanny Sue seems a bit lost for words as the assistant hands me three huge bags. "You bought a lot more than a pair of socks!"

"Just thinking ahead." I adopt a wise, motherly tone. "Children grow so quickly, you have to be prepared. Shall we go and get a coffee?"

"Starbucks?" chimes in Minnie at once. She's been watching me attentively and has insisted on wearing the size 7–8 pale-pink raincoat, even though it's trailing on the floor. "Starbucks-muffin?"

"We might have to go to a chain coffee shop." I try to sound regretful. "They may not have an organic health-food cooperative."

I consult the map—and to get to the food court, we're going to have to walk past all the designer shops. Which is fine. I'll be fine. I just won't look in the windows.

As the three of us start walking along, my eyes are focused straight ahead on that pointy metal modern sculpture hanging down from the ceiling. It's fine. It's good. Actually, I've got *used* to not shopping. I barely miss it at all—

Oh my God, it's that Burberry coat with the frills that was on the catwalk. Right there in the window. I wonder how much—

No. Keep walking, Becky. *Don't look.* I close my eyes until they're two squinty slits. Yes. This is good. If I can't actually *see* the shops—

"Are you all right?" Nanny Sue suddenly notices me. "Rebecca, are you *ill*?"

"I'm fine!" My voice sounds a bit strangled. It's been so long since I shopped. I can feel a kind of pressure building up inside me, a kind of bubbling desperation.

But I have to ignore it. I promised Luke. I promised.

Think about something else. Yes. Like when I did that labor class and they said you breathe to distract yourself from the pain. I'll breathe to distract myself from the shopping.

Breathe in . . . breathe out . . . breathe in . . . oh my God, it's a Temperley dress.

My legs have stopped dead. It's a white-and-gold Temperley evening dress, in a shop called Fifty Percent Frocks. It has stunning embroidery around the neck and it sweeps to the floor and it looks like something straight off the red carpet. And it has a sign by it saying EXTRA 20% OFF TODAY.

My fingers are gripped round my shopping bags as I stare through the window.

I can't buy this dress. I mustn't even look at it.

But somehow . . . I can't move either. My feet are rooted to the polished marble floor.

"Rebecca?" Nanny Sue has come to a halt. She peers in at the dress and clicks her tongue disapprovingly. "These dresses are terribly expensive, aren't they? Even on sale."

Is that all she can say? This is the most beautiful dress in the world, and it's a fraction of its full price, and if I hadn't made that *stupid* promise to Luke . . .

Oh my God. I have the answer. In fact, this could be the answer to a lot of things.

"Minnie." Abruptly, I turn to her. "My lovely, precious little girl." I bend down and cradle her face tenderly between my hands. "Darling . . . would you like a Temperley dress for your twenty-first birthday present?"

Minnie doesn't answer, which is only because she doesn't understand what I'm offering her. Who wouldn't want a Temperley dress for their twenty-first? And by the time she's twenty-one, it'll be a rare vintage piece! All her friends will be really envious! They'll all say, "God, Minnie, I wish my mother had bought *me* a dress when I was two." People will call her the Girl in the Vintage Temperley Dress.

And I could borrow it for Luke's party. Just to try it out for her.

"Muffin?" Minnie says hopefully.

"Dress," I say firmly. "This is for *you,* Minnie! This is your birthday present!" Firmly, I lead her into the shop, ignoring Nanny Sue's startled look. It takes me ten seconds to sweep the place and realize the Temperley dress is the best thing they've got. I *knew* it was a bargain.

"Hi!" I say breathlessly to the assistant. "I'd like the Temperley dress, please. At least . . . it's for my daughter. I'm buying it in advance, obviously," I add, with a little laugh. "For her twenty-first."

The assistant stares at Minnie. She looks at me. Then she looks at her colleague as though for help.

"I'm sure she'll be the same dress size as me when she grows up," I add. "So I'll try it on for her. Do you like the lovely dress, Minnie?"

"No dress." Her brows knit in a frown.

"Darling, it's *Temperley*." I hold the fabric up to show her. "You'll look gorgeous in it! One day."

"No dress!" She runs to the other side of the shop and starts climbing into an open stock drawer.

"Minnie!" I exclaim. "Get out! So sorry . . ." I add over my shoulder to the assistant.

"Muffin!" she yells, as I try to manhandle her out. "Want muffin!"

"We'll have a muffin after we've got the *dress*," I say soothingly. "It'll take no time—"

"No dress!" Somehow she extricates herself from my grasp and scampers into the window display. "Dolly! Mine dolly!"

Now she's grabbing a naked mannequin.

"Minnie, please stop that, darling." I try not to sound as rattled as I feel. "Come back here!"

"Mine dolly!" She drags the whole mannequin off its podium onto the floor with a crash and starts hugging it. "Miiiine!"

"Get off, Minnie!" I say. "It's not a dolly! She thinks it's a doll," I add to the assistant, aiming for a light-hearted laugh. "Aren't children funny?"

The assistant doesn't laugh back, or even smile.

"Could you get her off, please?" she says.

"Of course! Sorry . . ." Red-faced, I try to pull Minnie off as hard as I can. But she's holding on like a limpet.

"Come on, Minnie!" I try to sound relaxed and cajoling. "Come on, sweetheart. Off you go."

"No!" she shrieks. "Mine, dolleee!"

"What's going on?" snaps someone behind me. "What's that child doing? Can't someone control her?"

My stomach curdles. I know that whiny, toxic voice. I whip round—and sure enough, it's the elf who banned us from Santa's Grotto. She's still got purple nails and a ridiculous permatanned cleavage, but now she's dressed in a black suit with a badge reading *Assistant Manager*.

"*You!*" Her eyes narrow.

"Oh, hi," I say nervously. "Nice to see you again. How's Father Christmas?"

"Could you please remove your child?" she says in pointed tones.

"Er . . . OK. No problem."

I look at Minnie, still clinging on to the mannequin for dear life. The only way I'm going to remove her is by peeling each finger off individually. I'm going to need ten hands.

"Could we possibly . . . buy the mannequin?"

From the permatanned elf's expression, I wish I hadn't asked that question.

"Come on, Minnie." I try to sound brisk and jolly, like a mother in a soap-powder commercial. "Bye-bye, dolly!"

"Nooooooooooo!" She clasps it harder.

"Get off!" With all my effort, I manage to prize one hand off, but she immediately clamps it back down.

"Miiiiine!"

"Get your daughter off that mannequin!" snaps the elf. "Customers are coming in! Get her off!"

"I'm trying!" I say desperately. "Minnie, I'll buy you a dolly. I'll buy you *two* dollies!"

A group of girls holding shopping bags have stopped to watch us, and one starts giggling.

"Minnie, you will have a Naughty Ribbon!" I'm totally hot and flustered. "And you'll go on the Naughty Step! And you won't have any treats ever! And Father Christmas will move to Mars and so will the Tooth Fairy—" I grab her feet, but she kicks me in the shin. "Ow! Minnie!"

"Dolleee!" she wails.

"You know what?" the elf erupts savagely. "Take the mannequin! Just have the bloody mannequin!"

"Have it?" I stare at her, bewildered.

"Yes! Anything! Just go! *Go! Out!*"

Minnie is still lying full length on the mannequin, gripping it for dear life. Awkwardly, I pick it up with both hands, dragging it along between my legs as if it's a dead body. Somehow, panting with effort, I manage to lug it outside—then drop it and look up.

Nanny Sue has followed us out with my three shopping bags. Now she's watching me and Minnie silently, her face unreadable.

And suddenly it's as if I come out of a trance. I see everything that just happened through Nanny Sue's eyes. I swallow several times, trying to think of some lighthearted comment about "Kids, eh?" But I can't think of one and, anyway, my mouth is too dry with nerves. How could I have let this happen? No one on the TV series ever got chucked out of a shop. I'm *worse* than all the families with fridges in the garden.

What's she going to say in her assessment? What will she tell Luke? What will she recommend?

"Have you finished shopping now?" she says in normal, pleasant tones, as if we aren't being stared at by every passerby.

I nod silently, my face burning.

"Minnie," says Nanny Sue. "I think you're hurting the poor dolly. Shall we get off her now and buy you a nice snack? We can buy one for dolly too."

Minnie swivels her head and looks mistrustfully at Nanny Sue for a few moments—then clambers off the mannequin.

"Good girl," says Nanny Sue. "We'll leave the dolly here at her own home." She hefts the mannequin up and props it against the door. "Now, let's find you a drink. Say, 'Yes, Nanny Sue.' "

"Ess, Nanny Sue," parrots Minnie obediently.

Huh? How did she do that?

"Rebecca, are you coming?"

Somehow I manage to get my legs in gear and walk along with them. Nanny Sue starts talking, but I can't hear a word. I'm too sick with dread. She's going to file her report and say Minnie needs special treatment at a boot camp. I know she is. And Luke will listen to her. What am I going to do?

BY NINE O'CLOCK that night I'm in a total state, pacing around the house, waiting for Luke to get back.

This is the worst moment in our marriage. Ever. By a million miles. Because, if it comes to it, I *will* be forced to take Minnie away to a safe refuge and never see Luke again and change our names by deed poll and try to forget through alcohol and drugs.

You know. Worst-case scenario.

At the sound of his key in the door, I stiffen.

"Becky?" He appears at the kitchen door. "I was expecting you to phone! How did it go?"

"Fine! We went shopping and we . . . er . . . had coffee." I sound totally false, but Luke doesn't seem to notice, which just shows how observant *he* is.

"So, what did she say about Minnie?"

"Not a lot. You know. I expect she'll report back later. When she's come to her conclusions."

"Hmm." Luke nods, loosening his tie. He heads to the fridge, then pauses by the table. "Your BlackBerry's flashing."

"Oh, is it?" I say with stagey surprise. "Gosh. I must have a message! Could you listen to it? I'm sooo tired."

"If you like." Luke shoots me an odd look, picks it up, and dials voice mail while taking a bottle of beer out of the fridge.

"It's her." He looks up, suddenly alert. "It's Nanny Sue."

"Really?" I try to sound astounded. "Well . . . put her on speakerphone!"

As the familiar West Country vowels fill the kitchen, we both listen, motionless.

". . . full report to come. But I just had to say, Minnie is an enchanting child. It was a pleasure to spend time with her and your wife. Becky's parenting skills are second to none, and I can diagnose no problems in your family whatsoever. Well done! Good-bye."

"Wow!" I exclaim as the phone goes dead. "Isn't that amazing! We can put this whole episode behind us and get on with our lives."

Luke hasn't moved a muscle. Now he turns and gives me a long, hard look.

"Becky."

"Yes?" I flash him a nervous smile.

"Was that by any chance Janice, putting on a West Country accent?"

What? How can he even *say* that?

I mean, OK, it *was* Janice, but she disguised her voice perfectly. I was really impressed.

"No!" I bluster. "It was Nanny Sue, and I'm offended you should have to ask."

"Great. Well, I'll give her a ring to chat about it." He pulls out his own BlackBerry.

"No, don't!" I yelp.

Why is he so *mistrustful*? It's a massive character flaw. I'll tell him so, one of these days.

"You'll disturb her," I improvise. "It's antisocial to ring so late."

"That's your sole concern, is it?" He raises his eyebrows. "Being antisocial?"

"Yes," I say defiantly. "Of course."

"Well, then I'll email her."

Oh God. This isn't going the way I planned. I thought I'd buy myself some time, at least.

"OK, OK! It was Janice," I say desperately as he starts tapping. "But I didn't have any choice! Luke, it was terrible. It was a disaster. Minnie got banned from a shop and she stole a mannequin and Nanny Sue didn't say anything, just gave us that *look,* and I know what she's going to recommend, but I can't send Minnie away to some boot camp in Utah, I just can't do it. And if you make me, then I'll have to take out an injunction and we'll go to court and it'll be like *Kramer vs. Kramer* and she'll be scarred for life and it'll be all your fault!"

Out of nowhere, tears have begun pouring down my cheeks.

"What?" Luke stares at me incredulously. *"Utah?"*

"Or Arizona. Or wherever it is. I can't do it, Luke." I scrub at my eyes, feeling exactly like Meryl Streep. "Don't ask it of me."

"I'm *not* asking it of you! Jesus!" He seems absolutely stunned. "Who mentioned Utah, for fuck's sake?"

"I . . . er . . ." I'm not quite sure now. I know *someone* did.

"I hired this woman because I thought she could give us some child-care advice. If she's useful, we'll use her. If not, not."

Luke sounds so matter-of-fact, I blink at him in surprise.

He's never seen the TV program, I suddenly remember. He doesn't know about how Nanny Sue comes into your life and changes everything and you end up sobbing on her shoulder.

"I believe in listening to professionals," Luke is saying calmly. "Now she's seen Minnie, we should hear her recommendations. But that's as far as it goes. Agreed?"

How can he take a situation that seems like a great big tangled spiderweb and reduce it to a single thread? How does he *do* that?

"I can't send Minnie away." My voice is still shaky. "You'll have to prize us apart."

"Becky, there'll be no prizing," says Luke patiently. "We'll ask Nanny Sue what we can do that doesn't involve sending her away. OK? Drama over?"

I feel a bit wrong-footed. To be honest, I was all ready for a bit *more* drama.

"OK," I say at last.

Luke opens his beer and grins at me. Then he frowns, puzzled. "What's this?" He unpeels a place card from the bottom of the bottle. "*Happy Birthday, Mike.* Who's Mike?"

Shit. How did that get there?

"No idea!" I grab it from him and hastily crumple it. "Weird. Must have got picked up at the shop. Shall we . . . er . . . watch TV?"

The advantage of having the house to ourselves is we don't have to watch snooker all the time anymore. Or real-life crime. Or documentaries about the Cold War.

We're snuggled up on the sofa with the gas fire flickering away, and Luke is flipping through the channels, when suddenly he pauses and turns to me.

"Becky . . . you don't *really* think I would ever send Minnie away, do you? I mean, is that the kind of father you think I am?"

He looks quite perturbed, and I feel a bit guilty. The truth is, I did.

"Er . . ." My phone rings before I can answer. "It's Suze," I say apprehensively. "I'd better get this . . ." I head swiftly out of the room and take a deep breath. "Hi, Suze?"

I've texted Suze several times since our mini-row, but we haven't spoken. Is she still angry with me? Do I dare bring up the special shortbread thing?

"Have you seen *Style Central*?" Her voice blasts down the line, taking me by surprise. "Have you *seen* it? I've just had a copy biked round. I couldn't believe my *eyes.*"

"What? Oh, you mean, Tarkie's interview? Does it look good? Danny said Tarquin was really experimental—"

" 'Experimental'? Is *that* what he calls it? Interesting choice of word. I could have chosen a better one."

There's a weird, sarcastic edge to Suze's voice. What's up? Suze is never sarcastic.

"Suze . . . are you OK?" I say nervously.

"No, I'm not OK! I should never have let Tarkie go to that photo shoot without me! I should never have trusted Danny. What was I *thinking*? Where were Tarkie's advisers? Who edited the photo spread? Because whoever it was, I'm suing them—"

"Suze!" I try to interrupt the stream of words. "Tell me. What's wrong?"

"They dressed Tarkie up in leather bondage gear!"

she erupts. "That's what's wrong! He looks like a gay model!"

Oh God. The thing about Tarquin is, he can look sort of . . . metrosexual. And Suze is quite sensitive about it.

"Come on, Suze," I say soothingly. "I'm sure he doesn't look gay—"

"Yes, he does! And it's deliberate! They haven't even *mentioned* that he's married or has children! It's all about sexy Lord Tarquin with his *honed pecs* and *what's under his kilt?* And they've used all kinds of suggestive props . . ." I can practically hear her shudder. "I'm going to kill Danny. Kill him!"

She must be overreacting. But then, Suze can get quite mother-tiger-ish about anyone she loves.

"I'm sure it's not as bad as you think—" I begin.

"Oh, you think?" she says furiously. "Well, wait till you see it! And I don't know why you're defending him, Bex. He's screwed you over too."

I think Suze must be going a bit deranged. How on earth could Danny have screwed me over in an interview about his new collection?

"OK, Suze," I say patiently. "How has Danny screwed me over?"

"Luke's party. He's blabbed."

I have never moved as fast as I do now. Within thirty seconds I'm upstairs and online, clicking feverishly till I get to the right page. And there it is, right under the moody black-and-white photo of Tarkie chopping logs in a tight white T-shirt with his kilt slung almost obscenely low. (He does have good abs, Tarkie. I never quite realized.)

Kovitz is in talks to launch a furniture line and lifestyle website, reads the interview. *Does this fashion whirlwind ever have any downtime?* "Sure," laughs Kovitz. "I like to party. I'm heading to Goa for a couple weeks, then I'm com-*

ing back for a surprise party. Actually, it's for Luke Brandon, the husband of Rebecca Brandon, who brought this whole collaboration together." Thus the fashion world comes full circle.

I read it three times, breathing faster and faster.

I am going to kill Danny. *Kill* him.

From: Becky Brandon
Subject: URGENT MESSAGE!!!!!
Date: 13 March 2006
To: Subscribers@stylecentral-magazine.com

Dear Reader of Style Central,

While reading the latest issue of *Style Central,* you may have noticed a small reference by Danny Kovitz to a surprise party for my husband, Luke Brandon.

May I please ask you very sincerely to FORGET THIS and PUT IT FROM YOUR MIND. If by any chance you know my husband, please do not mention it. It is supposed to be a SURPRISE.

If you could rip out the page and destroy it, that would be even better.

With sincere thanks,

Rebecca Brandon (née Bloomwood)

People Who Know About Party

Me
Suze
Tarquin
Danny
Jess
Tom
Mum
Dad
Janice
Martin
Bonnie
Those three women who were listening at the
   next-door table
Gary
Janice's plumber
Rupert and Harry at The Service
Erica
Marketing directors of Bollinger, Dom Perignon,
   Bacardi, Veuve Clicquot, Party Time Bever-
   ages, Jacob's Creek, Kentish English Sparkling
   Wine
Cliff
Manicurist (I was so stressed out, I had to talk to
   <u>someone</u>, and she promised not to blab)
165 invited guests (not including Brandon C lot)
500 readers of <u>Style Central</u>

Total = 693

Oh God.

SIXTEEN

WHY DID HE have to mention it? *Why?*

And Suze is right: One of those pictures of Tarkie is *totally* inappropriate.

I left Danny about twenty messages, all getting more and more irate, until at last he called, when I was giving Minnie a bath, and left a message trying to defend himself. He has such a nerve.

"Becky, OK, look. That guy was out of line. I told him off the record! We were just chatting after the interview! Anyway, what does it matter? Nobody reads *Style Central*. No one Luke knows, anyway."

To be fair, that's true. And that's the one thing that gives me comfort: *Style Central* only has about five hundred readers. I mean, they're all very cool and important and influential in fashion and design, but the point is, they don't know Luke.

First thing the following morning, I got in touch with the editor and begged him to let me contact all the subscribers, and eventually he agreed to pass on an email asking them not to let on. Two weeks have passed and nothing seems to have seeped out yet. I think I've contained the outbreak. But I still can't relax.

In fact, I'm in a bit of a state all round. I'm not sleep-

ing well, and my hair looks terrible. In one sense the
party is more under control than it was, because I've
booked all the things I hadn't thought about, like
heaters and loos and flooring. But everything costs so
much *money*. All my credit cards are starting to bounce,
and it's getting scary. I had a really nasty conversation
with the Portaloo lady yesterday (I must be more careful about answering the phone), who wanted to know
why my deposit was being held up and wasn't at all
sympathetic about my recent emergency root canal.

I just hadn't realized . . . I mean, I hadn't quite
planned . . .

Anyway. Today is the big day. I'm going to march in,
wearing my smartest prospective-board-member suit
and killer heels. Trevor's back from his holiday and I've
got an appointment at eleven to see him. And I'm going
to ask for the Employee of the Year money, plus a raise.
Payable immediately.

As I arrive at work, I'm feeling quite jittery. I've never
asked for a raise before. But Luke always says it's perfectly normal and appropriate. He says he respects people who value their own worth correctly. Well, I value
my own worth at precisely seven thousand two hundred pounds more than I'm getting at the moment.
(That's how much I've worked out I need for the party.
Maybe I'll ask for eight, to be on the safe side.)

I'm not going to throw a tantrum about it. I'm just
going to be firm and to the point. I'll say, "Trevor, I've
assessed the market rate, and I calculate that a personal
shopper of my caliber is worth an additional eight
thousand pounds. Which I would like advanced today,
if possible."

Actually . . . let's make it ten thousand. That's a nice
round number.

And what's ten thousand pounds in the scheme of

things? The Look is a massive department store with a great big turnover, and they can easily afford ten thousand pounds for a valued employee and potential board member. I mean, Elinor spent way more than ten thousand pounds in my department in about five minutes flat. Which I might mention, if things get a bit sticky.

As I'm heading up the escalator, my BlackBerry buzzes with two new emails. The lighting company and the security firm have both finally got back to me. I read each of their quotes in turn—and when I've finished I feel so wobbly I nearly trip over the top of the escalator. They both want four-figure sums beginning with 4, with a 50 percent deposit payable immediately, due to the lateness of the booking.

So let's work this out. In total, I now need—

OK. Don't panic. It's very simple. To put this party on properly, I need . . . fifteen grand.

Fifteen grand? Am I seriously going to ask my boss for fifteen thousand pounds? With a straight face?

I want to laugh hysterically, or maybe run away. But I can't. This is my only option. I have to stay bullish. I have to *believe* I'm worth another fifteen thousand pounds. Yes. I am.

As I reach our department, I duck into one of the dressing rooms, lock the door, take three deep breaths, and face myself in the mirror.

"Trevor," I say as confidently as possible. "I've assessed the market rate, and I calculate that a personal shopper of my caliber is worth an additional fifteen thousand pounds. Which I would like today, if possible. Check or cash is fine."

I did it quite well. Apart from the shaky voice. And the gulping when I got to *fifteen thousand*.

Maybe I should start off asking for ten thousand.

And then say, "Actually, I meant fifteen," as he's about to write out the check.

No. Bad idea.

My stomach is turning over. This is where I wish I had "people," like Danny does. He never has to ask anyone for money; in fact, he behaves like money doesn't exist.

"Becky." Jasmine is knocking on the door. "Your customer's here."

OK. I'll just have to wing it. Or hope someone gives me a really, *really* big tip.

ON THE PLUS SIDE, it's a good morning. As I grab a coffee at ten-thirty, the place is full. Both Jasmine and I are in the middle of one-to-one appointments, and there are a few drop-in customers too. We always let our regular clients come and use the nice dressing rooms, even if they haven't made a consultation appointment. There's a cappuccino machine, and sofas, and bowls of sweets, and the whole place is feel-good. I even have a few customers who regularly meet here, for a chat, instead of at a café.

As I look around, listening to the familiar noises of hangers and zips and chatter and laughter, I can't help feeling proud. The rest of the store may be struggling, but my department is warm and happy and buzzy.

Jasmine is packaging up a load of Paul Smith shirts, and as she rings up the till, she arches her eyebrows at me.

"Look what I got online." She pulls out a plastic tabard reading OFFICESUPPLIES.COM. "I wear it when I deliver clothes. No one ever gives me any gip."

"Wow," I say, impressed. "That's thorough."

She nods. "My delivery name is Gwen. I've got a

whole second personality going on. Gwen doesn't smoke. And she's a Pisces."

"Er . . . great!" Sometimes I worry that Jasmine has gone a bit far with the whole cloak-and-dagger bit. "Hi, Louise!"

Jasmine's client has arrived at the till. It's Louise Sullivan, who has three kids and her own online food company and is constantly stressing over whether to have a tummy tuck or not, which is ridiculous. She looks great. It's not *her* fault her husband has zero tact and likes making crass jokes.

"Will you take your clothes now or have them delivered discreetly?" says Jasmine as she swipes Louise's card.

"I could probably take one bag now," says Louise, and chews her lip. "But no more than one."

"No problem." Jasmine nods in a businesslike way. "So . . . we'll deliver the rest in a computer-paper box?"

"Actually . . ." Louise reaches in her carrier bag. "I brought this." It's a flat-pack box, stamped with LIGURIAN OLIVE OIL.

"I *like* it." I can see Jasmine looking at Louise with a new respect. "Olive oil it is." She takes the box. "Tomorrow evening?"

"Which one of you is Becky?" comes a man's voice, and we all start. You don't often get men on this floor, but a guy in a leather jacket with a fleshy face is striding toward us. He's holding a box marked COMPUTER PAPER and wearing a deep scowl on his face.

I feel a sudden qualm. I really hope that's just a box of computer paper.

"Me!" I say brightly, as Jasmine stuffs the olive-oil box under the counter and Louise quickly melts away. "Can I help?"

"What the hell is going on?" He brandishes his box at me. "What's this?"

"Um . . . a box? Would you like an appointment with a personal shopper, sir?" I add hastily. "Menswear is actually on the second floor—"

"I'm not after menswear," he says menacingly. "I'm after *answers.*"

He crashes the box down on the counter and lifts the lid. Jasmine and I exchange glances. It's the Preen dress I sold to Ariane Raynor last week. Oh God, this must be Ariane's husband. The one who used to be a rock star, apparently, but hasn't had a hit for years. The one who tried to make a pass at the au pair and trims his pubic hair in front of *Desperate Housewives.* (We've chatted quite a lot, Ariane and me.)

"*Shop In Private.*" He pulls a piece of paper from his pocket and reads out loud in a sarcastic voice. "*Have clothes delivered in a cardboard box labeled* Computer Paper *or* Sanitary Products."

Shit.

"She's been shopping, hasn't she?" He thumps the leaflet down. "How much has she spent?"

My phone bleeps with a text and I can see Jasmine jerking her head at it. I surreptitiously click on it to find a message from her.

Ariane is here for her alteration!!!! I put her in dressing room 3 while you were in with Victoria. Shall I warn her?

I nod unobtrusively at Jasmine and turn back to Ariane's husband.

"Mr. . . ."

"Raynor."

"Mr. Raynor, I'm afraid I couldn't comment," I say smoothly. "I have to respect my customers' privacy. Perhaps you could come back another time?"

"Jasmine?" rings out Ariane's distinctive voice from the dressing room. "Could you look at this hem? Because I don't think—" Her voice breaks off abruptly, as though someone's muffled it—but it's too late. Her husband's face has jolted in recognition.

"Is that Ariane?" Incredulity spreads over his face. "Is she shopping *again*?"

"No, she's not, you oaf," I want to reply, "she's having an alteration done on a dress she bought two years ago. And, anyway, what about the Bang and Olufsen system you just insisted on replacing in your country house? That cost squillions more than a dress."

But instead I smile sweetly and say, "Our customer appointments are confidential. Now, if that's all—"

"It's not!" He raises his voice to a bark. "Ariane, you come out here now!"

"Sir, please, could you refrain from shouting in here?" I say calmly, while reaching for my phone and texting to Jasmine.

    Ariane's husband v. irate. Take her out back
    way.

"Ariane, I know you're in there!" he shouts threateningly. "I know you've been lying to me!" He makes for the entrance, but I block his way.

"I'm afraid I can't let you in." I smile. "Only customers are permitted in the personal-shopping area. I'm sure you understand."

"*Understand*?" He turns his wrath on me. "I'll tell you what I understand. You're all in this together, you witches. Computer fucking paper." He bangs a fist down on the box. "You should be in *jail*."

I can't help flinching. His blue eyes are bloodshot and I suddenly wonder if he's been drinking.

"It's simply a discreet packaging option." I keep my voice steady. "Not everyone wants to flaunt designer labels at this time."

"I bet they don't." He eyes me nastily. "Not to their mugs of husbands, they don't. Is this 'Who can fleece their man the most?' "

I'm so outraged, I can't help gasping.

"Most of my clients have their own incomes, actually," I reply, forcing myself to stay polite. "And I think it's up to them how they spend it, don't you? I believe Ariane's furniture business is going very well at the moment?"

I can't help a little dig. I know he's threatened by her success. She says it every time she comes in. And then she says she's going to leave him. And then by the end of the session she's crying and saying she loves him really.

Honestly, shopping beats therapy, anytime. It costs the same and you get a dress out of it.

"Ariane!" He starts pushing past me.

"Stop!" I grab his arm, absolutely furious. "I told you, only clients are permitted in the—"

"Get out of my way!" He throws my arm aside like I'm a doll.

OK. Now this is a matter of principle. No one barges past me, into *my* department.

"No! You're not going in!" I grab his shoulders, but he's too strong. "Jasmine!" I yell as I grapple with him. "Lead all the customers to safety!"

"You bloody well let me in!"

"This is a *private* shopping area—" I'm panting with the effort of restraining him.

"What on *earth* is going on?"

A deep voice booms right behind me, and I relinquish my grasp. I swivel around, already knowing it's

Trevor. Gavin is lurking behind him, face gleaming as though he's watching some kind of floor show. Trevor meets my eyes with a grim "There'd better be a very good reason for this" look, and I shrug defensively back, trying to convey "Yes, there is."

As Trevor turns to Mr. Raynor, his expression suddenly changes to one of awe. "My goodness! Is it . . . *Doug Raynor*?"

Trust him to know some ancient old rocker that no one else has even heard of.

"Yeah." Doug Raynor preens himself. "That's me."

"Mr. Raynor, we're extremely honored to see you here at The Look." Trevor launches into full obsequious-manager mode. "We're all huge fans. If there's anything I can do to help you—"

"There is, as it happens," Doug Raynor cuts him off. "You can tell me what *this* is all about. You might call it discreet shopping; I call it downright lying." He slaps the leaflet down on the reception counter. "And I'm calling the *Daily World* tomorrow. Exposing the bloody lot of you."

"What's this?" says Trevor, looking puzzled. "*Shop In Private*? Do I know about this?"

"It's . . . um . . ." My mouth feels like cotton wool. "I was going to mention it . . ."

I can feel blood filling my face as Trevor reads the leaflet in silence. At last he looks up, his eyes like two black holes of disapproval.

No. Worse than disapproval. He looks like he wants to murder me. Gavin is reading it over his shoulder now.

"You pretend to be *cleaning ladies*?" He gives a sudden snort of laughter. "Jesus Christ, Becky—"

"You think this is a responsible way to carry on?" Doug Raynor chimes in furiously. "You think this is the way a top department store should be acting? It's criminal deception, that's what it is!"

"Gavin." Trevor snaps into full damage-limitation action. "Be so kind as to take Mr. Raynor to menswear and offer him a new suit, with our compliments. Mr. Raynor, perhaps I can offer you a glass of champagne at the oyster bar when you've finished shopping, and you can express any concerns you have directly to me?"

"Yeah. And you'll be getting an earful from me, I can tell you." Doug Raynor is obviously torn between staying and shouting some more and getting a free suit—but at last allows himself to be led away by Gavin. Jasmine has vanished into the dressing rooms too.

It's just Trevor and me and an ominous hush.

"You—you said you wanted to know the secret of our success," I falter. "Well, this is it."

Trevor says nothing but reads the leaflet through again, his fingers gripping the paper hard. The longer he's silent, the less certain I feel. Obviously he's *angry* . . . but might he not be a bit impressed too? Might he say this is the kind of risk-taking chutzpah we need in retail? Might he say that this reminds him of the kind of crazy stunt he pulled when *he* was just starting out and how would I like to be his special protégée?

"Becky." He finally raises his head and my heart lifts with hope. His eyes aren't black holes anymore. He looks quite calm. I think it'll all be OK! "Were you planning to see me about this today? Is that why you made the eleven o'clock appointment?"

He sounds so reasonable, I relax. "Actually, no. There was something else I wanted to discuss."

There's another silence between us. Would this be a good time to bring up the raise? I suddenly wonder. I mean, yes, he's cross about the leaflet, but that won't affect my long-term prospects, surely? Especially not if I'm going to be his special protégée.

Right. I'll do it.

Except I won't ask for fifteen. I'll ask for ten.

No, twelve.

I take a deep breath and clench my fists by my sides.

"Trevor, I've assessed the market rate, and I calculate that a personal shopper of my caliber—"

"Becky . . ." He cuts across as though he didn't even hear me. "This so-called initiative of yours was unapproved, inappropriate, and dishonest."

He sounds so cold and distant, I feel a jolt of alarm. OK, forget the raise for now. I'll just go for the Employee of the Year money instead. I mean, he can't take *that* away from me, however cross he is, surely.

"Um, Trevor, you know how you said I was going to be Employee of the Year?" I try again hurriedly. "Well I was just wondering . . ."

"Employee of the Year? Are you joking?" His voice has such a steely edge that I step back nervously.

I suddenly notice how tight his lips have gone. Oh God, I was wrong. He *is* angry. In that horrible, quiet, scary way. My hands feel a bit clammy.

"You've behaved in a way that is to the detriment of The Look." His voice is inexorable. "You've deceived myself and other managers. You've contravened every good practice and protocol of this organization and caused a fracas in front of customers. This is a serious breach of professional conduct. Not to mention embarrassing the entire store in front of Doug Raynor, a major celebrity. Do you think he'll ever come and shop here again?"

"I know I should have got permission first," I say hastily. "And I'm very sorry. But that's why my sales are up! Because of Shop In Private! All my customers love it. I mean, they even wrote you letters saying how much they love it. The whole place is buzzy, everyone's happy, everyone's buying stuff . . ."

Trevor's not listening to a word.

"Becky, I'm afraid that, as from this moment, you're suspended until further notice." He looks at me as though I'm some lowly worm. "Take your things, please, and go."

SEVENTEEN

AS I SIT ON THE TUBE, I'm numb with shock. Two weeks ago I was the star. I was going to be invited onto the board. I was being presented with flowers.

And now I'm suspended in disgrace.

They're going to do an internal investigation. They're going to treat the matter "very seriously." Jasmine looked absolutely stunned as I gathered my stuff together out of my locker, but Trevor was standing right there, so she couldn't say anything other than "Call me!," which she muttered just as I was going.

And then Trevor escorted me right to the staff door, as though I might try to nick stuff or something. I've never felt so humiliated in my whole entire life.

Actually, on second thought, maybe I have. But this is *definitely* equal with all those other times.

No Employee of the Year money. No raise. Maybe no job at all. What am I going to do? How am I going to pay for the party? I'm trying to think it through calmly, but my chest keeps going into spasms of fear.

Could we do without loos, maybe, and tell everyone to go before they come? Could I get Dad and Martin to be the bouncers? I don't mind doing a bit of valet parking myself, if it comes to that. Oh God—

When I catch sight of my own reflection in the tube

window, my eyes are all wide and starey. I look like a demented crazy person. Maybe this is what happens. People decide to hold surprise parties and they end up cracking under the strain and their whole life falls apart. Maybe surprise parties are a major cause of mental illness. I wouldn't be surprised.

I've agreed to meet Janice and Minnie at Waterloo, and as I approach them I wince. They look so happy and carefree.

"We've had a lovely morning!" Janice enthuses as soon as I reach her. "Haven't we, Minnie? We did all my Easter cakes and popped them in the freezer."

"Thanks so much, Janice." I manage a weak smile. "I really appreciate it."

Janice has been such a star—as soon as she heard about Mum and Dad going to The West Place, she volunteered to look after Minnie while I was working. She's bought a whole cupboardful of toys, even though I begged her not to, and taught Minnie loads of new nursery rhymes. The only downside is, she keeps making even more pointed remarks to Jess about grandchildren and sighing loudly as she puts Minnie's finger paintings up on the wall.

"It was my pleasure! Anytime. So . . . have you heard from your mum?" she adds hesitantly.

"No. Have you?"

Janice nods. "They're having a super time! The apartment's lovely, apparently. They've been to the theater twice *and* had a mud wrap. Both of them, at once!"

"Great." I look down. "Well . . . I'm glad they're enjoying themselves."

"Are you two still not speaking, love?" Janice looks anxious.

"S'pose not."

Mum and I have never been not-speaking before. I don't know what the rules are, but if she didn't tell me about the mud wrap I guess the not-speaking must still be on.

"Well, I'd better let you go . . ." Janice hands me Minnie's mittens. "I'm off to a crafts fair now, start my Christmas shopping. Where are you and Minnie going?"

"Green Park," I say after a pause. Which is kind of true. The Ritz *is* right by Green Park.

As we come out of the tube at Piccadilly, gray clouds rush into the sky as though they've just been waiting for their chance, and there's a sudden smattering of rain. I put up Minnie's hood and trudge on miserably. Of all the things to raise my spirits, the prospect of tea with Elinor is really *not* one.

She's waiting for us in the same grand suite as before, wearing an ice-blue day dress, and on the table are three new jigsaw puzzles.

"Ladeeee!" Minnie's face instantly lights up and she rushes forward to give Elinor a hug. A flash of utter shock and discomposure passes across Elinor's face, and despite my mood I almost want to giggle.

"Well, Minnie," she says awkwardly, almost curtly. "You'd better sit down."

Minnie is still clinging to her, and, very stiffly, Elinor pats her shoulder. I wonder if any small child has ever hugged her before—well, Luke, I suppose. Before she left him. The thought of it makes my stomach ache.

The table is laid with a sumptuous tea, like last time, but I'm too churned up to feel like eating. I just want to get through this ordeal and go.

"Wait there, Minnie," says Elinor, as Minnie scrambles up beside me on the sofa. "I've bought you a special cake."

She heads to a nearby bureau against the wall. As she turns, holding a silver tray with a dome on it, her cheeks have turned the faintest tinge of pink, and . . . is that half a minuscule smile? Is Elinor . . . *excited*?

She places the dish on the table and lifts the silver dome.

Oh my sweet Lord. How much did *that* cost?

It's a heart-shaped cake, covered in perfect pink fondant icing, with pink truffles and glacé cherries arranged symmetrically around the edge and a name piped meticulously in icing in the center: *Minnie*.

"Do you see?" Elinor is gazing at Minnie for a reaction. "Do you like it?"

"Cake!" says Minnie, her eyes lighting up greedily. "Miiiine cake!"

"It's not simply a cake," says Elinor a little sharply. "It's a cake with your *name* on it. Don't you see that?"

"Elinor . . . she can't read," I explain gently. "She's not old enough."

"Oh." Elinor looks put out. "I see." She's just standing there, still holding the silver dome, and I can tell she's disappointed.

"But it's lovely," I say quickly. "Really thoughtful."

I'm genuinely touched by the trouble she's gone to—in fact, I almost wish I could take a picture of it with my phone. But then how would I explain it to Luke?

Elinor cuts a slice and hands it to Minnie, who stuffs it into her mouth, smearing cream and crumbs everywhere. I hastily grab a couple of napkins and try to contain the mess—but, to my surprise, Elinor doesn't seem as uptight about it as I expected. She doesn't even flinch when a glacé cherry rolls onto the immaculate Ritz carpet.

"Now, I've bought some new jigsaw puzzles," she says, sipping her tea. "This particular one of Notre Dame is interesting."

Notre Dame? For a two-year-old? Is she crazy? What's wrong with Maisy Mouse?

But, amazingly, Minnie is listening, entranced, as Elinor informs her about the different shades of gray and the need to start at the edges. When Elinor tips the puzzle out, Minnie watches with huge eyes and timidly reaches for pieces only when Elinor tells her to. She keeps looking up at me as though inviting me to join in, but I can't bring myself to do some stupid puzzle. There's a line of tension running through me like a steel thread, getting tighter and tighter. What am I going to do? What am I going to do?

My mobile suddenly rings and I practically leap off the sofa, I'm so nervous. What if it's The Look, telling me they've done their investigation and I'm fired? What if it's Luke and he hears Elinor's voice?

But as I pull out my phone, I see Bonnie's ID.

"Elinor, excuse me a moment," I say quickly, and head over to the other side of the massive sitting room. "Hi, Bonnie, what's up?"

"Dear, I can't speak for long." Bonnie sounds really flustered. "But we've had rather a setback."

"Setback?" I feel a jolt. "What do you mean?"

Please let it be something small. Please let it be that we've got another nut-allergy person. I can't cope with anything else big—

"I don't know if you're aware that Luke's been trying to set up a meeting with Christian Scott-Hughes? He's Sir Bernard Cross's—"

"—right-hand man," I join in. "Yes, he won't stop talking about it."

"Well they've set a date. The only date Christian can do. And it's April seventh."

I feel a nasty little twinge. "What time?"

"Lunchtime."

I breathe out. "Well, that should still be all right—"

"In Paris."

"*Paris?*" I stare at the phone in horror.

"They're planning to stay overnight. Luke's asked me to book flights and a hotel."

No. No. I can't be hearing this.

"He can't go to *Paris*! Tell him his diary's booked! Or phone Christian Scott-Hughes's office and tell them—"

"Becky, you don't understand." Bonnie sounds as hassled as I feel. "Christian Scott-Hughes is a very busy man. Getting this slot has been quite a coup. If we re-arrange, it will be in several months' time. I simply can't do it—"

"But what about that whole fake conference you set up?"

"Luke's missing it. He says it's not important enough."

I stare blindly at a gilt-framed painting of a girl in a red hat. My mind is whirling. Luke can't go to Paris on the day of his party. It just can't happen.

"You'll have to get him to reschedule," I say desperately. "Make up some reason. Anything!"

"I've tried!" Bonnie sounds at the end of her tether. "Believe me, I've tried! I've suggested that he really should be at the conference; I've invented a lunch with his financial backers—I've even reminded him it's his birthday. He just laughed. He won't listen to anything I say. Becky . . ." She exhales. "I know you wanted to surprise him. But I think you're going to have to tell him the truth."

"No!" I stare at the phone, aghast.

"But it's the only way—"

"It's not!"

"Dear, is the surprise really *that* important?"

"Yes!" I cry out, suddenly near tears. "It *is*!" I know she thinks I'm crazy and irrational. And maybe I am. But I'm not giving up now.

As I put down the phone, I'm trembling. It's as if the line of tension has been drawn up another 50 percent, till I can hardly breathe. Barely knowing what I'm doing, I head back to the sofa, reach for a tiny sugared bun, and stuff it into my mouth. Then another one. Maybe sugar will help me think.

How do I stop Luke from going to Paris? Pinch his passport? Kidnap him? Find some brilliant, watertight excuse?

Suddenly I become aware that Elinor has stopped reaching for pieces of puzzle and her chilly eye is resting on me. If she tells me my shoe is scuffed, I will honestly throw this bun at her.

"Rebecca, are you quite well? Have you had a shock?"

I automatically open my mouth to say, "Don't worry, I'm fine." But . . . I just can't. I'm not strong enough to keep up the happy façade. Not to someone who doesn't even count.

"To be honest, I've been better." With a shaky hand, I pour myself a cup of tea and stir three sugars into it, slopping some over the edge.

"Would you like a brandy? Or a stiff cocktail?"

I eye her a bit suspiciously. Elinor? Offering me a *cocktail*? Is she making a dig?

No. Her face is humorless. I think she means it. And you know what? It's the most welcome suggestion anyone has made to me for a long time.

"Yes, please," I say after a pause. "I'd love a stiff cocktail."

Elinor passes me the room-service list, and I order an apple martini; after about a nanosecond it appears. I sip it gratefully, and the alcohol hits my bloodstream and at once I feel a bit better. Once it's halfway gone, I stop trembling. God, I could do with about three of these.

Elinor is still calmly putting jigsaw pieces together as though nothing's wrong, but after a while she looks up dispassionately and says, "Have you heard some bad news?"

"Kind of." I take another sip of apple martini. There's something mesmerizing about sitting in this room. It feels totally detached from the real world, like we're in a bubble. No one even knows I'm here. It's like none of it really exists.

And suddenly I have an overwhelming urge to spill. I mean, if I tell Elinor, who can she blab to? No one.

"I've been organizing this party for Luke for his birthday." I stir my apple martini. "A big surprise party. It's in two weeks."

Elinor doesn't flicker, even though it can't be easy to hear that your only son is having a surprise party and you don't even know about it, let alone have an invitation.

"I couldn't invite you," I add bluntly. "You know I couldn't." *Even if I wanted to,* I don't add.

Elinor moves her head about a millimeter without replying, and I press on.

"There were already loads of glitches." I rub my face. "I mean, I was already pretty stressed out. But now I've just heard that Luke's arranged a meeting with this guy Christian Scott-Hughes on the same day as the party, in Paris. And we can't get him to change it. He's been wanting to meet Christian Scott-Hughes for ages. His assistant doesn't know what to do, nor do I. Either I pinch his passport and he's totally livid, or we move the whole party to Paris somehow, or I give in and tell him the truth . . ."

I trail off miserably. I so, so, *so* don't want to tell Luke. But I have a horrible feeling that's what it might come to.

"I've kept it a secret all this time." I nibble on the slice of martini-infused apple. "Luke has no idea what

I'm up to. I can't bear to spoil it. But what else am I going to do?"

There's a knock at the door and a waiter silently comes in with another apple martini. He takes my empty glass, replaces it with the full one, and glides out again.

I gape stupidly. Does that always happen here? Or is it just Elinor?

"Do you mean Christian Scott-Hughes who works for Sir Bernard Cross?" inquires Elinor, who has made no comment on the second apple martini.

"Exactly. Luke's desperate to make contact with Bernard Cross for some environmental client."

I take a sip of my new cocktail, which is just as delicious as the first, then glance up to see if I'm going to get any sympathy from Elinor. If this was anyone normal, they'd already be going, "You poor thing!" or even giving me a hug. But her face is as rigid and distant as ever.

"I know Bernard," she says eventually. "We met at Saint-Tropez on his yacht. A charming man."

Great. Just typical. Here I am, sharing my problems, and all she can do is boast about her superior social connections. And, by the way, does Elinor even *know* what the word *charming* means? Maybe she's mixed it up with *rich*. That would explain a lot.

"I'm sure you do know him," I say shortly. "Well done." I know I'm being rude, but I don't care. Does she think I *care* whose stupid yacht she's been on? I fish out the slice of apple from the second martini and stuff it in my mouth, but not before Minnie has spotted it.

"Apple! Miiiine apple!" She tries to reach inside my mouth and get it back out.

"No, Minnie," I manage to say, and remove her wriggling fingers from my mouth. "Not your apple. It was a grown-up apple and it's all gone now."

"Mine juice!" Now she focuses on the cocktail. "Miiiine juice—"

"I could speak to Bernard." Elinor's calm voice hits my ears. "I could explain the situation and arrange to have the meeting changed. Luke would never know who was behind it."

Startled, I meet Elinor's eyes. She looks so detached I can barely believe I heard her right. Is she actually offering to *help* me? Could she fix my problem, just like that?

Something is sparking in my stomach. It feels a bit like hope.

But already I know I have to damp it down somehow. I can't let myself even think about it, let alone hope, let alone . . . I mean, this is Elinor. *Elinor.* Luke would kill me if he even knew Minnie and I were here, let alone giving away information about his business, let alone inviting offers of help . . .

"No. You can't help. I'm sorry, but you just can't. If Luke ever found out I was even talking to you . . ." A familiar anxiety is washing over me and I get to my feet, dumping my cocktail on the table. "I've already stayed too long. We should go. Minnie, say, 'Bye-bye, Lady.' "

"Lad-eeee!" Minnie flings herself at Elinor's legs.

"So what will you do?"

She frowns with a kind of dispassionate interest, as though I'm one of her jigsaw puzzles and she wants to see how it comes out.

"I don't know," I say hopelessly. "I'll just have to think of something."

WHEN I GET HOME, the house is empty and silent and there's a note on the table in Janice's handwriting.

Nanny Sue's assistant rang. Please call to arrange meeting regarding Minnie.

In a reflex action, I crumple the note and throw it in the bin, then make myself a cup of tea, trying to keep my spirits up. Come on, Becky. Think positive. I can't let my problems get me down.

But even though I load my cup with sugar and sit down with a pencil and paper, no solution comes to my brain. I feel blank and empty and defeated. I'm just wondering whether I should mix myself another comforting cocktail, when the doorbell rings. In surprise I head to the hall and open the door, to see a grizzled old guy in overalls standing on the doorstep. His hands are filthy and he has about three teeth and there's a van pulled up behind him in the drive.

"Tent?" he says without preamble.

For a moment I stare at him uncertainly.

"Love?" He waves a hand in front of my face. "You want a tent?"

"Yes!" I come to. "Yes please!"

Finally, some good news. This is a sign! Everything is going to turn around for the better. Already, the thought of a canopy billowing in Janice's garden is making me excited.

"So, are you from Cliff's company?" I say as he undoes the back of the van.

"Sends his apologies. Most of the lads were called away to an emergency job in Somerset. It's manic."

"I thought everything was really quiet," I say in surprise.

"We had cancellations." He nods. "Then people change their minds, don't they? Lot of it about. Most of our tents have gone down to the West Country, but Cliff said you could have this."

He briskly unloads a pile of white tarpaulin onto the

drive, and I eye it uncertainly. It's not quite as *big* as I was expecting.

"Is that a formal tent?"

"Gazebo, innit? Got a bit of mildew on one side, but give it a go with some bleach; it'll scrub up." He's already back in his cab and switching on the engine. "Cheers, love."

"Wait!" I call out. "Where do I return it?"

A look of amusement passes over the guy's face.

"Nah, you're all right. We don't need that one back."

The van disappears out of the drive, and I take a tentative step toward the pile of white tarpaulin. Maybe it's bigger than it looks.

"Blanket!" Minnie rushes out of the house behind me, leaps onto the tarpaulin, and starts jumping on it.

"It's not a blanket! It's a . . . a tent. Get off, sweetheart. Let's look at it."

Gingerly, I lift up one of the layers and feel a pang of dismay. Underneath, it's green with mold. I lift up another panel—and there's a massive flapping rip in it.

I feel light-headed. This was the one bit of the party that was supposed to be *sorted*. It'll take me hours to clean this and try to mend the rip.

And it's not even a proper tent. It's tiny. How am I supposed to hold a party for two hundred in this?

My whole body is pulsing with compressed panic. But I don't have any options. It's this or nothing.

"Right!" I say as brightly as I can to Minnie. "Well . . . Mummy needs to clean this, doesn't she? Don't *touch*!" I whip her hand away from the green mold.

"Jelleeee!" she wails crossly. "Miiine!"

"It's not jelly! It's yucky!"

I find rubber gloves, bleach, and a scrub brush under the sink, and after I've parked Minnie safely in front of the TV, I start scrubbing. I thought the bleach would cut straight through the green grime, like in the telly ads. But it doesn't. The mold is stuck to the tarpaulin and caked over with mud in some places. It must have been there for years. It takes me ten minutes' solid scrubbing to remove about six square inches of crust, and then I sit back on my heels, exhausted.

I can't clean this whole thing.

But I have to. I can't afford anything else.

I scrub for another ten minutes, then dunk my brush in the bowl of water and bleach, which is now black with dirt. My back's aching. My head's throbbing. As I push my hair back off my hot face, I feel hollow with fear. For the first time, the worst-case-scenario, no-more-delusions reality of my situation is hitting me. Why did I think I could throw a massive grown-up party, all on my own? It's too big.

I want to cry.

No. I'm not going to cry.

Almost without meaning to, I slowly reach into my pocket and pull out my phone. And press Suze's speed-dial number with my thumb.

I'm not going to ask her for help. I can't bring myself to go that far. But if she *offers* again . . . then I'll accept.

"Bex! Hi!" She answers straightaway.

"Suze?" I say tremulously. "How's it all going?"

I won't bring up the subject directly. I'll just wait till she mentions the party and take it from there.

"I'm still furious!" Suze replies hotly. "Do you know what I did today? I got all Tarkie's team in for a meeting and I said, 'Why weren't you *there*? Why was no one at the photo shoot?' And do you know the worst thing? One of them *was*!" Her voice rises indignantly. "He said he did think it all looked rather odd, but he thought it must be the latest thing in fashion and he didn't want to interfere. I'm telling you, Bex, I'm becoming Tarkie's manager. Have you heard from Danny?" she adds. "Because I keep calling him, and he won't return my calls."

"No, he won't answer my calls either." I hear a sudden screaming in the background and a faint banging sound.

"Wilfie! Stop that! Bex, I'd better go. How are you, anyway?"

She hasn't even mentioned it.

And suddenly I feel a stab of humiliation. I can't tell her. I can't admit I'm knee deep in manky tarpaulin with no money and no job and no idea how I'm going to throw this party together.

"I'm . . . I'm good! I'll talk to you later, Suze . . ." I ring off and sit in complete stillness for a moment. The drive is becoming chilly and dark. I can see a light coming on in Janice's house and have a sudden thought. I scroll down my numbers again and press *Jess.*

I'll ask her round for a cup of tea and she'll see the tent and volunteer to help clean it. I know she will. I should have asked Jess ages ago. She's my sister, after all!

"Hi, Jess!" I say eagerly as soon as she answers. "Are you around? Do you want a cup of tea or anything?"

"Tom and I are in Staffordshire," she says, her voice sounding distant. "I've come to do some research at the museum here. I couldn't bear Janice a minute longer. You won't *believe* her latest stunt."

"What?"

"She stole our contraception! Took it! She denies it, but I know she did. Why else would *our* condoms have been in *her* bedroom drawer? I said to her, 'Don't tell me they're yours, Janice, because I won't believe you.' I mean, she's probably never even *heard* of fair-trade ethical condoms, let alone bought them. We had a massive row. Martin went and hid in the tree house, he was so embarrassed."

Despite everything, I can't help a half giggle as I try

to imagine Jess and Janice having a stand-up row about condoms.

"So we had to get out of there for a few days," Jess is continuing. "Becky, I can't stand her. What am I going to do?" Her voice dips away.

"Jess? Are you there?"

"Sorry! Listen, my phone's running out. Can I call you back later?"

"Sure!" I try to sound lighthearted. "Give my love to Tom!"

As the light in my phone dies away, the drive seems darker than ever.

My head droops down onto my knees. I feel exhausted. All my remaining energy has been sapped away by those two calls. I've got nothing left. I've got no hope, no plans, no answers. I don't know why I thought I could throw a party. I must have been crazy.

A tear suddenly rolls down the side of my nose, followed by another. I'm going to have to admit defeat. I'm going to have to cancel the party. I can't see any other way. It's just too overwhelmingly massive. There's no way I can pull it off.

I give a huge sob and bury my face in my hands. I can't believe I'm giving up. But what else can I do?

I'll call Bonnie and ask her to email all the guests. We'll make up some excuse. Luke can go to Paris. He'll never even know what I was planning. Life will just carry on. It's the easiest solution. It's the *only* solution.

"Rebecca?" My head jerks up and I blink at the tall, shadowy figure standing in front of me.

"*Elinor?*" I feel a choking panic. "What are you doing here? You can't come here! This is where I live! What if Luke saw you, or if my parents—"

"Luke isn't here," replies Elinor calmly. She's wearing the dove-gray Chanel coat which I sold her, belted tightly around her waist. "No one is here except you and Minnie. My driver ascertained these facts before I approached."

Her driver? Where did she get him from, MI5?

"I will be brief." Her eyes are focused on the middle distance, away from me. "I wish to offer you my assistance again. I believe you rejected it too hastily, for reasons which I can only surmise. However, it seems to me that you need a personal contact with Sir Bernard Cross. I can ask him to rearrange Luke's meeting, and I'm sure he will do so." She hesitates. "If you would like me to do this, then please let me know."

"Thanks," I say dully. "But there's no point now. I'm canceling the party."

For the first time Elinor looks at me directly, and I can see the flash of surprise in her eyes.

"*Canceling*? Why?"

"Because I can't do it." A fresh tear runs down my nose. "It's all a disaster. I bartered for this tent, but it's all moldy, and I'll never clean it in time, and it's not even big enough. And then I ran out of money, so I was going to ask for a raise, but I got suspended from work, and Luke's going to Paris anyway . . ." I wipe my eyes. "What's the point? What's the point even trying anymore?"

Elinor is running her gaze coldly over the tent.

"Do you have no one to help you with this endeavor? Your friend Susan, perhaps?"

God, I had no idea she even knew Suze's name.

"I kind of—" I break off and flush. "I told all my friends I didn't want their help."

It's getting really dark now and I can barely see Elinor. I'm psyching myself up to ask if she would like a cup of tea, hoping she'll say no, when she speaks again, sounding even more stiff and awkward than usual.

"I have remembered the conversation we had and considered it often over the past few weeks. You are a perceptive young woman, Rebecca. I have never given anything to Luke outright. There have always been . . . expectations attached. Now I would like to give him something. Unconditionally. And that is why I should like to help you."

"Elinor . . ." I wince. "It's kind of you. It really is. But like I said, there's no point. Even if Luke doesn't go to Paris, I can't put this party together in time." I lift up a moldy tent flap and let it drop. "You expect me to entertain two hundred people in *this*?"

"So you're simply giving up?"

I feel stung by her tone. What does she care? It's not her party. She's not even invited.

"I suppose so." I shrug. "Yes. I am."

"I find this disturbing." She eyes me stonily. "I have never known you to give up on any project before. You have been misguided, yes. Unpolished, yes. Impulsive, yes. Foolish, yes—"

Is she trying to make me feel better?

"OK, thanks," I interrupt. "I get the picture."

"—but you have always been tenacious," continues Elinor, as though I didn't speak. "You have always refused to give in, whatever factors are mounting against you. It is one of the things I've always admired about you."

She's *always admired* me? Now I've heard it all.

"Well, maybe this one is just too big, OK?" I say wearily. "Maybe I'm not Superwoman."

"If the will is there, anything is achievable with enough resources."

"Yes, well, that's the whole *point*!" I erupt in frustration. "Don't you understand? I've been suspended from work! My credit cards are all used up! I don't *have* any bloody—"

"I have resources," Elinor cuts me off.

I stare at her uncertainly for a few moments. Is she saying . . . She can't be . . .

"I have resources," she repeats. "We could . . . do it together."

Oh my God.

Together? Is she trying to come on board as joint hostess?

"Elinor . . ." The idea is so preposterous, I almost want to laugh. "You can't be serious. Luke would— He'd be—"

"Luke would not know. Luke would never know." She sounds so resolute, I stare at her, taken aback. She really means this, doesn't she?

"Mummy!" Minnie comes rocketing out of the house, then stops dead in astonishment. "Ladeee!" She throws herself on Elinor with delight.

"Elinor." I rub my forehead. "You can't just . . . Do you know how bad things are? Do you know how Luke would react if—"

"I do know. This is why I am asking you for this chance." Her face is as stony as ever, but suddenly I notice the tiny quivering by her eye that I noticed before.

Unless it's just the dusky light.

"It is impossible for me to give anything to Luke." Her voice is entirely without self-pity. "He has cut me out of his life. He mistrusts me. Any gift I attempted to make would be met with short shrift. If you say yes to my offer, then you are giving me the opportunity to make Luke an unconditional gift. Perhaps even to make my own reparation." Elinor pauses. "The kind of gift . . . that his real mother would have made to him."

What? Did she just call Annabel his *real mother*?

I swallow, several times. This is all getting too heavy. I'm not sure I can cope. It was easier when Elinor was just the big bad witch that we never saw.

"If you refuse my offer," she adds, as matter-of-fact as ever, "then you are denying me this privilege."

"Puzzle?" Minnie is tugging hopefully at Elinor's bag. "Puzzle?"

"Here you are, Minnie." Elinor reaches into her bag, pulls out one of the puzzles that she had earlier in the Ritz, and presents it to Minnie. Then she looks directly at me. "Please."

My mind is shooting back and forth helplessly, like a pinball. I can't . . . I mustn't . . . I could . . .

Luke would never know . . .

No, I *can't* . . .

But we wouldn't have to cancel . . . Luke would get his party . . .

"Perhaps you need time to think about it," says Elinor, and I focus on her as though for the first time. Standing there, holding her expensive bag with two gloved hands, her hair gusting a little in the wind, she looks pale and old and shadowy. And almost . . . humble.

This is maybe the most mind-blowing thing of all. Elinor Sherman, grandest, snootiest woman in the world, for once hasn't told me or bossed me or lectured me. She's asked. And now she's waiting meekly for an answer.

Or at least as meekly as you can when you're dressed head to toe in Chanel with your driver waiting.

"OK," I say and give her a sudden grin. "OK, Elinor. You're on."

"Thank you." Elinor hesitates. "Rebecca, I wish to say something else. I know you have been determined to throw this party yourself. I know you take pride in being independent. But you must not underestimate the pleasure it will give others to give to Luke, in whichever way is appropriate."

"My friend Suze said something like that to me too,"

I say slowly. "She wanted to help but I wouldn't let her."

I wince as I remember Suze's hurt voice saying, "It's not always about *you*, OK? It's not because we think you can't do it. It's because Luke isn't just your husband, he's our friend too, and we wanted to do something nice for him."

She really wanted to get involved. And I was too proud to let her. Even now I haven't actually asked, have I? I've waited for her to volunteer. Well, no wonder she hasn't.

I suddenly feel like the biggest cow there ever was.

"Elinor, excuse me a minute . . ." I take a few steps away, pull out my phone, and speed-dial Suze again.

"Bex?" She sounds surprised. "Are you OK?"

"Listen, Suze," I say in a trembling rush. "I'm so sorry. I wish I'd asked you to help with the party all along. I love your idea about the special shortbread; Luke would be so touched. And I was just going to say . . ." I swallow hard. "Is it too late? Would you help?"

There's a still, beating silence for a moment, then Suze says, "Be honest, Bex. Have you got yourself in a totally shit mess?"

"Yes!" I give a half laugh, half sob. "I have."

"Then Tarkie owes me a fiver," she says with satisfaction. "OK. When, where, and what do I need to do?"

KENTISH ENGLISH 🍾 SPARKLING WINE

SPANDINGS HOUSE | MALLENBURY | KENT

Ms. Rebecca Brandon
The Pines
43 Elton Road
Oxshott
Surrey

3 April 2006

Dear Ms. Brandon,

Thank you very much for your letter of 27 March.

I'm glad our consignment of fifty bottles of sparkling wine reached you safely and that, on tasting, you were so "struck" by its punchy and distinctive flavor. We're very proud of it!

However, I totally understand if, as you say, you have recently discovered the temperance movement and decided to make your party teetotal. We will arrange to have the bottles picked up without delay and hope your party goes with a (dry) swing!

Yours truly,

Paul Spry
Marketing Director

P.S.—We will shortly be launching a nonalcoholic sparkling wine, and I will be pleased to forward you ten bottles, with our compliments.

EIGHTEEN

SO MUCH HAS HAPPENED. There are only three days to go. I can't quite believe it. And finally, *finally*, everything is on track.

Elinor has the most amazing contacts in the world. She can just *make things happen*. She points her bony finger and it's instantly done. At least, she points her bony finger at an assistant, and he gets it instantly done.

So she's not exactly a riot. We don't exactly high-five each other when we get a result. And she doesn't seem to understand the function of chocolate, let alone want to share the odd Kit Kat. But the plus points are: 1) She wants Luke's party to be fabulous; 2) she's thrown a million smart parties before; 3) she has loads and loads and *loads* of money.

I mean, money's just not an issue anymore. Even Suze has been quite wide-eyed at the way Elinor doles it out without a flicker. Jess, of course, can't cope. Jess puts her hands over her ears and says, "I don't want to know." And then she takes them off again and lectures Elinor on sustainability and responsible sourcing. To my amazement, Elinor always listens gravely—and a few times she's even agreed to Jess's suggestions. (Although *not* the one about knitting woolly hats out of recycled yarn to hand out to guests, so we won't need heaters. Thank God.)

Honestly, the party's going to be just—

I mean, it'll be the most—

No. I won't say anything more. I don't want to jinx it.

It's even been quite fun, the five of us having our top-secret meetings (Suze, Jess, Bonnie, Elinor, and me). Elinor always leaves first, and the rest of us wait breathlessly till she's out of earshot, then erupt with hysteria at something she said or did. I mean, she's still totally ice queen most of the time. But even so, she's almost starting to feel—in a weird way—like one of the gang.

Luke has no idea. None. He still thinks I'm at work two and a half days a week, and I haven't put him right.

The only unresolved issue is the meeting with Christian Scott-Hughes. Bernard Cross has been at some retreat in Sweden and uncontactable. But he's back today. Elinor has stated she's going to get on the phone to him this morning and won't take no for an answer. And I believe her.

So the biggest challenge left is keeping the party secret from Luke between now and Friday. But we've got this far; we can make it till Friday, surely. Today, Bonnie's finally revealing to Luke's entire staff that there isn't a conference, it's a surprise party instead. There's bound to be a big buzz, and we decided I should keep Luke out of the office on some pretext. So we're going to see a possible school for Minnie this morning. (I told Luke we'd already left it really late, and he had to come too because otherwise they'd think we weren't committed parents and, no, I *couldn't* just tell him about it later.)

"Ready?" Luke hurries down the stairs, looking immaculate in a navy suit and his really expensive cashmere coat from Milan.

"Yes, ready." I finish doing my lipstick and survey myself in the hall mirror. The school we're going to see today has a red and navy uniform, so I'm wearing red and navy too, to show how keen we are. (I nearly bought the crested hat off the website, but then I thought that was going a bit far.)

"Nanny Sue called," Luke adds. "She's coming at six o'clock."

"Fine," I say after a pause. There's no point trying to argue Luke out of Nanny Sue. I've already tried.

"Good luck at the school!" says Janice, who has come over to watch Minnie. "Don't worry about us, we'll be fine, just the two of us!" I glance over and she gives me the tiniest of winks.

I've already exchanged about ten secret texts with Janice since breakfast. The tent guys are coming over to prepare her garden this morning, but neither of us mentions that, obviously.

As I'm heading out of the door, Janice pulls me back with an urgent whisper.

"Love, I heard from your mother yesterday."

"Oh, really?"

The estate agents are having a nightmare finding us a rental place, so Mum and Dad are still living it up in the The West Place, having mud wraps and champagne cocktails every day, I expect.

"She told me she's not invited to the party." Janice peers at me anxiously. "That can't be true, Becky, love."

That is *so* Mum. Trying to get everyone on her side. And, anyway, it's not true. She's had an invitation.

"Why does she want to come, anyway?" I know I sound sulky, but I can't help it. "She said it would be a fiasco."

"But, Becky, it's going to be a wonderful party." Janice looks all flustered. "You can't let her miss it."

"She can come if she wants. She knows where I am."
My phone bleeps with a text and I pull it out.

I have secured a brief interview with Bernard
today. I will keep you informed. Kind regards. Elinor.

Elinor has to be the only person in the world who
writes *kind regards* on text messages. Mind you, *kind regards* is a lot better than *I remain disapprovingly yours,*
which is how she once ended a letter to me.

Thx! I text back. Look forward to hearing!

I head out into the drive—and it takes me a moment
to notice what Luke is doing. He's unlocking the
garage. Shit. Shit! Where did he get the key from? I *hid*
it, precisely so he *wouldn't* open the garage and find the
moldy tent, plus 132 plastic-bag pom-poms. (Which I
am *not* disposing of, whatever Elinor says. I made them
for the party and they took me hours and they're
bloody well going in the party.)
"Nooooo!" Somehow I make it across the drive in
order to dive between him and the garage door. "Don't!
I mean . . . what do you need? I'll get it. You start the
engine. Get the car warmed up."
"Becky . . ." Luke looks astonished. "What's wrong?"
"You . . . don't want to get your nice coat dirty!"
"Well, you don't want to get *your* coat dirty," he
points out reasonably. "I'm only after the road map. My
bloody sat nav is on the blink." He reaches for the han-
dle again, but I block his way.
"We can buy one on the way."
"*Buy* one?" He peers at me. "Why would we do that?"
"You can always do with an extra road map." My

hand is clamped on the garage door handle. "It'll be fun. We can choose it together!"

"But we've already *got* one," he says patiently. "If you'd just let me into the garage—"

OK, I need extreme measures.

"Do you know how desperate I am to buy something?" I cry dramatically, my voice throbbing like a Shakespearean actress. "You won't let me buy any clothes. Now you won't let me buy a road map either! I need to spend some money or I'm going to go crazy!"

I break off, panting. Luke looks so freaked out, I almost feel sorry for him.

"OK, Becky. Fine." He backs away, shooting me wary little looks. "We can stop at a service station. No problem."

"Good." I fan myself as though overcome by emotion. "Thank you for understanding. So, where did you get the garage key?" I add casually, "I thought it was lost."

"It was the damnedest thing." Luke shakes his head. "I was looking for it, and I said aloud, 'Where is that key?' and Minnie led me to it at once. She must have hidden it herself!"

Honestly. That's the *last* time I include Minnie in any of the preparations. She's a total blab.

"You'll never guess where it was," Luke adds as he starts the car. "Inside your makeup bag. Can you believe it?"

"Incredible!" I try to muster an astonished voice. "What a little monkey!"

"By the way, do you want to come to Paris with me on Friday?" Luke adds casually as he reverses.

I'm so thrown I can't answer. I gaze blankly back at him, my mind skittering. What do I say? What would be the natural reaction?

"Paris?" I manage at last. "What do you mean?"

"I'm going to Paris for this meeting, remember? Just thought you and Minnie might like to come along. We could make a weekend of it. You know it's my birthday?"

The word *birthday* is like a hand grenade going off in the car. What do I say? Do I pretend I've forgotten? Do I pretend I didn't hear him?

No. Act normal, Becky. *Act normal.*

"Um . . . is it?" I swallow. "Wow, of course it's your birthday! Well, that sounds lovely."

"We'll have to spend Friday night with my clients, I'm afraid, but at least it should be a celebration. I mean, once we've seen Christian, we're well on the way to meeting with Sir Bernard himself!" Luke sounds ebullient. "I'll get Bonnie to make the arrangements. So that's agreed?"

"Fab!" I smile weakly. "I just need to text Suze about something . . ."

I reach for my phone and quickly text Bonnie: Luke wants to take us to Paris on Friday! Do NOT book tickets!!

Honestly, I'm going to crack up at this rate.

No, I'm not. It's fine. Elinor's on the case. Deep breaths. Only three days to go.

HARDY HOUSE SCHOOL is a much nicer school than St. Cuthbert's, I instantly decide. For a start, the secretary who greets us has a really cool Pippa Small necklace on. And there aren't any pupils called Eloise. (I asked.) *And* they make their own homemade biscuits.

As we sip our coffee and eat the biscuits, we have a view out to the playground, which is surrounded by horse chestnuts. I watch all the little girls running round and skipping, and I feel a sudden pang of longing. I can just see Minnie joining in with all of them. It would be perfect.

"D'you think Minnie'll get a place?" I turn anxiously to Luke.

"I'm sure she will." He looks up from his BlackBerry. "Why wouldn't she?"

"Because it's really oversubscribed!"

I glance again at the sheet of paper I've been given, entitled *Our Entry Procedure.* There are six stages to it, starting with filling out a form and ending with *Final Assessment Tea Party.* Now I can see why everyone gets stressed out by schools. I'm already terrified. What if Minnie grabs all the cakes and yells "Miiiine"? They'll never give her a place.

"Luke, stop looking at your BlackBerry!" I nudge him. "We have to make a good impression!" I pick up a leaflet on attainment grades and start flipping through it, just as the door opens and the secretary appears again.

"Mr. and Mrs. Brandon? Come this way, please." She ushers us along a short passage smelling of beeswax. "Here's the headmistress's office," she says, leading us straight into a paneled room with a mahogany desk and green upholstered chairs. "Our current head, Mrs. Bell, is leaving at the end of term, and the prospective head is with us for a few days, so we thought it would make more sense for you to see her. She'll be along in just a moment."

"Thank you," says Luke charmingly. "And may I compliment the school on your delicious homemade biscuits?"

"Thank you!" She smiles. "I'll be back presently with the new head. Her name is Mrs. Grayson," she adds as she exits. "Harriet Grayson."

"There," murmurs Luke. "We're making a perfect impression."

I can't reply. In fact, I've frozen. Don't I know that name?

OK. This could be bad. I need to get out of here, or warn Luke, or—

But the door is already swinging open again—and it's her. It's Harriet Grayson, MA, dressed in the same knitted suit. She comes forward with a professional smile—then recognition flashes onto her face.

"Professor Bloomwood!" she says in astonishment. "It *is* Professor Bloomwood, isn't it?"

There is no way out of this. None.

"Um . . . yes!" I say at last, blood flooding my face. "Hi!"

"Well, what a surprise!" She beams at Luke. "Professor Bloomwood and I have met before. Brandon must be your married name?"

"That's . . . that's right." I gulp.

I risk a tiny glance at Luke, then wish I hadn't. His expression makes me half want to burst into laughter and half want to dash out of the room.

"Are you in the art world too, Mr. Brandon?" she says pleasantly as she shakes his hand.

"The *art* world?" Luke says after a fairly long pause.

"No, he's not," I chime in hurriedly. "Not at all. Anyway, moving on to the really important subject, we'd like to send our daughter Minnie here. I love your playground. Beautiful trees!" I'm hoping we can move on, but Harriet Grayson, MA, looks puzzled.

"So, are you relocating from New York?"

"Um . . . that's right," I say after a pause. "Isn't it, darling?" I shoot Luke a brief, desperate look.

"Goodness! But what about your work at the Guggenheim, Professor Bloomwood?"

"The Guggenheim?" echoes Luke in a slightly strangled voice.

"Yes, the Guggenheim. Absolutely." I nod several times, playing for time. "Obviously I'll miss the Guggenheim very much. But I'll be . . . focusing on my own art."

"You're an artist yourself?" Harriet Grayson seems bowled over. "How wonderful! Are you a painter?"

"Not really." I cough. "My work is . . . it's quite hard to describe—"

"Becky's art form is unique," Luke suddenly chimes in. "She creates . . . unreal worlds. Fantasyland, some might call it."

I shoot him a tiny glare, just as there's a knock on the door.

"Mr. Brandon?" The secretary looks in tentatively. "You have an urgent message to call your office."

"I'm so sorry." Luke looks surprised. "It must be very important for them to interrupt me. Excuse me." As he heads out of the room, I grab the prospectus and flick randomly to a page.

"So!" I say hastily. "When you say the children read every day, what exactly do you *mean* by that?"

Thank God. For about five minutes Mrs. Grayson talks about reading schemes and I nod intelligently. Then I ask a question about the science building and I get another three minutes, and I'm about to move on to netball when the door opens.

I gape at Luke in surprise. His face is glowing. He looks like he's won the lottery. What on earth—

Oh my God. Elinor's done it!

OK, now I'm *dying* to check my texts.

"I'm so sorry," Luke says politely to Mrs. Grayson. "I've been called back to my office on unavoidable business. But Becky can stay and do the tour."

"No!" I jump to my feet as though I've been scalded.

"I mean . . . I'd rather see it with *you,* darling. I'm so sorry, Mrs. Grayson—"

"That's quite all right," she says smilingly. "And may I say again what a pleasure it is to see you, Professor? You know, your advice regarding little Ernest Cleath-Stuart was invaluable."

Beside me, I can sense Luke prick up his ears. "What's this?" he says politely.

"All in a day's work," I say hastily. "It was nothing to speak of—"

"I have to disagree! Professor Bloomwood cleverly spotted the potential of one of my pupils at St. Cuthbert's," Harriet Grayson tells Luke. "A young boy who was having a few . . . difficulties, shall we say. But he really has come out of himself since we gave him the art award. He's a different child!"

"*Ah.*" Luke nods in sudden understanding. "I see." His eyes are softer as they meet mine. "Well, Professor Bloomwood's very good at that kind of thing."

We head along the corridors and out of the school without speaking, slide into the car, and look at each other for a moment in silence.

"So." Luke raises a quizzical eyebrow. "Professor."

"Luke—"

"Don't tell Suze." He nods. "I got it. And, Becky . . . good for you. Except we can never send Minnie to this school now, you realize?"

"I know," I say gloomily. "And I really liked it."

"We'll find another." He squeezes my knee, then reaches for his phone and dials. "Hi, Gary? I'm coming straight in. I know, incredible news!"

Surreptitiously, I turn on my BlackBerry and it bleeps with incoming texts, the first from Elinor.

I have spoken to Bernard. Kind regards, Elinor.

Just like that. Sorted, with no fuss. The more I get to know Elinor, the more I realize she's an incredible woman. I think Luke must have got some of her genes. The determined, steely, crush-every-obstacle ones. Not that I'll ever say that to him.

"So . . . what's up?" I say innocently as Luke starts the car. "What's the big excitement at work?"

"You remember that trip to Paris?" Luke looks over his shoulder to reverse. "It's off, I'm afraid. We're not meeting Christian Scott-Hughes, after all—we're meeting the main man, this afternoon. Sir Bernard just decided to give us half an hour, out of the blue! Sir Bernard Cross himself!"

"Wow!" It's lucky I'm good at acting. "How *amazing*!"

"It's unheard of." Luke nods, his eyes on the road. "Everyone's in a state of shock."

"Well, congratulations! You deserve it!"

Thx Elinor I'm texting back. You are a total STAR!!!!!!!!

"What I *do* think"—Luke pauses as he negotiates a tricky roundabout—"is that someone has pulled some strings for us. This kind of thing doesn't happen out of the blue." He glances at me. "Someone, somewhere is behind it. Someone influential."

My heart seems to jump right into my mouth. For a moment my throat is too tight with panic to answer.

"Really?" I say at last. "Who would do that?"

"I don't know. Difficult to say." He frowns thoughtfully for a moment, then flashes me a tiny grin. "But whoever it is, I love them."

FOR THE REST of the afternoon, I'm on tenterhooks. It's all going according to plan—as long as each bit of the plan works out. As long as the meeting goes well; as long as Luke doesn't decide to go to Paris anyway; as long as no one at the office blabs . . .

I'm trying to do a seating plan but, honestly, it's worse than Sudoku, and I'm too preoccupied to concentrate. Janice keeps coming in and fussing about where exactly the tent entrance will be, and Minnie jams a pencil in the DVD player halfway through *Finding Nemo*. So basically it's five o'clock and I haven't got beyond Table 3 when there's the sound of a key in the front door. Hastily, I gather up my table charts and shove them in the cupboard, behind Dad's *Sounds of the Seventies* CD collection. When Luke comes in, I'm sitting on the sofa, reading a book, which I've just grabbed off the floor.

"Hi, how was it?" I look up.

"Great. Really good." Luke is glowing even more triumphantly than he was this morning. "Sir Bernard's a great guy. He wanted to listen, he was interested, we raised a lot of thought-provoking side issues . . ."

"Fantastic!" I smile—but I can't quite relax yet. I have to be sure. "So . . . you definitely won't need to go to Paris on Friday?"

"Afraid not. Although we could still go if you wanted?" Luke adds.

"No!" Relief sends my voice shooting sky-high. "God, no! Let's just . . . stay here. Chill out. Not do anything." I'm babbling, but I can't help it. "So, a good day all round." I beam at him. "We should open some champagne."

"Yes. Apart from one thing." Luke frowns briefly. "I had to give my assistant a verbal warning. Not really the way I wanted to end the afternoon. I may have to let her go."

What? My smile falls away.

"You mean Bonnie? But . . . *why?* You said you wouldn't say anything. What did she do now?"

"Oh, it's very disappointing." Luke sighs. "For months she seemed the perfect assistant. I couldn't fault her. But then she started making the inappropriate comments that I mentioned to you before. I've recently noticed she seems very distracted. And now I'm sure she's been making illicit phone calls of some kind."

Oh God, oh God. This is *all* because of me and the party.

"Everyone's allowed to make the odd phone call," I say quickly, but Luke shakes his head.

"It's more than that. I have my suspicions. At best she's moonlighting; at worst, stealing company information."

"She wouldn't do anything like that!" I say in horror. "I've met her. She's obviously completely honest."

"Darling, you're very trusting." Luke shoots me a fond smile. "But I'm afraid you're wrong. *Something's* going on. I came across Bonnie dealing with a pile of paperwork that quite clearly had nothing to do with Brandon Communications. Not only that, she looked as guilty as sin when I appeared, and she hid some papers under the desk. She clearly didn't expect me back for a while. So I had to have a stern word." He shrugs. "Not pleasant for either of us, but there you go."

"You were *stern*?" I say, aghast.

I can just picture what happened. Bonnie was going through the guest list with me this afternoon. That must be what she hid under the desk. I thought she rang off rather hastily.

"What exactly did you say?" I demand. "Did she get upset?"

"Does it matter?"

"Yes!" I feel a surge of frustration. "You stupid idiot!"

I feel like yelling. "Did it never occur to you she might be helping to organize your surprise birthday party?"

I mean, obviously I'm *glad* it didn't occur to him. But still. I hope Bonnie's OK. She's so mild-mannered and sweet, I can't bear the idea of Luke upsetting her.

"What's the problem?"

I can't say anything else. I'll give myself away.

"Nothing." I shake my head. "No problem. I'm sure you were right. It's just . . . a shame."

"OK," Luke says slowly, giving me a slightly odd look. "Well, I'll go and change. Nanny Sue will be here before too long."

The instant he's gone, I dash into the downstairs cloakroom, speed-dial Bonnie's number, and get voice mail.

"Bonnie!" I exclaim. "Luke just told me he gave you some kind of verbal warning. I'm *so* sorry. You know he doesn't understand. He'll feel terrible when he finds out. Anyway, the good news is, Paris is definitely off! So everything's finally falling into place. Have you told all the Brandon C lot yet? Call me as soon as you have a chance."

As I ring off, I hear the doorbell.

Great. That must be Nazi Sue.

TODAY NANNY SUE'S wearing her official blue uniform. Sitting on the sofa, with a cup of tea and a laptop open beside her, she looks like she's a policewoman come to arrest us.

"So," she begins, looking from me to Luke and then smiling down at Minnie, who's sitting on the floor with a puzzle. "It was a pleasure to spend some time with Becky and Minnie."

I don't reply. I'm not falling for her so-called friendly overtures. This is how she always starts on her TV show. She's all nicey-nicey and then she goes in for the kill, and by the end everyone's sobbing on her shoulder and saying, "Nanny Sue, how can we be better people?"

"Now." She taps at the laptop and a video screen appears with *Minnie Brandon* in black letters above it. "As you know, I filmed our morning together, as is my common practice. Just for my own records, you understand."

"*What?*" I gape at her. "Are you serious? Where was the camera?"

"On my lapel." Nanny Sue looks equally taken aback and turns to Luke. "I thought you'd informed Becky."

"You *knew*? You didn't tell me anything!" I round on Luke. "I was being filmed the whole time and you didn't *tell* me?"

"I thought it better not to. I thought if you knew, you might . . ." He hesitates. ". . . act unnaturally. Put on a show."

"I would never *put on a show*," I retort, outraged.

Nanny Sue is scrolling through the images, pausing every now and again, and I catch a glimpse of myself talking stagily about organic Play-Doh.

"That bit's not relevant," I say hastily. "I'd fast forward."

"So, what did you think, Nanny Sue?" Luke is leaning forward in his chair, hands clasped anxiously on his knees. "Did you spot any major problems?"

"Unfortunately, I *did* notice something that concerned me," Nanny Sue says seriously. "I'll show you now . . . Can you both see the screen?"

What did she notice? Whatever it was, she's *wrong*. I'm feeling a burning indignation. What gives her the right to come into our house and film us and tell us what's wrong with our daughter? Who said she was an expert, anyway?

"Wait!" I exclaim, and Nanny Sue stops the footage

in surprise. "Plenty of children have spirit, Nanny Sue. But it doesn't mean they're spoiled. It doesn't mean they've got *problems*. Human nature is a varied and beautiful thing. Some people are timid and some are feisty! Our daughter is a wonderful human being, and I'm not having her spirit crushed at some . . . oppressive boot camp! And Luke agrees!"

"I agree too." Nanny Sue's voice takes me by surprise.

"What?" I say feebly.

"I don't think Minnie has problems in the slightest. She could do with more structure and discipline in her life, but otherwise she is just a lively, normal toddler."

"Normal?" I stare at Nanny Sue stupidly.

"Normal?" exclaims Luke. "Is it *normal* to squirt ketchup at people?"

"For a two-year-old, yes." Nanny Sue looks amused. "Entirely normal. She's just testing the boundaries. Incidentally, when did she last squirt ketchup at anybody?"

"Well . . ." Luke looks at me a little uncertainly. "Actually . . . I don't remember now. Not for a while."

"She is willful. And at moments she does seem to have the upper hand. I suggest that I spend a day with you and give you some advice on controlling her wilder ways. But I really don't want you thinking that you have a problem child. Minnie is a *normal* child. A lovely child, in fact."

I'm so taken aback I can't find a reply.

"She's very intelligent," adds Nanny Sue, "which will be a challenge as she grows older. Intelligent children can often test their parents the most . . ."

She starts talking about boundaries again, but I'm too chuffed to listen properly. Minnie's intelligent! Nanny Sue said my child was intelligent! A genuine expert off the telly!

"So you're not going to recommend any boot camps?" I cut into her speech joyfully.

"Ah, now, I didn't say that." Nanny Sue's face turns graver. "As I said, I did pick up something in my observations. And it worried me. Watch this."

She presses a button and the film starts—but to my surprise, it's not Minnie on the screen. It's me. I'm in the taxi on the way to the discount mall, and the camera is zooming in on my hands.

"Where are you?" Luke peers at the screen. "In a taxi?"

"We . . . went out. Do we really need to see this?" I make to close down the screen, but Nanny Sue smoothly moves it out of my reach.

"We could pop into this new mall instead of the soft-play," I can hear myself saying on-screen.

"Becky, I'd like you to look at your hands." Nanny Sue points with a pencil. "They're shaking. Look at your fingers twitching. They began when we first saw the sign for the shopping mall, and I don't believe they stopped until you'd bought something."

"I've just got twitchy fingers." I give a casual little laugh. But Nanny Sue is shaking her head.

"I don't want to alarm you, Becky—but has it ever occurred to you that you might have an addiction to shopping?"

A sudden snort comes from Luke, which I ignore.

"Shopping?" I echo at last, as though I'm not even certain what the word means. "Er . . . I don't *think* so. . . ."

"Look at the tension in your jaw." She gestures at the screen. "Look at the way you're tapping the seat."

Honestly. Aren't people allowed to tap seats anymore?

"You have an air of desperation about you," persists

Nanny Sue. "To my eyes, this is a disproportionate reaction."

"No, it's not!" I realize I sound too defensive and immediately backtrack. "Look. I hadn't been shopping for a while, it's a new discount mall—I'm only human! They were giving away free gifts! They had Jimmy Choo at fifty percent off! And Burberry! *Anyone* would be twitchy!"

Nanny Sue looks at me for a moment as though I've been speaking gibberish, then turns to Luke.

"I'm starting a new series of adult programs. We're going to be tackling all sorts of disorders, from addiction to anger—"

"Wait a minute." I cut her off in disbelief. "You're saying you want *me* to go to boot camp? Luke, can you believe this?"

I turn to him, waiting for him to laugh and say, "What a ludicrous idea." But he has an anxious frown.

"Becky, I thought you said you weren't going to shop for a while. I thought we'd made an agreement."

"I *didn't* shop for myself," I say impatiently. "I only bought a few essential clothes for Minnie. And they were all on sale!"

"Your life is your own concern, of course," Nanny Sue is saying. "However, my worry is that Minnie may pick up your tendencies. She already has an advanced knowledge of brand names, she seems to have an unlimited amount of money to spend—"

This is the final straw.

"That is *not true*!" I exclaim indignantly. "She only spends her *pocket money*. It's all written down in a special book, which I showed you!" I reach into my bag and produce Minnie's pocket-money book. "Remember?" I thrust it at Nanny Sue. "I mean, yes, she has the odd little advance, but I've explained to her she'll need to pay it back."

Nanny Sue leafs through the book for a moment, then gives me an odd look.

"How much pocket money does she have a week?"

"Fifty pence a week," says Luke, "for now."

Nanny Sue has produced a calculator from her own bag and is tapping at it.

"Then, according to my sums . . ." She looks up calmly. "Minnie has spent her 'pocket money' until the year 2103."

"What?" I stare at her, discomfited.

"*What?*" Luke grabs the book from her and starts flipping through. "What the hell has she bought?"

"Not that much . . ."

The year 2103? Can that be right? I'm frantically trying to do sums in my head as Luke examines the entries in Minnie's book like the Gestapo.

"Six dolls?" He jabs at a page. "In one day?"

"They were a matching set," I say defensively. "And they've got French names! It'll help her language!"

"What's this?" He's already on another page. "Junior Dolce boots?"

"She wore them the other day! Those little suede ones. You said how nice she looked!"

"I didn't know they cost two hundred *quid*!" he erupts. "I mean, Jesus Christ, Becky, she's a kid. Why does she need designer boots?"

He looks really shocked. To be honest, I'm a bit shocked myself. Maybe I should have added up what she was spending a bit better.

"Look, OK, I'll stop her pocket money for now . . ."

Luke isn't even listening to me. He's turned back to Nanny Sue.

"You're saying that if we don't cure Becky, Minnie could turn into a shopaholic herself?"

I've never known him to look so anxious.

"Well, addictive behavior is known to run in families." They're both talking as though I'm not even here.

"I'm not *addicted*," I say furiously. "And neither is Minnie!" I snatch the pocket-money book from him. Nanny Sue must have added it up wrong. We *can't* have spent that much.

Minnie has been Hoovering her way efficiently through the shortbread biscuits on the coffee table, but now she notices the pocket-money book.

"Pocket money?" Her eyes light up. "Shops?" She starts tugging at my hand. "Starbucks—shops?"

"Not now," I say hurriedly.

"Shops! *Shops!*" Minnie is tugging at my hand in frustration, as though if I just understood, I'd do what she wanted. It's the same look Dad got in France, that time we wanted to buy an electric fan and all the French shop assistants stared blankly as he shouted, "Fan! *Fan! Électrique!*" and whirled his hands around.

"*Shops.*"

"No, Minnie!" I snap. "Be quiet now!"

Minnie looks as though she's racking her brain for another way to put it—then her face lights up. "*Visa?*"

Luke breaks off his conversation and stares at her, stricken.

"Did she just say 'Visa'?"

"Isn't she clever?" I give an overbright laugh. "The things children say—"

"Becky . . . this is bad. Really bad."

He looks so upset, I feel a sudden clanging in my chest.

"It's not bad!" I say desperately. "She's not . . . I'm not . . ." I trail off helplessly. For a moment no one says anything, except Minnie, who is still tugging my arm, exclaiming, "Visa!"

At last I draw breath. "You really think there's a problem, don't you? Well, fine. If you think I should go to boot camp, I'll go to boot camp."

"Don't worry, Becky." Nanny Sue laughs. "It won't be as bad as all that. It'll simply be a program of discussion and behavior modification, based in our London headquarters, with a residential option for those from far away. We'll be having workshops, one-to-ones, role play . . . I think you'll enjoy it!"

Enjoy it?

She hands me a leaflet, which I can't even bring myself to look at. I can't believe I've agreed to go to boot camp. I *knew* we should never have let Nanny Sue back in the house.

"The main thing is, Minnie's OK," Luke exhales. "We've been really worried."

Nanny Sue takes a sip of tea and looks from him to me. "Out of interest, what made you think she had problems in the first place?"

"I never did," I point out at once. "It was Luke. He said we couldn't have another baby because we couldn't control Minnie. He said she was too wild."

As I'm speaking, it hits me. He hasn't got any more excuses! Result! I whip round to Luke.

"So, will you change your mind now about having another baby? You *have* to change your mind."

"I . . . don't know." Luke looks cornered. "You don't just rush in to these things, Becky. It's a big step—"

"Everything in life is a big step!" I say dismissively. "Don't be a scaredy-cat. *You* think Minnie should have a sibling, don't you?" I appeal to Nanny Sue. "*You* think it would be good for her."

Ha. That'll teach Luke. Two can play at the getting-Nanny-Sue-on-their-side game.

"That's a very personal decision." She looks thoughtful. "However, it's sometimes helpful to discuss these things. Luke, is there a particular reason you don't want to have another child?"

"No," says Luke after a long pause. "Not really." He looks very uncomfortable, I suddenly notice.

Why is this such a sore point with him?

"Of course, babies are disruptive little creatures—" begins Nanny Sue.

"Minnie wasn't!" I defend her immediately. "I mean, only a tiny bit—" I break off in dismay. "Is it because of when she chewed up those papers that time? Because she was *teething,* Luke, and you shouldn't have left them on the bed, and you should have made photo-copies—"

"It's not that!" Luke cuts me off heatedly. "Don't be ridiculous. That wouldn't be a reason. That wouldn't be—" He breaks off abruptly, an odd, jarring note to his voice. His face is turned away, but I can see the tension growing in his neck.

What is *up*?

"I think there's more to this than child behavior, isn't there, Luke?" says Nanny Sue quietly, and I stare, agog. This is just like the TV show! "Take your time," she adds, as Luke takes a deep breath. "There's no hurry."

There's silence apart from Minnie chomping another shortbread. I don't dare move a muscle. The whole atmosphere in the room has changed and become stiller. What's he going to say?

"Having Minnie has been wonderful." Luke speaks at last, his voice a little gruff. "But I just don't feel as though I could give the same intensity of feeling to an-other child. And I couldn't risk that. I know what it is to feel abandoned and unloved by a parent, and I'm not going to do it to a child of my own."

I'm so gobsmacked I can't even utter a sound. I had no idea Luke felt this. None. *None.*

"Why do you feel abandoned, Luke?" Nanny Sue is

using the soft, sympathetic voice she always uses at the end of the show.

"My mother left me when I was small," says Luke matter-of-factly. "We did meet in later life, but we never . . . bonded, you might say. Recently we had a major disagreement, and as a result I'm fairly sure we'll never speak again."

"I see." Nanny Sue looks unfazed. "Have you made any attempts at reconciliation? Has she?"

"My mother never gives me a thought." He gives a small, wry smile. "Trust me."

"Becky, are you familiar with this situation?" Nanny Sue turns to me. "Do you feel that Luke's mother never gives him a thought?"

My face flames and I make a tiny, inarticulate noise that doesn't mean anything.

"Becky hates my mother even more than I do," chimes in Luke with a short laugh. "Don't you, darling? I'm sure you're heartily relieved that we never have to see her."

I gulp my tea, my face burning. This is unbearable. I've got about two hundred texts in my phone, all from Elinor, all about Luke. She's done nothing this week except devote herself to giving him the best party in the world.

But I can't say anything. What can I say?

"I was brought up by a wonderful stepmother." Luke is talking again. "She really *was* my mum. But even so, that feeling of abandonment never leaves you. If I had another child, and it felt abandoned . . ." He winces. "I couldn't do that."

"But why would it feel abandoned?" asks Nanny Sue gently. "It would be your child. You would love it."

There's a long silence—then Luke shakes his head.

"That's the trouble. My fear, if you like." His voice is very low and husky. "I don't see how I could have enough affection to be split so many ways. I love Becky. I love Minnie. I'm *done*." He turns to me suddenly. "Don't *you* feel that? Haven't you ever felt afraid you might not have the capacity to love another child?"

"Well, no," I say, a bit baffled. "I just feel like . . . the more the merrier."

"Luke, this is a very common fear," says Nanny Sue. "I've known many, many parents who express this worry before having a second child. They look at their first beloved child and all they can feel is guilt that there won't be enough love to go round."

"Exactly." His brow furrows deeply. "That's exactly it. It's the *guilt*."

"But each of those parents, without exception, has said to me afterward that there *is* enough love. There's plenty." Her voice softens even more. "There's plenty of love."

I feel a pricking at my eyes.

Oh, no way. I am *not* going to let Nanny Sue make me cry.

"You didn't know in advance how much you would love Minnie, did you?" Nanny Sue says quietly to Luke. "But that didn't stop you then."

There's a long pause.

My fingers are crossed tightly, I suddenly realize. Both hands. And my feet.

"I . . . guess not," says Luke slowly at last. "I guess in the end you just have to have faith." He looks up at me and gives a tentative smile, and I beam joyfully back.

Nanny Sue is the cleverest expert in the world, and I *love* her.

IT'S AN HOUR before we've said our last good-bye to Nanny Sue, promised to stay in touch forever, and finally got Minnie into bed. Luke and I tiptoe out of her bedroom, lean back against the wall, and look at each other silently for a moment.

"So," says Luke at last.

"So."

"Do you think we'll have a boy or a girl?" He pulls me toward him, and I sink into his arms. "Do you think Minnie wants a brother or sister to boss around?"

I can't believe he's talking like this. I can't believe he's so *relaxed* about it. Nanny Sue is such a genius. (Apart from the shopping-boot-camp bit, which looks hideous, and I've already decided I'll have to get out of it somehow.)

I close my eyes and lean against Luke's chest, feeling suddenly warm and blissful. The party plans are all sorted. Luke wants another baby. Minnie's a lovely, intelligent child. At *last* I can relax.

"We've got so much to look forward to," I say happily.

"Agreed." He smiles back, just as my phone rings. I see Bonnie's ID and extricate myself to answer.

"Oh, hi!" I say in a friendly but guarded tone. "I'm with Luke—"

"Does he have his BlackBerry on him?" Bonnie interrupts in a really un-Bonnie-like way.

"Er . . . he's switching it on, actually," I say, turning to look at him. (He'd turned it off while Nanny Sue was here, which just shows how much he respects her opinion.)

"Take it from him. Find an excuse! Don't let him see it!"

She sounds frantic, and I react instantly.

"Give me that!" I snatch the BlackBerry out of Luke's hand right as it starts buzzing and flashing. "Sorry!" I quickly cover with a laugh. "It's just . . . my friend from work wants to talk about different BlackBerry models. You don't mind, do you?"

"Don't let him look at his computer either!" Bonnie's voice is in my ear. "Nothing with emails on it!"

"Luke, could you make me a cup of tea?" I say shrilly. "Right away? In fact . . . I'm feeling a bit ill. Maybe you could bring it to me in bed? And some toast?"

"Well . . . OK." Luke gives me a slightly strange look. "What's wrong?"

"Bathroom!" I gasp, heading away. "Just make the tea! Thank you!"

I hurry into our bedroom, grab his laptop off the desk, and hide it in my wardrobe, then turn breathlessly back to the phone. "What's up, Bonnie?"

"Becky, I'm afraid a short while ago . . ." She's breathing fast. "I made a rather significant mistake."

A mistake? *Bonnie?*

Oh my God. The strain got to her. She messed up some piece of work and now she's getting me to cover up her tracks. Maybe she'll ask me to fabricate evidence or lie to Luke or delete emails off his computer. I feel simultaneously touched that she trusts me enough to ask me . . . and remorseful that I've driven her to such a state.

"Were you upset by Luke telling you off?" I demand. "Is that why you made a mistake?"

"I was a little flustered this afternoon," she says hesitantly, "yes."

"I knew it!" I clutch my head. "Bonnie, I feel so bad about what happened. Was Luke really angry with you?"

"He wasn't unreasonable, in the circumstances, but I was shaken, I must confess—"

"Bonnie, stop right there." My voice is trembling with resolution. "Whatever you've done, whatever mistake you've made, whatever losses Brandon Communications suffers as a result—there is no *way* it was your fault. I won't let Luke fire you. I'll defend you to the hilt!"

I have a sudden vision of myself squaring up to Luke in his office, holding Bonnie by the wrist and saying, "Do you *realize* what a treasure this woman is? Do you *realize* what an asset she is?"

"Becky, dear, don't worry! I haven't made any mistake regarding Brandon Communications." Bonnie's voice cuts into my reverie. "I'm afraid it's to do with the party."

"The *party*?" I feel a tremor. "What's happened?"

"As you know, today was the day I informed the company about Luke's surprise. I sent out the group email and all went smoothly. People are very excited and pleased."

"Right." I'm trying to quell a growing panic. "So . . ."

"I then realized that I hadn't mentioned the group birthday card. So I prepared a second email, informing the recipients that the card was in reception and would be presented to Luke at the party. I was just spell-checking when I thought I heard Luke's voice. In my confusion, I hastily sent the email and closed down my screen." She pauses. "I didn't realize my error till later."

"Your error?" My heart is pounding. "Oh God. You didn't send it to Luke, did you?"

"Yes, I'm afraid it went to Luke," says Bonnie after the briefest of pauses.

I feel a tiny flash of shock, like sparks in my head. Breathe in . . . breathe out . . .

"It's fine." I'm amazed how calm I'm being, like a trained paramedic. "Don't worry, Bonnie. I'll delete it off his computer and his BlackBerry. No harm done. Thank God you caught it, that's all—"

"Becky, you don't understand. Luke got it because he's on our general-contacts list. *That's* where I sent it by mistake."

"General contacts?" I echo uncertainly. "Well . . . who's that? Who's on the list?"

"Around ten thousand City analysts, pundits, and national press. I'm afraid it went out to all of them."

I feel another flash—but this one isn't tiny sparks. It's massive, crashing, overwhelming tsunamis of horror.

"Ten thousand people?"

"Of course, I immediately sent a retraction and asked for complete discretion. But I'm afraid it's not as easy as that. People have started responding. Birthday messages are arriving for Luke. His in-box is full. He's had fifty-six already."

With a shaking thumb I jab at Luke's in-box on his BlackBerry. As it opens up, a list of unread emails fills the screen.

    Many Happy Returns Buddy!

    Wishing You a Good One

    Happy Birthday and all the best from the mar-
    keting team at HSBC

I can hear Luke's tread as he comes up the stairs. I want to gibber with panic. I need to hide the Black-Berry. I need to hide everything, squash everything away.

"He'll guess it all!" I whisper in horror, ducking into the bathroom. "We have to delete them! We have to stop them!"

"I know." Bonnie sounds fairly desperate too. "But it seems people have been forwarding the email on. He's getting emails from all over the place. I don't know how we can contain them."

"But it's a secret!" I almost wail. "Don't they *realize*?"

"Becky." Bonnie sighs. "Maybe you've kept the secret for long enough. The party's only two days away. Isn't it time to tell Luke?"

I stare at the phone in utter shock. She thinks I should *give up*? After all this?

"Absolutely not!" I retort in a savage whisper. "No way! I'm giving him a surprise party, OK? A *surprise*. I'll just have to distract Luke so he doesn't see any emails or anything."

"Dear, you can't possibly distract him from his emails for two entire *days*—"

"Yes, I can! I'll lose his BlackBerry, and I'll deal with his laptop somehow . . . Get the tech guys to delete all the emails if they can. Keep me posted. Bonnie, I've got to go—"

"Becky?" Luke is calling from the bedroom. "Darling, are you OK?"

I ring off, gaze at Luke's BlackBerry for a heart-thumping moment, then quickly stamp on it, treading it into the tiled floor. There. Take *that,* ten thousand people all giving my secret party away.

"Becky?"

I open the door to see him standing with a mug and plate bearing two slices of toast.

"Are you OK?" He peers at me in concern, then holds out his hand. "Can I have my BlackBerry back?"

"I . . . broke it. Sorry."

"Jesus!" He stares in shock at the mangled remains. "How the hell did you do that?" He looks around the room. "Where's my laptop got to? I'll have to email Bonnie—"

"No!" My cry is so piercing he gives a startled flinch, and tea slops out of the mug. "Forget your laptop! Forget everything! Luke . . ." I cast desperately around. "I'm . . . ovulating!"

Yes!

"What?" He stares blankly at me.

"Right now!" I nod firmly. "This minute! I just did a test. They're very specific these days. So we need to get down to it! Quickly! Minnie's asleep, it's just you and me in the house . . ." I sidle up to him suggestively, take the mug and plate out of his hands, and dump them on a shelf. "Come on, darling." I lower my voice huskily. "Let's make a baby."

"Well, there's a thought." His eyes gleam as I start to unbutton his shirt and tug it out of his trousers. "No time like the present."

"Absolutely." I close my eyes and run my hand down his chest in my most sultry way. "I am *so* in the mood."

Actually, it's true. All the adrenaline pumping round my body is getting me quite hot and bothered. I pull his shirt off completely and move closer, breathing in his faint scent of sweat and aftershave. Mmmm. This was a *very* good idea.

"Right back at you," murmurs Luke against my neck. He's obviously in the mood too, in quite a major way. Excellent. I'm good for a few hours. He won't even think about laptops or BlackBerrys. In fact, if I play things right, this will take care of things till morning. And then . . .

Oh God. I've got no idea. I'll just have to think of something else. I've got plenty of time to work out a plan.

All I know is one thing. He's having a surprise on Friday night, if it kills me.

NINETEEN

OK, IT PRACTICALLY *is* killing me. It's seven-thirty the next morning and I'm totally sleep-deprived, because every time I was about to drop off, Luke would murmur something like, "I'll just check my emails," and I had to do my sultry nymphomaniac act all over again.

Which, you know, had its benefits. But now we truly are sated, both of us. I mean, really. We're done. (For the moment, at least.) And I know Luke's mind will be roaming. So far I've managed to keep him contained to the bedroom. I brought us all breakfast in bed, and he's sipping his second cup of coffee while Minnie eats a piece of toast. But any minute he'll start looking at his watch and saying—

"Have you seen my laptop?" He looks up.

I knew it.

"Um . . . have you lost it?" I prevaricate.

"It must be around here . . ." He pushes at the shirt which he discarded on the floor last night.

"I expect so." I nod wisely. I secreted it out of the room earlier and stuffed it behind the bottles at the back of the detergent cupboard in the utility room. Then I propped an ironing board and overflowing basket of laundry in front of the cupboard door. He'll never find it.

"I need to get in touch with Bonnie and explain the situation . . ." He's searching the room with more energy. "Where the hell *is* it? I had it last night! I must be going fucking *demented*. Can I use your BlackBerry?"

"Out of power," I lie smoothly. "I forgot to charge it."

"I'll use your parents' computer, then—"

"They've changed the password," I say hastily. "You won't be able to get in. More coffee, darling?"

The phone on the bedside table rings and I pick it up as naturally as possible.

"Hello? Oh, it's for you, Luke!" I muster tones of surprise. "It's Gary!"

"Hi, Gary." Luke takes the receiver. "Sorry, my Black-Berry's bust—" He breaks off and gapes at the phone. *"What?"* he exclaims at last. "But, Gary—"

I sip my coffee demurely, watching Luke and trying not to smile. At last Luke puts down the phone, looking shaken.

"Bloody hell." He sinks down on the bed. "That was Gary. I think he's having a nervous breakdown."

"No *way*!" I exclaim theatrically.

Good old Gary. I knew he wouldn't let me down.

"He said he needs to see me urgently, talk about the company, talk about his life, get away from the pressure. He sounded absolutely on the edge. *Gary*, of all people!" Luke looks staggered. "I mean, he's the last person I would expect to crack up. He's always been so steady. He said he can't face London, he wants to meet me at some remote place in the New Forest, for fuck's sake."

It's a holiday lodge Gary goes to with his family. It's got no phone signal, no Internet, and no TV. Gary and I had a little chat early this morning. He said he reckons he can keep up his nervous-breakdown act for the morning, and meanwhile we'll come up with more plans.

"You *must* make Gary a priority," I say seriously. "After all, he's your right-hand man. I think you should go to wherever he says and hear him out. He might do something stupid otherwise," I quickly add as Luke seems to hesitate. "You don't want to risk that, do you? Call Bonnie and see if she can rearrange your appointments."

Automatically, Luke claps his hand to his pocket for his BlackBerry—then remembers.

"Oh, this is a bloody joke." Cursing under his breath, he reaches for the landline phone. "I don't even know her direct line."

"It's—" I bite my lip just in time. Shit. I'm getting careless. "It's probably more sensible to go via the switchboard," I cover hastily. "Look!" I proffer an old Brandon Communications notepad; laboriously, Luke taps in the number, a deep scowl on his face.

I have to bite my lip hard so I don't smile. He's so *crabby*.

"Hi, Maureen. It's Luke. Can you put me through to Bonnie?" He takes a slug of coffee. "Bonnie. Thank God. You will not *believe* the fiasco on this end. I haven't got my BlackBerry or my laptop, I've just had a crazy call from Gary, I have *no* idea what I'm doing—" He breaks off, and I can see the ripples gradually calm on his face.

"Well, thanks, Bonnie," he says at last. "That would be great. Talk to you soon. Have you got this number? . . . OK. And . . . thanks." He puts the phone down and looks at me. "Bonnie's going to bike another laptop over here while I'm seeing Gary. If you take delivery, I can pick it up on my way back to the office."

"What a good idea!" I exclaim, as though this is news to me and I haven't already exchanged about fifty emails on the subject. "Good thing Bonnie's so efficient, isn't it?" I can't resist adding.

Bonnie's sending over a specially modified laptop, which will be unable to access the Internet due to a "server flaw." The tech department has also disabled Luke's email account and set up a dummy one. Bonnie's going to fill it with enough emails to keep him busy and unsuspicious—but nothing else. Basically, we're cutting him off from virtual civilization.

"And she's sorting out a car to take me to wherever the hell Gary is. It should be here in about twenty minutes." Luke looks around the room yet again, his brow furrowing. "I'm *sure* I brought my laptop back last night. I'm *sure* I did."

"Don't worry about your laptop," I say soothingly, as though he's a psychotic patient. "Tell you what, why don't you get Minnie dressed?"

My BlackBerry has been vibrating with incoming calls, and as soon as Luke's out of earshot, I grab it and answer without even checking the screen.

"Hi, Bonnie?"

"No, it's Davina."

I'm so focused on this morning's events, it takes me a nanosecond to realize who it is.

"Davina?" I can't hide my surprise. "Hi! How are you?"

"Becky! You poor thing! This is *terrible*!" For one mad moment I think she's talking about the party nearly coming out. Then I realize what she means.

"Oh, that." I wince. "Yes, I know."

"What *happened*?"

I really could do without going over the whole thing again. I'd kind of managed to forget about it for now.

"Well, my boss found out about the Shop In Private service." I keep my voice low. "And he didn't like it. So I'm suspended and they're going to do an investigation." To be honest, I've been so frantic over the last few days I've barely given the investigation a thought.

"But you saved our lives!" Davina sounds impassioned. "We're all agreed, we're not standing for it. We had a meeting yesterday, a few of your regular clients. Jasmine was the one who spread the word, then we all got on a group email—"

"*Jasmine?*" I'm quite taken aback at the idea of Jasmine rallying the troops.

"We're not letting this go. We're going to take action. And that boss of yours will wish he never messed with you."

She's so fierce, I feel touched. By Jasmine too. Although, to be honest, what on earth can any of them do? Maybe they're all going to write a joint letter of complaint.

"Well . . . thanks, Davina. I really appreciate it."

"I'll keep you posted. But what I wanted to ask is, are you OK, Becky? Is there anything I can do? Anything at all? I've got the whole day off, so if you need to talk, if you want cheering up . . ."

I feel a wash of gratitude. Davina's such a sweetheart.

"Thanks, but not really." *Not unless you can somehow distract my husband—*

Ooh. My thoughts have stopped abruptly in their tracks. Davina's a doctor, isn't she? So she could maybe—

No. I can't ask that. It's too big a favor.

But it would save my life, and she *did* offer . . .

"Actually, there is something that would really help me out," I say cautiously. "But it's massive . . ."

"Anything! Just tell me!"

Davina is a *star.* By the time Luke comes back into the room with Minnie, the plan is in place. Both Davina and I have texted Bonnie; everything's set. I hastily whip my BlackBerry back under the duvet and smile at Luke, just as the phone rings on cue.

"Oh, hi, Bonnie!" I say innocently. "Yes, Luke's here. Did you want him for something?"

I hand over the receiver—and this time I have to bite my lip even harder as Luke's face becomes more and more aghast.

"An emergency *medical*?" he expostulates at last.

Oh God, I mustn't laugh. I mustn't.

"You can't be serious!" he's exclaiming. "How can it be an *emergency*, for fuck's sake? Well, tell them I can't." I can see him getting frustrated. "Well, tell the insurance company to sod off. Well . . ."

Good for Bonnie. She must be acting absolutely implacable on the other end.

"Jesus Christ." At last he crashes the phone down. "Apparently I have to have a full medical this afternoon. Some sort of insurance cock-up."

"What a pain!" I say sympathetically.

Davina's promised to give Luke the most full-on medical going. It'll last at least six hours, he'll be in a hospital gown, unable to use his laptop or a mobile phone, and no one will be able to get to him.

"This is the most fucking *ludicrous* day—" He thrusts two hands through his hair, looking totally beleaguered.

Luke *really* isn't used to things being out of his control. I'd almost feel sorry for him—if I didn't want to giggle.

"Never mind." I squeeze his hand fondly. "Just go with it." I glance at my watch. "Won't your car be here any moment? Shouldn't you get ready?"

As Luke is putting on his jacket, a text buzzes through on my BlackBerry and I surreptitiously click on it. It's from Bonnie, and it's very short and to the point.

Becky. Have you seen YouTube?

• • •

OK. JUST AS I THINK everything's happened that possibly can, something else does.

The marketing department at Foreland Investments has made a video in which everyone says, "Happy Birthday, Luke!" to the camera, and they've posted it on YouTube under the heading *Happy Birthday, Luke Brandon!*

I'm torn between being really, really touched and really, *really* climbing the walls. I mean, YouTube, for God's sake! Could they have done anything less discreet? Couldn't they have waited till tomorrow evening to post it? Every time I watch it I have to have a squirt of calming Rescue Remedy afterward.

By ten o'clock it's already had 145 hits, only about ten of which are me. By eleven o'clock, when Janice and Suze arrive, it's up to 1,678—and to my disbelief, two *more* videos have been posted. One is from Sacrum Asset Management, in which *Happy Birthday Luke Brandon* has been spelled out in paper clips on someone's desk. The other is from Wetherby's, where the whole marketing department sings "Happy Birthday" to the camera.

"That's so *cool*!" Suze gapes at my laptop in disbelief.

"I know." I can't help feeling proud. I mean, all these people must really like Luke to bother to do a video for him. But I can't help feeling jittery too. "What if he sees it, though?"

"He won't see it," says Suze confidently. "Why would he search on YouTube? I bet he never goes on YouTube. He's too busy. It's only tragic cases like you and me who are always online."

I'm about to object that I am *not* a tragic case, when the doorbell rings and we all start.

"That's not him, is it?" says Janice in a gasped whisper, clapping a hand over her heart.

Honestly, Janice does overreact. I hardly spilled my coffee at all.

"Of course not. It'll be the tent guys."

But it's not them; it's Danny. He's standing on the doorstep, wearing a battered leather coat over ripped jeans and silver Converse, and holding a pile of garment bags.

"Costumes, anyone?" he says, deadpan.

"Danny, you star!" I seize on them. "I can't believe you did this!"

I peek inside one of the bags and see a flash of gold brocade trimmed with twinkling lace. Oh my God. These will be perfect.

"Well, I had to. Jesus. That mother-in-law of yours is like Stalin. She's the worst boss I ever had." He looks around, haunted. "She isn't here, is she?"

"Not right now," I say reassuringly. "But Suze is. So beware. She's still furious with you about that photo shoot."

"Oh." Danny looks uncomfortable and takes a step away. "The thing with that is, Suze just didn't understand the aesthetic. You have to remember, she's not a creative person—"

"Yes, she is! She's an artist! Look at her photo frames!"

"Right." Danny tries a different tack. "Well, OK, she is a creative person, but she *totally* didn't get the look I was going for . . ."

"Yes, I did!" Suze's voice rings out scornfully behind me. "I got 'the look' perfectly! You set Tarkie up, Danny! Admit it!"

Danny looks at her silently for a moment. He seems to be considering his next move. "If I admit it," he says finally, "will you forgive me instantly, no questions, move right on?"

"I . . ." Suze hesitates. "Well . . . I suppose so."

"OK, I set him up. Love you too." Danny plants a kiss on her cheek and heads past me into the house. "Do you have any coffee? Janice!" He greets her flamboyantly. "My style icon! My muse! What *is* that fetching shade of lipstick?"

"He's . . . impossible!"

Suze looks so infuriated, I'm about to offer her a squirt of Rescue Remedy. But a noise from outside attracts my attention. A big lorry is pulling in to Janice's drive. Its reversers are bleeping and a guy in jeans is beckoning it in. That must be the tent!

OK. This party really is starting.

BY FOUR O'CLOCK that afternoon, the tent is up in Janice's garden. It isn't decorated yet, but it still looks fab, all big and billowy. (My little gazebo is up too, at the side. Elinor's tent guys haven't stopped teasing me about it.) I'll have to make sure Luke doesn't catch a glimpse— but by the time he gets back tonight, it'll be dark, anyway. Janice wanted me to sew all the curtains together, but I think that would just be *weird*.

Gary managed to spin out his nervous-breakdown act for three hours, and now Luke's with Davina, doing his medical in some basement suite at her hospital. She's just phoned to give me an update.

"I've got him on the treadmill for an hour to assess his heart. He's *really* not enjoying this," she adds cheerily. "So where will he go after me?"

"I . . . don't quite know," I admit. "I'll call you back."

I haven't yet formulated the next part of the Luke-

containment plan, and it's starting to worry me—
especially as now there are thirteen "Happy Birthday,
Luke Brandon" videos on YouTube. All day, Martin's
been going online to look and shouting out, "There's a
new one!" And now someone's created a Web page
called happybirthdaylukebrandon.com, which has
links to them all and invites people to post their
funny/fond/rude stories about "The City's King of
Spin," which is what they're calling Luke.

The whole thing makes my mind boggle. Who's *done*
that? Danny's theory is, no one in the City is doing any
work at the moment and they're all dead bored, so
they've seized on this as a diversion.

"Number fourteen's just gone up," calls out Martin
from his laptop as I put the phone down. "Some girls
from Prestwick PR, singing 'Happy Birthday' like Mari-
lyn Monroe. In the nude," he adds.

"Nude?" I hurry over to see, followed swiftly by Suze.

OK, so they're not totally nude. Their crucial bits
are hidden by office plants and files and corners of
photocopiers. But honestly. Don't they know Luke's
married? Especially that one with the dark curly hair
and the swivelly hips. I hope *she's* not coming to the
party.

"What are you going to do with Luke next?" says
Suze, who overheard me talking to Davina. "I mean, he
can't do a medical all day, can he? He must be spitting
by now."

"I know." I bite my lip. "I thought I'd get Bonnie to
send him loads of emails. Like, pages of really dense
paperwork, saying it's urgent and he's got to read it all
at once."

"And tomorrow?" persists Suze.

"Dunno. More paperwork, I suppose."

Suze is shaking her head. "You need something

bigger. What is the one thing that you can guarantee will grab his attention? Like with Tarkie I know exactly what I'd say. I'd say the Historical Society phoned with evidence that Great-Great-Great-Uncle Albert *didn't* fire the cannon, after all. He'd drop everything instantly."

"Wow." I stare at Suze in admiration. "That's really specific. Who was Great-Great-Great-Uncle Albert?"

Suze makes a face. "It's quite boring. Do you really want to know?"

Hmm. Maybe not.

"The point is, I know what presses Tarkie's buttons," Suze is saying. "And you know Luke. So what will get him going?"

"A work crisis," I say after a moment's thought. "That's all I can think of. He always jumps when some big client is in trouble."

"Can you invent a work crisis?"

"Maybe." On impulse, I reach for my phone and call Bonnie.

"Hey, Bonnie. Have you seen the latest YouTube?"

"Oh, Becky," begins Bonnie miserably. "I feel so wretched. If only I hadn't sent that email—"

"Don't worry about that now," I say quickly. "But maybe we can *use* the fact that everyone knows. Could you email his clients and say we're trying to distract him till tomorrow night and ask them to invent a crisis that will keep him busy?"

"What sort of crisis?" says Bonnie doubtfully.

"I don't know! They could pretend they're going bust, or make up some sex scandal—anything! Just to keep him occupied for a few hours. Tell them that anyone who comes up with any ideas should call you and you can coordinate them."

One of his clients will come up with something

clever. I mean, if they can make videos, they can invent a crisis, surely?

Already my phone is ringing again, and I glance at the ID as I answer, but it's not a number I know.

"Hello?"

"Rebecca?" booms a jolly voice.

"Yes," I say cautiously. "Who's this?"

"Eric Foreman, *Daily World*. Remember me?"

"Eric!" I exclaim in delight. "How are you?"

Eric is a journalist at the *Daily World,* and I first met him when I was a financial journalist. I wrote pieces for him, in fact, but then I gave that up and we lost touch. How come he's tracked me down?

"I'm good, my beauty. Just putting together a piece about your husband's birthday for the City diary and I was after a quote from you. Or, even better, him? Is he around?"

"*What?*" I stare at the phone, aghast. "Why are you doing a piece about his birthday?"

"Are you joking? Prime bit of gossip like this? Have you seen YouTube? Have you seen how many hits he's got?"

"I know," I say desperately. "But that wasn't supposed to happen. It was supposed to be a secret!"

Eric's guffaw of laughter nearly deafens me. "Is that your quote?" he says. " 'It was supposed to be a secret'? I've been emailed about it eight times today already. I thought this was your own viral campaign, my love."

"No! I want it to stop!"

He roars with laughter again. "You can't control it now. It's all over the place. Even people who don't know him are passing it on. You know that the marketing team from Atlas Fund Management is on retreat in Kent? They've written *Happy Birthday Luke* with their cars in the car park. Just sent me the picture. I'm going to print it tomorrow unless I get a better one."

"No!" I nearly shout in horror. "You can't! I'm throwing Luke a surprise party! Which means he's supposed to be *surprised*." I feel hot with frustration. Doesn't anyone *get* this?

"Oh, this gets better and better. So he has no idea, does he?"

"None!"

"And the party's tomorrow night?"

"Yes," I say automatically, then curse myself. Eric might be my friend, but first and foremost he's a tabloid journalist.

"Don't let him near the *Daily World*, then." Eric gives a laugh. "I'll be featuring this as my main story. The City needs a good cheer-up after all that's happened recently. You, young lady, have given everyone a reason to have a bit of fun. I'm not spiking that. General features editor'll be onto you too, I'm sure."

"But—"

"And we won't be the only ones. So you'd better keep your old man away from the press."

"No! You can't!"

But he's gone. I stare dumbly at the phone. This can't be happening. My top-secret surprise party, which no one was supposed to know about . . . is being printed in the *newspapers*?

BY THE EVENING, I'm just about holding it together, even though there are now twenty-three YouTube tributes, and Eric has already put a piece about Luke's party on the *Daily World* online City page. I've sent a desperate email out to all the guests and Brandon Communications clients, telling them the party *is* still a surprise and asking them to please, please not contact Luke.

Bonnie has biked round a big pile of paperwork to distract Luke tonight, and a couple of friendly clients have agreed to try to occupy him tomorrow with various made-up issues. But none of them sounds that convincing. To be honest, I'm stressed out. We still have a whole night and day before the party, and the entire world knows about it, and there's a massive great tent flapping next door. I mean, how am I going to keep this a secret?

"Don't worry. Not long now." Suze gives me a kiss, her coat and scarf already on. "I'll be off now. See you tomorrow for the big day!"

"Suze." I catch her hands. "Thanks so much. I don't know what I would have done without you, and Tarkie, and . . . and everything—"

"Don't be silly. It's been fun! Anyway, Elinor did most of it. And Bex . . ." She pauses, suddenly more serious. "Luke *will* be blown away. He really will."

"You think so?"

"I know it. It's going to be sensational." She squeezes my hands. "I'd better run, or he'll see me."

As the front door closes, my phone rings yet again and I look at it wearily. I've been on the phone so long today, I feel like my vocal cords are wearing out. At last I summon the energy to pick it up. I don't recognize the number, which is no surprise.

"Hello? Becky here."

"Becky?" comes a soft female voice. "You don't know me, but my name is Sage Seymour."

What?

A huge spurt of adrenaline shoots through me, like three cans of Red Bull and winning the Olympics, all at once. I'm talking to Sage Seymour? She knows my *name*?

Sage Seymour is sitting somewhere, holding a phone, talking to me. Ooh, I wonder what she's wearing. I mean, not in a pervy way. Just in a—

Come on, Becky. *Answer.*

"Oh. Oh, hi." I'm trying desperately to sound cool, but my stupid voice has shot up three octaves. "Um, hi! Hi!"

I can't seem to move off the word *hi.*

"I've hired your husband to do some publicity work," she says, her lilting voice totally familiar now. "But I guess you know that."

My mind scampers in panic. Do I know? I mean, obviously not officially. But if I say Luke hasn't told me, does it sound weird? Like he's not interested or never talks to his wife?

"It's so exciting!" I swallow. "I'm a huge fan."

I want to shoot myself. I sound so *lame.*

"It was a bit 'out there' as a choice. But, you know, I was so sick of Hollywood bullshitters. Your husband had more sensible ideas for me in ten *minutes* than any of those bozos."

I feel a flash of pride. I *knew* Luke would do a good job.

"So, I heard about your party," Sage adds casually. "Sounds like a big deal."

G'uh? How does she—

"Y-yes," I stutter. "I mean, pretty big—"

"I went on YouTube. Awesome tributes. Then my assistant got the email from Bonnie. You need to distract Luke, right?"

"Yes! It's all got out on the Internet and it's supposed to be a big surprise and—"

"How about I keep him busy for you?" says Sage calmly. "I could demand that he come to the set. Throw a diva hissy. I can put on a good show. Once he's at the set, we'll take care of him. Show him around, keep him occupied till you need him. Then we'll send him off in a car."

"Wow." I gulp. "That would be amazing."

I am so jealous. I want to go to the movie set. *I* want to be shown around. I'm frantically trying to think of an essential reason why I should go there too, when she adds, "You used to be on the telly, right? *Morning Coffee?*"

"Yes!" I say in amazement.

"I watched you when I was off work. You were funny."

"Well . . . thanks!" I gulp.

"We should have a drink sometime."

It's like the world tips on its side. I grip the phone, wondering if I just dreamed that. Sage Seymour has suggested we have a drink? A top, Oscar-winning movie star has suggested we have a drink? My whole *life* I've fantasized about this moment. I mean, I always felt it was meant to be. Didn't I say? Didn't I know all along I was meant to mix with movie stars?

Maybe we'll become best friends!

Maybe I'll be a bridesmaid at her wedding. You know, if she gets married or anything. I wouldn't need to be the one standing next to her. I could be three along.

"That would be . . . great." I somehow manage to get the words out.

"Cool. Well, don't worry about Luke. It's in hand. And good luck tomorrow! Bye, Becky."

And just like that, she's gone. Feverishly, I save her number in my phone. Sage Seymour. In my phone. Sage Seymour. Just like she's any of my friends.

Oh my God, this is so cool.

I'm just sending a quick text to Gary and Bonnie—

Good news! Sage Seymour says she will take care of Luke tomorrow till party

—when I hear the crackling sound of Luke's key in the front door. I thrust my phone away and grab a magazine.

OK. Act natural. I have *not* just been chatting with my new best friend Sage Seymour.

"Hi there!" I say, glancing up. "Good day? How was Gary?"

"Fuck knows." Luke shakes his head. "He was making no sense at all. I've told him he needs a holiday." He grimaces as he takes off his coat. "Bloody hell. My arm. I've had five thousand jabs."

"Oh, dear!" I say sympathetically. "Well, I'm sure they were all necessary. If it's a matter of your health—"

"I've never known a medical like it. That doctor made me run for an *hour*." He looks incredulous. "And there were *six* questionnaires, all repeating one another. Whoever devises these things is an utter imbecile."

Davina told me earlier that Luke was the stroppiest patient she'd ever had and that he'd given her a lecture on how inefficient and time-wasting her medical was. Which is fair enough, given that she spun it out for four hours longer than normal.

"Poor you." I stifle a laugh. "Well, I'm afraid a whole pile of paperwork arrived for you to read urgently . . ."

Just in case you thought you were escaping for a minute.

I drag over the box that Bonnie couriered round this afternoon, which is full of contracts and letters. That should keep him busy.

"Let me get online." Luke perks up. "Is this my new laptop? Excellent."

I feel prickles of alarm as he unpacks it from its box. Even though I know it's safe. They promised me. Sure enough, after a little while Luke curses again.

"Bloody thing's got no Internet access!" He jabs at it a few times. "What's wrong with this bloody *server*?"

"Oh, dear," I say innocently. "Never mind. Well, why not just deal with the paperwork? You can sort out your laptop tomorrow. Have you eaten? Would you like some risotto? Janice brought some round."

I'm heating up the risotto in the kitchen when I hear Luke's phone ring.

"Luke Brandon." I can just about hear him answer. "Oh, Sage! Hello there. Wait a minute . . ."

The living-room door is shut. Damn.

I hesitate for a moment—then tiptoe through the hall and press my ear to the door.

"Well, I'm sorry to hear that," Luke is saying. "Of *course* you're our number one priority. Sage . . . Listen, Sage . . . No one's saying that, Sage—"

Yes! She's obviously giving a brilliant show. Well, of course she is. She's an actress.

"Well, of course I can—eight *a.m.*? At Pinewood . . . OK, fine. I'll see you there."

There's silence from the living room, and I'm wondering whether to tiptoe away when I hear his voice again.

"Bonnie? It's Luke here. Just had Sage Seymour on the phone. I'm afraid she's confirmed every suspicion I ever had. Nightmare woman. She's insisting I come to her movie set first thing tomorrow." He pauses. "I don't *know* why! This has come out of nowhere! She was talking gibberish about press statements and strategies; she seems totally self-obsessed, paranoid that we're not taking enough interest . . . Anyway, I'll call you when I'm on my way back to the office." He lowers his voice, so I have to press even harder against the door to hear.

"Thank goodness I didn't tell Becky. Something told me to wait until we knew it was going to work out—" He breaks off. "No! Of course I haven't mentioned that to Becky yet. It's only a possibility. We'll cross that bridge when we need to."

My ears prick up. What's a possibility? What bridge?

"I'll see you tomorrow, Bonnie. Thanks for that."

Shit. He's coming. I dart back to the kitchen, where of course the risotto has burned at the bottom of the pan. I'm briskly stirring the burned bits into the rest when Luke comes in.

"I've got an early start tomorrow, by the way," he says guardedly. "Seeing a client."

"Have some food, then." I put a plate down in front of him, like a perfect, unsuspicious wife. "Big day tomorrow. Your birthday, remember?"

"Shit. Of course it is." Alarm briefly crosses his face. "Becky, you haven't made any plans, have you? You know we've got this big company training program? It'll go on into the evening. I don't know when I'll be back—"

"Of course." I manage an easy tone. "No worries! We'll do something nice on Saturday."

Oh God. I can't cope. My mouth keeps twitching with faint hysteria, and I feel as if thought bubbles must be floating above my head.

There's a tent outside the window! It's your party tomorrow! We're all in on the surprise except you!

I can't believe he hasn't guessed. I can't believe I've kept it secret for this long. I feel like there's only the thinnest curtain hiding everything in my brain and any minute he'll sweep it aside and see the lot.

"Becky . . ." Luke is surveying me with a perplexed frown. "Is something up? Are you upset about something?"

"What?" I jump. "No! Nothing! Don't be silly." I grab my glass of wine, take a swig, then beam at Luke as convincingly as I can. "Nothing's up. It's all good."

Keep it together, Becky. Just keep it together. Less than twenty-four hours to go.

People Who Know About Party

Me
Suze
Tarquin
Danny
Jess
Tom
Mum
Dad
Janice
Martin
Bonnie
Those three women who
   were listening at the
   next-door table
Gary
Janice's plumber
Rupert and Harry at
   The Service
Erica
Marketing directors of
   Bollinger, Dom Perignon,
   Bacardi, Veuve Clicquot,
   Party Time
   Beverages, Jacob's Creek,
   Kentish English Sparkling
   Wine
Cliff

Manicurist (I was so
   stressed out, I had to talk
   to <u>someone,</u> and she
   promised not to blab)
165 invited guests
   (not including Brandon C
   lot)
500 readers of <u>Style Central</u>
Elinor
Ritz waiter
   (I'm sure he was listening)
Elinor's staff (6)
Caterers (how many actu-
   ally know? Maybe only
   one or two?)
35 Brandon C staff
10,000 Brandon C contacts
97,578 users of YouTube
   (In fact, 98,471, has just
   gone up)
1.8 million readers of
   <u>Daily World</u>

Total = 1, 909, 209

OK. Don't panic. As long as
they all keep quiet until tomorrow.

TWENTY

AND SUDDENLY it's three clock the following day. Less than *four* hours to go.

I haven't sat down all day and my legs are aching and my wrist is stiff from clamping my phone to my ear . . . but we're there. We're really there. Everything's in place and it all looks breathtaking. Everyone's in position. The team leaders have had their final meeting. Elinor's in overdrive. She and Jess have become a sort of sub-team, ticking off lists and double-checking every detail obsessively together. In fact, there's a competitive spirit growing between them to locate all the glitches and find solutions as fast as possible, like ace party trou-bleshooters.

Jess keeps telling Elinor that she's a talented woman, and she should come out to Chile and use her organi-zational skills for something *worthwhile,* and has she ever thought about volunteer work? To which Elinor just puts on that blank, stony expression. (I couldn't help retorting to Jess yesterday: Who says a *party* isn't worthwhile?)

Luke is still with Sage on her movie set at Pinewood, and she keeps sending me updates by text. Apparently everyone's in on the secret, the whole cast and crew. They confiscated his new mobile phone as soon as he arrived and plonked him on a director's chair with earphones. When he got restless, they showed him around all the sets and trailers. Then they gave him lunch. Then Sage made up a load of stuff to complain about. Then they plonked him back on the director's chair. Every time he tries to speak to her, she says, "Shh! I have to concentrate!" or the director tells him off.

So basically he's taken care of until six o'clock. Then Bonnie is going to ring him and say she sent over a vital contract to the house by mistake and it needs signing today, so could he go and sign it and fax it to her? And the car will bring him back here. And I'll greet him at the door. And then . . .

Every time I think about it, I get goose bumps. I can't wait. I can't wait!

The caterers are scurrying about in Janice's kitchen. The tent is lit up like a spaceship. Janice's garden is like a festival of bunting.

Now I just need to have a bath and do my nails and get Minnie ready—

"Hello, Becky, love."

Mum's voice nearly makes me drop my cup of tea all over the floor. She must have let herself in without me hearing.

My stomach flips with apprehension as she comes into the room. I'm not ready for this. The only communication I've had with Mum has been cryptic back-and-forth texts during the last few days via Janice's mobile.

It all kicked off when Janice asked Mum and Dad for drinks before the party, whereupon Mum replied that if her own daughter wasn't going to invite her, then she wasn't going to come. Janice texted back that she was sure Mum *was* invited; didn't she have an invitation? Mum replied touchily that she'd been *disinvited*. So I told Janice that Mum was only disinvited if she wanted to be. And Mum said that she wasn't going to impose herself where she wasn't welcome. Then Dad chipped in and rang Janice and said we were all being ridiculous. And that was kind of where it was left.

"Oh." I swallow. "Hi, Mum. I thought you were still at The West Place. Where's Dad?"

"Outside, in the car. So, the party's tonight, I take it?"

Her voice sounds so stiff and hurt, I cringe, simultaneously feeling a bit resentful. She's the one who's been living it up with mud wraps and cocktails. How come *she* gets to be stiff and resentful?

"Yes." I pause a moment, then add with a shrug, "You were right, by the way. It *was* all nearly a disaster. Turns out I couldn't do it on my own."

"Love, no one ever said you had to do it on your own. And I'm sorry I said . . ." Mum trails off awkwardly.

"Well, I'm sorry too," I say, a bit stiffly. "I hope I don't let you down tonight."

"I wasn't aware that I was invited."

"Well . . . I wasn't aware that you weren't."

We're standing at angles to each other, our chins averted. I'm not sure where we go from here.

"Oh, love." Mum's cool façade crumbles first. "Let's not argue! I'm sorry I ever mentioned . . . you-know-who. Mr. Wham. 'Club Tropicana' fellow. 'Wake Me Up Before You Go-Go.'"

"I know who you mean," I say hastily, before she does the whole of Wham Rap.

"I didn't mean to put you down. I was just *anxious* for you, love."

"Mum, you don't need to worry about me!" I roll my eyes. "I'm a grown-up, remember? I'm twenty-nine. I'm a *mother.*"

"And *I'm* a mother!" She claps a hand to her chest dramatically. "You wait, love! It doesn't go away! Ever!"

Oh my God. Is that true? Am I still going to be stressing about Minnie when she's twenty-nine and married?

No. No way. I'm nothing like Mum. I'll be on a Caribbean cruise by then, having a good time.

"Anyway," Mum's saying. "Dad and I have done a lot of talking over the last few days, in the steam room and during massages . . ."

Honestly. Have my parents once made it out of the spa?

"I can see why you might have felt you needed to mislead us about the house," Mum presses on, her face pink. "I'm sorry I overreacted, love. And I realize I've been a bit . . . *tense* these last few weeks." She sighs gustily. "It's just been a tricky time, what with all of us in the house . . . and the Cutting Back didn't help . . ."

"I know." Instantly I'm full of remorse. "And we've been so grateful to live here—"

"You don't need to feel grateful! This is your home, love!"

"But even so, it was too long. No wonder we all got a bit tetchy. I'm sorry all our stuff stressed you out, and I'm sorry about fibbing . . ." My cool façade has totally crumbled too. "And of *course* I want you to come to the party, if you want to."

"Of course I want to! Janice says it's going to be wonderful. She says she's doing touch-ups! She's bought three extra tubes of Touche Éclat!"

I *have* to talk to Janice.

"It is going to be wonderful. Just wait." I can't help bubbling over. "Wait till you see the birthday cake, Mum. And the *decorations*."

"Oh, love, come here." Mum holds out her arms for a hug and squeezes me tight. "I'm *so* proud of you. I'm sure it'll be wonderful! Janice says it's a *Pride and Prejudice* theme now? Luke'll look super as Mr. Darcy! I've bought a bonnet and Dad's got some breeches, and I'm going to curl my hair—"

"*What?*" I draw away. "It's not bloody *Pride and Prejudice!* Where did *that* come from?"

"Oh." Mum looks taken aback. "Well, I'm sure Janice said she was wearing that lovely blue dress from the community theater production—"

For God's sake. Just because Janice is wearing her Mrs. Bennet costume, suddenly the whole thing is *Pride and Prejudice?*

"It's not *Pride and Prejudice.* And it's *not* Japanese. So don't get any ideas about kimonos."

"Well, what is it? *Is* there a theme?"

"Kind of." I debate internally for a moment—then make a snap decision. "Come and see."

I pull her into the kitchen, unlock my file box, and pull out Danny's drawings. "Here are the designs. Top secret. Don't say a word to anybody."

Mum peers at them uncertainly for a moment—then recognition flashes over her face.

"Oh, *Becky,*" she says at last. "Oh, *love.*"

"I know." I can't help beaming. "Isn't it amazing?"

It was me who insisted it should be an individual, bespoke party that would be more meaningful to Luke than to anybody else there. And it was me who came up with the actual idea. But, to be truthful, it was Elinor who made all this happen. Elinor and her multimillion-dollar clout and her multimillion-dollar checkbook and her complete refusal to take no for an answer.

"But how on earth . . ." Mum is leafing through the pages, looking stunned.

"I've had help," I say vaguely. "Lots of help."

The only people who know about Elinor's involvement are Suze, Jess, Bonnie, and Danny. Somehow Elinor's managed to orchestrate everything from the background. As far as all the caterers and serving staff are concerned, I'm in charge and I'm paying for everything and I'm the boss. Even Janice has no idea.

Which is making me feel more and more uncomfortable as time goes on. I mean, Elinor has done so much. She should get the credit. But what can I do about it?

"So what have you done with Luke?" Mum looks around, as though I might have stuffed him in a cupboard.

"He's fine. He's on a film set with this new client of his."

"Film set?" Mum goggles.

"Shh! I'm not supposed to know about it! He's being taken care of for another three hours." I glance at my watch. "Then he's coming here and . . . surprise!"

"And what are you going to wear, Becky love?" Mum interrupts my thoughts, her eyes suddenly bright and inquisitive. "Have you bought something new?"

For a while I pretend I didn't hear the question. I've been avoiding thinking about this.

"Becky? Have you bought something?"

"No," I say finally. "I haven't. I'm going to pick something out of my wardrobe."

"Darling!" Mum sounds astonished. "That's not like you!"

"I know." I sink down into a chair and pick at my nails, my spirits deflating a little. "But I couldn't go shopping, could I? Not after I promised Luke."

"He didn't mean for a *party*, surely. I mean, surely he'd make an exception—"

"I didn't want to risk it. You don't understand, Mum; he's taking it all really seriously. Nanny Sue said I'm a shopaholic," I add gloomily. "She said I need to go to boot camp or Minnie will turn into one too."

"*What?*" Mum looks satisfactorily outraged. "What nonsense! Don't listen to a word of it. Moneymaking charlatans, all of them. Boot camp sounds like *rip-off* to me. You're not going to go, are you, love?"

I love Mum. She always says the right thing.

"Dunno. Maybe. The point is, Luke totally believed her." I sigh. "And after all, it's *his* birthday. It's *his* day. How would I be making it his day by buying myself a new dress?"

I don't want to admit the scenario I'm secretly afraid of—which is that I organize a brilliant surprise party but then ruin it when he asks me how much my new shoes cost and we end up having a row.

"So I've decided, Mum." I raise my head. "It's something out of my wardrobe. I'm adamant."

"Well . . . good for you, love." She gives me an encouraging smile. "Tell you what, let's go and look in your wardrobe right now. See what we can find. Chop, chop!"

As I follow her up the stairs, my feet are heavy. This is why I've been putting off the whole outfit moment. Everyone else will have a new dress tonight, even Minnie.

Anyway. Never mind. I made a promise and I have to make the best of it. It's not like I don't *have* any clothes.

"So, did you have any ideas?" says Mum as we enter the room. "What's already in your wardrobe?"

"Maybe my black lace dress?" I'm trying to sound upbeat. "Or that blue dress I wore before Christmas? Or maybe—" I open the wardrobe door and stop midstream. What's that?

What's that brand-new posh garment carrier from The Look, hanging right in the middle of my wardrobe? And why has it got a big red bow on it?

"Open it!" Mum says excitedly. "Go on!"

Shooting her looks of slight suspicion, I pull it open. I see a glimpse of sumptuous dark green silk and inhale sharply. *No.* That can't be—

I drag the zip all the way down, just to be sure . . .

And it flows out of the garment carrier, like a deep-green glimmering river.

It's the Valentino.

It's the Valentino dress with the single jeweled shoulder which came into The Look a month ago. I must have tried it on about twenty times, but there's no way I could *ever* afford it and—

I suddenly spot a gift card tied to the hanger and open it with scrabbling fingers.

To Becky. A little something for you to pick out of your wardrobe. With love from Mum and Dad.

"Mum." Tears have shot to my eyes and I blink furiously. "You shouldn't. You *shouldn't*—"

"It was Janice!" Mum can't contain herself any longer. "She told me you weren't buying yourself anything new. Well, we couldn't have that! Not our little Becky! And, this way, it's in your wardrobe! Do you see? Do you get it, love?" She's beside herself with triumph. "It's already *in your wardrobe*! You're keeping your promise to Luke!"

"I get it, I do," I say, half laughing, half tearfully. "But, Mum, this is Valentino! It costs a fortune!"

"Well, it wasn't nothing!" Mum sucks in breath. "You know, Wendy's Boutique in Oxshott does *very* reasonable evening dresses, and I do sometimes wonder why you girls—"

She breaks off at my expression. We've disagreed about Wendy's Boutique many times over the years.

"Anyway. I asked your nice colleague Jasmine what I should get and she suggested this dress at once. *And* she gave it to me at the discount staff rate, plus another big discount for damage!" she ends in triumph.

"Damage?" I peer at it. "It's not damaged!"

"She snipped the hem," says Mum conspiratorially.

"She's clever, that one. And then all your nice friends rallied round and chipped in. So it's from them too."

"What friends?" I'm not following this at all. "You mean Jasmine?"

"No! All your shopping friends. Your clients! They were all there, you know. They signed a card too—where is it?" She starts to root around in her bag. "Here we are."

She presents me with a plain Smythson card, on which someone has scrawled: *Have a great time tonight, Becky, and see you back at The Look VERY SOON! With all our love from Davina, Chloe, and all your loyal friends.*

Underneath are about twenty more signatures, and I read them in growing bewilderment.

"But what were they all doing at the store at once?"

"Getting refunds!" says Mum, as though it's obvious. "Didn't you know? They've started a campaign to reinstate you!"

She hands me a bright-pink printed piece of paper, and I take it in disbelief. Is *this* what Davina was talking about?

BRING BACK BECKY!!!

We, the undersigned, would like to protest at the treatment of our esteemed friend and fashion consultant, Becky Brandon (née Bloomwood).

As a result of her callous and unjustified treatment by The Look, we will be:

Boycotting the Personal-Shopping Department
Spreading the word among our friends and contacts, and
Unshopping with immediate effect.

"Unshopping?" I look up with a giggle. "What does that mean?"

"They're returning everything they've bought," says Mum with satisfaction. "Quite right too. There was a whole line of them, beautifully dressed, all bringing back expensive things still in their wrappers. All getting the money back on their gold cards. I dread to think how much it was all worth. One woman had three long dresses. Yves Saint whatsit? Five thousand pounds *each,* apparently. Blond woman from Russia or some such?"

"Olenka?" I say in astonishment. "Those dresses were special order. She *returned* them?"

"She threw them down on the counter like this." Mum demonstrates with a flamboyant gesture. "Quite dramatic, isn't she? '*Thees* is for Becky and *thees* is for Becky.' Then the manager came down to the department." Mum is warming to her tale. "I can tell you, he got the heebie-jeebies when he saw how long the queue was. Quite flustered, he was. He said, 'Ladies, please reconsider.' Offered them all a free cappuccino. But they laughed at him."

"I bet they did!" I can just imagine Trevor trying to keep control of all my clients. They're a pretty sassy lot.

"So if he isn't on the phone to you apologizing within the day, then I'm a monkey's uncle," says Mum comfortably. "From what I heard, you should be claiming from *them,* love."

"Wait." Suddenly the blood is pulsing in my face. "Wait a minute. Mum, I never told you I'd been suspended from work."

"I know you didn't," she says equably. "I was a bit surprised, I must admit. I mean, I knew it was your day off. I didn't realize *every* day was your day off now!" She laughs merrily.

"So you came here . . . ." I say disbelievingly, "and you knew I'd been suspended and you didn't say a word?"

"What's there to say? You'll work it out. We do worry about you, Becky. But we've got faith in you too." Mum pats my hand. "You'll be all right."

"Oh, Mum." I look from the Valentino to her kind, cozy face, feeling the tears rise again. "I can't believe you bought me a dress."

"Well, love." She pats my hand again. "We've had such a super time at The West Place. We wanted to say thank you. Shoes too!" She nods at a shoe box at the bottom of the wardrobe.

"Shoes *too*?" I grab the box.

"Yes, Cinderella!" Mum twinkles. "I hear even Jess is wearing a lovely new frock for the occasion?"

"She is *now*." I roll my eyes.

Jess's dress has been such a saga. At first she was going to order this drab unbleached cotton shift from the worthy-lentil catalog. So I said she had to wear something more glam, and she got on her high horse and said why should she support throwaway consumerism just for one night? Whereupon I said, "I meant you should *borrow* something—all the celebs do it, and it's *far* more green than buying something out of a catalog." To which she couldn't find an answer. So she'll be in an exclusive Danny Kovitz number, and there's no way she can get out of it.

I'm ripping the shoe box open in excitement as my mobile rings.

"I'll get it, love." Mum reaches over to the chair where my mobile's lying. "It's—" She peers more closely at the screen and her mouth drops open. "Sage Seymour? Sage Seymour the *actress*?"

"Yes!" I giggle. "Shh! Be cool!"

I expect Sage will be giving me another update on

Luke. Last time she phoned, he was eating a burrito and talking to the choreographer.

"Hi, Sage! How's it going?"

"He's gone!" She sounds desperate. "I'm so sorry. We've lost him."

"*What?*" I sit back on my heels, a piece of tissue paper trailing from my fingers. "But . . . *how?*"

"He just upped and left. Booked himself a car and went. Didn't even pick up his mobile from the floor manager. I was in makeup, I had no idea—"

"How long ago?"

"Half an hour, maybe?"

Half an *hour?* My pulse is quickening in alarm. "So, where's the car gone? Can you find out?"

"No! It's not even one of ours. Apparently he'd been saying he needed to go, and the line producer had been promising to get him a car as soon as one was ready, you know, stringing him along . . . But I guess he couldn't wait."

That is so typical of Luke. He can't just sit still and enjoy being on a movie set like any normal person. He has to organize himself a car and go back to work. Celebrities are *wasted* on him.

"I need to get back," Sage is saying. "But, Becky, I'm sorry. We fucked up." She sounds genuinely apologetic.

"No! Don't be silly! You did an amazing job. It's not *your* fault he left. I'm sure I'll find him."

"Well, let me know how it works out."

"Of course." I turn off my phone, breathing hard, and look at Mum. "You won't believe this. Luke's gone missing. No one knows where he is."

"Well, ring him, love! He'll have his mobile—"

"He hasn't *got* a mobile!" I almost wail. "I broke his BlackBerry and he had some crappy substitute, which he's left behind. I don't know what car company he's using. I mean, I guess he's heading back to the office, but I don't know . . ."

I feel a drumbeat of panic as the enormity of this sinks in. What if he's not on his way to the office? What if he's coming here? He could stumble on the whole thing before we're ready.

"OK." I snap into action. "We need to warn everybody. I'll call Bonnie, you tell Janice, we'll call all the car companies—we'll track him down."

WITHIN TEN MINUTES, I've got everyone gathered in Janice's kitchen for an emergency crisis meeting.

It's all even worse than I thought. Bonnie has just forwarded me an email from Luke, which he sent before he left the studio, using the film's email account. He told her he wouldn't be able to get back to the office in time for the company training program, sent his apologies, and told her to have a good weekend.

What the fuck is he *doing*? Where is he *going*?

OK, Becky. Stay calm. He'll turn up.

"Right," I announce to the assembled group. "Oxshott, we have a major problem. Luke has gone AWOL. Now, I've drawn a map." I point to my hastily constructed flip chart. "These are the directions he might have gone in from the Pinewood Studios. I think we probably can rule out north—"

"Ooh!" Suze suddenly exclaims, looking at her phone. "Tarkie says one of the royal family has seen the YouTube clips and wants to send Luke a happybirthday text. They're out shooting together," she explains bashfully as everyone looks at her, agog.

"Which member?" Janice clasps her hands. "*Not* Prince William!"

"Tarkie didn't say. It might be Prince Michael of Kent," Suze adds apologetically.

"Oh." Everyone subsides a little in disappointment.

"Or David Linley?" Janice perks up. "I do love his furniture, but have you *seen* the prices?"

"Stop it!" I wave my arms frustratedly. "Focus! Who cares about furniture? This is an *emergency*. First, we need a lookout stationed outside, so if Luke comes back here we can head him off. Second, we need to think hard where he might have gone. Third—"

"Your phone," says Mum suddenly. My BlackBerry is vibrating on the table, with a central London number I don't recognize.

"It might be him!" says Dad.

"Shh!"

"Quiet!"

"Put him on speaker!"

"No!"

"Everyone *quiet*!"

It's as though the terrorist kidnapper is on the line after days of waiting. Everyone goes quiet and watches as I answer.

"Hello?"

"Becky?" Luke's voice is unmistakable. And relaxed. Doesn't he *realize* how stressed we've all been?

"Keep him talking!" whispers Mum, as though she's a federal agent trying to triangulate his position.

"Hi, Luke! Where are you? At the office?"

That was good. Play completely ignorant.

"As it happens, no. I'm at the Berkeley Hotel." There's a smile in his voice. "And I want to invite you and Minnie to join me for a little birthday celebration. If you're up for it."

What-what-what-what-what?

I sink down onto a chair, my legs rubbery, trying to block out all the questioning faces around me.

"What do you mean?" I falter at last.

If he has arranged his own birthday party without telling me, I will *murder* him. I mean it.

"Darling, I could tell you were disappointed last night when I said I'd be at the training program," he's saying. "I could see it in your face."

"No, I wasn't!" I want to yell. *"I wasn't! You're all wrong!"*

"Oh yes?" I manage.

"And it got me thinking. It's my birthday! Fuck it, we should celebrate. We've got through a hell of a year and we deserve a treat. Let's meet up, the three of us, have some dinner, drink some champagne . . . then we can put Minnie to bed next door and see about making her a little sibling." His voice is as seductive and teasing as I've ever heard it. "What do you think? I've ordered the champagne already."

I cannot believe what I'm hearing. Any other time, I would die and go to heaven to hear this invitation. *Any other bloody time.*

"Right," I say weakly. "Well . . . that sounds wonderful! Just . . . hang on a minute . . ."

I clamp my hand over the phone and look desperately round at everybody.

"He wants me to come to a hotel room and drink champagne! For his birthday!"

"But it's the party!" says Janice, who is clearly out to get the Most Obvious Comment prize.

"I *know* it's the party!" I say, almost savagely. "But how can I say no without looking suspicious?"

"Do both?" says Suze. "Champagne, celebrate, whatever, whiz back here?"

I think it through frantically.

Champagne. Food. Sex.

We could get it done in . . . half an hour? Forty minutes max? We'd still be back in good time.

"Yes." I come to a decision. "I'll go up there, play along, and bring him back as quickly as I can."

"Don't hang around, love." Janice looks anxious.

"Traffic can get nasty this time of day," Martin chips in. "I'd grab him and go."

"Can I leave Minnie with you, Mum?"

"Of course, love!"

"OK." I take a deep breath and turn to the phone again, trying to sound as syrupy as possible. "Hi, Luke. I'll be there as soon as I can. But without Minnie. Mum's here and she's going to babysit. I think we need to be *a deux*, don't you?"

"Even better." He gives that growly laugh that I love and my insides clench. Why does he have to choose *tonight* to turn into the perfect husband?

Anyway. Whatever. I must get going.

"I'll see you soon!" I say breathlessly. "Love you!"

LUKE'S BOOKED A SUITE, and as he opens the door he's holding a glass of champagne. Low, jazzy music is playing, and he's in a robe. A *robe*.

"Well, hello there." He smiles and bends to kiss me.

Oh God. This is all more extreme than I realized. He's completely switched gear. His rhythm is slower, his voice is lazier; I haven't seen him look so relaxed since we were on our honeymoon. The suite is amazing too, with paneled walls and plushy sofas and a massive bed. If this were *any* other time . . .

"Hi!" I pull away. "Well, this is a big surprise!"

"Total impulse." Luke grins. "In fact, this is your doing," he adds over his shoulder as he heads to the cocktail bar.

"*Mine?*" Is he joking?

"All the times you've told me we should relax more,

enjoy ourselves, take it easy—you were right. I hope you're impressed."

"Yes," I say shrilly. "This is fab."

"So let's just kick back. We've got all night." He hands me a glass and kisses my neck lingeringly. "Shall I run a bath? It's big enough for two."

A *bath*? How long will that take? I have to nix that idea at once. I have to speed things up. I glance at my watch and feel a twinge of alarm. It's already later than I thought. We have a party to get to. There is *no time for a bath*.

But then . . . look at his face. He'll be crushed. And he's gone to so much effort, and I bet it's a lovely bath . . .

We could have a really quick bath. In, out, done.

"Good idea! I'll do it!" I hurry into the sumptuous marble bathroom and whack on the taps.

Oh wow. Asprey toiletries. I can't help opening the bath oil and smelling it. Mmm.

"Isn't this great?" Luke has come up behind me and wraps his arms around me, firm and strong. "Just us, all night long. There's no rush, no hurry . . ."

OK, we have *not* got time for any of this all-night-long business.

"Luke . . . um . . . we have to have quick sex." I turn round, thinking desperately. "We have to have really, really fast, speedy sex because . . . I want to conceive a boy."

"What?" Luke looks dumbfounded. As well he might, since I'm making this all up as I go along.

"Yes." I nod seriously. "I read a book about it, and it said that you have to have sex really fast. No foreplay. Just . . . boom."

"*Boom?*" echoes Luke dubiously.

Why is he looking so reluctant? He should be *pleased*. I mean, if you knew how many times—

Anyway. Not relevant right now.

"Boom," I say firmly. "So . . . come on!"

Why isn't he moving? Why is he crumpling his brow and sitting on the edge of the bath and looking as though some deep problem has occurred to him?

"Becky," he says at last. "I don't feel comfortable aiming for one particular sex of baby or another. I love Minnie. I'd *love* another Minnie. And if you feel in any way that I've been hankering for a son—"

"No! I don't think that!" I say hurriedly. "It's just . . . why not? And later on we can try for a girl! Even it up!"

Even *I* can tell I'm making no sense, but luckily Luke is used to that.

"Bath's ready!" I rip off my top. "Come on!"

OK, so I don't feel it necessary to go into the details of what happens next. And, anyway, there hardly *are* any details. Except we start off in the bath and end up in the shower and we still only take fourteen minutes, and Luke has no idea I'm subtly chivvying him along.

Well, to be honest, I kind of forgot about the chivvying, once we got down to it. Or, to put it another way, we were both chivvying each other along. I don't want to boast, but I reckon we could have got an Olympic medal in the "underwater-pairs formation," maybe. Or the "synchronized freestyle program." Or the—

Oh. OK, then. Moving on.

The point is, what a fab way to start the evening. I feel so glowy I won't even need blusher. And if we get dressed and leave right now—

"Want something to eat?"

As I head into the living room, hastily drying myself, Luke is back in his robe, lolling on the sofa.

"Have a look at these." He gestures at the platter on the table. "Fashion cakes."

Fashion cakes?

In spite of myself, I have to hurry over—and I can't

help gasping in delight. It's a whole plate of dinky little cakes in the shape of shoes and bags.

"Each one is inspired by a different fashion item." Luke looks pleased. "I thought you'd like them. Have one." He hands me an iced over-the-knee boot.

It's scrummy. I almost want to cry. This is the most perfect evening, and I've got to drag him away from it . . .

Maybe I'll have just one more cake.

"More champagne?" Now he's refilling my glass.

And one more glass of champagne. Just a quick one.

"Isn't this wonderful?" Luke pulls me against him and I nestle into his chest, feeling lulled into relaxation, feeling his heart beat against my skin. "This has been quite a day."

"I couldn't agree more." I take a deep gulp of champagne.

"Losing all my technology has been weirdly liberating. I've been forty-eight hours now without emails or Internet or even a proper phone. And you know what? I've survived."

"I knew it." I turn my head to look at him. "I think you should have a BlackBerry-free day every week. It'd be good for your health."

"Maybe I will," says Luke, his hand edging up the inside of my leg again. "Maybe we'll come *here* every week. That would be great for my health."

"Yes, definitely!" I giggle. "Here's to that!" As I lift my champagne glass, my own BlackBerry rings, and I stiffen.

"Ignore it," says Luke comfortably.

"But it's Mum," I say quickly, glancing at the display as I grab it. "It might be about Minnie. I'd better get it . . . Hello?"

"Becky!" Mum's voice is so high-pitched and anxious, I jump. "Janice has just seen a traffic alert! Terrible snarl-up on the A3. How are you doing? Have you left yet?"

I feel a jolt of panic.

Oh God. What I am *doing,* drinking champagne and eating cakes? I glance at Luke. He's lying back on the sofa in his robe, his eyes closed. He looks like he could stay here all night.

"Er, not yet . . ."

"Well, I'd get cracking, love! You don't want to get stuck!"

"I will! We're on our way. See you soon."

"What's up?" Luke opens one eye as I put down the BlackBerry. I have about ten seconds to think of a full-fledged convincing story.

OK. Got it.

"Luke, we need to go right now," I say urgently. "Minnie's hysterical because neither of us kissed her good night. So we need to go back to Oxshott, kiss her good night, make sure she's settled, and come back. Quick! Get dressed!" I'm already pulling on my under-wear.

"Go *back*?" Luke hauls himself to a sitting position and peers at me. "Becky . . . are you crazy? We're not going back!"

"Minnie's in a terrible state! Mum said she was going to make herself ill. We can't just leave her!"

"She'll be fine. She'll fall asleep and she'll be fine." He calmly takes a sip of champagne, and I feel a stab of in-dignation. I mean, OK, so Minnie isn't really in a state, but what if she was?

"How can you say that? She's our child!"

"And we're having a night off! It's not a crime, Becky. If we go back to Oxshott, I guarantee she'll be asleep before we even get there."

"But I won't be able to relax! I won't be able to enjoy myself! How can I sit here and drink champagne when my little girl's having"—my mind roams wildly—"convulsions?"

"*Convulsions?*"

"Mum said she was seriously worried for Minnie's health. She said she'd never seen anything like it." I stare defiantly at Luke. "I'm going, even if you're not!"

For a frozen moment I'm petrified he might say, "Fine, you go, see you later." But at last he puts his glass down heavily and sighs.

"Fine. Whatever. We'll go and kiss her good night."

"Great! Perfect!" I can't hide my relief. "It's still early; we can still have a good evening. Let's take the cakes and the champagne," I add casually. "Just in case we're hungry on the way."

No *way* am I leaving those gorgeous little cakes behind. And as soon as I'm dressed, I hurry into the bathroom and scoop all the toiletries into my bag. I'm not leaving those behind either.

I'm just about ready to go and Luke is putting on his overcoat when my BlackBerry bleeps with a text.

R u on way to Oxshott yet? All looks fab here and everything in place!!!!! Suze.

Nearly! I text back. C u soon!!!!!

As we travel down in the lift, I smile nervously at Luke. It's suddenly hit me: We're nearly there! It's nearly his surprise! After all this time, all this planning . . .

Excitement rushes up through me like a glittering firework, and I can't help giving him a hug. "All right?"

"I suppose so." He raises his eyebrows wryly. "We'd better be getting special parenting angel points for this somewhere."

"I'm sure we will." Somehow I manage a normal-ish

voice—but I can hardly contain myself. This is it! In less than an hour we're going to arrive and Luke's face is going to drop and he's going to be so blown away he won't even be able to *speak* . . .

I hurry him out of the lifts and into the foyer. My legs feel light; my whole body is fizzing with anticipation.

"You check how long the bar's open," I improvise. "I'll see if I can hail a cab."

I've got a car service waiting outside. I'll pretend I just found it on the street.

"Luke? Luke Brandon?"

A balding businessman leaning against the concierge's desk has looked up. He's had quite a few drinks, I instantly realize from his bloodshot eyes.

"Oh. Hello, Don." Luke smiles briefly. "How are you? Donald Lister from Alderbury Consulting." He introduces me. "This is my wife, Becky."

A delighted realization is dawning on the man's flushed face.

"Wait a minute. Shit! Luke Brandon! It's you!" He points at Luke as though he's won the prize and is claiming his ten quid. "Bloody hell! Happy birthday, old man! So how was it?"

The world goes blurry for an instant.

OK, we have to leave. Now. Trying not to give away my panic, I put my arm through Luke's and tug gently, but he doesn't move.

"Good, thanks." Luke gives a polite, surprised smile. "How on earth did you know?"

"Are you kidding? *Everyone's* been—" The man breaks off as he sees my face. "Shit." He gives an awkward guffaw. "Haven't given the game away, have I?"

I want to say something quick and sharp that will neutralize him, I want to rewind, I want to smother this stupid man, get rid of him, go *away*—

"Is the bash tonight?" The man claps a hand over his mouth. "Were you on your way—Oh bugger."

I want to launch myself at him like a tigress and rip his head off with my teeth. *Shut up, shut UP.*

"Sorry, sorry! Didn't say anything." He pats the air a few times as though to bury his words, then hastily heads away across the marble floor.

But he can't bury his words. They're out there, like flying ants wheeling in the air.

For the first time ever, I wish I were married to some stupid, unperceptive, Neanderthal-type moron.

But Luke's no moron. And I know him too well. He might look impassive to a stranger, but I could see his mind crunching. I could see exactly when the truth landed. Now his face is carefully blank, but it's there in his eyes. He turns and smiles.

"Well . . . I've got no idea what *that* was all about," he says, his voice a little too hearty.

He knows.

I feel numb.

TWENTY-ONE

DURING THE LONG TAXI RIDE, we hardly talk. At first I try to keep up a jolly façade, but everything I say sounds false and hollow to my own ears. We turn off toward Oxshott and we're nearly there and I should be bubbling with excitement—but it's not like I planned at all.

A sudden tear rolls down my cheek, and I brush it away quickly before Luke can see.

"Becky—" Luke sounds agonized.

Great. He did see. Even my own stupid *body* is giving it all away.

For a moment we just stare at each other, and it's as though marital telepathy is finally kicking in between us. I know what he thinks. I know what he feels. He'd give anything to rewind; he'd give anything not to know. But he can't un-know.

"Becky . . ." Luke looks tortured as he scans my face. "Please—"

"It's fine. I just—"

"I don't—"

Everything we say is meaningless half sentences. It's like neither of us can risk edging near the truth. Then suddenly Luke seems to come to a decision and pulls me close.

"I'll be surprised," he says in an intense, low voice.

"I will. I don't know anything. If you knew how touched—" He breaks off, breathing hard. "Becky, please don't be upset . . ." He grabs my hands and crushes them so tight, I wince.

I can't speak. I can't believe we're having this conversation.

"We'll be there soon." I wipe my eyes at last and check my makeup. Suze is all primed with my dress, and Danny is in charge of Luke's outfit too.

It's fine, I tell myself sternly. Even if it's not exactly what I planned, it's fine. Luke's here, I'm here, he's going to have his party, and it's going to be fabulous.

"Happy birthday, darling," I murmur as the taxi pulls in to Janice's drive, and I squeeze Luke's hand.

"What—Why are we pulling in *here*?"

Luke is heroically trying to sound like the most astonished person in the world. I wish he wouldn't. He's not very good at it.

"Get out." I flash him a smile—and even though I know he knows, I can feel the excitement fizzing up again. I mean, he doesn't know *everything*. I pay the taxi driver and lead Luke through Janice's darkened house. The catering staff is either hiding in the kitchen or already in the tent, but even so, I don't dare turn on the lights.

Ow. I just bumped my hip on Janice's stupid table. Why does she have *tables* everywhere?

"OK, outside . . ." I push him forward, through the French doors into the garden. There's the tent, all decorated with twinkly fairy lights and lit up inside—yet completely silent, as though two hundred people aren't gathered inside.

"Becky—" Luke stops dead and stares. "I can't believe this. I can't *believe* what you've—Did you arrange all this yourself?"

"Come on!"

I drag him along the matting to the entrance, my heart suddenly racing. They'd better all be there.

Of course they're there.

I take a deep breath—then pull open the flap to the tent.

"SURPRISE!!"

The noise is phenomenal. A massive throng of lit-up faces is turned toward us. I recognize only some of them. Janice is near the front, in her Mrs. Bennet dress, and Jess is in the most amazing sculptured black sheath, with dramatic makeup to match. As I look around I can't help a twinge of pride. Fairy lights are strung up and silver balloons are bobbing with *Happy Birthday, Luke* printed in the Brandon Communications logo font. All around the tent are glossy mock promotional posters and blown-up newspapers, each with a different headline and story about Luke Brandon. (I wrote them all myself.) The pièce de résistance is a massive backlit graph, just like the ones they produce for Brandon C press launches. It shows pictures of Luke every year, from a baby right up to adulthood, and is headlined: LUKE—A BUMPER YEAR.

And right above our head, all around, are my pompoms. We strung fairy lights through them and hung them in garlands—and they look *amazing*.

"Happy birthday to you . . ." Someone launches into singing, and the crowd follows lustily.

I dart a glance at Luke.

"Wow!" he exclaims as though on cue. "This is such . . . I had no idea!"

He's making the hugest effort to look supremely shocked. I have to give him that.

"For he's a jolly good fellow . . ." the crowd is now singing. Luke keeps spotting faces in the crowd and acknowledging them with waves and smiles, and as soon as the singing finishes, he takes a glass from a waitress and raises it toward the general melee.

"You bastards!" he says, and there's a roar of laughter. The little three-piece band in the corner strikes up with some Gershwin, and people surge round Luke, and I watch his face as he greets them.

He wasn't blown away. He wasn't speechless with surprise. But then . . . I knew he wouldn't be. The minute that guy opened his mouth in the Berkeley Hotel.

"Becky! This is fantastic!" A woman from Brandon Communications whose name I've forgotten (but I remember that amazing Alexander McQueen dress) descends on me. "Did you do all these decorations yourself?"

Erica and her staff are circulating with canapés, and I can see Janice approaching a chic blond girl with a powder compact. For God's sake. I told her, *no touchups.* I have to head her off, quick.

But before I can, a graying man hands me a cocktail and introduces himself as an old colleague of Luke's and asks me how long it all took to plan, and then his wife (floaty dress, too much lipstick) asks me excitedly if I've seen the clips on YouTube, and about fifteen minutes go by and I haven't done anything except talk to strangers. I don't even know where Luke is.

There's a bit of a draft coming through the flaps of the tent too, and everyone's gradually huddling away from the entrance.

"People! A word if you please." Luke's commanding voice fills the tent, and at once all the Brandon Communications people stop talking and turn to attention, as though he's about to make some company presentation. The others follow suit, and the whole place falls silent with incredible speed.

"I just want to say . . . thank you." He surveys the

crowd of smiling faces. "To all of you. I can't believe so many old friends are here and I look forward to catching up. I can't believe you all *knew* about this, you devious lot." There's an appreciative laugh around the tent. "And I can't believe how clever my wife has been." He turns to me. "Becky, take a bow."

A spattering of applause breaks out, and I dutifully make a little bow.

"Was it a total surprise, Luke?" calls out the woman with too much lipstick. "Did you have absolutely no idea?"

Luke darts the wariest of glances at me; you'd hardly notice it.

"Yes, absolutely!" He sounds forced. "I had no idea until I stepped into the—" He breaks off. "At least, obviously I suspected *something* when we got into the taxi—" He stops again and rubs his face awkwardly, and there's a curious, expectant hush around the tent.

"Here's the thing." Luke looks up at last, and his usual polished veneer is gone. "I don't want to lie to all of you. I don't want to put on an act, because this is too important to me. I want to say what I really feel. Someone *did* give the game away earlier on. A little. So, yes, I was expecting . . . something. But you know what? A party like this isn't about the surprise factor. It's about someone going to so much trouble that it just . . . overwhelms you. And you think, *What did I do to deserve this?*" He pauses, his voice trembling a bit. "I am the luckiest man alive, and I'd like to propose a toast. To Becky."

I'm glancing at my phone. It's been buzzing with texts throughout, and I've only had half an ear on Luke's speech. But now I look up.

"OK, Luke." I allow myself a smile. "You're wrong. This kind of party is *all* about the surprise factor. Take your drink. Take your coat. And step this way, please.

Everyone, if you could collect your coats and follow us . . ."

Out of nowhere, Daryl, Nicole, Julie, and three of their friends have materialized and are efficiently pushing in rails of coats. All the guests are looking at one another, flummoxed. Daryl winks at me—and I wink back. He's a total star, Daryl. He got in touch a week ago and said he'd really improved on the fire-eating and did I want to audition him again? Whereupon I said no thanks—but there was another job he could do. All six teenagers are dressed smartly in white shirts and waistcoats, and Nicole's wearing her Vivienne Westwood shoes, I notice.

Luke hasn't moved a muscle. He looks utterly gobsmacked.

Ha!

"Becky . . ." He wrinkles his brow. "What on earth—"

Ha! Ha!

"You think *this* is your party?" I nod at the tent derisively.

I almost want to skip with glee as I lead him back through Janice's house to the drive. And they're here. Right on cue. Four massive coach buses, parked outside. They're jet black and on the side is printed in white:

LUKE'S REAL SURPRISE PARTY.

"Wh—"

Luke's jaw has dropped. He seems unable to speak.

Yessssss!

"In you get," I say blithely.

I KNOW, I know, I didn't tell you. I'm sorry.

I *wanted* to. But I was afraid you might blab.

• • •

THE ATMOSPHERE in the coach is fantastic. The whole level of festivity seems to have gone up ten notches. I keep hearing snatches of "Where are we *going*?" and "Did you know?" and gales of laughter.

And Luke just seems stunned. I've never *seen* him so stunned. I must surprise him more often.

"OK, blindfold on," I say as we reach the turning.

"No." He starts to laugh. "You can't be serious—"

"Blindfold on!" I lift a mock-stern finger and waggle it at him.

This is quite a power trip, actually. He's totally under my control. I yank the ends of the blindfold really tight and peer out of the front of the coach. We're nearly there!

I text Suze: **Five minutes** and immediately get back: **OK.** She's there, waiting for me, along with Mum, Dad, Minnie, Danny, and the rest of Team 2.

Oh yes. I had two teams. Well, actually, that was Elinor's idea.

I know Elinor's still there too, because Suze sent me a text a few minutes ago saying that Elinor had been checking every last-minute detail fanatically, and all the staff were petrified of her.

As we head up the long avenue of trees, I can see all the guests peering curiously out of the coach windows, and I furiously make a finger-to-lips gesture. Not that Luke would guess, probably. He's only been to Suze's new house once.

I say "house." What I mean is, "stately home with parkland."

It was such a last-minute decision to come here. We'd planned to hire a venue, and Elinor was poised to bribe some other event to move (she's totally ruthless, like a trained assassin), when Suze suddenly said, "Wait! What about Letherby Hall?"

I think sometimes Suze actually forgets how many

houses she and Tarquin possess. She certainly had no idea how many bedrooms it's got.

Anyway. Once we'd made *that* decision, everything fell into place. Or at least was shoved very quickly into place. And it's the perfect, dreamiest, most romantic setting for a party. I can hear people oohing and aahing behind me as they catch sight of the house, with its two grand wings and central dome and Doric pilasters all over the place. (I know they're Doric pilasters because Tarkie told me. In fact, I'm quite hoping someone asks me about them.)

There's a breeze in the air as we all pile out of the coach and crunch forward over the gravel. The front entrance is open and lit up, and I usher everyone in silently, still guiding Luke. We cross the ancient stone floor and soon we're all assembled, standing in front of the grand double doors to the Great Hall.

I can hear the whispers and giggles and "shh!"s going on behind me. I can feel the anticipation now. I almost feel frightened. This is it. This is the moment.

"OK." My voice shakes a little as I untie his blindfold. "Luke . . . happy birthday."

As I open the double doors, the gasp behind Luke is like hearing the rush of water. But I'm looking only at his face. It's ashen.

If I wanted blown away and speechless . . . then I've got it.

He takes a step forward wonderingly. Then another . . . then another.

The whole of the Great Hall has been transformed into the stage of that vintage toy theater he bought for Minnie—the toy theater of his childhood. All the *Midsummer Night's Dream* sets have been painstakingly reproduced. There are the same bushes and trees and castle spires, there's a brook and moss. Little tables and chairs are nestled among the foliage. A band is playing low, magical music. Set here and there in the trees, like big flowers, are more of my pom-poms. I can't help feeling proud. They *do* look good.

"This is—" Luke swallows hard. "It's exactly the same as—"

"I know." I grip his hand tight.

This was always my idea. But I could never have done it as spectacularly as this if it weren't for Elinor.

"Daddeeeee!" Minnie comes running out from behind a tree, dressed in the most beautiful, gossamer fairy dress with wings that Danny made for her. "Happy! Happy Daddy!"

"Minnie!" Luke looks overwhelmed as he scoops her up. "Where did you—How did you—Suze! Jane! Graham! Danny!" He's turning his head in bewilderment as they all pop out from their hiding places.

"Happy birthday!"

"Surprise!"

"Say something, Luke, love! Give us a little speech!" I can't believe Mum's pointing a camcorder at Luke's face. She *knows* we've hired a professional cameraman.

"*Bonnie?*" Luke looks even more shellshocked as Bonnie emerges from behind the waterfall in a spectacular aquamarine dress, an abashed smile on her face. "Please don't tell me *you* were in on all of this."

"Just a little."

"This is . . . unreal." He shakes his head and looks around the magical room again. "Who *else* knows it's my birthday?"

"Who else? Um . . ." I meet Bonnie's eyes and want to laugh. "Quite a few people. Most of the City."

"The readership of the *Daily World*," adds Bonnie. "And the *Standard* City Diary, and the *Mail* just ran a little piece."

"You've got messages from three members of the royal family," puts in Suze brightly.

"Don't forget YouTube!" adds Dad. "Hundred thousand hits at the latest count!"

Luke looks as though we must have gone mad. "You're joking," he says, and we all shake our heads.

"Wait till you see the tributes!" says Mum. "And you've got your own happy-birthday website!"

"But . . . this is crazy." Luke puts a hand to his head. "I *never* celebrate my birthday. Who on earth—"

"Becky's been very busy," Bonnie says.

"Trying to keep it *secret*!" I exclaim indignantly. "Trying to *stop* people blabbing and posting stuff on the Internet! It's been like trying to keep control of an octopus."

"A drink, sir?" A stunning male model wearing one of Danny's *Midsummer Night's Dream* costumes appears from nowhere. His thighs are clad in fur and there's a wreath of leaves round his head, and his chest is bare and tanned, and *very* honed. (I think this is Danny's own fantasy interpretation of *A Midsummer Night's Dream*—i.e., basically just a forest full of hot men.)

The male model is holding out a wooden tray which looks like a slice of tree, bearing cocktails with silver tags. "I can offer you a Brandon, a Bloomwood, or a Minnie. And then if you and your wife would like to get changed before the show?"

"The show?" Luke turns to me. I raise my eyebrows mysteriously and squeeze his hand again.

"Wait and see."

IT'S THE MOST INCREDIBLE blow-your-mind party. It just is.

I mean, I know I helped organize it and everything, so I shouldn't boast. I should be all modest and self-deprecating and say, "Oh, it was OK, I suppose," or "As parties go, it wasn't bad," and shrug and change the subject and talk about the weather.

But too bad, I'm not going to; I'm going to tell you the *truth*. Which is that it's the most out-of-this-world party and everyone's said so, even people who go to loads of parties, like the Right Reverend St. John Gardner-Stone, who turns out to be a total sweetie with a good line in knock-knock jokes.

Everything so far has gone perfectly. When Luke had put on his dinner jacket and I was in my divine green dress, we took our seats in the hall on little chairs, drinks in hands, and a circus dance troupe performed the most amazing acrobatics all around us in the trees of the forest, with thumping music and laser lights flashing.

Then came the fire-eaters—a Czech troupe that does all kinds of amazing stunts. (They included Alonzo/Alvin in the routine, because I told them they had to, and he looked totally terrified and exhilarated all the way through.)

Then a massive screen came down from the ceiling, another soundtrack played, and all the YouTube tributes to Luke began, and I nearly cried.

OK. I did kind of blink away a few tears.

Not that any of them were any *good*. I mean, seeing a bunch of marketing executives from Kettering do a rubbishy "Happy Birthday, Luke da Man" rap into a shaky mobile phone isn't exactly *The Shawshank Redemption*. But it was the fact of them. People I don't even know, wishing Luke a happy birthday.

Then we had video messages from all the friends who couldn't be here, like Luke's dad and Michael, followed by the text messages from the website, flashing up one after another. And finally a clip I didn't even know about, which Suze had been emailed ten minutes before we arrived, apparently. It starts off with Sage

Seymour on her film set, sitting on a director's chair, saying, "Luke, honey, where the hell *are* you?" and pretending he's supposed to be doing a scene with her, and it ends up with all the cast and crew wishing him happy birthday. Even the really famous ones.

As soon as Sage appeared on the screen, Luke's head whipped round to me, and he said, "How the *fuck*—"

And I couldn't help giggling and whispering in his ear, "Luke, just face it. There's no point trying to keep any secrets from me."

I was expecting him to laugh, but he didn't. To be honest, he looked a teeny bit freaked.

Then we sat down for the most amazing feast in the Long Gallery, which was decorated with flower garlands and yet more plastic pom-poms. (I really did make a *lot*.) There were loads of speeches, and Luke thanked everyone a zillion times and I thanked everyone a zillion times. Then Luke made a really touching speech about Annabel and the toy theater and how special those memories were to him, and how he'd bought the same theater for Minnie and hoped she would have the same memories of *him* one day. And everyone dabbed at their eyes.

Oh, and he said some nice stuff about me. You know.

Then the coffee came round with Suze's special *Luke's Walnut Shortbread*, and everybody oohed and aahed again. I met Suze's eyes and silently mouthed, "Thank you."

After that, the band appeared on stage in the East Hall (all Suze's rooms have names). And now there's dancing in that room and mood-music-and-lounging-around-on-sofas in another huge room, and people are still milling around the *Midsummer Night's Dream* room, and later on, there'll be ice cream and fireworks and a stand-up comedian, only Luke doesn't know that yet.

I'm watching him from my perch by the brook. He's surrounded by old friends, holding Minnie in his arms, and I haven't seen his face lit up like that for . . .

I don't know. Way too long.

I'm just wondering which kind of cocktail to move on to next when Suze comes swooshing up to me in her dress—which, I have to admit, is almost more fabulous than mine. It's dark purple with a train, and she got it in Paris from Christian Dior and wouldn't tell me how much it cost, which means it was a *squillion*.

"Bex, I don't know what to do about . . ." She pauses, then mouths, "Elinor."

"What about her?" I look nervously around to check that Luke isn't in earshot.

Suze leans close and breathes in my ear, "She's still here."

I feel a bolt of shock. She's *here*?

Elinor told me a million times that she wasn't staying for the party. She said she was leaving half an hour before we arrived. I just assumed she had.

"But where—" I look wildly around.

"It's my fault." Suze's face crumples. "I couldn't *bear* for her not to see any of it. Not after everything she's done. I knew she couldn't actually *come* to the party . . . so I asked, would she like to hide in the Priest's Passage and watch?"

Suze glances up meaningfully, and I follow her gaze. There's a tiny iron balcony at first-floor level, which I've never really noticed. But it's empty.

"I don't understand," I say stupidly. "Where is she?"

"Hidden behind a secret panel, looking out through a spy hole." Suze chews her lip anxiously. "She said she only wanted to see you and Luke arrive and know that everything had worked. She said she'd slip away after that. But I just got Tarkie to go and check her car—and it hasn't left. She must still be there! She hasn't had any food, she's standing in this tiny space . . . and I'm worried. What if she gets ill? I mean, how *old* is she?"

Oh God. This could all go horribly wrong.

I glance over at Luke—but he's laughing at something and doesn't even notice me. "Come on, let's go."

The stairs up to the Priest's Passage are tiny and narrow and musty, and I clutch my precious Valentino dress to me. As Suze cautiously pushes open the old wooden door, it's Elinor's shoulders I see first—narrow and rigid. Her face is pressed right up to the panel in front of her and she looks like a statue. She hasn't even heard us.

"Elinor?" I whisper, and she whips round, a fleeting look of panic on her pale face.

"It's fine! It's Suze and me. We've brought you a snack." I offer her a plate of mini desserts from dinner, but she shrinks away.

"I must go."

"No! You don't have to. We just wanted to make sure you were all right."

"Luke doesn't suspect I'm here?"

"No. Not at all."

There's silence. Elinor resumes her watch and I glance at Suze, who gives me a "What do we do now?" shrug.

"Luke and Minnie seem very close," says Elinor, her eye pressed right up against the spy hole. "He has a natural manner with her."

"Um . . . yes."

"With your parents too."

I don't reply. This is all too surreal. How did I get into this situation? How can I be standing in a tiny, cramped hole with my rich bitch mother-in-law, both of us hiding from the man who links us?

And how can I be feeling like I want to give her a great big, warm, proper family hug? Like I want to gather her in, away from this dark, distant hiding hole, into the light and warmth of the party? She's never seemed so vulnerable and alone as she does right now. And it's because of her that we're all having the time of our lives.

"It's just wonderful down there." I put a hand out cautiously and squeeze her arm. "Everyone's said it's the best party they've ever been to."

"Luke has enjoyed it?" She turns.

"Oh my God, yes! He's bowled over! Did you see his *face*?"

"You've made his year!" Suze nods enthusiastically. "He's so touched. He's been round the whole forest, looking at every detail. It's so clever."

Elinor says nothing, but I see the tiniest flicker of satisfaction in her eyes. And suddenly I can't bear it. This is all wrong. I want Luke to know. I want everyone to know. There was a massive driving force behind tonight, and it was Luke's mother.

"Elinor, come down." The words spill out before I can stop them. "Come down and join the party." I hear Suze's astonished gasp but ignore it. "Come on. I'll make things OK with Luke."

"I fear that will be impossible."

"No, it won't!"

"I must leave. Now. I have stayed too long." Elinor has unclasped her handbag and is pulling on a pair of kid gloves. Oh God, I've frightened her away.

"Look, I know you've had difficulties, you two," I say cajolingly. "But this is the perfect time to mend them. At his party! And when he knows you were behind all this . . . he'll love you! He'll *have* to love you!"

"That's precisely why I cannot go down." Her voice sounds so harsh that I flinch—though it might just be because of the dusty air up here. "I did not fund this party in order to win Luke's love in some ostentatious way."

"That's not—I didn't mean—"

"I will not go down. I will not join in the festivities. I will not have him knowing that I was any part of tonight. You will never tell him. *Never*, do you hear me, Rebecca?"

Her eyes flash at me furiously, and I recoil in fright. For all the vulnerability she can still be pretty scary.

"OK!" I gulp.

"There are no conditions attached to tonight. I have done this for Luke." She's looking again through the spy hole. "I have done this for Luke," she repeats, almost as though to herself.

There's a long silence. Suze and I are glancing at each other nervously, but neither of us dares speak.

"If I went down, if I was to make myself known as benefactor, I would have done it for myself." She turns and regards me evenly, her eyes giving nothing away. "As you said so clearly, an unconditional act does not require reward."

God, she's hard on herself. If it was me, I'd make up some reason why I could do it all for Luke, be the noble benefactor, *and* go to the party.

"So . . . you'll never tell him?" I venture. "Ever? He'll never know it was you?"

"He will never know." She looks at Suze dispassionately. "Please stand aside so I can leave."

That's it? No high-fives, group hugs, let's-do-this-again?

"Elinor . . . wait." I hold out my arms, but she doesn't react, so I shuffle toward her in the tiny space. But she *still* doesn't seem to know what I'm doing. So at last I wrap my arms gingerly around her bony frame, feeling like Minnie when she randomly hugs a tree in the park.

I can't quite believe this is happening. I'm hugging Elinor.

Me. Hugging *Elinor.* Because I *want* to.

"Thanks," I murmur. "For everything."

Elinor draws away, looking stiffer than ever. She nods briefly to me and Suze, then slips through the wooden door.

"Will anyone see her?" I mutter anxiously to Suze, who shakes her head.

"There's a back way out. I showed her earlier."

I lean against the dusty old wall and breathe out heavily. "Wow."

"I know."

Our eyes meet through the dimness, and I know Suze is thinking all the same thoughts I am.

"D'you think he'll ever know it was her?"

"Dunno." I shake my head. "I just . . . don't know." I glance through the spy hole again. "Come on. We'd better get down."

THE PARTY IS in full swell downstairs. Guests are milling around everywhere, holding drinks, wearing their silver party hats (we had crackers at dinner), wandering around the midsummer forest and looking round the waterfall, which is now lit up with amazing colored lights, or gathered around the roulette tables. The catering staff is circulating with tiny little passion-fruit sorbets on individual spoons. Danny's models are stalking around in their spectacular *Midsummer Night's Dream* costumes, looking like they've popped in from a magic faraway land. There's echoing laughter everywhere, and chatter, and the *thud-thud* of the band reverberating through the floor, and every so often the flash of a laser from the show. I must go and dance again in a minute.

I head toward the cocktail bar, where a bartender flown in specially from New York is entertaining a small crowd with cocktail-shaker tricks. There, to my astonishment, I find Janice and Jess clinking glasses with massive warm, friendly smiles.

What's going on? I thought they hated each other.

"Hi!" I touch Jess's shoulder. "How's it going? Doesn't Jess look *amazing*?" I add to Janice.

"Absolutely super!" agrees Janice. "What a wonderful outfit!"

"It's a nice dress," says Jess, tugging awkwardly at it so the neckline goes crooked. "Nice and plain. And the fabric's sustainable."

She's always the same. The minute I compliment her appearance, she gets uncomfortable and starts trying to sabotage it.

"Jess borrowed this from Danny," I tell Janice as I patiently adjust the neckline back again. "It's a prototype from his new eco-couture collection. You know it's probably the most expensive dress in this room?" I add airily. Which is true, even if Suze did pay a squillion. "It's more expensive than mine," I add for good measure.

"What?" Jess blanches. "What are you *talking* about?"

I want to burst into laughter at her expression. I've kind of been saving this tidbit up.

"Oh yes. Because it's made of hand-spun, free-range silk," I explain. "They have to wait for the cocoons to fall naturally from the trees, and they don't use any machines, and all the artisans are paid really generously. Only about three of these will ever be made. In Browns, it would cost . . ."

I lean forward and whisper the price in Jess's ear. She looks like she wants to expire on the spot.

"Plus, no one in the world has worn any of the

pieces from this new collection yet," I inform her. "You realize you're an exclusive fashion story?"

Anyone else in the world would be thrilled to be an exclusive fashion story. Jess still looks completely freaked out.

"*Enjoy* it! You look *fab*." I put an arm round her shoulders and squeeze tight until she reluctantly laughs.

"So are you having a good time? Have you danced yet?" I can't help smiling at Janice's beatific face. She looks like she's had a good few cocktails.

"Oh, Becky!" Janice bubbles over. "Guess what, love, guess what? Jess is having a baby!"

What? I look, staggered, from Jess to Janice, to Jess's stomach, to her cocktail, and back to her face. She can't be—

Oh my God, did Janice's fertility drug *work*? And why is Jess looking so happy about it?

"It's only a possibility," corrects Jess, rolling her eyes. "And he's not a baby. He's three."

"He's the dearest little angel!" Janice acts as though Jess hasn't even spoken. "Can we show Becky the picture?"

I watch in bewilderment as Jess reaches into her evening bag. She pulls out a photograph and turns it around to show a grinning little boy with dark floppy hair and olive skin and a few freckles scattered over his nose.

Instantly, my heart melts. He looks so goofy and endearing, I almost want to laugh, except it might hurt Jess.

"Is that—"

"Maybe." Jess is glowing. "It's early days."

"You should really think of adoption, you know, Becky." Janice is puffed up proudly like a pigeon. "As I said to your mother, it's the *only* responsible way to have a child these days. Angelina showed us the way, of course."

Angelina showed us the way? Is this the woman who was having hysterics about five minutes ago because her son might not carry on his genes? I roll my eyes at Jess, but she just laughs and shrugs.

"Well, good luck!" I say. "When do you . . . you know. Get him?"

"Like I say, it's early days." Jess immediately looks cautious. "We may not be approved; we may still fail on all sorts of counts . . . I shouldn't have shown you the picture, really."

Yeah, right. Like Jess is going to fail at anything.

I'll be an aunt! Minnie will have a cousin!

"Well, I'm so happy for you." I squeeze Jess's arm. "And I'm glad you're having a good time, Janice."

"Oh, love, it's amazing! I know it was a huge effort for you." Janice sweeps a tipsy arm around. "But it was all worthwhile."

"Yes," says Jess, before I can reply. "It was worthwhile." She meets my eyes and gives a little smile.

Jess and Janice head off to find Tom, and I order myself a drink. As I'm standing there, almost lost in a happy dream, I spot Luke in the mirror behind the bar. He's standing at the roulette table, with Minnie next to him, peeping over the top. He looks totally, utterly, 100 percent happy. Everyone's focused on one massive pile of chips, and when the wheel comes to a standstill there's an almighty roar. Everyone laughs and claps one another on the back, and Minnie is crowing in delight.

As the croupier starts her patter and players begin to place new bets, Luke suddenly notices me watching him. He jerks his head at a quiet sofa nestled in the corner and peels away from the crowd, Minnie's hand clutched in his.

"Sweeties!" Minnie says triumphantly as they reach

us, and brandishes a handful of red and green gambling chips at me.

"They're not sweeties, darling." I want to laugh. "They're chips!" Now she looks totally confused. "Not eating chips, *special* chips. You make money with them at the magic table! Or . . . lose," I add hastily as I see Luke's raised eyebrows. "Often you lose. So you shouldn't ever gamble, Minnie. Gambling is very *bad*."

There. A quick zap of responsible parenting.

Luke sinks down onto the sofa and I follow suit. My ears are ringing from dancing next to the band, and my feet are starting to ache . . . but the rest of me is almost trancey with exhilaration. The party's been so utterly perfect. It's been better than I could ever have hoped. And it hasn't even ended yet. We've still got some of the best bits to go!

"Were you surprised?" I say for the millionth time, just to hear him say it.

"Becky . . ." Luke shakes his head incredulously. "I wasn't *surprised*. I was absolutely blown away."

"Good," I say in satisfaction. I take a sip of my cocktail (a Brandon) and nestle back on the old plushy sofa, Minnie on my lap and Luke's arm around both of us. For a few moments we're both quiet, just taking in the scene around us.

"That Christmas wish," Luke says suddenly. "You made a wish about me. In the shopping mall. Remember?"

Oh God, I *knew* he heard. And he's kept quiet about it all this time.

"Was your wish about this party?" he's saying. "Is that why you rushed to shut the elf up?"

My mind flashes back to the words I scrawled on the Christmasy paper. It seems a million years ago now.

"Yes," I say after a pause. "That's right. I wished that

I could plan you a surprise party and you really *would* be surprised. And you were!"

"You got your wish." He smiles.

"I did." I survey his face, then reach up and run a hand gently down his cheek. "I really did."

"So, tell me." His eyes glint with amusement. "Exactly which bits of your strange recent behavior can I ascribe to party planning?"

"I haven't been *strange*." I hit him.

"My love, you've been bordering on lunacy. Conceiving a boy, so we have to have sex very, very quickly?"

"Party." I grin.

"Ovulating?"

"Party."

"The Botox? The so-called 'boob job'?" I can't help giggling at his expression.

"Party. I'd been meeting Bonnie for the first time. Oh, and don't bollock her about mentioning your shower gel anymore!" I add sternly. "It was *me* who told her to mention it. And the gym. And anything else that sounded a bit strange."

"You?" He stares at me. "Oh, for fuck's—" He shakes his head as it obviously all starts to fall into place. "Why the hell didn't I *realize*? I should have known she wouldn't become that erratic overnight. What about the sixteen coats?" he adds suddenly. "Was that a party thing too?"

"Er . . . no," I admit. "That really was Minnie. Naughty girl, Minnie," I add reprovingly.

"But what I really don't understand is . . . how did you *achieve* all this?" He sweeps the air with a hand. "I mean, Becky, this is beyond spectacular. This is . . . ." He trails off.

I know what's underlying his words. He doesn't want to say it, but he's worried I took out some massive loan for all this and I won't tell him till tomorrow, when I'll reveal we're broke.

Honestly, he could have more *faith*.

But there's no point pretending this evening didn't cost shed-loads of money. Any moron can see that it did.

"I had . . . help," I say. "Major, *major* help. With everything. Bonnie was amazing," I add quickly, before he presses me more on exactly who helped with the finances. "She coordinated everything, she arranged the guest list, she sent out the invitations—"

"And of course that's why she was looking so shifty the other day." Luke exhales, looking rueful. "OK. I get it. I've really fucked up. I owe her a big bunch of flowers."

"*Not* lilies," I put in. "You always get them, and she can't stand them but she's too polite to say anything. Get sweet peas and ranunculus. Or I could tell you all her favorite Jo Malone products."

Luke shoots me an astonished look. "Anything else?"

"Loads, if you're interested," I say blithely. "Bonnie and I are such good friends now. We tell each other everything."

"Oh, you do, do you?" Luke looks as though he's not sure what he thinks about this.

"We really bonded over this whole thing. It's been such a saga." I take a swig of cocktail and kick off my shoes. Talking everything over with Luke, it feels as if some wound-up part of me is finally starting to relax. "You can't imagine. Trying not to let you see the Internet, and breaking your BlackBerry . . ."

"I still can't believe you did that." He raises a half grin—although I'm not sure he's *totally* had a sense of humor about his BlackBerry.

"And the worst thing was that bloody meeting in Paris! Oh my God, I nearly *killed* you!" I can't help starting to laugh. "We were all like, 'What do we do? How do we move it?' And you were so bloody *pleased* with yourself—"

"Shit." I can see the realization hitting Luke. "Of course. The meeting was supposed to be today—" He breaks off. "Wait a minute, though. You're not saying—" I can sense the cogs whirring in his brain. "You couldn't have been behind *that,* surely. You're not telling me that you personally somehow arranged for Sir Bernard Cross to decide he wanted to give me a meeting?" He gives an astonished laugh. "I mean, I'll believe many things of you, Becky, but *that . . .*"

I keep smiling, but inside I'm kicking myself. I've said too much. Let's move on, quick.

"Not me, exactly. Oh God, and the *tent*—" I hastily launch into a full account of bartering for the tent, and Luke laughs at all the right places, but I can tell he's preoccupied. When I've finished, we lapse into silence and he sips his drink pensively, and I know exactly where his mind is roaming.

"I always knew someone influential was behind that meeting," he says at last, staring into his drink. "I said so at the time. I could sense some powerful person behind the scenes, helping me out. And now I think I know who it was." He looks up, straight at me. "It's obvious. And it's obvious why you don't want to tell me."

My heart has stopped. My hand has frozen round the stem of my glass. Luke's so sharp. His mind's so quick. I should never have let anything slip out.

Is he angry?

I lick my lips nervously. "Luke, I really can't say anything."

"I understand." He takes a deep slug of his drink, and for a while neither of us speaks.

As we sit there, the party thrumming around us, I keep darting cautious looks at him. He hasn't ex-

ploded. He hasn't stormed out, saying that the whole
evening's spoiled for him now. Is he not as bitter as I
thought?

I keep thinking of Elinor, hidden away in her tiny,.
musty hole. If I'd just persuaded her to stay . . . could I
somehow have worked things out between them?

"But, Becky, you realize this isn't just some tiny little
favor." Luke breaks in to my thoughts. "This is immense.
I mean, all this." He gestures around the room and lowers his voice. "This . . . person. They were behind that
too, weren't they?"

Slowly, I nod. If he knows, there's no point pretending.

Luke exhales sharply, cradling his drink. "You know
I'm going to have to say thank you, Becky. Somehow.
Even if they don't want to be thanked."

"I . . . I think that would be nice, Luke." I swallow.
"Really nice."

I can feel a pressing of tears behind my eyes. Just
like that, things have been mended. We'll meet up
and, yes, it'll be stilted and awkward, but they'll talk.
And Luke will see his mother with Minnie. And he'll
realize there's a different side to her.

"No time like the present." Luke gets to his feet with
a sudden energy. "You know, I didn't say anything—but
all along I half-suspected Tarquin. How do he and Sir
Bernard know each other? Go shooting together, do
they?"

It takes a moment for me to catch up with what he's
saying. He thinks all this was *Tarquin*?

"And of course he's been desperately trying to repay
me for that help I gave him earlier this year," Luke is
saying. "But really, such extraordinary generosity was
uncalled for." He looks around the room as though
with fresh disbelief. "I don't know *how* I can ever thank

him properly. And to Suze too. I assume they were in it together?"

Noooo! Wrong! You've got it all wrong!

I want to say something; dislodge him off this track. But what can I do? I can't betray Elinor's confidence, not after everything she said.

"Wait a minute!" I scramble to my feet, depositing Minnie on the sofa. "Luke, you mustn't say anything—"

"Don't worry, Becky." He smiles. "I'm not going to give the game away. If they want to stay incognito, so be it. But if somebody goes to all the trouble of doing something as exceptional and special as this . . ." His face is shining. "They deserve a public thank-you. Don't you agree?"

My heart is tying itself into knots. He should know what his mother did for him. He should know, he should know.

"Come on, Minnie, Daddy needs to make a little speech." Before I can react, Luke is striding into the East Hall. "Suze?" he beckons to her cheerfully as he passes. "Could you come in here a moment? And Tarquin?"

"What's going on?" Suze says as she follows us in. "What's Luke doing?"

"He thinks it was all you," I mutter under my breath. "You and Tarkie. He thinks you fixed Sir Bernard and paid for all this. Now he wants to say thank you."

"You're joking!" Suze stops dead, her eyes dark and troubled. "But . . . we didn't!"

"I know! But how can I tell him that?"

For a moment we stare at each other anxiously.

"Does Luke suspect Elinor had *anything* to do with it?" says Suze at last.

"Nothing. He hasn't mentioned her once."

He's mentioned everyone else in the world. All his

family. All his friends. He toasted them all in his speech. But not her.

Luke has already bounded up onstage between songs, and the lead singer of the band has handed the microphone to him.

"Ladies and gentlemen, a moment if I may?" Luke's voice booms around the room. "There've been many thank-yous tonight. But I just want to draw attention to one very, very special couple. They have opened this beautiful house to us, provided us with stunning hospitality . . . and much, *much* more besides, which I won't go into here . . ." He pauses meaningfully, and I can see Tarquin darting a puzzled look at Suze. "But please know, Suze and Tarquin, I will never forget what you did. To the Cleath-Stuarts." Luke raises his glass, and all the guests on the dance floor echo him, then break into applause.

Suze is trying to smile charmingly as people turn to her, applauding.

"I feel terrible," she murmurs desperately through her smiles. "What about Elinor?"

"It was her choice," I murmur back. "There's nothing we can do."

I think of Elinor speeding home through the night, shoulders rigid. With no one toasting her, no one smiling at her, no one even giving her a passing thought. And suddenly I make a silent vow to myself.

Luke'll know one day. He'll know one day.

"Give us 'New York, New York'!" someone yells at Luke, and the room breaks into laughter.

"No chance." Luke flashes a smile and hands the microphone back to the band singer, who immediately counts the band into a new song.

"Suze, darling." Tarquin has made it over to us, looking perplexed. "What on earth was Luke—"

"Just thanking us for being good friends," she says brightly. "You know."

"Ah." Tarquin's brow clears. "Generous chap." He has an ancient school name tape poking out of his dinner jacket, I notice. It says *WFS Cleath-Stuart*. Which is his *father*.

"Tarkie." I beckon him over. "Piece of fluff." I push the name tape back inside his collar and wink at Suze, who just shakes her head with a rueful grin.

We watch as Luke threads his way slowly through the throng, chatting and nodding to people as he goes. As he pauses to talk to Matt from Brandon C, I suddenly notice Minnie reach for Matt's cocktail glass and take it to her lips. Matt hasn't even noticed.

"Minnie!" I charge forward and grab it. "No! You *don't* drink cocktails! Luke, did you see what she did?"

Once upon a time, Luke would have hit the roof. Now he just swings her up and frowns at her mock-sternly.

"Come on, Minnie. Don't you know the rules? No gambling and no drinking. Got it? And no online shopping. Not till you're at least . . . three."

"Happy Daddy!" Minnie pokes him with a glittery cocktail umbrella.

"Now, you go to Grana a minute." He puts her down and shepherds her toward Mum. "I just need to have a little chat with Mummy." As he leads me off the dance floor, I feel a bit surprised. What does he need to chat about?

It's not the Valentino dress, surely. It can't be. I've *told* him it was a present from Mum.

"I was going to leave this till later," he begins as we reach a quiet spot in the *Midsummer Night's Dream* glade. "But why not now?"

"Absolutely." I nod, slightly apprehensive.

"Although you're probably in the loop already." He

rolls his eyes ruefully. "I mean, you obviously know about Sage Seymour being a client."

"We party planners make it our business to know everything." I smile sweetly. "Even secrets our husbands *were trying to keep from us*."

"And you've spoken to her."

"Several times, actually." I flick my hair back nonchalantly. "We got on really well. She said we should have a drink sometime."

Suze nearly *died* when I told her. She asked, could she come along and be my assistant?

"So . . . you know everything?" persists Luke. He's clearly driving at something, but I'm not sure what.

"Er . . ."

"You *don't* know everything." He's scanning my face as though trying to work it out.

"Maybe I do," I parry.

Damn. Why don't I know everything?

"The estate agent just called and left a message with Bonnie." He appears to change tack completely. "They've found us a rental place. But, of course, it all depends."

"Right." I nod wisely. "Of course. It all depends. On . . . many things." I'm tempted to add, "On cabbages and kings."

"Becky . . ." Luke gives me a strange look. "You have absolutely no idea what I'm talking about, do you?"

Oh, I can't keep the pretense up any longer.

"No!" I exclaim crossly. "I don't! Tell me!"

"You have no inkling of what I'm about to say." He crosses his arms, looking as though he's enjoying himself.

"It's probably really boring," I shoot back. "So I do know but I forgot, because it's so dull."

"Fair enough." He shrugs. "Never mind. Not really important. Shall we go back?"

God, he's maddening.

"Tell me." I glare at him. "At once. Or you can't have a party bag. And they're really *good* party bags."

"OK." Luke relents. "Well, to recap what you probably already know . . ." He shoots me a grin. "I've started working for Sage Seymour."

I feel a little twinge of glee. My husband's working for a movie star! It's so cool!

"And she likes the idea of having someone from outside the film business giving her a fresh take on things. In fact, she likes it *so* much"—Luke pauses, his mouth twitching—"that she's asked me to go and work for her in L.A. for a little while. I'd work with her team, make some contacts, and maybe, if things go *really* well, open a media division of Brandon Communications. Becky." His face changes to alarm. "Are you all right? *Becky*?"

I can't speak. L.A.?

Hollywood?

"And—and we'd all go?" I stutter as soon as I've got my voice back.

"Well, that was my idea. Gary can take care of things here for a while, so I was thinking three months. But obviously your job is a big consideration." He looks anxious. "I know it's been going well for you, I know you were hoping to make it onto the board—"

My job. Fuck. He doesn't even know about my job.

"You know what, Luke?" I say as earnestly as I can. "We're a partnership. A *team*. And if my career has to take a backseat for a while, so be it. That's what marriage is all about. Plus, they have shops in L.A., don't they? And I've got a green card, haven't I?"

"Well . . . great!" He lifts his glass toward me. "Looks like we have a plan."

He really means it? Just like that?

"So . . . we'd be in Hollywood," I say, just to be sure. "For three months."

"Yup."

"I've never been to Hollywood."

"I know." He grins. "Fun, huh?"

My heart is leaping around like a fish. Hollywood! Me, Becky Brandon, née Bloomwood, in Hollywood!

Luke's saying something else. His mouth is moving. But I can't hear him. My mind is too stuffed with alluring images. Me Rollerblading down a boardwalk, all tanned and fit. Me driving down Sunset Boulevard in a convertible. (I must find out how to drive American cars.) Me and Sage Seymour hanging out by her shell-pink pool, wearing bikinis from some really hip downtown boutique, while Minnie looks adorable in a sundress.

People will call me the Girl with the English Accent. Or maybe the Girl Who's Best Friends with Sage Seymour. Or maybe . . . the Girl in the White Sunglasses. (Yes. I'll get some tomorrow. That can be my look.)

And it'll be sunny all the time! And we can drink smoothies on Rodeo Drive! And maybe we'll go to the Oscars . . . maybe we'll meet Johnny Depp . . . maybe I can be an extra in a film . . .

"Becky?" Luke's voice finally impinges on my consciousness. "What do you think?"

I feel as if my smile is going to break my face in two.

"When do we go?"

THE 📌 LOOK

601 OXFORD STREET   LONDON W1

Ms. Rebecca Brandon
The Pines
43 Elton Road
Oxshott
Surrey

11 April 2006

Dear Rebecca,

Thank you for your letter of 10 April.

I'm sorry that you are unable to take up my offer of
reinstatement at The Look, with board directorship and
increased salary. Obviously your family life comes first,
and please be assured that your position will be open as
and when you return from Los Angeles.

With best wishes for your trip.

Trevor Holden
Managing Director

P.S.—Please could you ask all your clients to STOP
bringing clothes back? We're desperate.

NANNY SUE ENTERPRISES

Where family life comes first . . .

Counseling | Workshops | Media | Parenting Aids | Guest Speaking

Ms. Rebecca Brandon
The Pines
43 Elton Road
Oxshott
Surrey

12 April 2006

Dear Rebecca,

Thank you for your letter of 10 April.

I'm sorry you will be unable to attend our Spending
Addiction Program after all, due to your trip to California.
I can understand how disappointed and "wretched" you
feel about this.

If it is any consolation, I'm sure that you will find similar
groups in Los Angeles and could perhaps pursue a course
of therapy there?

With all very best wishes,

Julia Summerton
Child Program Director

**CENTRAL DEPARTMENTAL UNIT
FOR MONETARY POLICY**

5th Floor • 180 Whitehall Place • London SW1

Ms. Rebecca Brandon
The Pines
43 Elton Road
Oxshott
Surrey

13 April 2006

Dear Rebecca,

Thank you for your letter of 10 April and all best wishes
for your upcoming trip to Los Angeles.

Unfortunately, I am fairly sure that *The British Journal of
Monetary Economics* does not have scope for an "L.A.
correspondent," as you suggest. Nor is the editor
"planning to branch out into other, more-interesting
areas, like movies and gossip."

However, should any other such opportunities arise, I will
be sure to let you know.

All the best—and Bon Voyage!

Yours sincerely,

Edwin Tredwell
Director of Policy Research

Santa's Grotto

Christmas Wish
(post in the Wishing Well for Santa to read your wish!!!)

Dear Father Christmas,

It's Becky here again. I hope you're well.

I wish for a Zac Posen top in aquamarine, the one with the bow, size 10.

Also those Marni shoes I saw with Suze, not the stack heels, the other ones.

A sibling for Minnie.

And, above all, Father Christmas, I wish that Luke could be completely, 100% happy, relax, and forget all the shit*. Just once.

Thanks. Love Becky xxx

*sorry

ACKNOWLEDGMENTS

Huge thanks to my editor Susan Kamil, Noah Eaker, and the rest of the fantastic team at The Dial Press.

I am supported by so many wonderful people—in particular Araminta Whitley, Kim Witherspoon, Harry Man, David Forrer, Peta Nightingale, my family, and the Board. Grateful thanks to all—I couldn't do it without you.

The name "Nicole Taylor" occurs in this book as a result of an auction in aid of The Children's Trust, which I was delighted to support. The Children's Trust provides specialist care for severely disabled children and is an inspiring cause. I would like to thank Nicole for her generous bid.

And finally, I'd like to thank all my readers for loyally supporting both Becky and me over the years—and a big hello to everyone on my Facebook page!